Georgina Wroe is a freelance journalist who moved to Moscow in her twenties. She covered stories ranging from wars in the former USSR to serial killers, for magazines including *GQ*, *Esquire*, and *Marie Claire*. She now lives in Suffolk and London, and returns to Russia on assignment.

Also by Georgina Wroe

SLAPHEAD

Fleeced

Georgina Wroe

HEADLINE

First published in 2000
by HEADLINE BOOK PUBLISHING

10 9 8 7 6 5 4 3 2 1

ISBN 0 7472 7551 3

Typeset by
Letterpart Limited, Reigate, Surrey

Printed and bound in Great Britain by
Mackays of Chatham plc, Chatham, Kent

HEADLINE BOOK PUBLISHING
A division of Hodder Headline
338 Euston Road
London NW1 3BH

www.headline.co.uk
www.hodderheadline.com

To Helena Wroe,
with love

In the 1999 elections to the Russian duma, more than 1,000 of the 6,700 candidates had a criminal record.

Russian Ministry for the Interior,
December 1999

CHAPTER ONE

I

Dominic Peach used the corner of a half-written press release to clean the nails of his left hand. They were uncharacteristically dirty, embedded with soil from Mr Orlovski's garden. But at least the paper was fulfilling some useful purpose. For an agency devoted to conservation, the number of trees it was responsible for pulping was criminal. Dominic's press release was designed to draw attention to a rise in the use of an unspecified luxury wool in the Home Counties. Unlikely to take the news agendas by storm, but that had been his intention. Six-foot three and twenty-three weeks off thirty, Dominic Peach worked on a strictly Benthamite theory of human happiness. The less work he generated, the less work he made for other people, so the happier they were. And, obviously, the happier he was.

Blessed with above-average looks and height, it was difficult for Dominic to do anything other than look down on people. That wasn't just his opinion; generally he was less aware of his looks than others were. But he liked it that way, people responded to diffidence. He also benefited from GM: general misapprehension. Namely, that as the only child of the director of an international tobacco company, who had, since he joined the firm at the age of sixteen, been encouraged to smoke sixty a day, Dominic was soon to inherit a fortune.

He straightened the press release and an arc of dirt formed a moustache on the nose of a lion on the letterhead, part of the Save Our Species logo. Dominic's girlfriend, Antoinette, had objected to the sage-green and gold-embossed animals. She said lions were autumn and fell into the fire spectrum. Dominic told her you couldn't apply a colour chart to an animal. She told him she couldn't take seriously the advice of someone so unrelentingly winter. Antoinette was a colour consultant.

Dominic re-checked the press release, turning the p and the r into capitals. For an English graduate it went against the grain, but in his experience you didn't get anywhere in PR without the widespread misuse of capital letters. He also struck out any reference to wealth. The last thing he wanted was to be besieged by reporters from the *Daily Telegraph*. This way he limited himself to a couple of calls from a rag in Henley that, in his opinion, encouraged an almost morbid interest in threatened animals among its readers. Dominic yawned.

'Dommie, do you do horses?' Deborah, who referred to herself with the emphasis on the second syllable, stuck her head over the parapet of the MDF dividers. Deborah was twenty-four and one month out of the press office of an international cosmetics company. Dominic remained seated.

'I'm sorry?' Dominic looked up from examining the knees of his black jeans, half wedged under a grey melamine desk and tinged a faint green from kneeling on grass. 'Do I *do* horses?' Though he knew exactly what she meant, he thought a casual lack of comprehension might make him look mockingly intellectual. He stressed the second *do* to make it sound as if she was suggesting he had relations, possibly sexual, with them.

'Yeah, you know, do them. Or is it Don?'

Deborah was dressed in a black mini-skirt with workman's boots straining to contain calves the colour and shape of a huge stick of rock. When Dominic imagined her in underwear, which boredom levels sometimes demanded, her knickers were grey and worn

2

through at the gusset. But on the phone she had the voice of an 0990 number, the vocal embodiment of one of those cards stuck up in telephone boxes. Looking at her, Dominic hoped she'd find a new career before video-phones.

'You're asking now if Don *does* horses?' He tried a sardonic smile. Even though he couldn't possibly fancy Deborah, he always tried for a lofty superiority at work. The same attitude he used for Antoinette's friends and in shops outside London.

'For Christ's sake, Dommie. It's a woman's magazine asking about HRT. Hormone replacement therapy comes from frigging horses. In case you didn't know.' Now *she* sounded superior. Irritatingly, despite having no interest in horses or menopausal women, Dominic found himself intrigued.

'Which bit?'

'Which bit what?'

'Which bit do they use?'

'How the frig should I know? Just tell me if it's you or Don.'

Dominic pretended to key HORSE into his computer. The drifting cloud of the screensaver evaporated to reveal a recently abandoned game of patience. After a half-minute pause during which Deborah resumed her conversation with the journalist, he shouted over the partition, 'It's Don.'

Deborah doodled as she spoke. 'I'm afraid you'll need to talk to our horseman, Don Gilson. But I'm afraid Don appears to be away from his desk at the moment. Can I get him to call you when he gets back?'

Dominic studied the length of his fingers as they rooted in a paper bag for another pineapple chunk. One press release a week was his limit. He rolled the sweet contemplatively over the roof of his mouth, which was still painfully sore from sucking the last. A lacerated mouth was one of the hazards of a non-smoking office. He sucked harder; lacerated mouth syndrome could well turn out to be the RSI of the new millennium.

Dominic heard the phone being slammed back into its cradle. Deborah always replaced the receiver with a crash.

'Tosser,' he heard from beyond the partition.

'Who?'

'That bloody woman. How the hell am I supposed to know where HRT comes from? Could be frigging pasteurised milk for all I know.' Dominic paused the game of patience. Could women be *tossers*?

'Well, there is the small point that you do work in the information department of an animal protection agency,' he said.

He wondered if Deborah was aware that by some freak internal window configuration he was able to see her picking her nose, even though she generally did it behind a pamphlet from the Cats' Protection League.

'Yeah, right. Like you know where it comes from.'

Dominic knew little about female hormones, HRT included, but it sounded as if Deborah's had gone out of kilter. That or her calorific level was dangerously low. Deborah spent most of her time on diets, filling the office fridge with an array of slimming aids that included most chemicals on the periodic table. None of them seemed to make any impact on her body, which strained to explode from its dark stretchy shrouds.

Dominic sighed and curled his toes in pleasure at the knowledge he'd got one over on them. Don never used to be horses. It was only in what Dominic internally referred to as the Great Animal Reshuffle of 1999 that Don had copped for more species than a head count on Noah's Ark. Dominic had used the student placement from the University of Harpenden as a pretext for redistributing the office workload. Overnight he'd come up with a database that flashed up the name of the officer responsible for each animal. It operated on strict and varying rotation – occasionally Deborah, mostly Don, but never himself.

With one exception. Dominic's responsibility to the endangered species of the world – he felt there should be one – extended to one animal group only. Sheep. No one in their right minds, Dominic reasoned – not even Concerned of Henley – could care about sheep.

4

Tigers, majestic and sleek, yes. Elephants, lumbering and loyal, yes. Sheep, dumb, easily led and covered in their own shit, no.

So it was that Dominic, less in deference, more by way of reassurance, kept a picture of a flock of them cut from a glossy travel article on New Zealand pinned to the green felt of his partition. At a conservative estimate the camera had captured somewhere in the region of twenty thousand sheep in repose. And that was just one flock in one country. No, Dominic felt he could sleep easy – he could even count them in his dreams with impunity – safe in the knowledge that sheep could *never* become endangered.

Dominic revolved the pineapple chunk across the roof of his mouth.

'Where is Don anyway?' Deborah's voice sounded as if it was coming from under her desk.

'Bank,' said Dominic.

'Really, why?' came Deborah's muffled reply. He could see her size eight boots sticking out from under her partition, lodged against the photocopier.

'Pass.' Dominic knew the reason for Don's rare absence from SOS was to arrange a mortgage, because he'd asked his girlfriend and her twelve-year-old son to move in with him. Dominic wondered why Don preferred to keep it to himself. Maybe it was because Deborah would inevitably label it bourgeois. More likely it was because altruism disturbed him.

'Dommie dear, put the kettle on. I'm herbal.' As she spoke, Deborah lobbed a porous tea bag towards him. Dominic, who had stood up, watched it sail past him and drop on the brown carpet tiles a few feet from the communal kettle.

Standing, Dominic saw the back of the head of SOS's managing director poring over another Lottery grant application form. SOS was into its fifth summer and, like most of the charities fuelled by the Diana-led decade of sharing, was, in the new millennium, suffering from compassion fatigue. The agency had grown up alongside the National Lottery and securing a significant grant from it was Tony Beecham's main aim in life.

The agency, once called SOT, Save Our Tigers, started as a one-man envelope-stuffing operation in the glory days when every china plate advertised in middle market Sunday supplements were of the Princess of Wales or an Amurski tiger. Today, as Tony was fond of telling people, the world of animal conservation was dog eat dog. But the beneficence of the National Lottery had come like a steroid shot in the arm.

From Tony's enclave the World Service beeped out the signal that meant another hour had been done away with. It had been his tight-trousered dictat to keep a radio constantly tuned, listening for leads to keep them 'ahead of the pack'.

His was the only individual office, separated from the others by a Japanese screen made from balsa wood and crepe paper, which protruded like a triptych into the room. The effect was more Tokyo lean-to than corporate chic, but he made up for it on the far wall with a dozen framed pictures of himself and some of the biggest names in animal conservation. Trophies for a lifetime devoted to goodness. Tigers were Tony's thing. There was a kudos attached to saving tigers that was not altogether wasted on big-game hunters. 'Inadequate men like to be identified with the powerful,' said Antoinette in one of her less introverted moments, making Dominic wonder if that analysis didn't, in her mind, apply to their seven-year relationship.

Deborah was lying on the floor filling out the answers in a women's magazine survey. Dominic suspected, though couldn't see, that Gill with a G, the office manager, had her head lowered over the Take-a-Break elevenses crossword. Sometimes it surprised him that there were so many animals left on the planet.

'Sorry, Debs, no tea for me,' said Dominic. 'Got to see a man about a dog.'

'Naughty, naughty. You know as well as I do that Don's dogs.' The words came out slightly breathlessly as she levered herself to her feet. Seconds later her phone rang.

'Save Our Species, Deborah speaking. How may I help you?' Without waiting for a reply, she added, 'Please hold the line.' She looked expectantly at Dominic with her hand held over the receiver.

'Sorry, Deb, must dash.' Dominic headed for the door, lighting a cigarette as he went.

'Piss off, then.' She took her hand from the receiver and purred, 'I'm afraid Don Gilson is the person you need to speak to and he's in a meeting. Can I take a message?' She covered the receiver with her hand again and said to Dominic, 'Anyway, it's urine.'

'I'm *sorry*?'

'Hormone replacement therapy comes from the urine of pregnant mares. I just read it.'

Dominic let the fire door suck in on itself behind him. Whether from the glimpse of the top of Deborah's hold-ups, a dodgy pork pie at lunchtime, or the HRT revelation, he felt slightly queasy.

He shrugged on his leather jacket with a fleecy lining that was, Dominic had been assured by the Camden vendor, genuine sheepskin. Standing with Antoinette by the canal lock last winter, the size of the rack and the smell of leather had comforted him, though today it was far too warm for sheepskin. With a nervous knot of tension in his stomach fuelled by the smell of baking tarmac and ozone, he knew spring was finally over. He clung to his jacket like a security blanket. For Dominic, June was always the cruellest month. This year's was to be no exception.

II

Mr Orlovski was, according to the agency, Polish. Dominic had no reason to doubt them. Ethnically they'd never got any of his visits wrong, including Mrs O'Leary (Irish) and Mr Singh (Hindu). So when Dominic found two books, *Krakow Between the Wars* and *Exploring Warsaw*, which he'd specifically joined Acton library to

7

borrow, propping up the TV aerial, he'd merely assumed the 'mutual interest' wasn't going to be history.

Dominic's interest as a volunteer for Elderly Alert was far from mutual. It stemmed from the fact that, according to the estate agents on the corner, period two-bedroomed terraces in W12 were fetching nearly £200,000.

At worst what Dominic was doing was cynically exploiting the elderly, though he preferred to look at it as putting inner London housing stock back in the hands of the English working class. Or redistributing wealth. Ever since he'd learnt that he wouldn't in fact be inheriting so much as a packet of Benson & Hedges, he thought it only fair he should be allowed a go at someone else's inheritance.

After a secret backroom chat with an independent financial adviser, unbeknown to Antoinette, Dominic had realised Elderly Alert's 'Adopt an Elderly' scheme was the only way for him to get a foot on the property ladder. Though now Dominic preferred to think of it as less of a foot, more a mortgage-free entire body. And it wasn't as if they, the visitee, didn't get something out of it while they were alive. After all, they got him.

Mr Orlovski's house was a two-up two-down terrace just off Shepherd's Bush Green. Dominic parked his bike outside and padlocked it to the drainpipe. He liked the area, which was important. He'd twice had to reject visits because the area had been unsuitable, once in East Acton, once an Ealing council estate. (He'd told the agency that in both cases he'd struggled to find a mutual interest.)

A tail wind down the incline of Holland Park Avenue and ease of traffic around the Green had made him early. But under the sheepskin he was sweating and knew that it would only get worse in the hothouse conditions of Mr Orlovski's front room. Because of his proximity to Loftus Road, home of QPR, with its seasonal Saturday afternoon fallout, Mr Orlovski's was one of the few roads in the area not to have been colonised by people-carriers – the badge of the media professionals from the nearby BBC. Only Mr Orlovski's and a couple of council-owned houses had maintained their pre-war dignity by withstanding the DIY fads of the last decade.

Dominic had his own key. With one thumb fixed to the bell, he stooped to collect a bottle of milk from the doorstep. As he pushed the door inwards from the street, a belch of the house came at him, smelling of stale ashtrays and fungal infection. Oddly, Dominic found it comforting.

'*Dzien dobry, Mr Orlovski, to jest Dominic.*' He pushed the door against the week's delivery of free papers. He said the same thing every time. It was the only Polish Dominic knew. 'Hello – where are you?' It was both convention and politeness on Dominic's part, because in the eleven months he had been visiting, Mr Orlovski had never moved from the front room. Dominic heard the television before he entered.

'Got the papers here, Mr Orlovski. And the milk. Fancy a cup of tea before we start?' Dominic was feeling virtuous. If anyone asked, he was the big-hearted volunteer from Elderly Alert, driven by the selfless need to help others. Mr Orlovski nodded as Dominic flicked his hair and made his way along a pitch-black corridor into the kitchen.

Light and air were barred from the room by a pair of filthy net curtains, shrouded by heavy red velvet. There was an old day bed in the corner that looked as if it had come from a Parisian salon. Mr Orlovski sat with his hips far back in an upright chair. Skeletal legs jack-knifed from his body. The chair's varnished wooden arms were the same colour and translucency as the dark stains on the back of his hands. His skin was the consistency of filo pastry and the colour of a toad's.

On his first visit Dominic had pointed to an unframed photo on the mantelpiece that the heat from the gas fire had turned brittle. 'That your sister, Mr Orlovski?' The age of the woman in the picture was, Dominic thought, about twenty. She was blonde and as thin as Wallace Simpson, wearing a cotton dress that tried to catch hold of, rather than cling to, her hips.

'No, my wife.' His voice sounded like pebbles being dragged over the shore.

'Where is she now? In London?' asked Dominic casually as he leant against the fire, legs crossed, inhaling the spent fumes from the gas.

'Lost.'

'What, you mean dead?' Dominic asked quickly but not, he hoped, unsympathetically.

'No, lost.'

'Are there any Orlovski children, then?'

'Maybe there was.'

Dominic found himself becoming disproportionately irritated. 'I'm sorry to hear that. Are they dead?'

'Perhaps.' Mr Orlovski seemed to have less interest in his family than most people invested in their luggage. Dominic, though he could understand it, was perplexed. Poles, everyone knew, had fanatical family loyalty.

Dominic set down the tea tray on a footstool. Mr Orlovski took his black in a china cup with a spoonful of jam in it.

The Scrabble was in a cupboard by the day bed, ringed on top by crop circles of glasses, though as far as he knew Mr Orlovski never drank anything other than tea. Dominic felt put out.

'You can get a cleaner, you know,' he called over his shoulder on his haunches. 'From the agency.' He shook the box. 'If you wanted. It would be free.'

Mr Orlovski didn't reply. Dominic passed him a wooden letter rack and held out the Scrabble tiles to him in a drawstring Elle make-up bag that Dominic had stolen from Antoinette.

'Right then, Mr O. You start.'

Mr Orlovski was Dominic's fourth, and the one to whom he attached the most hope. Booty from the others had been pleasant but not outstanding. An eighteenth-century hallmarked hip flask from Mr Singh when he died from a stroke in January. Then there was Milky from Mrs O'Leary in Osterley, whom Dominic had only consented to visit because she was detached with a large garden. Mrs O'Leary was a one-time dinner lady to whom he'd become quite attached, despite the fact that, though childless, she still paid council rent. Bingo had been their mutual interest. He'd even applied to the agency for a wheelchair, two weeks before she'd died, to take her to the Ritz on the High Street. He wondered to this day if it had been the excitement that had brought on the fatal angina attack.

Milky was Mrs O'Leary's cream-coloured cat. It might have started off white but, like everything in her front room, had become discoloured by nicotine. Mrs Ross at the Elderly Concern presented Milky to him in a Walkers crisp box with air holes bored into it. She'd said that without checks Milky should have gone to the Blue Cross but, because of Dominic's background with animals, he could keep her. The rest of Mrs O'Leary's stuff went to the Caribbean home help.

'*Zajecie*,' said Dominic in three syllables as Mr Orlovski put his tiles down. 'Good one.' He counted the score in his head. 'Fifty, you're on the double.' He wrote the score on a jotter. Sometimes Mr Orlovski translated it from the Polish, sometimes he didn't.

Dominic thought as he inflated his chest. 'P-H-O-T-O.' He exhaled, placing the word underneath and thereby making four new words. Though Mr Orlovski said nothing, Dominic added by way of explanation, 'Zo, alternative spelling of zho, a cross between a Himalayan yak and a cow, and jo is, of course, a beloved.' He smiled. 'Scottish.' Dominic took a sip of tea. Mr Orlovski looked unmoved.

Dominic sat back and tried to imagine him before pleats of slack skin had engulfed him. His hair was grey and scraped over his scalp, his eyes were a translucent rheumy green, like sun shining through a leaf. Dominic looked away. No longer young enough to think of himself as immortal, Dominic was repelled by old age. He concentrated on the room instead. It was cluttered, old papers under tables, junk mail stacked in size order. Plastic bags Mr Orlovski washed and hung out on the line before folding and storing under the window.

'*Zona*,' said Mr Orlovski, putting two Scrabble tiles down. 'Wife.' They rarely used the Polish dictionary that Dominic had bought from a second-hand bookshop off Charing Cross Road – unless pique drove him to it, when Mr Orlovski 'bingoed' or got rid of all his letters.

'Wife? Really? *Zona*, who'd have thought,' said Dominic ponderously. He knew it was an opening. Though the women he visited rarely ceased talking about their families – Mrs O'Leary's infertility treatments lived on in Dominic's memory – the men were more reticent. It could lead to all sorts of problems with wills.

'What about your *zona* then, Mr Orlovski? Are you still in touch?' Dominic offered him a cigarette that he accepted, though usually he smoked roll-ups.

'No, not now.'

'You were then—'

'Mr Peach, my private life is my affair. I would prefer not to speak of it.'

It was one of the longest speeches Dominic had ever heard Mr Orlovski make and made him wonder if he didn't use Polish as an excuse to give him the edge on the Cs, Js and Zs in Scrabble.

'Fair enough. It was only conversation. I was just thinking that if you had any family over here I might be able to help find them.'

Mr Orlovski curtly shook his head, suggesting no further dialogue was on offer. After about forty minutes and a ninety-point advantage to the old man, Dominic said, 'Actually, Mr O, I've got to get away pretty sharpish. Do you mind if we have a roll-over week?'

'I'm sorry?'

'You know, start again the next time I see you.'

'As you wish, Mr Peach.'

It was nearly six when Dominic stood up to leave. He walked the tea tray along the narrow corridor into the kitchen. 'I'll put those geraniums in next time I'm here.' Dominic hunched his jacket. Mr Orlovski nodded.

'Right then, see you next time, Mr O.'

Mr Orlovski raised a papery hand but didn't look up. On an impulse Dominic tried to shake it, but it was withdrawn quickly enough to avoid a connection. Its texture, Dominic was startled to discover, was that of a used condom.

Dust from the curtain over the door caught in the back of his throat. Dominic needed a drink and was surprised to discover it was due to thirst as much as anything.

He had a faint metallic taste in the back of his throat from the black tea and the beginnings of a headache. He reached into his top pocket for two Advils. He knew the reason for the pain in the top of his brain, which was tingling nervously as if steeling itself for trepanation. It was always like that these days. When he had an appointment with Antoinette.

His narrow-legged black jeans were needlessly gripped by a pair of bicycle clips as he mounted his bicycle gracefully, scooting along on the left pedal before easing his other leg over the seat like the hero in a black and white film. Sometimes it was only Dominic's sense of himself as another person that kept him going.

III

The thing about Antoinette, and they both knew it, was that she was a trophy bird, tall, blonde and symmetrical. And the thing about trophy birds, and they both knew this too, was that unless under the extenuating circumstances of serial misadventure or insanity (and even then not always), they never got dumped. As far as Dominic was concerned, that was the essence of their seven-year relationship.

From Antoinette's point of view, it was Dominic's height. He'd once heard her tell a friend at a party that, *geneswise*, she could only date men taller than herself. Antoinette was five foot eleven. And in any case, *timewise*, she'd invested too much in him to look back. Then, of course, there was the general misapprehension, the belief that she would be the heiress of a fortune from tobacco.

So, like the Grecian hunter-gatherer who waited seven years for an olive tree to bear fruit and woke up finding himself stuck as a farmer, there was an encroaching inevitability to their relationship.

He watched her speak. '. . . then we could turn the pantry into a shower room.'

He put his pint down. 'You want people to shower in a *pantry*?'

'Not in the pantry,' said Antoinette testily. 'It won't be a pantry, it'll be a shower room.'

'So you'll have naked wet people going through the kitchen.' Dominic picked up the brochure; it referred to an area of London he'd never heard of.

'No, idiot, the kitchen will be in the bathroom.'

Dominic put the brochure face down on the table. 'Have you got any pound coins?' He stood up as he sorted through his trouser pockets, dredging up a few coppers, an opened packet of Advil, and two pineapple chunks.

'In my purse.' Antoinette hauled out a black leather wallet from a matching bag which she had had locked between her Cuban heels under the table. Antoinette always matched, apart from on 'multi-coloured' days, which she said were an evil necessity of Boho chic.

Dominic estimated that he knew what Antoinette was talking about ten per cent of the time. She ignored his interruption, halting only to drag a highly stylised hand through her bob, which because of its close proximity to her mouth Dominic noticed was the same colour as her lips. Which were animated, though Dominic couldn't quite understand what was coming out.

'Just going to the fag machine.' Dominic moved towards the

darkness at the back of the bar. It was still early and the pub had the sickly sweet lingering smell of last night's unfinished glasses and stale cigarettes.

Something seemed to connect in her brain. 'How's your father?'

'I'm sorry?'

'Your dad. How is he?'

'Yeah, OK, he's got a ticklish sort of cold at the moment.'

Antoinette didn't know that Dominic hadn't spoken to his father in four years. He liked to tantalise her with medical details that suggested he was on his way out.

'Still smoking?'

''Fraid so,' said Dominic.

'Good.'

'*Good?*' said Dominic with mock surprise.

'Well, you know, good that he hasn't fallen for all this politically correct stuff.' She smiled.

Unlike the bars in town which, by 6 p.m., would be spilling onto the pavements with suits, the Dog and Duck did most of its trade after hours, or in half-hour bursts after TV programmes had finished. A couple of teenagers were draining pints of lager over the pool table. They were wearing vests like the white cotton vests Dominic's mum sewed his initials (D.P.) into that made them call him *damp proof* at school. Their chunky gold chains swung like metronomes over the pool table when they dipped for a shot. There were two discarded matching tartan shirts on the red velour next to them. A sheet of handwritten darts fixtures was tacked to the wall. Someone had crossed out a name and written 'twat' on it in red.

Dominic liked the Dog and Duck not least because he knew Antoinette couldn't stand it. Thanks to the familiarity of his surroundings, and three Advil, his headache was evaporating. Last week their meeting in a Soho bar had actually brought on a focal migraine.

When he returned to the table Antoinette was mid-shriek.

'Sorry, darling, got to dash.' She snapped the phone shut and slammed it on the table. Not to be outdone, Dominic countered with a packet of Camel lights. 'Bloody woman thinks she can haggle me down. No bloody way.' Antoinette made it sound as if every word was a sentence. 'Dodo, why do we have to drink in this bloody awful pub?' She hoovered up several gulps of vodka and tonic with a straw. *Hygienewise* she always insisted on straws in bars outside zones one and two.

Antoinette's job had, Dominic was dimly aware, a seasonal element to it. As the earth rotated, so too did the in colours, and so too did Antoinette's clients. 'People will always need to know their fundamental tones,' she said. Fundamental tones put Antoinette in the top taxation bracket.

'I mean it's not like we even know anyone round here.'

'I do,' said Dominic petulantly.

'Who?'

Dominic paused. 'Well, John there, and Mr Ahmed in the paper shop, and the Italian at the dry cleaners.'

'But Dodo, you don't *know* them, know them.' He was on a losing tack but had temporarily made her forget the stack of estate agents' details in front of her.

'What?' Dominic said sarcastically. 'You mean you *know* those tossers you hang around with?'

'You mean our *friends*?' Antoinette's mouth drew back in disgust, causing a curve like a punctuation bracket to appear at either side, placing her lips in parenthesis. 'Yes, I think I have more understanding of our friends than I do of Mr Ahmed, yes.' She flicked a column of cigarette ash angrily, which missed the ashtray, and rearranged herself in a way that suggested she was leaving.

Dominic wanted to tell her to fuck off but he was aware it wasn't the response of a 29-year-old man and no way to speak to a girlfriend of seven years.

They'd both started university as approximately the same people, but by the end of their courses, like a light source diffracting through a crystal, they were at odds. Antoinette had used higher education to gentrify herself beyond all reference to her suburban childhood. And Dominic had yet to invent his adulthood. They were like lovers in a metaphysical poem, except rather than being twin points on a pair of dividers, they were no longer in the same geometry set.

She softened gradually. 'Look, Dodo, I said I'd meet Susie in a North African place in Clerkenwell. Do you fancy it?'

'What sort of a place?'

'What do you mean, "What sort of a place?" A Rabat sort of a place.'

Dominic hadn't really known what he'd meant but he'd been reluctant to turn it down straight off. For a start, it meant Antoinette hadn't envisaged their drink lasting more than half an hour. He felt another stab of annoyance.

'Better not.'

'OK, fine,' said Antoinette and got up to go. Her skirt had ridden above her knee and Dominic thought that if he hadn't been her boyfriend he would have fancied her. She thrust her phone back in her bag. Dominic knew that what he really wanted was to be persuaded.

He sounded hurt. 'It's just that I think we should . . .'

'What?' said Antoinette, her annoyance subsiding.

'Well, you know.' He shrugged.

'No,' she said cautiously, sitting down again.

'Talk. You know, about the move. Us.' He was playing a dangerous game.

'Well,' said Antoinette, 'I suppose I don't have to go.' She pulled her phone out, 'I'll call Sus—'

'No, you go,' said Dominic, pretending hurt. 'You should see your friends. Anyway, I've got work stuff to do.' Inwardly he grinned. He'd only intended to prove to himself that he could get her to stay if he wanted. But in less than a minute she'd notched up *uncommitted* and *selfish* on the relationship blacklist. He tried

17

to hide his victory as she stormed out. He picked up his pint, adding *pre-menstrually unstable* to the tally. He contemplated a kebab. It hadn't been a totally wasted evening.

IV

Hidden by the maze of partitions, Dominic was staring out of the window. It was the fourth cloudless day in a row. Even cycle couriers snaking past him on the way to work had shed a layer of Lycra. Dominic knew that he could no longer get away with ironing only the front of his shirt.

For him, June meant fear. For years it had been exams. Now it was Antoinette's house hunting fever that started with an irritable restlessness in late May and reached a sweaty peak in mid-August. It began to tail off in late September with a mild recurrence around Christmas and, depending on the interest rates, then lay completely dormant until May. He knew from the estate agents' details on display last night that the campaign had already started. For the last four years, aided by the rise in London prices, a hike in the cost of borrowing and judicious gazumping by a Scottish couple on a Georgian terrace in Barnsbury, he'd managed to escape commitment.

'The toilet duck says we should start.' Deborah swung her hips sullenly as she sucked on a liquorice stick.

'What?'

'The toilet duck says,' Deborah put two fingers to her eyes, sending the liquorice stick into her hair, and squeaked in a Japanese accent, 'you must staaaart.'

Tony Beecham was known around the office as Tony San because of his obsession with Japanese management techniques (despite Don Gilson's objections to Japan's poor record on animal rights). Tony had a girlish waist, slim and very high up. He emphasised it by a tight belt that gave shape to his hips, elongated his bottom and stressed the winking half-moon of his buttocks under his Y-fronts as he walked. This, and his obsession with longevity, had caused most of his colleagues at SOS to speculate that he was gay although in fact Tony wore his trousers like that because he thought it made him look like Bruce Lee. Today's meeting was based on the Japanese management technique of *kiesan*.

'What I think she's trying to say is that Tony has told us to start the meeting,' said Gill with a G, the office manager about whom Dominic had never felt the same after he'd seen a can of vaginal deodorant in her bag. She wore fake gold belted skirts and drove a Peugeot 306 and had a teenage son called Mark who spent most of his time in young offenders' institutions. She had recently started hinting at the 'special relationship' she had forged with Tony.

In the conference room, someone had laid out a convenience-store breakfast. Each banana had a 73p price sticker attached to it, which Dominic recognised as having come from the nearby Egyptian Lodge community store. The oranges were unpriced.

'Come on, who's supposed to start this bloody thing, then?' Deborah's concession to the weather was to wear a pair of denim dungarees turned into a dress.

'Tony is,' said Gill. 'As if I haven't got better things to do than sit around with you lot.' Gill had colour-treated hair and wore a lot of manmade fabrics.

'But the whole point is that this meeting is *without* Tony,' Don said. 'We discuss ways that we think the agency could be improved and then report back.'

'Bollocks,' said Deborah. 'Pass me one of those mango yoghurts.'

Don started to take charge. 'The whole point of *kiesan* is that it isn't a leadership thing. It's all about continuous improvement.'

Deborah, after licking the lid of the yoghurt pot, threw it sticky side down on the table. It was priced 73p, Dominic noticed.

Dwight, the office junior, was slumped with his head face down, resting on his crossed arms. A £1.73 can of Red Bull stood six inches from his head.

His voice was boyish. 'Are you sure I have to be here? I feel like shit.' He lifted his head just off the table. He was wearing an orange cropped top and silver drawstring trousers. Dominic thought he caught a glimpse of glitter on his left cheek. Gill had once told him that Dwight was thinking of applying for a sex change on the NHS. Gill had counselled against it. She'd read that a black man's high level of testosterone made the operation virtually undoable and she'd dated a security guard from Charing Cross who reckoned that ninety per cent of transsexuals regretted the op and returned to the unit with an axe. 'Attacked the surgeon with a chopper,' she'd said with a nicotine laugh, 'as it were.'

Don wore half-moon glasses and, now the weather had improved, open-toed shoes without socks. His feet were in impeccable order, neatly trimmed toes in perfect descending size. He had a faint northern accent that the office associated with honesty and suffering.

He stood up. 'So can anyone suggest parts of their workload which, given the overall strategy of the company's policy, could be improved on?'

'Come again?' said Gill as she reached for a banana, her blouse stretching across her back, showing her bra straps as she leant over. Then for no reason she stood up and breathed in hard, allowing a clutch of blouse to fall over her waistband. She sat down and started to peel the banana. 'My *workload* would be improved if I didn't have to spend half an hour at the Egyptian Lodge getting this stuff.'

'Toilet duck says it's breakfast and a gift from management,' said Deborah.

'Dominic?' Don's glasses slipped down his nose as he turned to him. Dominic had deliberately positioned himself away from the table to show his lack of enthusiasm. It would have been outright disdain if Tony had been chairing it, but Dominic liked Don. He shrugged and opened his fists, which were resting on the table.

'Why do you call him toilet duck?' Dwight asked Deborah.

'Because he's a tosser and Tony San sounds like a bathroom cleaner.'

Dominic sighed, looked at his nails and made a note of the For Sale sign on a flat above Shoe Express in the High Street. Antoinette would hate it, but it showed he was making an effort.

'Can I have a banana?' said Deborah, looking at Gill. In an unexpected show of anger, Don ripped one from a bunch and slammed it down in front of her.

Deborah was unmoved. 'No, I mean, Gill, am I allowed a banana? I'm food combining this week.'

Gill scrunched up her eyes in thought. 'You've had a yoghurt?'

'Dairy.'

'Then you can't.'

Deborah grunted.

'Have another yoghurt,' said Gill.

'Too many fat units.'

'Go on,' said Gill. She wore a ring on every finger of both hands, with the exception of the wedding finger.

Don ignored them. 'Well, I have one suggestion to make.'

'Oooh er,' said Gill.

Dwight pulled his head off the table. 'I think I'm going to chuck up.' He pushed his chair back and sat staring at the table, silently belching, with his hand clamped to his chest.

Don continued, 'In my opinion a fresh perspective is what's needed, new eyes and all that. I think if we were to redistribute our species database, we might all feel the benefits.'

Dominic abruptly sat up, as if someone had pulled a string attached to his collar.

'For example,' Don went on, 'Deborah, which species are you responsible for?'

'Can't remember.' In the absence of a spoon she was using her finger to scoop up the yoghurt.

'And Dom, you're what, exactly?'

'Exactly . . .' Dominic paused and nodded his head from side to side as if to indicate that the number of animals he was responsible for was difficult to articulate. 'Exactly, I.' He stopped.

Don sat down.

Dominic said, 'My point is that as regards lists, Don, I'm not sure we really should be doing anything as hasty as that.' Don's rapid descent into his chair dislodged the air in the room. Suddenly everyone, even Dwight, was looking at Dominic. He continued, 'I mean, experience counts for everything in this game. I mean, how many of us would have your touch with elephants, or Tony's with tigers? Or even Deborah's with,' he paused, 'pregnant mares?' He shifted his chair round towards the table. 'No, I think in order to get this agency on the map we need an altogether different approach.' He smiled to signal the end of his speech.

'Like what?' asked Deborah.

'Well,' said Dominic, 'something new and exciting. Really new and really exciting.'

'Such as?' Don looked genuinely aroused.

At that moment the door burst open with such ferocity that the Labradors of the World calendar swayed left to right on its drawing pin. Tony stood before them. He held his hands together and said, 'It looks like we're saved. In its wisdom the Lottery Commission has granted SOS a grant of fifty thousand pounds to,' he looked at the letter he was holding in his left hand, 'continue the sterling work with refugees for the oppressed and their families. Providing essential—'

'You what?' said Deborah.

'I'm only reading it,' snapped Tony, anxious not to have his good news knocked. 'Providing—'

'That's going a bit far, isn't it, calling them families?' said Deborah, scraping yoghurt from her front. 'I mean I wouldn't refer to a pair of elephants as a mummy and daddy exactly.'

'Sounds spicy,' said Gill.

Dwight raised his head. 'You're probably not allowed to call animals *animals* any more,' he said. 'Not PC, probably got to call them people. I mean, like, we're not people any more, we're co-workers.'

'Co-worker yourself,' said Gill.

'Look,' said Tony, 'they can call them the Duke and Duchess of York for all I care. What it means is that we've got some funding at last.'

'That's brilliant news, Tony.' Don had crossed the room and was shaking Tony by the hand. 'That really means we can get a few worthwhile projects under way. Congratulations.'

'Yes, well done,' said Dominic. He stood up and glanced at his watch, tapping the face pensively. 'Look, unfortunately I've got an appointment with my contact at the IFA.' He shrugged. 'Sorry, but I think he's got a new lead.'

'Oh,' said Tony, disappointed. 'I thought we could go out and celebrate, discuss new things, see how the *kiesan* meeting went, bond a bit.' He smiled. 'Come on. Who fancies a spot of early lunch?'

Only Don nodded.

Tony continued, 'Sushi? On me?'

'Oh yeah. Which bits?' said Gill.

Deborah shook her head. 'Sorry, I can't have protein.'

Dwight moved towards the door. 'I really am gonna chuck up.'

CHAPTER TWO

I

Tim the First, the only democratically elected leader of Belugastan, had never seen a genuine pair of the boots after which he had named himself. He would have called himself Timberland, but it might have caused legal problems. Tim knew from *Forbes* magazine how litigious Americans could be.

But he was aware that the boots stood for strength and reliability, which was good, because strong and reliable was how Tim thought of himself. There had been another reason – it had the chilling resonance of the Mongol leader Tamerlane who, second only to Bill Clinton, Tim admired most in the world, excluding his mother and his almost-fiancée. The name struck the right balance between tyrannical dictatorship and entrepreneurial zeal. As a bonus, the boot company's website expounded a corporate creed so close to philosophy that Tim had decided to make it the state religion. The third reason for an electoral nom de plume was to shed his former identity as Feodor Barinov. As Barinov, he was wanted for fraud by the regional prosecutor. As the elected Tim the First with a place in the Russian Duma, he was not.

Out with the old and in with the new had been Tim's winning election slogan, along with a manifesto promising to make pit bull terrier fighting the national sport. The $100 bill presented to every voter who put an X against his name on the ballot paper hadn't, history would record, gone amiss.

It was a new dawn but very little in Belugastan had changed. The unwieldy party apparatchiks still ran the show, cutting deals and carving up the country's resources the same as they had done for the last seventy years. Only today they were allowed to show off their wealth in Hugo Boss suits and hearse-black Japanese jeeps. What the West didn't realise was that what they called the biggest players in the Russian Mafia were dyed-in-the-wood communists. Under communism they'd been limited to a fortnight's summer holiday in Bulgaria and limitless caviar and Soviet champagne. Now the booty was limitless.

What *was* new in Belugastan was the twenty-storey palatial hotel in which Tim found himself. It was not only palatial in the way that the Swedish hotel chain had intended it, it was palatial in the sense that the ruler's official residence took up the entire thirteenth floor, which due to superstition was the only floor neither long-term leased nor occupied.

Tim was six floors below his official suite, in room 74, the sometime home of Anna Arbatova, his girlfriend, to whom in the past half-hour he'd proposed marriage, a place in the cabinet and oral sex. She had refused all three. Tim disapproved of opposition, but in Anna's case he made an exception. As, still in bed, he struggled to pull on his underpants, the solid gold nuggets of his four rings danced like 24-carat finger puppets beneath the sheets.

Finally he levered himself out of bed to open the window, which led onto a small balcony overlooking Peace Square. The smell of diesel fumes hit him before the heat. The current heat wave was testing even to the population of a country at the heart of the world's biggest landmass. An unfair scalding of weather had arrived too early and claimed the lives of twelve people. Not, as in other countries, the old and the weak; in Belugastan the sunstroke victims were young vodka-charged men drowning in local reservoirs. Tim drew an arm across his wet forehead.

'Why won't you?' he asked again. For a man half an inch over six foot four and weighing sixteen stone, Tim's voice was quieter and more refined than people expected.

'Why won't I what?' Though Anna knew what he meant.

'Take the job.'

'Because I already have a job.' Anna sat up and tried to pull the sheet over her breasts.

'I am asking you to help me, and the country,' said Tim, 'and you are refusing to come to your nation's service. Am I right?' He hadn't meant it aggressively. Tim's displays of aggression were never directed towards women, for whom he had 'more than average respect' – his phrase.

He had been born Feodor Barinov on 12 April 1961, the day Yuri Gagarin became the world's first cosmonaut. As the capsule whizzed through the atmosphere, Mrs Barinova had been undergoing a thirty-two-hour labour in maternity hospital 54. Gagarin's module plummeted to earth in a Saratov garden after 10 hours and 55 minutes, and just under twelve hours later she was delivered of a ten-pound baby boy. Feodor's father wanted to call him Yuri, but his mother, a professor of English and Russian literature, correctly anticipated a glut in the name and called her first and only son after Dostoyevsky. That evening as her son was taken to be wrapped in swaddling she predicted, cosmos or not, that he would be touched by stardom.

At the age of fifteen, Feodor encouraged his mother to translate English and American detective fiction into Russian, which he pirated on a homemade printing press and sold at a rouble per publication, Conan Doyle being the market leader. Less than ten years later, at the age of twenty-four, he was on the way to becoming a multi-millionaire with a fortune carved out of an illegal pyramid scheme built on shares in the local Aftonat factory.

When the factory and the scheme collapsed in 1994 and the militia were called in, Feodor's career in politics began. Feodor knew election to the presidency of Belugastan would come with an automatic seat in the Russian Duma where, along with the rest of the criminal element, approximately ten per cent of all politicians, he would be exempt from prosecution. Though in any other country a politician who had profited at the expense of a ruined electorate would stand little chance of election, in Belugastan, like Albania, voters seemed to respect a crook. For that Feodor was duly grateful. In case they changed their mind he operated under an alias.

He lay back on the bed and tried to pin Anna down by stretching his right arm out over her. Anna Arbatova had hair as close to the colour of cream as anything he'd ever seen. Her skin was like steppe hay in August.

She pushed his arm away. 'Tim, I don't want to be your Minister of Women's Culture.'

'*For* women's culture,' Tim corrected.

'Whatever. It still sounds like a cure for thrush.'

'Haven't women got a place in our new society?' asked Tim plaintively. The fortune Tim had amassed had been unscrupulous but not as underhand as most Russian money piles, and he wanted something honest for Belugastan. He wanted the nation to be built on principles. Anna, who was standing in front of a mirror, pulling a pair of jeans on over a red G-string, agreed.

'Of course.'

'Well, then.'

'But I have a job.'

Tim moved to the edge of the divan and buttoned his shirt from top to bottom. 'Some job.'

Before she met Tim, Anna had been the principal dancer of the country's ballet company. When she met Tim she was still a principal dancer, though at a lap-dancing club. With the end of Soviet subsidies, the national ballet company had closed. On Tim's persuasion she'd taken a behind-the-scenes job as the club's manager.

She flicked her hair into a ponytail. 'Can't you get someone else to do it?'

'Like who?' Tim smelt his sock. 'It has to be a woman.'

'Your mum?' She was inches from the mirror, using a brush to apply lipstick.

'I cannot,' Tim sighed, 'get my mother to be the Minister for Women's Culture.'

Anna blotted her lips. 'Why not? She's not that old.'

'No,' he said slowly, 'but she *is* the Foreign Minister.' He paused and looked at Anna. 'Have you no interest in helping your country?'

'No, I mean yes. Yes, of course. Look, I've got to dash. Are you coming tonight?'

'Yeah. We've got a cabinet think-tank.' He said the words hesitantly in English as Anna kissed the air over her shoulder. She hadn't even asked what think-tank meant.

'I love you,' he called after her as the door closed on him. He shook his head as he pulled up his Armani jeans and simultaneously clicked on his Rolex, checking to see if it was time for his presidential jeep to arrive. It was with a sense of sorrow, as he threaded his leather belt, that he realised the Rolex was older than the country he ruled.

Belugastan was to be five years old on 1 August. A funnel-shaped country the size of Wales, its apex was a twenty-kilometre stretch of the Caspian, which it clung to like a drunk to a bottle. In the boom days of caviar production the country's sliver of coast had entitled it to fish the sea for its grey-green prize of primeval ooze.

Now even the sturgeon faced their future with apathy – fewer and fewer bothered the up-water swim along the polluted Volga to spawn. Apart from a few die-hard poachers, most of Belugastan's 90,000 population had returned to a nomadic lifestyle, living in yurts in the mountains and scratching out a living from goats, sheep and camels.

Whereas other territories had fought bloody wars to free them-selves from the Soviet oppressor, Belugastan, or Kalkukia as it was known in Soviet times, had slipped away like a gatecrasher at a party. The Kalkukia National Front had fortuitously chosen the day that Boris Yeltsin had swiped the world headlines by drunkenly conducting a German brass band as the day that it would chug, undocumented, into autonomy. The move involved little more than a declaration from the local TV station and a new flag run up the mast in Peace Square.

Even if the Russian President hadn't been otherwise indisposed, few in the Kremlin would have lost sleep over the loss of Kalkukia. Unlike Chechnya with its strategic place on the Caspian oil pipe's route to Europe, Kalkukia made the Soviet graveyard of Norilsk look like a boom town.

In deference to the glory days of caviar production, the secessionists, a huddle of bespectacled nationalist factions who, after seventy years of oppression, survived only two of freedom, named the country Belugastan. Even the new flag was a black lump of Beluga on a red, blue and white background.

It was a quiet transition which fitted the place. In its entire history the country had only appeared once in Soviet texts, as the arid region where Catherine the Great banished St Petersburg prostitutes in the eighteenth century. That was why the country's only resource was a glut of highly attractive women, some of whom were of questionable virtue.

But, as resources went, it was a start.

II

The start of June was the best time to get them, second only to the start of the summer holiday when Erik usually looked forward to a schoolgirl special. Topicality was the magazine's watchword. Take the war in Kosovo, when he'd done an army special. He'd even borrowed a tank from the nearby military base where the commandant had promised to throw in a couple of Migs for an extra twenty dollars. But Erik knew his limitations; he couldn't fly and he'd never get the girls to travel. He'd got a mate from his national conscription days to park the tank in Leninski Park, effectively ending four chess games and a football league final. But on the brighter side, he had picked up eight more subscribers.

Twenty-eight-year-old Erik Marchenko had the dark thin looks of a Tartar, though he was Ukrainian by descent. In his opinion he had two principal physical traits that set him aside from the ordinary – dark, near pupil-less eyes which he exaggerated by wearing black-rimmed specs with no magnifying power, and charisma. The latter was an underrated commodity throughout the former Soviet Union.

His prey was a girl buying apples from an Armenian street seller. Even though Erik couldn't see her face, he knew from her good calves and the attentiveness of the Armenian that she was attractive.

She was wearing tights under a knee-length blue cotton dress and high slip-on shoes. Experience had taught him not to approach women wearing flat shoes, which demonstrated a lack of interest in personal maintenance. Ironically, he thought, they objected more than the good-looking ones to taking their clothes off for money.

He crossed the road as she was putting the kilo of apples in her bag.

'Excuse me. I saw you from across the street and I was wondering if you wouldn't mind showing me your breasts?' The hot weather made his job so much easier. His December edition, which saw two topless girls posing with shovels in the snow – Edition 12, topical issue, *The Reburial of Tsar Nicholas II* – had caused him no end of problems. It was impossible to gauge chest size in a fur coat.

'I'm sorry?' She was a brunette with short hair. Readers' letters suggested a preference for long hair, but Erik wasn't totally unaware of the women's movement and felt he should move with the times. She had a haughty expression, which was common at this stage. Erik knew straightaway that her clothes were too cheap to be deliberately down-at-heel.

'I was wondering if I could see your breasts.' As he spoke Erik thrust his hands in his trouser pockets like a schoolboy. He needed to come across as a younger brother with a natural curiosity about the female body. Sex overcomplicated his work.

'Why?' It had worked. She was not offended, not even shocked. If anything, she was amused.

'I think you can help me.' This was the time to look away, embarrassed.

'You think my breasts can help you?' She was starting to edge away. Erik knew he had to root her physically to the spot. He lit two cigarettes and offered her one.

'What's your name?'

'Lisa.' She stressed the first syllable and exhaled a mouthful of smoke with the second.

'Work locally, Lisa?' Erik moved his glasses to the top of his head.

'I'm a student.' Erik could make out the hard edges of books she was carrying in a plastic bag with a picture of the Marlboro man on it. Her legs were so thin they barely pulled her beige tights taut.

He inhaled again and smiled. Erik had a theory about women that rarely let him down. Compliment beautiful women on their intelligence and intelligent women on their beauty. He'd only known it once to have occurred together and she, he was glad to say, wasn't up for negotiation.

'Look, I'll be blunt. You look like the sort of woman I can talk to.' He inhaled. 'I run an art house magazine with several erudite columns and I wondered if you might think about contributing to it.'

She hid her confusion and disappointment, Erik was pleased to note, with a smile.

She blushed slightly. 'But what's that got to do with my breasts?'

'No, the breasts were a mistake.' He tried to look embarrassed. With a slight backward flick of the head he let his glasses fall back onto his nose.

'I'm sorry?'

'Your breasts. At first I thought you might make it as a model, but now I can see your talents lie in other directions. You should be pleased.' He smiled and rotated his foot over the butt of his cigarette on the pavement. He liked the definition of his thigh muscles prominent under his jeans when he did this.

'But . . .' Lisa was pulling in her stomach muscles and using the top of her arms to tighten her dress over her breasts.

'Look, it depends on this month's model quotient. We'll see. Only now,' he said looking at his watch, 'I'm in a bit of a rush. Could I take your number?'

'Well . . .'

'OK, then, we'll leave it.' He made to look round.

'347 0292.' Because she was breathing in so hard she struggled with the number and exhaled loudly at the end. Her breath smelt faintly of onions. He pulled a Biro from his top pocket and jotted it on the back of his hand.

'I can't promise anything but we'll see.' He extended a hand to Lisa who shook it limply. All the haughtiness had gone. Erik smiled. He hadn't even had to mention money and, despite her short hair, she might make a saucy American bank teller for Edition 74, topical issue, *Can IMF Loans Really Help the Former Soviet Union?*

Now Erik had to hurry. He had left his Dneiper motorbike and sidecar on the corner of Andropov Street half a kilometre away. He started to sprint, cutting through the smell of a hotdog stand, the weight of his mobile phone thudding satisfyingly against his hip. A car backfired as he dashed across the road, swerving through a ragged line of street urchins selling out-of-date newspapers to drivers as they waited at the traffic lights. Erik didn't have time to check out the opposition, the cabinet meeting started in twenty minutes. Aside from being an amateur pornographer, or even because of it, Erik was Belugastan's Minister of Culture.

III

Tim paused as he crossed the square towards the Palace of Culture, former home of the National Ballet School and now the head-quarters of his club – Come Dancing, the former Soviet Union's premier lap-dancing club. He was weighing up the scene in terms of the pluses and minuses of the last five years. From where he stood the minus side was in debit.

The Palace of Culture had been built in the shape of a combine harvester. Few architects would have embarked on so ambitious a project, but the 1960s were the heyday of Soviet achievement, the satisfied post-Stalin belch during which the capital of Belugastan had been created. The town, if it had been known for anything, was renowned as the centre for combine harvester production and its central factory, now virtually defunct, was called simply the Kombinat. The factory doubled as the Aftonat factory where Tim had launched his pyramid scheme. Today on the left flank of the building, which residents took to be a wheel, on top of a fresco that had once read 'We are building Communism', was an advert for Israeli toothpaste. On the other wheel, basking in the evening sun, a huge poster advertised Zhubelovski vodka, with a picture of a beaming man in an open-necked shirt holding a bottle and pointing at a hologram of himself on the neck. Tim knew that on both images Vladimir Zhubelovski's facial warts had been air-brushed out. Due to an empire built on vodka and narcotics, Zhubelovski was the richest man in the country.

Opposite the Palace of Culture in the central square were two cast bronze busts, one of Dzhungar, the fourteenth-century Mongol who, according to folklore, founded the country, the other of Lenin. Tim was aware that other states had celebrated their independence by removing all traces of their Soviet past. Tim had it on his to-do list but he hadn't got round to it. In his defence, he maintained that Belugastan shouldn't be afraid to remember its past which, though inglorious, had allowed some, including himself, to become exceedingly well off. Also in his mental in-tray was the re-ignition of the eternal flame which had gone out eighteen months ago in a power cut.

Trolley buses clattered around the square driven by men and women who had last received a pay cheque more than a year ago. They drove with a barely concealed sense of anarchy, as if, unpaid, they no longer had to comply with the laws of the road. Since neither teachers nor medical staff, street cleaners or bin men had been paid in anything other than a consignment of Kazakh gherkins exchanged for a combine harvester, he hoped they weren't setting a precedent.

The blue-uniformed traffic GAI, secreted at vantage points around the square, swooped only when they saw the coloured number plates of a foreigner, of which there were few, or the more familiar insignia of a foreign car, of which there were many.

Tim blinked as he went into the dark entrance. The main hall where Come Dancing was housed was next to an empty cavernous cloakroom. Unused in summer, its space was jealously overseen by two old women dressed in grey housecoats. On their left was a closed sportswear concession called Reebuk. The building smelt of dampness and changing rooms, and out of the early evening sunshine, the interior seemed even gloomier than usual.

It was an unusual venue for a governmental cabinet meeting. But it served in the absence of a parliament, which was still being converted from the Palace of Youth by Turkish builders. Also it was on the bus route home of Mrs Barinova.

'Would anyone like a drink before we start?' They were sitting in a green plastic alcove at the furthest point from the main stage.

Apart from a few bar staff getting ready for the evening ahead, the club was empty. It held a pre-party sort of expectation that Tim liked.

'Mum?'

'A gin and tonic would be nice, darling.'

'Erik?'

'Bacardi and cranberry juice, please.' Erik had one hand in the pocket of a pair of grey combat trousers, from where he was drawing on a cache of sunflower seeds. A discarded pile of husks lay in the ashtray.

Tim called over a waitress wearing a pair of blue trousers, a short-sleeved shirt and a pink badge with her name on it. Friday afternoon was the Kids' Kabaret, when the club opened its doors to the under-twelves of Belugastan's apparatchiks, Tim's recompense for the way that their avarice and corruption kept the country going. Tim had based it on the *Zolotoya Molodzh*, the Golden Youth of the Communist Party, who had also believed it was never too early to start networking.

'Anna not coming, dear?' asked Mrs Barinova, crunching on an ice cube.

'No,' said Tim, not looking up. 'She can't, she's working tonight.'

'Still with the computer firm?'

'Yeah, that's right.' When he'd first told his mother that his girlfriend was a lap-dancer, she'd claimed to mishear and ever since maintained Anna was a laptop enhancer. He could see no reason to put her right. Tim had been amazed his mother had known what a laptop was. She said she'd read about them in *American Psycho*.

Erik had known Tim since the days of the pyramid scheme, at the Aftonat factory, where Erik had worked as a post-perestroika *tolkach*, the youngest in the firm's sixty-year history. A *tolkach* was a communist fixer. During a period when ordering a new light bulb could take a month, a *tolkach* had the contacts to duck the stranglehold of Soviet bureaucracy and keep industry running.

Now Erik used his flair to track down attractive women. In essence, the technique was the same.

Out of the corner of his eye Tim saw Igor the stagehand and bouncer sweeping the floor for the 9 p.m. performance.

Erik said, 'Where is everybody else?'

'Business,' said Tim.

'What sort of business?' asked Erik. Even though there was no one around worth impressing, he pushed his glasses onto the top of his dark hair.

Tim said, 'A *razborka*.' A *razborka* was a settlement of accounts which in Belugastan was more likely to be done with rocket launchers than pocket calculators.

'Anyone we know?' asked Mrs Barinova.

'Tseltralny versus the Kombinat.' He made it sound like a football match. In other countries it would have been a football match, but in Belugastan the gangs belonged to workers from the central metalworks and the Kombinat.

'Ouch,' said Erik, grimacing.

'Look,' said Tim, looking at his watch. His law and order platform had already been dented by the recent disappearance of half a dozen women from the town, even though no bodies had been found. 'Can we move on?' He signalled to the waitress for another Coke. He was keen to finish before the start of Anna's shift.

Mrs Barinova bent to pick up a ball of wool that had fallen onto the floor.

Tim put down his Coke and said, 'As you all know, the challenges that face us, the first democratically elected government of Belugastan, are, not to put too fine a point on it, immense.' He looked at each one of them gravely.

'Hear, hear,' said Erik, starting his second Bacardi and cranberry.

Tim went on, 'We have to build on what we've got. And what is that exactly?'

Tim had meant it rhetorically so was annoyed when Erik said, 'Girls.'

Mrs Barinova shook her head.

'Yes, Erik,' said Tim, 'women will be a valuable resource, but we have another valuable and beautiful resource.'

'Not those bloody combine harvesters,' said Erik.

'No, we have one of the most beautiful *countries* in the world.' He put his palms flat on the table. 'I say we open Belugastan up for tourism.'

Nobody said anything. Mrs Barinova sucked the end of her knitting needle contemplatively. After thirty seconds she said, 'What about virtual casinos?'

'That's not a bad idea,' said Erik, weighing it up. 'On-line gambling is going to be huge.'

'But,' said Tim, 'what about *tourism*?'

'Well, I can't really see it catching on,' said Mrs Barinova, trying not to offend. Mrs Barinova was old-style Russian intelligentsia. She was five foot one and, though she loved her lumbering son with every cell of her tiny frame, she did sometimes wonder if the nurses at the maternity ward hadn't handed her the wrong swaddling bundle. The woman in the next bed to her had been a javelin thrower. It did happen.

'Who, in their right minds, would want to come to Belugastan?' said Erik. 'It's hardly Saint-sodding-Tropez. Sorry, Mrs Barinova.'

'Well, it might be,' said Tim petulantly. 'What about two-week split yurt breaks?'

'What the hell,' Erik was contemptuous, 'is a two-week split yurt break?'

'Holiday-makers spend their first week in a yurt,' Tim spoke as if he was reading from a brochure with the words already fixed in his head, 'experiencing all the excitement of a nomadic way of life—'

'The excitement of a nomadic way of life?' repeated Erik incredulously. His tone was starting to annoy Tim. 'When was the last time you experienced the nomadic way of life? Probably never, because if you had you would know that it is about as exciting as watching sheep shit dry, which, incidentally, is what nomads spend ninety-five per cent of their time doing.' The speech seemed to exhaust Erik because in one movement he drained his Bacardi and cranberry and collapsed back into the booth. 'Anyway, what does the second week of this once-in-a-lifetime extravaganza entail? Seven days at a nuclear reactor?'

'No, a week's sturgeon fishing on the Caspian,' said Tim.

'What a thrill. The water's so polluted you're more likely to need an asbestos suit than a rod,' said Erik sulkily. 'Can I get another drink?'

Tim put his hand up to catch the waitress's eye. 'Same again?' He was trying not to take it to heart. 'OK then, what's your great idea?'

Erik waited for a moment. 'Lyposuction.'

'I'm sorry?' said Tim.

'Lyposuction.'

'What are you talking about?' asked Tim irritably.

'What does every woman in the world want?'

Mrs Barinova looked up. Erik continued, 'To be thin. Take this from someone who knows. Someone who spends his entire day studying the female form. I estimate, and I think you'll find that official statistics will back me up on this, that the average woman is now four kilos heavier than her Soviet sister. Of course, the Snickers and McDonald's revolution is to blame. Fast food is now the enemy of the people.'

'I like the filet o' fish,' said Mrs Barinova.

'Exactly,' agreed Erik. 'What I propose is turning the Kombinat into a lyposuction and health farm.'

'Oh, for Christ's sake,' said Tim.

'OK,' Erik conceded. 'I have another idea.'

The club started to fill up. Most were men wore sunglasses and cheap Turkish leather coats. The women were short-skirted and showing off an early summer tan in variously coloured boob tubes. The drinks, like the conversation, were strictly segregated; men drinking neat vodka shots while the women sipped glasses of luridly coloured viscose liqueurs. The body language at the tables meant they didn't know the women, or maybe just weren't drunk enough. Tim recognised a few of them from his Feodor Barinov days, before the pyramid scheme, when he'd been a small-town hustler. Now he and his country were going straight, he wanted to keep a distance.

'Go on,' said Tim cautiously.

'What have Scotland and Nepal got in common?'

'Is this some sort of joke?' Tim tapped his watch.

'No, think about it.'

'I love a riddle,' said Mrs Barinova.

'Give up?' asked Erik.

'Yeah, I give up,' said Tim. 'To be honest, I'm not so sure where Scotland is.'

Erik smiled. 'Really, it's more a Himalayan kind of thing.'

'Scotland is in the *Himalayas*?'

'No, you prat. The thing in question.'

'Is Himalayan?'

'Not exactly.'

'For Christ's sake, what is it then?'

Mrs Barinova put down her knitting. 'I know,' she sucked on a needle. 'Yetis,' she said excitedly.

'You're on the right lines, but more woolly,' said Erik.

IV

Anna chose not to park in the allotted space that, under Tim's instructions, had been marked Director. Not only did she consider it a ridiculous title for the manager of a strip club, if she parked on the pavement with the other German-made cars she stood less chance of having the Mercedes stolen. The creak and coolness of the leather was comforting and she was reluctant to leave the bubble of Teutonic efficiency to start another shift at Come Dancing.

After leaving Tim earlier that day she'd spent the afternoon shopping. It was her grandfather's birthday in a couple of days and, as she had done every year for the last sixteen years, she'd offered to make a cake. She was guessing again that a fruit sponge was his favourite. She had to guess because she'd never met him. In fact he was, as far as she knew, dead, which in many respects made his parties a bit of a non-event, but her grandmother insisted on them.

The results of her shopping, though no more than two bagfuls, had taken an afternoon of queuing and were littered over the back seat of the car, together with a birthday card with a bear and balloons on it, another tradition. She righted a carton of soured cream that had fallen over as she swerved to avoid a pothole and tried to feel optimistic about the coming six hours.

The car beeped and sealed itself shut as she headed across the cracked pavement carrying her shoulder bag and walked into the Palace of Culture.

'You've just missed them,' said the cloakroom attendant who looked as if she had been on duty since the 1917 revolution. Reporting on people, whether because of her age or because she'd spent fifty years being nosy for the security services, came as second nature to the old crone. Anna nodded. She presumed the woman was referring to Tim and the cabinet meeting.

Anna had avoided them on purpose. Not only would she have been roped in to the latest saving Belugastan initiative, there was also a stronger than odds-on chance that Tim would have proposed to her again, and making excuses was getting tiresome. And the more she rejected him, the likelier it was that he would go somewhere else.

She unlocked the door to her office and flicked the overhead light on. The office, previously used by male dancers as a changing room, was windowless and on hot days Anna was sure she could still smell the athletes' feet.

Inside, next to the fax, she saw a note with Tim's unmistakable backward sloping writing on it. 'Darling, I've gone to the banya. Why don't you come round after your shift finishes? I love you. Tim xxx. PS. We missed you at the cabinet meeting. PPS. Does lyposuction mean anything to you?'

She screwed the letter up and flicked it at the bin. If it went in, she reasoned with herself, her plan would work; if it missed, her scheme would fail. The paper ball fell neatly into the metal grey bin and Anna swallowed a smile. Superstition meant a lot to her.

She flicked back her hair, two blonde, shoulder-length plaits underneath a baseball cap, and sat down. On weekday evenings Come Dancing operated with a staff of a dozen dancers, one DJ and three bar staff, two of which were women who, if sickness demanded it, could double up as dancers. Lap-dancing, as Anna knew, had more to do with a well-trimmed bikini line and maintaining eye contact than a fantastic body or dancing skill.

The first few days of really hot weather always put their takings up. Not only did the sun leave the men dehydrated and gasping for beer, but the sight of women dressed in summer clothes left them wanting more. It was reassuring that men were predictable to the point of being barometer-led. For the moment she had the advantage over Tim – hormonally he couldn't get enough of her. By putting herself out of reach, it would stay that way. If she married him he would have a mistress in a month and she would steadily lose her influence. This way she had him just where she wanted him.

A green light flashed momentarily before the phone rang. When it warbled like that, it meant an international call. Cautiously she picked up the receiver and answered in English. She also stood up, partly out of nerves.

'This is Anna Arbatova speaking.'

'Hello, Anna. This is John in Huston. We need to talk.' He sounded relaxed. Anna always appreciated Americans' ability to get to the point.

'Yes, we do.' She smiled as she sank back into her swivel chair and coiled the phone cable around her finger. The chair dropped and bounced slightly under her weight. Something about the American's voice made her think of dollar signs.

CHAPTER THREE

I

The head-tossing, lip-pursed refusal by Antoinette to accompany Dominic to Tony's flat in Lewisham did not surprise him. In fact, it had been the certain knowledge that he would be turned down in favour of, as it happened, a visit to her chiropractor that had made Dominic ask her. As he recalled, it had been an Indian head massage that had caused her to miss SOS's cherry blossom celebration in April. He filed them both under *no interest in my work*, his list of her transgressions to be used against her at a later date.

Tony was calling it a *hoshin kanri* meeting. As he put it the day before, 'Policy deployment, a breakdown of strategy, execution and process change.' It was the usual sort of bollocks, but served the dual purpose of a free meal and an evening pass from Antoinette, with the prospect of a couple at the Dog and Duck on his way home.

It was weekend London. The suits had evaporated to leave the indigenous gangs of teenage girls, smoking and sullenly dragging platform shoes behind them. The girls wore long trousers and their skin was red under their vest tops. They gave off the thrill of night-time expectations along with a puff of bubble gum. Another side effect of growing up, the loss of the hormonal need to go out on a Saturday night, made Dominic despair.

Georgina Wroe

The train pulled out of Charing Cross to clatter through Battersea's two-up two-downs, where the landscape was more northern industrial than urban. The carriage was empty apart from a man in Lycra shorts with a mountain bike. On the seat opposite, the headline of Friday's *Evening Standard* screamed 'London Property Prices Set to Soar.' A fall in interest rates was apparently once more on the horizon.

After three years of studying lending rates as keenly as the head of the Bank of England, Dominic knew it could be a double-edged sword. Antoinette would either be tense – they had missed the boat – or relaxed – it would be stupid to buy. Though the unfocused dread of moving in with Antoinette exercised him for several hours a day, the exact reason *why* was more difficult to pinpoint.

It wasn't just the permanence that scared him. Permanence was possible, though not sought after. It was nailing his colours to a mast that worried him. The realisation that this would be the sum total of the parts of Dominic Peach. He gave himself until the age of thirty before he had to do anything drastic. Jobwise, property-wise or relationshipwise, as Antoinette would say.

This gave him 156 days, timewise.

Lewisham was a new area of London for Dominic. It even smelt different. London, for him, had increasingly the smell of a foreign city, a holiday destination rather than a home.

He clung to Tony's handwritten directions like a treasure map, all too aware that, even at the weekend, few pedestrians would be able to identify the next street. Among the stresses of living in the late twentieth century, no one mentioned the stress inherent in not being able to name the road fifty yards from your home.

Tony lived in a block of purpose-built four-storey flats from the 1980s which, depending on the politics of the borough, were installed with either entry phones (Conservative) or chair lifts (Labour). Tony's was a mutant cross, with the cataracts of dirty net curtains at some windows and long-stemmed flowers in blue vases at others. Dominic guessed Tony's to be the one with a mobile of aluminium stars jingling in the wind.

As he approached, an old woman rattled a shopping trolley in front of her as she ploughed out of the doorway. She looked at Dominic suspiciously. A fountain of grey hairs sprouted from a mole on her chin.

'You from the council?'

'No,' said Dominic.

'Got any ID?'

'No.'

'Then piss off.' She rammed her back, swathed in two coats, against the door to make sure it clicked shut before edging her trolley down the set of three stairs.

Dominic buzzed and waited for the metallic reply.

'Hello, Tony? It's Dominic.' The invitation to dinner had been a bolt from the blue. Dominic assumed it was a celebration of the Lottery money, though every time he said the word 'assume' in his head, he heard Antoinette stating, 'Never say *assume*, it just makes an ass out of u and me.'

He wished he'd stopped off for a couple in the Eagle on the corner.

'Hi,' said Tony, 'come up. It's on the second floor, first left.'

Dominic pulled the door. Inside, the stifling glass hallway smelt of furry carpet tiles and free papers left to bake in the sun.

Dominic didn't like mixing the Venn diagrams of work and free time. Seeing colleagues away from work was like catching your parents in bed. It revealed a new and disturbing side to them, one you didn't want to see or admit existed.

'Hi, come in, Dominic. Come on in.' Dominic had mapped out a couple of opening gambits in his head as he climbed the stairs. He was staggered to see dimly that the hall was lit by a dull bare bulb, and that Tony was wearing, unless Dominic was mistaken, a skirt.

Dominic tried hard not to look down. He thrust a bottle of red wine, anonymous in green tissue paper, into Tony's hand, out-stretched to be shaken.

'Nice place.' Dominic was in a dark room, turned pitch black as an internal door closed shut, sucking the light from the hall. Tony had disappeared as well. Then he seemed to re-emerge from an airing cupboard with a pair of black silk ballet shoes in his hand.

'Slippers?' he said.

'Great, yeah.' Despite his unspecific dread at being greeted at the threshold of a doll's house by a man in a skirt, Dominic's real worry was whether, verrucawise, or smellwise, he could get away with slippers. He decided he had no choice.

Tony had disappeared again, through a door where a crack of light was visible. Dominic slipped off his trainers and pushed his socks as far into them as he could, like a man planting bulbs.

'Couldn't your girlfriend make it?' Tony appeared in the door-way, illuminating Dominic as he levered his feet into the slippers, balancing himself against the wall. 'Do they fit all right?'

'Yeah, fine. Um, no. She, I mean Antoinette, had to see her chiropractor.' Dominic followed Tony through the doorway.

Tony said, 'Nothing wrong, I hope.'

For the first time it occurred to Dominic that a visit to a chiropractor often denoted pain. He wasn't sure why Antoinette went.

'Lower back trouble,' he said.

'Too much sitting at a desk, no doubt,' said Tony.

'Probably.' Dominic looked round the room which, in contrast to the hall, was white. This made it seem slightly larger than a box room. Streamers covered in Japanese lettering fell from a broad black picture rail. The floor was wooden and segmented by a silk screen. The flat smelt of stale joss sticks and boiled rice. It was tidy not in a minimalist sort of way but because there wasn't room for any objects.

'Take a seat,' said Tony and pointed to a futon. 'Has she tried any Chinese medicine?' he asked.

'Er, I'm pretty sure she's done some aromatherapy,' said Dominic tentatively. 'Probably.' He sat down, his buttocks jarring on a cushion he had wrongly expected to be soft.

'I was thinking more traditional. You know the three fundamentals – shen, qi and jing. Has she got bad jing, do you know? She might have been born with it.'

'Possibly,' said Dominic. 'Qi, QI right?'

'Mmm,' said Tony in a way that made Dominic think he took recreational drugs.

'Fantastic,' said Dominic.

'She has fantastic qi?' asked Tony as he sat on the floor, his outstretched feet touching Dominic's slippers.

'No, fantastic Scrabble word. If you haven't got a U.'

'Right,' said Tony, standing again. He said, 'I'll open this, then.' He went into the kitchen which was separated from the sitting room by a bead door.

Dominic was anxious. Tony's skirt, which he'd been hoping was a bath towel, was, in the light of day, a sarong that gaped dangerously when he sat down. Dominic wondered what Don Gilson would have said. Don was probably too in touch with his feminine side to notice. Questions of Tony's true sexuality came unbidden to Dominic.

'When are the others getting here?' he said in the direction of the kitchen. The size of the flat meant he didn't have to raise his voice.

'What others?'

'You know, the work lot, the gang.' He tried to sound jovial.

'No, Dom, it's just you.' He handed Dominic a glass of red wine. 'Or would you prefer a sake?'

'No, this is fine.' He sipped the drink and felt his teeth coated in tannin. He'd hoped in the mêlée of bottle-offering to upgrade his £3.49 Bulgarian. 'So then, it's just me. That will be nice.'

Tony returned to the kitchen.

Dominic started flicking through his Rolodex of excuses. He

continued, 'It's a great area here. Close to the station. What is it into town? Twenty minutes? Maybe Antoinette and I should think about buying in south London.'

Tony ignored him. 'How long have you been at SOS now, Dom? You don't mind if I call you Dom, do you?'

'Not at all.'

'And we still know so little about each other, don't we?' Tony sipped his drink. 'I strive for a family atmosphere at work. It's important, don't you agree?'

'Absolutely,' said Dominic, noticing that the window closest to the kitchen was steaming up.

'And families should be able to tell each other everything. Am I right?'

'Oh, yes, Antoinette and I share—'

'Care for another glass?' Tony swirled a measure of sake into his own glass, which threatened to spill over. After half a glass of silence, Tony said, 'Well, I guess we could get down to it now.'

'Get down to what, exactly?' asked Dominic noncommittally, his knees clamped shut.

'There's no point in beating about the bush,' Tony took a slug of sake and Dominic refilled his wine glass. 'I couldn't speak to Don about it, he would be heartbroken. But I've got to tell someone.'

Dominic was nodding as his buttocks clenched their way along the futon. 'Right,' he said. 'Whatever your problem, I'm sure we can all help.'

'I do so hope so.' Tony looked straight at Dominic and clutched his knee. Dominic let out an involuntary yelp.

'Yoko Ono?' asked Dominic, pointing his head towards the hi-fi.

'Sakamento,' replied Tony.

Dominic's palms started to sweat. 'Look, Tony, what's this all about? If you're trying to let it be known to the office via me that you fold origami for the other side, then that's fine. It's really no big deal. No big deal. I mean, look at Dwight.'

Tony recoiled with such speed, Dominic was afraid he would lose the sarong entirely. 'What are you talking about? Origami? I don't know any origami. Dwight? What's Dwight got to do with this?' As Tony moved, a cat that Dominic had thought was a cushion leapt onto the window ledge. 'Are you mad? I'm talking about the grant. The Lottery grant!'

'Oh.' On a couple of levels Dominic was disappointed. He had even less interest in the supposed injection of funds into SOS than in Tony's sexuality. 'What about the Lottery grant?'

Tony was sitting on a black ash chair opposite Dominic. Forgoing eastern convention for the fourth time, he poured himself another shot of sake, which he downed in one. 'That fifty grand we got from the Lottery Commission, to save SOS?'

'Ye-es,' said Dominic cautiously.

'All that crap about saving the oppressed, allowing them to live free, etc, etc. Remember? Well, it turns out they intended the money for another SOS. Not ours.'

'Which SOS?'

Tony was close to talking through clenched teeth. 'Swing Out Sisters.'

'Isn't that a pop group?'

'No,' said Tony sadly. 'It's a refuge for the victims of lesbian domestic abuse.'

'Oh.' They paused. Dominic said, 'Can lesbians be the victims of domestic abuse?'

'Unfortunately so. In Aberdeen, they call it lesbian on lesbian violence,' replied Tony glumly.

'In Aberdeen?'

'Apparently, Aberdeen is the biggest centre for lesbian on lesbian violence in Europe.'

Dominic was sage. 'Right.'

'Not good,' said Tony, sipping sake. 'I hate to break it to the others, it'll destroy Don.' They sat in silence for a while. Dominic asked if they had sent the cheque. Tony said that when he'd called

51

the Lottery Commission on Friday he'd been told they'd have it by Monday.

'I'm buggered if I'm going to let a lot of bloody dykes have money that could save species.' Tony, who up until then had only looked Dominic in the eye at the end of sentences, fixed him directly. 'There's one hope.'

Dominic looked up. 'Ye-es?'

'What do you know about Belugastan?' asked Tony.

Dominic frowned. 'Beluga what?'

II

From their vantage point halfway up the hillock, Erik could keep an eye on the motorcycle and sidecar, less as a precaution against theft, more in care a dog pissed on it.

'You know what you're like?' As Erik spoke a scream more pig than dog rent the air.

'Surprise me,' replied Tim unhappily.

The crowd took a collective inhalation of breath. One of the pit bull owners, a woman in cut-off denim shorts and a sun top, shouted encouragement.

'A saiga.' A saiga was the Russian equivalent of an African wildebeest albeit only two and a half feet tall. Its chief characteristic was a bulbous drinker's nose which warmed the winter steppe air as it breathed.

'Since when did you drop pornography to take up natural history?'

'No, I read about it last night, during my research. Let me tell you about the saiga. By the time the male saiga has chased down and successfully impregnated his mate, he is so exhausted he keels over and dies.'

'Relevance?' Tim stopped looking at the woman in the shorts and sun top and turned to Erik.

'You and Anna, man, you're getting obsessed trying to get her to marry you.'

'Haven't you got any pornography to do?' asked Tim irritably.

They were standing on the hill five metres from the rest of the crowd. Tim's low-profile election campaign meant that few of his electorate, ninety-three per cent of whom had voted in his favour, actually recognised their elected leader. Using a blow-up of a male model from *Four-Wheel Drives Today* as his poster had, according to Erik, not only improved his chances among the female voters but also lessened assassination attempts. Now, the electorate was kept informed of his true identity strictly on a need-to-know basis.

The blistering weather, so close to the end of the fighting season, guaranteed a good turn-out. There were twenty dogs on the fight list, thirteen Staffordshire pit bulls and seven American. The makeshift fighting ring was at the bottom of the dell that had once been the yard of the Cultural Club of Chemists, five kilometres south of the capital. The car park was stacked with smoke-glassed foreign cars watched over by crew-cut bully boys who, both in looks and temperament, were not very different from the dogs in the ring. Windows that weren't frosted as a security feature were clouded with the condensation of panting pit bulls inside.

The heat meant the average bout lasted no more than twenty minutes and the crowd was getting agitated, complaining the level of gore hadn't been worth their coming. A group of six rabble-rousing women fanning themselves with their palms had travelled overnight from Astrakhan. The weather left the dogs wheezing and apathetic. They lunged half-heartedly at necks and skulked deject-edly in corners. There was a rumour, put about by the small man in open-toed sandals with the fight list, that a mastiff and a Dalmatian would be fighting at three thirty.

'You see that,' Erik gestured with a roll-up cigarette towards the ring. 'My point entirely. There you go. The female is, and always will be, more aggressive than the male.' He looked at Tim. 'And not just in the animal world,' he said in a voice Tim thought was supposed to be sinister.

Tim knew that Erik was referring to what he called the 'balance of power' in his relationship with Anna.

'Why don't you mind your own sodding business?' said Tim quietly.

In the ring a pugnacious tiger-striped bitch, her face covered in scars from previous battles, was salivating and straining at the leash, high on powerful haunches, to get at her opponent. A cry of derision went up around the clearing and a couple of women spat in disgust as the black and white dog opposite retreated in defeat towards its master.

As the crowd mooched and regrouped, Tim spotted the back of the vodka magnate Vladimir Zhubelovski with his hallmark three-quarter-length black leather coat, worn in all weathers, and long blond hair, occasionally worn in a ponytail though today freely flowing down his back almost to his waist. Two bodyguards on either side formed a protective layer of muscle.

'Look there! That bitch there!' Erik was pointing towards the ring. 'She's beaten her opponent before the fight. You see her – she's walking off in disgust.'

A boy of about eight with a sunken bare chest approached them. He was carrying a shopping bag full of money.

'Door,' the boy said. He was wearing grubby blue and white striped shorts and his knees were covered in scabs. His buoyant lack of both respect and recognition of his President irked Tim. There was incognito and there was taking the piss.

He searched his calfskin wallet, its stitches strained to the limit, and pulled out a bundle of low denominations sterlets, the official currency.

'Christ's sake, I wouldn't wipe my arse with that stuff.' The boy looked at Tim in disgust as he put a 500,000 sterlet note in the bag. On the official currency exchange rate it was worth 0.005 US cents. 'What else have you got?' He sounded like a baby league highwayman. 'What about dollars?'

Erik swiped the kid softly on the back of his head with his cuff. Good humouredly, he said, 'What's the matter with you? This is your national currency.'

The boy mistook the gesture as one of violence and pulled the bag away defensively. 'Shut up before I tell my mum on you.' He pointed to the woman in the denim shorts, now outside the ring, fussing over the tiger-marked pit bull terrier.

'Do you know who I am?' asked Tim.

The boy looked at them intently. He nodded towards Erik. 'You're the bloke who does them dirty magazines. My mum says you're a pervert.'

Erik looked shocked. It had been some time since the editor's column had been printed with his by-line picture. Heeding his own advice, he now used a picture of Bill Gates to lessen reprisals.

Erik nodded at Tim. 'What about him?' he asked.

'Look, what is this? Guess the name of the punter? It's ten dollars so either pay up or get lost,' said the boy.

'What's your name?' asked Tim.

'Igor,' said the boy.

'What's your mum's name?' Tim put two $10 notes into the plastic bag.

'Natasha.' Before they could ask anything else, Igor lolloped down the hillside towards his mother.

Another fight was in full flow. Two forty-pound beasts of slathering hate were locked together. Blood and spittle started to fly in the dirt ring, making a dark paste on the ground. The windless dell had started to smell of dog shit.

Tim sank onto his haunches. He was wearing a pale coffee-coloured Kenzo suit, or as the Uzbek label called it, Kenco. Despite the fact that he had two originals at home he didn't want this one covered in grass stains, dog piss and grease from an old McDonald's wrapper left in Erik's sidecar.

He bit on a stem of grass. 'Do they enjoy it?'

'What?'

'Dog fighting,' said Tim. 'I mean, the Romans did it and the ancient Egyptians.'

'Really,' grunted Erik.

'But is it the image we want to give of a liberal up-and-coming democracy?'

'Sure. You wouldn't want to deprive them of their right to fight, would you? That's not fair. You wouldn't do that to people. It wouldn't be right.'

It was logic, thought Tim, of a type. And the dogs did seem to be enjoying themselves. In many respects, if he was going to clamp down on anything it should be gang violence, but then again, they seemed to enjoy that too.

'See the black one? They can trace his pedigree all the way back to the American Kennel Club. I've got a hundred riding on it.'

'Sterlets?' asked Tim hopefully.

'Dollars,' replied Erik, not taking his eye off the fight. 'Go on, you beauty, bite. Bite him,' he screamed.

As he yelled, Tim sat back. It didn't feel like an appropriate time to remind Erik that he was the Minister of Culture. He'd tried to call Anna that morning, but she wasn't at Come Dancing, her palace suite, or her grandmother's dacha. The sun dodged behind a cloud that had scudded across the steppe. There was a breeze strong enough to combine the smell of dog breath and benzene, but not enough to disperse it. A few mosquitoes flitted above their heads; it was too hot and too uncomfortable. Tim thought of a swim.

'Shit, man,' Erik collapsed beside him. 'If that dog can trace its pedigree to anything more than a tin of dog food then I'm a—' He paused.

Tim said nothing.

Erik exhaled a sigh and lay back staring at the sky.

Tim said, 'Your proposal from the other night?'

'Mmmm,' said Erik, still replaying his lost money in his mind.

'You sure you could organise it? How would it get advertised?' Tim lay back alongside him.

'You, my friend, are not a media person. Whereas I am. I have the contacts. There are whole magazines in the West and websites devoted to the pursuit.'

'Really?'

'Of course. It would take a couple of calls. A few adverts. We could get your mum to help with the websites.'

Tim raised himself on an elbow. 'They'll pay fifty thousand dollars each?'

'Minimum,' said Erik.

An unfamiliar stab of doubt, becoming more familiar with every passing day of his presidency, gnawed at him. 'What if it doesn't work? Is it illegal?'

'Is dog fighting? I mean, Christ, who's to know?' Erik shrugged. 'Isn't that what politicians do? Make decisions on behalf of their people?'

About twenty metres to their left Igor and Natasha were shepherding a pit bull into the back of a rusty green Lada estate. Both her unprepossessing charges looked at her adoringly. She draped her arm loosely over her son's shoulder and said something to make him laugh. The dog, only slightly bloody from the scrap, nuzzled his armpit. Also Tim couldn't help notice, in a respectful sort of way, how Natasha's shorts rode up her bottom as she leant over to put her bag full of bloodied towels in the back. As she re-emerged from the boot she turned and, seeing them, smiled. Her hair was ginger blonde and her smile almost perfect.

Erik was staring at her longingly. 'Christ, what a fool I've been.'

Tim nodded.

'It's been here, under my nose for years.'

'Exactly,' said Tim, smiling as he watched the car pull away.

Erik got up. 'Edition 76, special topic, *Pit Bull Fighting, Are Women the New Supremos?*' He touched Tim's shoulder lightly with his foot. 'Come on. Do you need a lift back into town?'

As Tim followed him down the hill, trying not to inhale the fumes of the jeeps as they pulled away, he looked back to where they'd been sitting. The crowd had gone, its silhouette obliterated by the liquid steppe sky.

III

Anna Arbatova drove as she moved, with the assurance that, even at twenty-nine, she was one of the best-looking women in the country. In fact she drove with even more assurance. Whereas most of Anna's friends relied on their looks to get by, Anna knew she needed something in addition if she was to succeed as she intended to. That was why she was one of the few women drivers in the country. Driving made her beautiful *and* independent. It wasn't vanity, it was realism. Her looks were an advantage, like Tim's ability to make money, but to turn them into a real asset required skill. Managing Tim was half of it. Using his position the other 50 per cent.

The grey high-rises on the road out of town had given way to huge castle-like brick dachas built within a stone's throw of her grandmother's one-storey wooden home. If her grandmother's dacha looked like the cottage in the gingerbread tale, these castles were the ogre's mansion at the top of the bean stalk – the imposing half-built weekend retreat-cum-fortresses of the country's nouveaux riches.

She pulled out in front of a Series 5 BMW, slipping down a gear to overtake. She hated to think of the neighbourhood she'd grown up in going to the dogs, for her grandmother's sake. Anna had more than usual affection for her grandmother. For as long as Anna could remember, she had been her mother.

Anna had a theory on parenting. The best, the most well-adjusted people in the world were brought up by grandparents. Grandparents expected less of children than parents so were less disappointed when they failed to succeed and less bitter. And children, because they felt a keen debt of gratitude, were less spoilt.

It was one of the reasons she was reluctant to have children of her own.

Anna's parents had died when she was six months old. She blamed their death on their divorce. She blamed herself for their divorce. Herself, and a strip of black ice on the road to Astrakhan.

Anna's parents divorced when she was born. In those days it was common. Not because of the increased workload or sleepless nights (the marriage, he a production line manager at the Kombinat and she a book-keeper, had been happier than most). Anna's parents separated as the only way to double up on their living accommodation. In Soviet days, a lifetime of togetherness hinged on a successful divorce.

On separation they were issued another apartment, the home of an alcoholic *kolkhoz* manager who had drunk himself to death, leaving a one-bedroom flat badly in need of redecoration. On the night of 13 February 1971, the baby Anna was being driven to her aunt's house in Astrakhan to save her precious nose from the noxious fumes of refurbishment when the car hit a strip of black ice. When the police reached them, her mother and father were dead and Anna, protected by layers of winter swaddling, was alive.

She was taken to her grandmother's the next day, where she remained for the next eighteen years, when she was able to take possession of the two flats she'd inherited.

Her grandmother, who had brought her own daughter up single-handedly after her husband died in the Great Patriotic War, called Anoushka her little miracle. Her parenting skills were rusty but effective. So when Anna showed promise as a ballerina at the age of seven, her grandmother encouraged her but without the mania of the other girls' mothers, women who refused to forgive their daughters for their sprouting breasts or allowing their hips to fill out.

Anna's hips, though, stayed boyish, and her breasts small enough to let her pirouette her way up the ranks of ballet school. Anna, in womanhood, looked so much like her grandmother that it shocked her.

Anna parked the Mercedes well away from the dacha. For as long as she could remember, her grandmother could not tolerate anything German. She remembered the Nazi occupation in 1942 when she was just married and she blamed the Germans for the wholesale deportation that followed. Anna walked round the shaded veranda and joined her grandmother at the back.

Anna's grandmother had not been shrink-wrapped by age or the wrinkles that seemed to dry out and condense other bodies. She was still tall. Her hair was white, which it had been since her forties, and her skin brown and unblemished.

'Let's try this cake. I'm sure your grandfather, God bless him, would have enjoyed it too.'

The format was the same every year. The only variant in the tradition over twenty years was where the cake ingredients came from. For the first decade they had been entirely Soviet; today it was an Icelandic cake base and Polish jam.

Anna stooped over the table to cut the cake, like a croupier bending over a table. She gave the first slice to the place set at the head of the table for her grandfather. She offered her grandmother one and then she took a plate for herself. For no obvious reason they had dispensed with candles in the 1980s. They sang Happy Birthday, as was the tradition, and Anna opened a bottle of Russian champagne. A glass went first to the head of the table.

'Do you still want me to do this when you're dead?' asked Anna as she picked at the cake. 'I mean, I will, you know.' The other good thing about grandparents, as far as Anna could see, was that they had no pretence, or even interest, when it came to their own mortality.

'No, that would be morbid.'

'This isn't morbid then?'

They were sitting in the garden under the shade from an apple tree, on chairs that had been brought outside around a flaking table. Both women were wearing *khalat*, cotton flowered housecoats tied across the stomach.

'It's a party.'

'How old is he today, Gran?' asked Anna.

'Today your grandfather is eighty-nine,' said her grandmother, who always referred to her late husband in the present tense and said she would continue to do so until the Party notified her officially that he had died.

Anna put her plate down, picking up a leaf that had fallen on the table and slicing chunks out of it with her nail. If it disintegrated on an even number it meant she would succeed, on an odd number that she would fail.

She had reached a point where success prevailed when a neighbour leant over the fence and said there was a call for her. Yekaterina Maximova's house was painted the same green as Anna's grandmother's, although it had something pointing from the roof that Anna had told them both was a satellite dish. It was rumoured her son was a fridge magnate in the Mafia. Yekaterina had been her grandmother's neighbour since the deported people had been allowed to return home nearly half a century ago. Anna, who had known Yekaterina all her life, scarcely noticed that the old woman looked as sun-shrivelled as a mummy from the Al-Tai mountains.

'It's Feodor for Anoushka,' said the old woman over the fence that separated her vegetable plot from her neighbour's. Few who had known Tim before the election could bring themselves to call him anything but Feodor.

Anna shook her head. 'Tell him I'm not here,' she said, reaching into her bag to make sure her mobile was switched off.

The neighbour looked blank, ignoring the younger woman and turning to one her own age to explain. 'She's not here, Yekaterina

Maximova,' Anna's grandmother said. 'Tell him you haven't seen her.'

She nodded silently and, bent nearly double, hobbled back into her dacha.

'You know, Anoushka, you really shouldn't lie like that. Why don't you want to speak to him? Don't you love him?'

Anna's grandmother had known all Anna's boyfriends who included, not in date order, two ballet dancers, a musician, three traffic cops, a hairdresser and a taxi driver from Kiev who had formerly worked in the Pavlov Institute. Of all of them she preferred Tim, but in Anna's opinion that wasn't saying much.

'You know he loves you.' Anna's grandmother stirred a spoonful of jam into her tea. Anna was thoughtful and rested her head on her grandmother's shoulder. She smelt of cotton not properly aired. 'Remember, child, women aren't sturgeon.'

'What?' Anna sat up abruptly. 'What are you going on about?'

'Sturgeons. The older they get, the more eggs they produce. If I remember correctly, in her fiftieth year a female Beluga produces three million of them.'

'I think you spent too long at the canning factory,' said Anna moodily. 'Anyway, I'm not a fish.'

'No, of course not.'

'Just you remember that,' she added defiantly.

The garden was now in total shade. The shadow was not cast from her grandmother's tumbledown dacha, window frames cracked like a spider's web, but by the giant mansions in the background. For half an hour, they dozed and talked until Anna said, 'I really ought to go.'

'Are you working tonight?'

'Mmm.' Anna stood up. 'Will you be all right, Gran? You won't sit out too long, will you?'

'No, sweetheart. I've just got a few things to say to your grandfather, then I'll go inside.'

Anna bent down to kiss her on the cheek and gathered up the

plates. 'Leave that glass for your grandfather, Anna,' she was told as she tried to clear the table. Anna understood that her grandmother's morbid superstitions were gene deep. And that she had probably inherited them.

Inside her grandmother's dacha it smelt of sour milk and apples. Late afternoon light streamed through the mosquito netting tacked to the windows in shafts. The wooden floor was covered in a rag rug, in which Anna could trace the dresses of her childhood. She opened a window and picked up her clothes. She laid the *khalat* on the divan in the corner of the room. As she reached in her bag to pull out a cardigan, she saw her grandmother in the garden smiling like a teenager at the empty chair.

IV

There was an unwritten rule at SOS that no one got in early on a Monday. It started as a special dispensation for whoever had read the Sunday papers, looking for leads, the day before. Now though, despite no one reading them, everyone, apart from Don, took the extra two hours.

For the second week it was over 30 degrees, a cloying heat that sapped Dominic and caused indecent underarm leakage. He sucked on a Starbucks coffee and, in the same move as he pushed the SOS door open, smelt under his arms to see if he'd remembered deodorant.

'Good weekend, Don?' asked Dominic. Friendly, yet not inviting more than a monosyllable of reply.

'Not bad, what about yours?'

'Tolerable.' On inspection, Don looked exhausted, drawn and pale. His unwashed hair confirmed Dominic's thoughts on mortgages in general and cohabiting in particular.

'Where is everyone?'

'Dunno. Tony's been in and gone out again.'

'How did he seem?' asked Dominic cautiously.

'A bit ferrety.'

'Like what?' asked Dominic sitting down, disappearing from Don's line of vision.

'Shifting stuff. Fidgety.'

Dominic extracted the *Guardian* from his inside pocket and pulled off his bicycle clips. His Saturday night with Tony had disturbed him. He'd hoped that by Monday morning he would have forgotten about it. But the conversation had been so pertinent to him, *the future of Dominic Peach*, that the rush of adrenaline had frozen it in his short-term memory.

Tony: 'How are you on the former Soviet Union, Dom?'

Dominic: 'Russia?'

Tony: 'Ish. It's Russia-ish.'

Dominic, reaching for Advil: 'What is?'

Tony: 'Really it's more of a Stan.'

'More of a Stan?'

Tony: 'From Russia, you go down a bit, then left a bit and up a bit.'

'What is?'

Tony: 'Belugastan. The home of the Beluga argali argali.'

'The what?'

Tony: 'The Beluga argali argali, one of the rarest, most endangered sheep in the world. I looked it up on the database, Dominic. You are sheep.'

'I am sheep,' repeated Dominic limply.

Tony: 'Sheep, Dom, are going to be *the* endangered species of the new millennium. Forget tigers and elephants. And SOS will be leading the field. You, Dom, are going to be the sheep man. Not *a* sheep man, *the* sheep man. You're going to do what Linda McCartney did for—'

'Wings?'

'I spotted it on the internet. They're advertising hunting

licences for $50,000. It breaks every rule in the endangered species handbook.'

The sound of the World Service time signal brought Dominic back to the office. He looked over at Don. 'Got anything in the pipeline, Don?' He left it vague, covering almost anything from holiday plans to bowel movements. What he'd intended was an idea to deflect Tony from endangered sheep in the former Soviet Union.

'Mmmm? How do you mean?' Don spoke as if he was reading something from his screen.

'You know, animals. Saving them. Saving the species. Elephants, tigers, emus.' His brain froze as he realised he didn't know the names of any more animals. He stared round. 'Cats, dogs, rabbits, etc.' He said ETC out loud to make it sound more official.

'Are you all right?' Don was on his feet staring over at Dominic.

'What? Yes, fine.'

Just as Dominic was pushing the *Guardian* to the back of his desk, under a video on saddle-making in Ethiopia by the International League for the Protection of Horses, Tony walked in.

'Good morning, workers.' He smiled, continuing to glide towards his office. 'No Deborah, no Dwight, no Gill?'

'Going through the Sundays,' said Dominic. He caught a glimpse of Don's arm raised in a Soviet-style salute.

'Good, good,' said Tony. 'Dominic, can I have a word?'

'Fuck,' said Dominic under his breath. 'Don, quick, I don't suppose you've got a new conservation technique on you, have you?'

'Not *on me*,' said Don, 'no. Why?'

'No reason.' As he spoke, the phone on his desk started ringing. 'Get that, can you, Don? Extension 231. It'll be Antoinette. Tell her I've gone to see the AI inspector.'

Dominic closed the door of Tony's office behind him, then opened it again briefly like a jack-in-the-box to remind Don, 'If it's to do with work, don't forget, I only do sheep.'

He sat down. 'You know, Tony, I have an appointment with my MRM at midday.' Dominic knew from Friday's pork pie wrapper that MRM stood for mechanically recovered meat. Tony was a vegetarian. He had been saving it for an occasion such as this.

Tony's room was cooler than the outer office. It had the yeasty odour of vitamin pills and black coffee.

Tony asked, 'Get home all right?'

'Yes, fine,' said Dominic.

'Look,' said Tony staring at him, 'about what we were talking about the other night.'

'Swing Out Sisters?'

'The dykes, exactly.'

Dominic looked nervously at the door.

'We've got to move fast—'

'You know,' Dominic tried to stem the flow, 'I've got a pretty big workload here at the moment, Tony. There's the MRM, the ISA, a couple of IFAs on the go. And developmentwise Antoinette and I are looking to buy.'

'Dom, you *are* sheep?' He said it half question, half statement.

'Mmmm,' Dominic replied, thinking, half man, half sheep.

'Good, because you're booked on a flight next week. I'm sorry if it's short notice. Blame Swing Out Sisters. I'm sorry but it's muff eat muff out there.' Tony looked at his desk purposefully in a way that suggested the briefing was over. 'I mean dog eat dog.'

Dominic tried to stand up.

'Of course, we'll need daily reports. We need to expose these men in the press for the evil sheep hunters they are. The detail I'll fill you in on as and when. How do you feel about it, Dom? Confident?'

Dominic rose weakly, shut the door behind him, inhaled and watched in silence as Deborah peeled the back off a pot noodle.

'What's the toilet duck want?'

He tried to sound nonchalant. 'I don't suppose you want to swap horses for sheep?' Dominic was aware the question sounded like a playground game but was unable to rephrase it.

'Bugger off,' said Deborah, throwing a plastic case of soy sauce at him.

CHAPTER FOUR

I

It was far too hot for cemeteries, though Anna hadn't seemed to notice when she'd asked him to meet her by her parents' grave at 3 p.m. Either that or she didn't associate heat with memories inappropriate to the surroundings. Tim didn't know what it signified. At best she was introducing him to her family, at worst she was gathering enough evidence of personal suffering to dump him guiltlessly.

Tim had cut short a Korean trade delegation after lunch to make it. The Koreans were hoping to start a joint venture logging company to hack away at the country's birch forests and turn them into office accessories for the South American market. Tim and his most trusted economic adviser, Natalia Timofevna, who looked like a bulldog and whose diminutive name of Nasty suited her, had agreed, subject to contract.

Nasty had returned to the security agency where she was director in charge of training women as bodyguards and Tim had been driven in the presidential Shogun to Cemetery Number 56 on the edge of town. As meetings went, it hadn't been entirely successful. The Korean delegation was being housed at the Palace Hotel. It was, apart from a pliable looking young secretary, exclusively male. All bar one had complained in a humourless way that their sleep had been disturbed by incessant phone calls from women asking if they wanted company. Only one of them, a short man in his fifties, almost as wide as he was tall, with eyebrows like a stage pelmet, whom Tim had seen when he was looking for Anna the night before at Come Dancing, looked rested enough to have taken advantage of the offer.

As far as women were concerned, the blood-curdling presence of Nasty as an economic adviser, in the face of the Koreans' teenage secretary, gave Belugastan the 1–0 moral advantage. Nasty, Tim was pleased to say, represented how far ugliness had come under his democratic rule. So when he hinted that the calls were, rather than anything unusual or illicit, merely a Beluga welcome, like a garland of flowers in the Pacific, they seemed to accept it.

Tim resolved to have words with Alexander, the six foot seven inch doorman, who let the girls know which rooms foreign men were in. The reason why Alexander knew when a trade delegation was in town was because his twin Pavel was Tim's driver. Both men looked identical and were identifiable only by the size of the key fobs that hung from their tree-stump waists, Alexander's having the edge. Tim liked to think of his coterie as close-knit, though others, he conceded, might have used the word corrupt.

The cemetery was still bathed in sunlight as Tim headed towards the plot. An occasional thread of cloud dragged itself across the sun, but not enough to cool the afternoon. In the south-east the peaks of the Al-Tai Mountains were visible on the horizon, rising out of the steppe like a distant cream-topped pie crust. Even in July the peaks were still capped in snow.

Cemetery 56 was known universally as *novi*, but for a burial ground recently opened, it was filling fast. In Orthodox style, the graves all had images of the deceased, taken from photographs, imprinted onto stone. The dead who hadn't been cut down by a Mafia bullet were mostly frozen in contented middle age rather than sagging infirmity. The intention, Tim guessed, was to show some sort of vitality. To his mind the images were cruelly out of place, like advertising something that had already sold out. He wondered if the photograph that would be used to adorn his tombstone had already been taken. He wanted to look solid and respectable.

Through the gravestones, Tim caught sight of Anna sitting opposite her family plot. Her back in a strapped sundress was curved so that the ridge of her spine was visible, like a fossil, showing the notches of her vertebrae. Her hair was loose and fell over her face. As Tim got nearer he saw she was paring an apple. She looked towards him as she heard the crunch of his feet on the gravel.

'Hello,' she said and offered him a slice of apple.

He sat next to her. 'How are you doing? I tried to get hold of you at—'

'I know.' She put down the apple.

'How is everything?' he repeated.

'OK.' In her left hand she was holding a bag of toffees. She was in a quiet mood that Tim recognised. She called it melancholia. Whatever it was, Tim was too busy for it.

She looked up. 'Do you know what these are?' Anna offered him a toffee and as he put his hand in the bag to accept, she made a fist to stop him taking one. Had he not had more than average respect for women, and their hormonal imbalances, he would have raised his voice.

'They look like caramels,' said Tim.

'They were my mum's favourite,' she said, adding, 'apparently.'

'Really?' said Tim trying to sound interested but wondering if it had been worth cutting the Koreans short for this. He tried to hold her hand.

'They were recovered from my mum's pocket on the night of the crash.' Anna was unwrapping one. The bag was old and greasy with a brand name in red capitals that Tim had never heard of. Two young pioneers hand in hand were dancing on the packet.

Anna picked at the sweet with long unpolished nails to get the paper off and then she ate it. Tim could tell by the speed her jaws were moving that the toffee was soft.

'Isn't that dangerous?' asked Tim. He thought he'd been summoned to discuss their future. 'Haven't they gone off by now?'

'Tim.' Her mouth was full of toffee. 'Have you heard of,' she sucked, 'trans sub station?' He had missed the last three syllables. He thought she was referring in general terms to a transport system.

'I'm sorry.' Tim looked away. 'I can't understand a word you're saying.'

She chewed more and then said, 'Transubstantiation.'

'Is it some sort of Metro terminal?' replied Tim. 'I'm guessing, though, babe.'

Anna swallowed. 'It's when bread and wine are changed into the blood and body of Jesus Christ.'

Tim nodded. It sounded like a type of pirating that was new, even to Belugastan. 'Do they do it here?'

'Do what?'

'The trans substation thing.' Tim was resting his elbows on his knees, one of which he was pushing out to touch Anna's thighs, though he would guess she hadn't even noticed.

'Tim, it's a religious thing.' She sounded disappointed. She turned to him. 'Don't you see what I'm getting at?'

Tim spun his wrist and waited a split second before his Rolex flicked into line. 'Babe, it's just that . . .' Tim was thinking improper thoughts, given their location.

Anna said, 'If my mum and dad hadn't been killed that night, Mum would've eaten these toffees. So when *I* eat one, that means,' she bit her lip, 'well, it's like a communion. Like I'm communing with her.' She smiled.

'Through toffees,' said Tim, trying to massage her leg with his outer thigh, subtly.

'That's it, exactly.'

'Anna,' Tim spoke slowly, 'you haven't been seeing anyone, have you?'

'Like who?' She was folding the bag of toffees and neatly putting them away.

'One of those American missionary people that book into the Palace,' he said. 'Or a shrink.'

'No, of course not. I've always thought it. Ever since I was a little girl. Every time I get depressed about the accident, I have a toffee and think of them.'

'Has this got anything to do with your grandmother?'

'No.' Anna stood up and smoothed the back of her dress, indicating that the meeting was over.

Tim remained seated. Erik was right, Anna might have a great, possibly legendary arse, but she was definitely on the top scale of high maintenance. Inwardly he sighed. Probably Bill found it so with Hillary. It was what gave them stamina to become great leaders.

'Is that what you brought me out here to tell me?' Tim sat back and crossed his legs, intending to show disbelief. 'To tell me how sucking a twenty-year-old sweet brings your relatives back to life?'

A block of clouds, dense but not dark, was propelling itself across the sky, casting a shadow like a grease stain over the cemetery.

'No, not just that.' Anna bobbed down, giving in to Tim's refusal to leave. 'I've also decided that I want to join the cabinet.'

'Great,' said Tim. 'What as?'

'I thought Minister for the Environment. Ecology is so important.'

Tim's smile was intentionally broad. 'No problem,' he said, pulling out a pair of Armani sunglasses. He had tried to give the impression of control. But more and more he had the feeling that events were unfolding that he knew less and less about.

As he left her, Anna sighed. Only one man had ever passed the cemetery test.

★ ★ ★

At just after four it wasn't worth going back to the Palace. Leaving Nasty's mobile number as a contact for the Korean delegation meant they would be unlikely to call. He watched Anna drive away from the cemetery with an unexpected feeling of gloom. That was a knot he had to tie up, but it was an elaborate bowline that left him stumped.

Pavel was waiting for him in the car, sitting at a ninety-degree angle to the passenger seat. The Shogun door was open and his huge legs reached the ground. His keys dangled from his belt like a golden scrotal sac. Tim had seconded the jeep from customs after they had impounded it from a team of American seismic geologists looking for oil. He watched the blue tattoos on the back of Pavel's hand blur past as he took the wheel. His left hand read Pasha, his own pet name; the right, Sasha, his twin's pet name.

Both men were ex-Spetsnatz, the Russian secret service, and had fought in Afghanistan and Chechnya. Pasha had a shaved head, grey wolf's eyes, crooked teeth and a fierce loyalty to anyone who was paying him, which was why, like his brother, he'd left Spetsnatz when the wages dried up. As Erik said, they were good boys to have on your side.

Tim liked to see the reassuring back of his head as he started the car, with its double roll of loose skin at the edge of the hairline over a starched white shirt and leather blouson-style brown jacket.

'Just drive, Pasha,' said Tim as he sank into the back seat of the Shogun, wondering if the dark glass made everything look worse than it was, or if it really was that bad. At the gates of the cemetery a coven of women was selling a selection of plastic flowers and light refreshments to mourners. None looked up as the Shogun spun off a layer of dust as it launched itself from the car park. Most of those six foot underground at the *novi* cemetery were there because they'd been underground in life, drug dealers, smugglers, extortion racketeers. There was a lawlessness to Belugastan that made governorship surprisingly easy. With no framework of law, businessmen – many called them Mafia – operated on an ad hoc basis, carving their own deals, selling off the country's resources. And the voters were too busy trying to survive. Tim made a token effort as the country's figurehead, but he too had his own agenda – staying out of jail. Central to his success was owning the radio station, which shamelessly advertised the President along with the latest brand of German sausage.

The dedications on the huge upright gravestones, rooted in a blue sea of lapis lazuli, were to mobsters mostly slain in their twenties. Some of the lads were even etched on the tombstone in bas relief wearing leather jackets and flat hats carrying the keys to a BMW.

It was an inexplicable devotion to the prestige of a car. Maybe it was exclusively Russian. Did the Sicilian Mafia rate themselves only by the horsepower of the car they drove? Tim knew why and it was the reason his pyramid scheme – which promised a new car to every man, woman and child – had flourished before it collapsed. Under communism, owning a car was one of the few ways to put yourself ahead of the pack. It gave you independence and freedom from the iron grip of the state. Greed and prestige had formed the framework of Tim's empire, but its driving force was mobility.

His scheme was simple. In Soviet times you had to wait for a new car not in weeks, or months, but in five-year plans. He knew this because when he started his adult working life as a production line worker at the local Kombinat he put his name down for a Riva 500. As he progressed up the production ladder, he grew no nearer to getting his car. So in 1989 when he was moved from being production manager of combines to cars, he took the law into his own hands.

They produced the Soviet legend, the little 100cc engine, Aka known around the country as the virgin because it was white, hard to get going but eventually responded well to good handling. All of them were shipped up the Volga to Moscow. In 1991, in the first days of perestroika, Feodor saw his chance and broke away to form a private co-operative, Aftonat, nominally to promote Aka car sales. What followed was not strictly legal, though it was not strictly illegal.

His chance came when, three years later, Mikhail Gorbachev issued a decree to stimulate the automobile export market. Aftonat transformed itself into a nationwide car dealership. The law stated that, for example, a Riva 500 made for export would cost $3,500, but internally it would still cost $7,000. It was easy. While thousands of cars, on paper, left the factory to go abroad, they remained in the country and were sold for $7,000.

That made him a rouble millionaire and gave him the idea to make more. Four years later he revealed plans for the new Yenesei, a so-called people's car, soon to be available at half the usual price of a Lada. Investing in this utopian dream would cost a Russian a not insignificant amount of the roubles required to build a new car factory in Latvia. The Russians lapped up the dream and bought into the firm.

At this stage, Feodor still believed in the factory. He already had Erik on board as his right-hand fixer. It was only when the money poured in and the problems started to mount that Feodor decided it might be better, as with all dreams, to leave them unrealised.

It was six weeks later that the Russian police's organised crime division disagreed. Tim was arrested. According to Erik, the only choice available was for him to become a politician. The investors were never repaid, but even if he hadn't changed his name, he was confident they would vote for him. Several well-respected Russian politicians had illegal pyramid schemes in their past. The electorate, who hated success and loved to see enterprise fail, seemed to appreciate the effort. Besides that, he gave all the electorate a new $100 bill as an incentive to vote him into a position of legal immunity. It was a refund – showing some degree of natural justice. Even after the bribe, he was still several million in the black. So he invested in the Palace Hotel, a resource from which all, he believed, could derive benefits.

'Any direction?' asked Pasha, rotating his head a degree anti-clockwise. His accent, like Gorbachev's, was southern. Tim thought the twins came from Odessa.

'Yeah,' said Tim. 'Maybe out towards Lenin Hills.' Tim had considered renaming Lenin Hills but decided against it, because it would mean changing the street maps again. The hills rose gradually from the plain. In the range's lee the capital had been built. Traditionally it was where newlyweds had their photographs taken. On a Monday it would be deserted, but the idea of going there appealed to Tim, if only to restore his faith that there was still a place where women wanted to marry.

A few Ladas had parked on the brow of the hill overlooking the city. A flea market clung to one side and a hot-dog stand under a Coca-Cola umbrella was selling German sausages with mayonnaise. The market men and women stood behind pieces of cardboard stacked with a few tatty possessions. One man in his sixties wore a string vest under a brown cotton jacket displaying war medals on the lapel. He was hawking an album opened on the ground to show enamel badges from around the Soviet Union that must have once belonged to his son. Another woman in a pink hair-net stood over the contents of a kitchen drawer.

'Don't stop, Pasha,' said Tim, feeling a wave of guilt, responsibility and depression rear up inside. 'Let's get back to the Palace.'

In the front seat he watched the crease of the driver's neck unfold as he nodded and slid the gear stick into first. They drove past a kiosk selling newspapers and vodka, where a drunk was arguing with the bare-chested young proprietor. His red-faced drinking partner, with his hand round the neck of a vodka bottle, was slumped on a low brick wall alongside.

Tim knew something had happened before he saw her. The Shogun had slowed down, stuck behind an old Zhiguli in the outside lane and something in the nearside. He heard Pasha swear and jam the hard part of his palm on the horn before flicking the indicator to show he was overtaking. Then he slipped down a gear.

As the car pulled out, Tim saw the reason for the hold-up. The black Volga 420 in front was exercising a dog. An extended leash linked the animal to the inside of the driver's door. The dog was panting twenty metres behind the car which was travelling at, Tim guessed, forty kilometres an hour. As they drew level with the dog, Tim recognised it as the tiger-coloured pit bull terrier from Sunday's fight, spewing a trail of saliva from its gritted jaw.

As the Shogun overtook the car, Tim peered into the driver's seat. A woman in her early thirties was singing the jingle to Radio Plus. Both windows were down. She was Natasha, Igor's denim-wearing mother from the dog fight.

'Slow down, Pasha, I want to speak to her.' Tim furiously rolled down the nearside window, smelling a burst of warm diesel-scented wind.

'Hi there,' he said. She didn't flinch, though she stopped singing. 'Don't you know what you're doing is illegal?'

She looked over at Tim in large dark glasses. 'Yeah? Who says so, the frigging President?' Her voice was gravelly, as if she smoked too much. She tried to accelerate, but must have felt resistance from the dog because she slowed down.

She was wearing a flowery dress with a gypsy collar pushed off the shoulder. On the seat next to her Tim saw a satchel, though he was more aware of her thin brown thighs.

'Do you fancy a drink?' he asked.

She was chewing gum. She poked her tongue through a strand of it and smiled. 'Maybe.'

'Palace Hotel tomorrow night seven o'clock. I'll meet you in the lobby.'

With the timing of a military campaigner Pasha put his foot down to prevent further discussion. It was at times like this that Tim knew why he paid him.

II

'Don't you think her left nipple is a little on the large side?' Mrs Barinova, still with her sheepskin coat slipped over her shoulders, was sitting on the edge of her chair in front of the Apple Mac. Erik had bought the computer in Moscow, clutching a note handwritten in an old woman's script stating the model and other 'specs'. The electrical store on the Novy Arbat was so Western and new that you didn't have to hand your bags in to an armed coat check.

Erik didn't know Moscow well but remembered the store had been round the corner from where a huge stars and stripes flag pinpointed the American embassy, and a few blocks up from the White House, the Russian parliament. He'd waited outside while Tim consulted a Georgian lawyer, called something like Askanvilli, about the exemption from prosecution of his forthcoming election. Erik had wanted to see where Yeltsin's tanks had gouged holes in the parliament building in 1993. Now, though, said Tim, thanks to the exacting standards of Turkish workmen, it was as good as new.

Mrs Barinova and Erik were in Erik's kitchen, a room he'd converted into his editorial heartland. The dark shadow where the oven had once stood was covered in post-it notes, mostly reminding Erik about the reader. 'The *Erik* reader is aged between 27 and 42,' said one. 'He is a home and car owner and currently involved in his third serious sexual relationship.' Mrs Barinova had once asked him on what the information was based. And though Erik hadn't told her in so many words to shut up, he'd made it clear that was what he meant. Mrs Barinova didn't mind, she was used to young men resenting the interference of older women. In any case the post-it notes were Russian-made, meaning the adhesive was weak so that most of the notes littered the lino floor, fuzzy side up.

Erik, sitting with his back to her, and working with his knees either side of a fridge, twisted and looked over his shoulder. The nipples, and the breasts, belonged to Lisa, the student he'd recruited buying apples in Andropov Street a few days ago.

Erik was working on text and, so close to a deadline, was tetchy. 'Some nipples *are* bigger than others are. The *Erik* reader appreciates that true beauty is imperfection.'

Mrs Barinova wondered if that had come from a post-it note. 'But this one is extremely, almost unnaturally, large. Do you want me to even them up a bit? Or alternatively,' she moved the mouse across Erik's old chopping board, 'I could blow the whole breast up.' The arrow on the computer screen hovered ominously at Lisa's aureole. Mrs Barinova was the only one on the staff, which amounted to three if you included Erik's cleaner, who understood the graphics programme PhotoShop. Artistically, Erik realised, it put the editor at a disadvantage.

'Some men like flat-chested. Some men like uneven nipples. We cater for all tastes.'

Mrs Barinova recanted. 'If you say so, dear.' She imagined, after all, that Erik was more au fait with the modern nipple than she was. 'What exactly is she supposed to be doing?'

Lisa, the centrefold for Edition 74, topical issue, *Can IMF Loans Really Help the Former Soviet Union?* was sitting behind a desk, topless – other than a tie and sucking a ballpoint pen and counting out gold coins. The backdrop was the foyer of the Palace Hotel, which Erik was allowed to use during the hours of 3 a.m. to 6 a.m. weekdays.

'She's a saucy bank teller,' said Erik. 'I would have thought that much, at least, was obvious.'

'What are those gold things?'

Erik, who today of all days didn't expect his artistry to be called into question, said, 'Coins.'

'They look chocolate to me.'

'Yes, they are actually chocolate. Those were the only gold coins I could find. Satisfied?'

'No need to be irritable, dear.'

'Does it matter?' Erik ran his fingers through his hair and adjusted his reading glasses. 'Our readers expect more from a centrefold than viable currency.'

'Exactly.' Mrs Barinova spoke under her breath. 'Even nipples for a start.'

'The editor's word,' Erik spoke in a way that suggested it was going to be the last on the subject, 'is final.'

Apart from the cathode ray hum from the Apple Mac and the occasional squeak from Erik's Sony laptop, the room was silent. As Mrs Barinova worked, her lips moved slightly and sometimes her tongue stuck out of the corner of her mouth in concentration.

The kitchen looked out over a quadrangle. A cluster of silver birches gave shade to a playground used more by drunks than children. At night, with no curtains, the image of Mrs Barinova and Erik was reflected back into the kitchen, blurred and imprecise, as if they had been melted. Erik's makeshift winter double-glazing, a layer of polythene, was still tacked to the frame so they couldn't open the window. Because of it, the room was airless and smelt of cardboard boxes and stale fat from takeaway cartons. Erik was using the cap of an empty beer bottle as an ashtray.

There had been a time when Erik thought he should tidy up before Mrs Barinova came round. He lived alone, paying $100 a month to a Second World War veteran, called simply Granddad, to live with his daughter and son-in-law's family during the winter, and at his one room dacha through the summer.

Granddad kept a key and, as far as Erik could understand, still considered the flat his own. Last Friday, Erik had returned from a date with Edition 73's centrefold – a nursery nurse called Galina – to find him drunk and insensible on his bed, having drunk a bottle of Erik's vodka. Erik had tried to pull him onto the divan next door but his legs, in a pair of frayed tracksuit bottoms, were like bricks. In the end Erik made a bed for himself in the kitchen. He tried to put the incident down to dementia and resolved not to keep strong liquor in the fridge. Due to Granddad's status as a war veteran Erik decided not to ask for a rent rebate.

One day Erik wanted to upgrade his living accommodation. Tim had already offered him a suite at the Palace, but the flat suited him for the moment. Erik was an artist and, like his hero Boris Kustodiev, the revolutionary painter, he knew that all significant art came out of suffering.

The brown flock walls were plastered in covers of not only his favourite model Alya, a physics teacher who six months ago answered a small ad for a waitress and was now living in Munich, but editions that he felt captured the essence of tasteful pornography. The tank edition stood out, as did the Winter Olympics edition showing a naked speed skater, who had threatened a law suit due to damage to an undisclosed weak chest. It was actions like hers that had given Erik a morbid fear of litigation.

As well as Erik's covers there were two portraits by Kustodiev, one of the Russian singer Feodor Chaliapin standing in the snow in Gorky Park. Chaliapin was wearing an engulfing knee-length fur coat. A pit bull terrier was looking up at him adoringly. It confirmed, said Erik, the operatic bass's status as a dog fighter. The other, called Russian Venus, was of a naked blonde beating herself with birch twigs in the banya. That was taped up on the wall opposite the bed.

After three minutes of silence Erik said, 'Sorry, Mrs Barinova. I shouldn't have snapped.' He looked up from his screen. 'You know what it's like on press day.'

'I'm signing off this page then sending it. I'm going to save this in J-Peg,' said Mrs Barinova, making Lisa disappear with a click of the mouse. 'I'm calling them Uneven 1, 2, 3 and 4.'

'Great,' said Erik.

'Erik, it's not my fault the woman has got uneven nipples.' She sounded put out. 'You chose her.'

Erik turned to her. He reminded himself that it wasn't just him who cared about the magazine. He smiled and changed tack. 'Fantastic job you made of the hunting web page,' he said.

'Thank you, dear.' She smiled and huffed the shoulders of her coat up a bit. 'Now all we have to do is register the domain, which we can do on line, and that'll be it. Shall we have a look to see how many hits we've had?'

Erik grunted. He had returned to his piece, a story set in the Moscow office of an international bank where the dashing Wall Street trader, Chandler Worthington, had fallen for the slim-hipped Masha and was gratuitously exploiting her in the security vault. It was, of course, a metaphor for the exploitation Russians had suffered at the hands of the IMF. As a working title he was calling it 'How Russians Are Screwed', though he accepted it was on the crude side.

The presses, in the same building as *Belugastan Today*, the formerly communist daily though now owned and run by the vodka magnate Zhubelovski, rolled at midnight. Mrs Barinova hung around as she did every month to oversee any production problems. This edition was especially important. There was a quiet expectation, in Erik's eyes, that this issue would be the one to break through the two thousand mark. Which was why Erik was more than usually touchy about having a flat-chested centrefold with uneven nipples. It was daring, he conceded as he took a swig of Pipsi, a Ukrainian cola drink. But all artists had to take chances.

'Shall I see how many hits we've had, Erik?' Mrs Barinova repeated. As Erik had no idea what she was talking about, he decided to pull rank.

'Must you do it right now?' he asked.

'I just thought—'

'OK then, if you must.' Whether Mrs Barinova was in her sixties or not, she was staff, and staff required discipline. Erik heard the discordant fizz as she logged onto the Internet. He returned to Chandler Worthington's sizeable injection.

'Oh my goodness, sixty-seven hits and four e-mails. Shall I print them off?' said Mrs Barinova excitedly. From the other side of the wall came the rhythmic thud of the neighbours making love. Erik looked at his watch: 10.20. The neighbours were shift workers at the Kombinat. Erik knew from the intensity and speed that he must be on a late start at eleven. Despite his and Mrs Barinova's current occupation, Erik didn't like to be around live pornography in front of his best friend's mother.

'Yes, good idea. Why don't you? And then log off. We might need the line.'

She muttered to herself as she signed off, filing the e-mails and then printing them. The pages slid into the printer's tray.

'Oh, my dear! One from Ohio, one from New York, one from Montana and one from Texas.'

'Wait a minute, hang on.' Erik was finishing with Chandler's hefty withdrawal which had left Masha severely depleted. 'Right, carry on.' He spoke forcefully to drown out next door's shaking headboard.

Mrs Barinova, who seemed unconcerned about the noise, looked perplexed. 'I'm sorry, I can't read it.' She shook her head. 'It's the English.'

'But you're a professor of English,' said Erik. 'What is it? Is the print too small? Here, take my reading glasses.'

'No, it's not that.' She tried to read the first e-mail.

Slowly, out loud she read, 'Dear Fellow Hunters from Across the Seas. I was real glad to log on to your site. Me and my sun have been huntin' for years and are intrested in joining yur next hunt for that dammed varmit sheep. Please furward all the details plus costs.' She showed it to Erik. 'What do they mean?'

Erik said, 'I imagine the writer is illiterate. It's very common in America especially if you cross-section the general population with the hunting community.'

'I had no idea,' said Mrs Barinova, genuinely concerned. She picked up the last e-mail. 'This one looks a bit better.' She read, 'To whom it may concern, Belugastan Ministry of Wildlife and Fisheries.' She looked up. 'Good, that, isn't it? I made the ministry up. I hope Feodor doesn't mind.'

Erik, still thinking of nipples, said, 'Go on.'

Mrs Barinova read on in barely accented English, 'I have been a hunter of wild sheep for many years. In America I have been lucky enough to take a grand slam of sheep trophies. It was therefore with some great interest that I encountered your website. I am extremely keen to take advantage of the opening up of the borders between our two great countries in particular to hunt wild sheep. For this reason I would be grateful if I could join your hunt at the earliest opportunity. Please let me know what your tour price includes. I consider the licence fee reasonable. I would also intend to bring on the trip my two trusty hunt guides. I look forward to hearing from you. Yours truly, S. A. Webster.'

'What do you make of that?' asked Erik.

Mrs Barinova touched her hair. 'I think it looks like you're in business.'

'*We're* in business, Mrs B. You're the Minister of Foreign Affairs.'

'It was your idea to convert your motorbike into a fictitious sheep.'

The phone to Erik's right was ringing. Mrs Barinova picked it up, holding the receiver as if she wasn't quite familiar with it, though she spoke with quiet efficiency. After a brief conversation she replaced the phone upside down in its cradle. Erik reached across her to right it.

She said, 'That was the printers. They wanted to know if they should adjust the nipples on page fourteen.'

Erik sighed, then remembered that few great artists were understood during their own lifetime.

III

Dominic touched the contours of the mobile phone in his jacket pocket tentatively as he cycled. It nestled snugly beside a packet of

Marlboros, as if it had always been there. Which it hadn't. For Dominic, things had happened unnaturally quickly in the last forty-eight hours.

His excuse for leaving the office had been an appointment with AI. He'd meant artificial insemination but Deborah had taken it to be Amnesty International. Not that it mattered now. Dominic might have come straight out with a request to take Mr Orlovski to Elderly Alert's summer fete and Tony wouldn't have batted an eyelid. Dominic was now what Tony called key personnel.

Dominic thought back. The phone call he had dodged as he went in to see Tony had been from Antoinette. She called back in the afternoon. She'd found a three-storey house in Islington and though it was, council estatewise, very cheek by jowl, it was a *tremendous* bargain. The bargain was currently on the market for £425,000. Dominic had stalled.

'Sorry, darling, something's really come up at work. It's top secret. I'll have to get back to you.'

'But Dodo, we've got to act fast. We—'

'Darling, I'll call you ba—' One of Dominic's maxims was that if you were going to hang up you did it while you were speaking. It made the caller less suspicious.

Shortly after that came the mobile phone. Tony had called him into the conference room.

'Listen, you'll need this.' He handed it to him like an unlicensed firearm.

Idiotically Dominic had said, 'What is it?'

Tony thought he meant what network.

'Dunno. Vodafone, Orange? Some sort of roam-around service. I've checked. It definitely works in Belugastan.' Tony lit a cigarette, though Dominic had never seen him smoke before. 'Have you brought your passport?'

Dominic took an old British passport from the breast pocket of his shirt.

'Good, the visa people will need this,' said Tony.

'Tony, is there really any need for all this cloak and dagger stuff? You'll have Dwight making a suit out of blankets next. It's not the Great bloody Escape.'

'Certainly there is an utmost need for secrecy. What we're doing defies every law in the Lottery Commission rule book.'

'Does the Lottery Commission have a rule book?' asked Dominic.

'Of course it does. And, listen, not a word to anybody, specially Deborah. You never know, she might be working for the opposition.'

'What opposition?' asked Dominic tiredly.

'The muff divers. Just look at her. Listen, I'm making contact in an hour. Logging on to their website and sending them an e-mail.'

'Great stuff, Tone.' He was being sarcastic, but the whole thing seemed to have gone beyond sarcasm. Dominic looked at his watch. 'I'd love to join you but what with this DVD thing looking the way it does . . .'

'Sure thing, Dominic. You get to it. See you tomorrow.'

It was another hot day which meant that Dominic's tyres left a print in the tarmac. A mousy woman driving a blue Espace people-carrier hooted savagely as Dominic waited a split second too long at the lights. Dominic loathed people-carriers with a mania that verged on dementia. They were so often driven by self-important, sexually-frustrated, career-frustrated, reproductively smug little shrews. He hated them because he worried that for him it spelt the future. Dominic deliberately steered slowly across the Espace's lane of traffic. The driver was wearing a sleeveless checked shirt and, though he couldn't see them, he guessed her legs were chunky and clothed in khaki shorts, with flat sandals on stumpy feet. To his amazement, her bat features framed by an Alice band solidified as she accelerated towards him. Had he not been able to fling himself into an empty lane signposted to Hanger Lane, she'd have run him over. He swore at her and she V-signed back. He was still replaying the incident in his mind when he pulled into the Ealing office of Elderly Alert.

The office was staffed exclusively by women. It had the smell of council funding: unread pamphlets mingled with the unfettered rage of people unremunerated for doing good works. In Dominic's experience the amount people were paid directly related to how much control they felt they ought to have over the nitty-gritty running of the office. Few city traders gave a toss whose turn it was to buy the milk. In Elderly Alert and SOS it was vital. Other signs of the registered charity were there: the communal fridge, the rotas, the posters that hinted at personality, the inevitable picture of Colin Firth as Mr Darcy, the volunteer sector's pin-up of choice.

An eccentric-looking fifty-something woman with her hair in a bun came to the door to meet him. 'Call me Jane,' she said with an outstretched hand. It surprised Dominic because she implied he'd been calling her inappropriately by her surname. As far as he could tell, he'd never seen her before. 'It is Dominic, isn't it?'

He smiled and nodded.

'You're . . .' She peered over a pair of bifocals attached to a length of what looked like bale string round her neck.

'Mr Orlovski,' said Dominic. 'He's making his own way here.'

'Aged bus scheme?'

Dominic hesitated. 'Do you mean London transport?'

'No, no,' she laughed. 'We run a free bus service linking the Elderly Alert offices,' said Jane. 'In west London, of course.'

'Of course.'

Jane suddenly smiled as if someone had pulled a cord in her spine. Then she stopped. She said, 'Look, do come through. Everyone's dying to meet you.'

The office was split level with a first-storey window facing the road. There were bay windows at the back looking onto a small garden. The office had, Dominic knew from Antoinette, what estate agents called cross ventilation. Dominic followed Jane's long back through the office, passing a series of coloured cardboard warnings, all written in black felt tip and cut with pinking shears around the edges. 'Do not leave unwashed mugs,' said one. 'Last person to leave bathroom switch overhead fan off,' said another. 'Do not throw glass in the big bin.'

In the garden the women clung to the shade. A frenzied air of patronage filled the garden with the smell of souring milk. Dominic had thought if he were an hour late, the do would be just about over. He peered round for Mr Orlovski who, it appeared, had had the sense not to attend.

'Dominic, do you know everyone here?' asked Jane, assuming ownership and displaying him like a prize bull. The women looked up from their elderly charges and visibly rallied, in the way of middle-aged women who rarely meet men that they aren't related to.

'Oh, do have some tea, Dominic,' said a short woman with short dark hair. 'Oooh, how lovely to have a man about the place,' she added, despite the three men sitting in wheelchairs around her.

'Just in time for the group phots,' said another, pronouncing the word like fots.

'Well, hang on, Mr Orlovski isn't here yet,' said Jane. 'We must wait for all the visitees.' As she spoke, Mr Orlovski appeared in the doorway wearing a loose-fitting grey cotton suit with a white shirt and yellow and grey swirling cravat.

Dominic felt an unexpected burst of pride.

'Mr Orlovski.' Dominic went to meet him, extending one hand to be shaken while the other offered a white plastic garden chair. 'I'm glad you could make it. How did you – I mean I could have collected you.'

'Bus,' said Mr Orlovski, dragging a handkerchief the colour of his suit across his damp forehead. Dominic had never seen Mr Orlovski look so well.

'Let me get you,' said Dominic, 'what? Water? Tea?'

'Tea,' said Mr Orlovski. There was a smell of what Dominic's grandmother called fustiness to him. Jane hovered with a plate of diabetic butterfly buns.

'Now before you get stuck in, we must do the photos.' She put the butterfly buns on a trestle table next to a plate which had a pinking-sheared message *gluten free* stuck into an egg sandwich with a cocktail stick. 'First of all, there's the individual pictures of visitors and visitees, then the group photo, which will go in next month's newsletter.' She smiled again. 'OK, everybody?'

She turned to Dominic and said bitterly, 'The bloody local rag promised to turn up.' She made the bl of bloody last for two seconds as she assessed Dominic to see if he was a blasted or bloody type. 'As usual, no support for community projects.'

Two wheelchairs were manoeuvred into position successfully. The third, pushed by the woman with dark hair, got its wheel stuck in a lump of turf. 'Stupid, sodding, bloody thing,' said the pusher, reversing hard.

In the individual shot Dominic stood with his hand on Mr Orlovski's shoulder like a Victorian patriarch with his wife. In the main shot he was positioned in the back row centrally. Jane, who took the picture using an instant Polaroid, wanted him central to encourage, or 'bump up' as she put it, the number of younger visitors. She called Dominic an 'inspiration'. He felt a stab of guilt. Then he reconsidered. After four unrewarded years with Elderly Alert, even Dominic knew he was only pretending to be in it for the money. He had a niggling affection for his charges that, had he stopped to examine it, might have disturbed him.

'Say Camembert,' said Jane. The back row, with the exception of Dominic, laughed. Just after the shutter went down Dominic jumped to the jingle of a chorus of 'Yankee Doodle Dandy'. It was only when Jane sing-songed 'Whose is that?' and women scurried to their handbags that Dominic realised it was his new mobile. The women made the sort of indignant noises people make whose phones haven't just rung.

Dominic stared at it as if it was an unexploded bomb and stabbed at a button with the green phone at a jaunty angle. He was amazed when the trilling stopped.

'Hello,' he said unsurely.

'Dom, it's Tony here. Can you talk?'

Dominic instinctively retreated to the gloaming at the bottom of the garden. He found himself standing over a pile of garden waste.

'Yes, Tony, I can talk.' He emphasised the word *can* to reflect the ridiculous nature of the question.

'How's the AI meeting?'

'Very informative indeed. Excellent BBs.' BB stood for butterfly bun.

'You know, I've been thinking about this whole Belugastan sheep thing.'

'Mmm,' said Dominic.

'It's not going to work.'

Dominic's foot stood on a still smouldering cigarette. 'Do you know, Tony, I've been thinking exactly the same thing myself.'

'Hang on, I haven't finished yet,' said Tony. 'It's not going to work if they *know* you're from an animal conservation organisation.'

'Mmm,' said Dominic. Jane was gesturing to him – he'd spent too much time away from the group.

'What I mean is that it's going to need a different name,' said Tony. '*You're* going to need a different name.'

'But what's the point of changing my name if I still come from SOS?'

'That's my point, Dom. In one. That's why you will be Seamus O'Shaunnessy, the famous Irish sheep hunter.'

'You *are* joking,' said Dominic, kicking a lump of dog shit that had turned white with the toe of his left foot.

'Think about it. It's the perfect cover. Also the initials are the same, SOS. Do you see?'

'I see that, Tony, I do see that. It's just that I'm not sure it's the way ahead. I mean I don't know anything about sheep hunting.'

'What's to know?' asked Tony. 'You see a sheep, you shoot it. Or, in Seamus's case, you pretend to shoot it.'

'Tony, I'm afraid you're cracking up.'

'What?'

'I can't hear you. You're cracking up.' Dominic, even though the line had been perfect, indented the phone icon with his finger. As he did so Jane came over and grabbed him by the elbow.

'Dominic, do see the photos. They've come out awfully well.'

A gallery of wheelchairs and their carers was laid out alongside a fruitcake. A woman in a trouser suit passed him a picture of himself and Mr Orlovski. The chemicals around the edges hadn't dried and duck-egg blue, the same colour that Dominic used to paint his Airfix kits, had run into the darker olive colour of Mr Orlovski's eyes. He stared at the photo, aware suddenly that the sum of his parts was no more than several coloured chemicals.

'It's a super likeness,' said the trouser-suited woman, looking over Dominic's shoulder. Dominic nodded absently and put it in his back pocket. 'You can keep that one, but if you want a copy of the group one, you should write to Jane.'

Dominic nodded. 'I'll make a note,' he said.

IV

The brass plaque on the second-storey office door of the Ministry of Internal Affairs read Colonel Nikolai Nikolaivitch Pertsov. The door was the same green as the nameplate which, though not exposed to the outdoors, had an encroaching verdigris that threatened to engulf it, making it look like a map of the evaporating Aral Sea.

Colonel Pertsov was Eastern European thin. His greying hair was shaved and he had the gaunt good looks of a May forty-fiver. He was known universally as Kolya. In his entire thirty-nine-year history only one man, as it happened his wife's lover, had ever consistently referred to him as Nikolai. The last time it had happened had been an hour before, when he'd been trying to get into the bathroom. It irked him. But then familiarity with your wife's lover wasn't ideal. Nor was living with him and his mother.

It wasn't his wife that he missed so much; in fact if the truth be known he couldn't stand her. It was more the lack of space combined with the lack of intimacy. Physically his world was getting smaller. Mentally he felt there was nothing left to connect him to the present and before long he would evaporate into the Russian ether. It was whimsical, but such was his mood after being kept awake half the night, prevented from sleeping by noises that he'd never made his wife make in sixteen years of marriage.

The room was colourless and dark, like a TV set with the contrast turned down. You got to it through an airier antechamber, intended to make you blink when you entered. Kolya liked that; he thought it gave him the upper hand. The antechamber was carpeted in a red hessian rug that extended not towards his door but away from it, directly to the desk of his heavily made-up secretary, Tatyana.

Four days a week Tatyana wore a faux Dior two-piece that, in texture and colour, seemed to be cut from the same hessian. It gave the impression of a tableau where the artist had only one shade of red. On the fifth day she wore a dress uncannily like the brown curtains in his office. It had more than once given Kolya, a detective of fifteen years, pause for thought.

His was the only room on the second floor of MID not furnished in 1970s Italian, leather sofas facing a large walnut table.

Uniquely in the Belugastan police headquarters, he retained the interior of the Soviet days. His reassurance came on Wednesday nights with the dubbed version of *NYPD Blue* which backed up his view that, even in America, good detective work was not based on slick interiors.

Tatyana announced herself not by a knock but the sound of her tights rubbing between her thighs. Though thick-legged, her impressive chest meant she had more than once made a fantasy appearance in Kolya's bedroom. She put a cup of tea on a pile of paperwork which lay at odd unread angles like a Braque painting.

Kolya was at the window staring at the cars spread out along a colonised strip of wasteland moated by a six-inch gully. The recent hot weather so soon after the last snow had meant a seismic splitting of the tarmac. Not for the first time he wondered why, among the two Ford off-roaders, two Series 6 BMWs and one 98 Volvo, his was the only Lada, albeit estate.

He put his pen down. 'Tatyana, would you call me a good detective?'

'What do you mean, good?' She sat down sulkily.

'At detecting crimes.' He spoke without sarcasm.

''Spose,' said Tatyana. 'What's brought this on?' Kolya ignored her.

There was a reason why Tatyana was moody at times other than the three days preceding her menstrual cycle. They both knew she was punishing him for not having a Cherokee jeep and a Panasonic push-button fax and answer machine. The absence of Western accessories meant that she was looked down on by the other secretaries in the police canteen. It was only fair she should take it out on her boss.

A hut-like food kiosk with a foot-square grill overlooked the car park. Though it looked like a shed, it passed as a credible retail outlet in most parts of the former Soviet Union. It was run by an ex-con who, fearing a takeover, slept inside on a camp bed, grazing on the kiosk's toxic produce. He only left to relieve himself against the wall at the back. Kolya guessed he kept a semi-automatic at the side of his put-me-up bed, to stave off any takeover bids. A takeover bid in Belugastan meant two armed thugs evicting you. It wasn't an ideal scenario, especially in the car park of the country's police headquarters.

Tatyana slurped the cup of tea she'd just brought in for Kolya. She looked at him. 'Oh yeah, there's been another one,' she said.

'Another what?'

Tatyana picked a cuticle with her teeth. 'Disappearance.'

Kolya sat down abruptly. 'Who, a woman?'

'Yeah, duty manager at the Kombinat.'

'Why didn't you tell me this before? When did it happen? Was she murdered?'

'Last night,' said Tatyana moodily. 'Her mum's only just called. I forgot.'

'Jesus Christ, Tatyana, give me the details. Don't you know that most crimes are solved in the first twenty-four hours?'

'Not round here they're not,' she said and stirred another spoonful of sugar into her tea.

Kolya grabbed his jacket from the back of his chair, one of his favourite *NYPD Blue* moves, and headed for the door. It was insubordination, but she did have a point.

V

They were sitting on a picnic bench of a pub off Cloudesley Square. Antoinette, who was eating polenta and squid and drinking Italian mineral water, tanned faster and more perfectly than anyone Dominic knew. With her blonde hair scraped off her face and a breathless healthy glow, she reminded him of a Nazi propaganda poster. He'd just landed the Belugastan bombshell.

'You know, Dodo, my mum was right about you. If you weren't

committed to us buying together, you should have said so from the start. You don't know what you're doing.' She inhaled. 'You sleep on a friend's floor, you work for some bloody Save the Whale outfit, and you cycle around like a hobo. For Christ's sake, you're almost thirty.'

'No, I'm not.'

'You're almost thirty. Face it, directionally, you're losing it.' Dominic could see where her eyebrows were growing back and a fine layer of hair above her upper lip. She went on, 'I've got plans. I can't wait. No, I won't wait for you to get your shit together. You might drag me down with you. I'm a growth person. Some people have energy, other people sap it. You're a sapper.'

As far as Dominic knew a sapper was a private in the Royal Engineers. He wondered if Antoinette had started seeing anyone; not another man, Dominic couldn't imagine that, but a therapist.

'I can't be sapped, Dominic, I can't.'

Suddenly Dominic was feeling as if a bath cube had been dropped into the liquid part of his brain. Something was happening that he wasn't prepared for, that he didn't like. Antoinette was dumping him. It called for drastic action.

'Darling, of course you can't be sapped. I never meant to sap you. I'm sorry. Look, I'll get the money out of the SNCF account. We'll look at the place when I get back. It's only for a week. We have a future together.'

After ten seconds she turned to him and smiled. 'Oh, Dodo, you scare me sometimes. I just want the house to work so much. I didn't mean all those things about your work and stuff. You're not a sapper.'

In quarter of an hour Antoinette was back talking about education authorities and *the children* with such precision that it was only after his fourth pint of cloudy Belgian beer that he realised that far from talking in the abstract, she meant her children, *their* children. On the fifth pint he got used to it. On the sixth, before she left to go to the bathroom, he joined in.

'They've got the most marvellous hemp toilet roll covers,' said Antoinette as she sat down.

Dominic felt another cranial bath bomb explosion. He saw the future and the future was people-carrier. When she stood up to leave, he decided to go to Belugastan and never come back.

CHAPTER FIVE

I

Tim was reclining. It was the third week of heat wave and the number of deaths by drowning stood at thirty-five. This was aside from the spate of disappearances of women that was capturing the headlines. Tim had toyed with the idea of making a public address to calm people, but due to his policy of anonymity he shied away from TV appearances. That left the radio. He put it on his to-do list.

From his window over the square he saw an ectoplasm trail of thin clouds. It was too hot to work, which was lucky because government business was slowing down. He'd spent the day with Nasty going over profit and loss in the Kombinat, where the director wanted to convert the factory from combine harvesters to jeeps. It was a chilling transformation project, despite the plans he'd set out before them. Nasty had told them to give it another quarter.

From his king-sized divan, Tim looked around the presidential suite. He knew every joint, every shape and colour of it so precisely he thought he would never, could never forget it. He knew the unchanging silhouette from his R&R position of choice, horizontal with his left hand behind his head, the right hand clasping the remote control and one sockless foot resting on the other.

What he hated most about the suite was how it felt. Not

emotionally, tactilely. The textures of the international hotel room. A nylon bed cover that slid too often onto the floor, the static carpet that gave you an electric shock when you touched the stainless steel bulb doorknob. The plastic menu and fire escape instructions in Swedish and Dutch. They weren't the textures of a family home. The place smelt of cleaning products rather than of cooking. Even the bowl of seasonal fruit left by the maid, when she had one spare, came in a crinkle-wrapped shroud.

Tim lived in the Palace because, in the past, it had suited him. From a security point of view he was safer out of an apartment block, with every stairwell a sniper's heaven. Tim didn't anticipate trouble, he just knew that as a successful businessman and democratically elected leader he was at risk. That, of course, had been another reason to use someone else's photograph in his election campaign and why he preferred the bull bars of his Shogun to the sharp black menace of the presidential ZiL. While Tim wanted the best for Belugastan, he was increasingly interested in getting the best for Feodor Barinov.

Maybe it was his age but now he was thinking more and more of a place where he could loll in an armchair, comfortable, with his young family running around, not slide about on a dusty nylon sheet watching cable sport. On the bedside wood-look table, two discarded pink wax earplugs looked like a pair of mutilated nipples. It was impossible to sleep in the hotel with the sonic boom of people above and below him.

He felt so well rested that he was reluctant to move. A low blood sugar, early evening torpor brought on by a sweltering day was making it difficult to stand up. He was even beginning to regret suggesting to the dog woman Natasha that she join him for a drink. He'd got one girlfriend and it had never been the thrill of the chase that had interested him. He couldn't understand men who married and divorced and then remarried and re-divorced, only to do it again ten years later. If it wasn't going to work the first time, what made them think it'd succeed the next? Erik would be like that. He'd spend years searching for the perfect union, never realising until it was too late that it was the format, not the players, he'd got wrong.

Tim stretched. As it was, his body was too long for the bed. He brought his legs into his chest and then let the weight of his legs on the floor lever him into a sitting position. He considered where to take Natasha. There was an Uzbek place on the corner of Gagarin and Alexei Tolstoy Street that had recently, with the widespread availability of monosodium glutamate, re-invented itself as a Chinese restaurant called the Golden Board. Tim knew the owner, Mr Pompek. In communist times the diminutive Mr Pompek was renowned as a prolific exporter of bear gall bladders to the Pacific rim. It wasn't the type of credential that lent itself to haute cuisine.

They could stay in the Palace but the hotel was midway through a *remont*, or refurbishment, intended to coincide with Belugastan's fifth-year celebrations. Tim was determined to contribute financially to the party; he still felt he owed the country after the collapse of the Yenesei pyramid scheme. A firework display was planned on Lenin Hills. The fireworks were a gift from the Korean logging delegation in return for favourable land rights. There was to be a funfair in the square near the Kombinat.

Dressed in a pair of stone-coloured trousers by Kevin Cline – written small enough not to be noticed – and a white T-shirt he left the room and slipped the plastic key into his back pocket.

The evening was too early for people to be out; he heard only the muffled noise of TV sets as he passed the rooms. He walked lifting his feet like a cosmonaut, rather than letting them slide, to reduce the static. Even though the Palace had been designed in Stockholm, Russian convention demanded at least one room on each floor was given over to the *djurnaya*, an elderly woman who kept an eye on the guests. Inevitably, in Soviet times, it had been intended less for customer care and more for the security services. But it was a tradition that had stuck.

Downstairs in the lobby bar, he ordered a drink from George, the Tanzanian barman who when not at the Palace was DJ on the local radio station. George was from Aruba and had been sent to Russia to study medicine. By the time the money for his education, sent from Moscow to Dar es Salaam and back again, had run out, he'd already given up medicine and, calling himself the Black Russian and married to a local girl, had taken to spinning records at a local disco.

Tim ordered a Borzhomi mineral water. 'How's the show going?' he asked.

'So so. The problem is,' said George, 'Russians have got no taste. Music to them is techno.'

It wasn't a statement Tim felt he could comment on. 'You don't know how long this is going on for, do you?' he said, nodding towards the refurbishment in the corner.

'Erik was in earlier. I think he knows,' said George, unscrewing the bottle. 'Stalin's favourite.'

'Who, *Erik*?'

'Borzhomi. It's Georgian.'

'Oh.' George knew more about Russian history than anyone Tim knew, apart from his mother. He took a sip of the salty water. 'George, I'm going to have to do a presidential slot on your show,' he said. 'It's about these disappearing women. According to the papers another one has gone.' George nodded. 'It's not good for my law and order platform.'

'What's not?' Natasha put her hand lightly on his waistband in a proprietorial sort of way that he liked. He spun round and sloshed some of his drink onto a beer mat. Close up she was much smaller than he had imagined, maybe just over five foot.

'Hello.' He was flustered. 'Oh, nothing.' With post-presidency friends Tim kept his job secret. 'I didn't know whether you'd—' He put his drink down. 'What would you like?'

'A vodka and tonic, please. No ice. Lime, if they've got it.'

George smiled and swivelled towards the optics without moving his feet. Tim wished he'd offloaded some of his nervous excitement earlier. Suddenly he felt slightly out of control.

'I've heard him on the radio,' she said.

'Yeah. Yes, he's got a show. That's right, eh, George?'

The bartender put the drink down. 'Tuesday nights at seven.'

'Don't you mind being called the Black Russian?' Natasha asked, raising the glass.

George looked at her, expressionless. 'Why should I?' He picked up his cloth. 'It's better than being a white Russian.' Sometimes George's comments smacked of racism.

Tim turned to face Natasha so that their hips were directly opposite each other. 'Shall we sit down?' Tim put his hand on the small of her back. He couldn't tell if he was pushing her or she was leading him, but he liked it.

'Let's recap all the evidence.' Kolya Pertsov had to speak in the breaks when the hammering from the corner stopped.

'Must we?' Tatyana crossed her legs and her red skirt rode up above her knees. By anyone's reckoning they were formidable legs. From where Kolya was sitting opposite her, he could see a dark crevice at the top of her thighs, like a forbidden cave. He continued rotating the beer mat in his hand.

She spoke first. 'What do you think they're making there?' Kolya recognised it for what it was, a diversionary tactic.

'Some sort of fish tank, by the look of it,' said Kolya.

'Why would you have a fish tank in a hotel lobby?'

'I don't know. Now, can—'

'Some sort of detective you are, then.' She laughed in an unkind way. Kolya pretended to adjust the handcuffs attached to his belt. The cuffs were more for a show of strength than an actual arrest. He didn't know whether Tatyana knew they came from a basement sex store on the corner of Engels Square. His gun, though, a Beretta, was real enough. He had no ammunition however.

'Probably something to do with the restaurant. They'll keep

fresh lobsters there and kill them as they're required.'

'Ugh,' said Tatyana theatrically. 'Can I have another drink, please?' She had her arms crossed and resting on the top of her stomach.

'Same again?' asked Kolya reluctantly.

'Yes, please.'

It wasn't just that Kolya didn't like asking the dapper black barman, a celebrity in his own right, for a slow comfortable screw, Tatyana's cocktail of choice, it was that they cost ten dollars each. Some weeks Kolya's entire take-home pay wouldn't have covered a round of slow comfortable screws. But it had been his idea to take her out for a drink, though going to the Palace had been Tatyana's. One of the problems of being the only uncorrupt policeman in the national squad meant that you had no one to bounce ideas off. Before they'd arrived, half an hour earlier, he had thought that even Tatyana was better than nothing. Now he wasn't so sure.

Kolya put her drink down next to her. It started off blue and then changed to orange. Two straws were poking out of it, and Tatyana was gnawing at them absently. Kolya was drinking a Russian beer called Tverskaya. Its advantage was that it was the cheapest alcoholic drink on the bar list; on the minus side, it tasted very yeasty. He belched.

'Pardon you,' said Tatyana.

Kolya ignored her and reached into a plastic bag that doubled as his attaché case. He pulled out half a dozen photographs which he fanned out across the table.

'These are all the women who have disappeared in the last two months,' he said. 'In age, they range from the youngest at twenty to the eldest at thirty-nine. What does that tell us?'

'She needs her roots doing,' said Tatyana, zeroing in on the picture which was nearest to her in age.

Kolya chose to encourage her interest, even though it was misguided. 'Elizabet Krusikova, twenty-eight, a nurse. Originally from Moscow, moved to Belugastan with her parents who both worked at the canning factory.' Kolya tapped the side of his beer mat.

'How do you know they've disappeared?' asked Tatyana. 'They might just have gone off. I mean, my mum did.'

'Good point,' said Kolya, who liked to give praise where it was due. 'Excellent point. In essence we don't. Though none are women who are given to that sort of thing.'

'They're *just* the sort. You should have known my auntie, she—'

'And we have the evidence of a seventeen-year-old mechanic in the latest abduction, yesterday's in fact, who saw the victim, Mrs Roviskaya, aged thirty-seven, being pushed into the Volga.'

'The river?'

'The car.' Kolya took a swig of beer.

'Maybe it's aliens,' said Tatyana. Though she'd started drinking her cocktail, the colour formation was unchanged.

'We don't know much about alien life forms, Tatyana,' Kolya said patiently, 'but I think we can suppose that they have progressed further in technology than a nineteen eighty-two Volga.'

''Spose so. What about the white slave trade? Selling them into Western brothels.' She was slightly breathless, 'My auntie—'

'That might have been a credible line of inquiry, admittedly, were it not for the fact that some of them were, how shall I put it? Getting on a bit.'

'Yeah, I see what you mean.' Tatyana picked up a photo of a woman in her late thirties. A couple who had been sitting very closely together in the corner got up to leave. Tatyana watched them. She was small and blonde, he was tall and well-off. Tatyana felt an immediate stab of jealousy. Her nail print sank into the face of the woman in the picture.

'Cow,' she said viciously, looking at the woman in the photo, who was thin and looking up from under a parasol. 'And *she* definitely needs her roots doing.'

Kolya looked up. He couldn't understand women. How could

Tatyana dislike an abduction victim? Then he thought about what she'd said. He jigged the photos into order.

'Brilliant,' he looked at her. 'Tatyana, that's superb.' He picked up the photos one by one and studied them. 'They're all blondes, but with dyed hair. Brilliant.' He could have kissed her. He might make a detective of her yet. The hammering from the corner had started again. Kolya sat back in the euphoria of a breakthrough. What were the chances of seven victims all having blonde hair? He moved his head sideways, slowly and purposefully, like on the credits of *NYPD Blue*. Out of the corner of his eye he saw a dark green Shogun pull out of the car park.

The flat was on the top floor of a yellowing four-storey Andropov building. As he'd parked the Shogun in the shade of a birch tree, he'd seen washing dancing on a line. Natasha had wanted to get back early because Igor was on his own. He hadn't complained. The noise of the aquarium was starting to get on his nerves. And from the minute he'd started thinking impure thoughts about Natasha, approximately two seconds into their meeting, it worried him that they might be spotted by Anna or his mum.

'Where is Igor?' he asked as he followed Natasha into the flat.

'It's OK, he's on the roof, laminating.'

Tim knew as much about building as he did about childcare.

'Does that work?' he asked.

'What?' Natasha had taken her outdoor clothes off and was wearing a blue wrapover housecoat which reached to just above the knee. There was a strong perfume in the room that he liked and a lesser one, more like rancid butter, that he couldn't identify.

'Laminating a roof. It can't be very waterproof.'

Natasha frowned and looked at him. 'No, not the roof. He's got a laminating plant up there. Well, it's not exactly a factory.' She was smiling as if she'd heard something that she liked. 'Come up, I'll show you.'

The stairs to the roof were at the top of another set that didn't seem to go anywhere. Around the base of the ladder was a collection of beer cans and the yellow paint was pitted black where cigarettes had been stubbed out.

'Kids,' said Natasha apologetically. He noticed that she hadn't locked her door. When he pointed it out, she said she had nothing to steal. Tim let her climb up first, on instinct hoping he'd be able to look up her housecoat as he followed.

'Come on, scaredy,' she called down from the skylight. The evening sun was shining through it, Tim felt slightly giddy. The air smelt fresh after the corridor and there was a breeze.

By the time he pulled himself onto the roof, Natasha was standing with her arm round Igor, waiting for him. He pushed himself up off his left knee and half crouched to brush off some dirt.

'Hi,' said Tim, extending a hand to the boy. 'We met at the fight.'

'Yeah, you were with the pervert.' He said it under his breath and his mother missed it. He was wearing blue knee-length shorts and a Dynamo Kiev T-shirt. 'Do you need anything laminating? Wedding photos, menus, table mats? Reasonable prices,' recited Igor.

Natasha had disappeared. Tim hadn't noticed the two hammocks low slung from a lean-to shed to a clothesline. One was rocking and twitching and yelping.

'Oh, my poor darling,' Natasha turned back towards Tim with an explanation that left him none the wiser. 'He can't always get out, you see.'

Igor tutted and returned to his price list. 'Impress your clients with your shiny cards, your friends with easy-to-clean mats . . .'

Tim had forgotten about the tiger-coloured pit bull. Natasha scooped it out of the hammock into her arms. As she did so a black and white rabbit flopped out of the smaller hammock.

'Meet Whitey.'

Tim was expecting a loose-jawed pugnacious face but the dog was bright-eyed and cute with ears that disappeared into the back of his head when they were stroked.

'People expect them to be tough, but they're softies,' said Natasha. Straight on, the dog was like an inverted triangle with squat black legs and huge hunched shoulders. He nuzzled and whimpered into Natasha's breast.

'Why do you call him Whitey if he's striped?' asked Tim.

'I thought it might give him a complex, make him fight harder,' said Natasha. 'You know.'

Tim didn't, but he smiled anyway. He was starting to feel jealous of the dog.

She went back to cooing in the dog's ear. 'Come on, cherub,' she said, 'time for your run.'

Past the hammocks, Tim hadn't spotted the Treadex in the far corner of the roof. It was crudely made and generated, not by electricity, but by the dog's own movement, like a giant hamster wheel.

'Mum, look at these menus I've just done, for the Golden Board.'

Natasha looked at Tim and then at Igor. 'Yes, darling, they're super.' She had the dog under one arm and with her free hand stroked Igor's head.

'Altogether twenty bucks, or thirty cents a pop. *And* he wants his pictures of the Shanghai gardens laminated because they get covered in oyster sauce. *And* he says I can do his gall bladder cards.'

Natasha smiled at him and walked with Tim to the edge of the roof. Their block was the smallest of the *microrayon*, which meant it was the oldest. On three sides it was surrounded by twenty-storey towering Brezhnev houses, already rundown and streaky. On her roof, in the opposite corner to the Treadex where Whitney was puffing, were two canvas chairs looking out, past the high-rises on the left and right, to an uninterrupted view of the Lenin Hills.

They stayed on the roof watching the sun set until it sank beneath the top of one of the blocks. She started to shiver and he suggested they move downstairs. She made tea while Tim got the courage to ask her about Igor's dad. As she came out of the kitchen with a wooden tray, Tim saw how so little in the flat was artificial. Natasha sat down on the arm of a leather chair by a stained oak desk. She slotted her hands between her thighs and looked thoughtful.

'Igor's dad was in the GAI. We split up a couple of years ago.' Tim was relieved. 'He used to drink and then he beat me up. Since then I've had this thing about men. I can't stand uniforms.'

Tim nodded sympathetically. 'I guess that's understandable if—'

'No,' said Natasha, 'it's actually more than that. It's got so that I can't abide men in positions of authority at all.' She looked up. 'Don't take this the wrong way, but that's why I like you. You seem so, kind of, well, *minor*.' She smiled in a way that meant he wasn't to be offended. Which he was.

She went on, 'What is it that you said you actually do?' She handed him a cup of black tea.

'I'm a carpenter,' said Tim without hesitation.

'Cool,' said Natasha. 'I can see we're going to get along fine.' Did he imagine it, or had she allowed her housecoat to fall open?

II

Vladimir Zhubelovski, had he chosen to, could have prefixed everything about himself with the word impressive. And on the few times he doubted it, like after a drinking bout had left him physically and mentally weak, he paid his staff to remind him. Tick the box marked impressive: physique, home, income, empire. Even his age, thirty-nine, had the ring of greatness about it – to have achieved so much, and yet with so much time still to spare.

There was only one thing about him that wasn't impressive. Actually two. His parents in the singular, or, his mother and father, with their tainted genetic background, in the plural. Zhubelovski needed to balance what they'd done to him and in his own impressive way he was doing just that.

He was sitting legs akimbo behind a birchwood and stainless steel easel that he'd brought back from Amsterdam on his last trip. Apart from a pair of monogrammed silk boxer shorts and a gold medallion, he was naked. Behind the easel, four metres from his claw-footed embossed stool, stood a gilt-edged seventeenth-century mirror from the same trip. He wasn't painting entirely from memory; he had clipped a photograph of himself to the top of the easel with a hair slide. In the picture he was lying in trunks on a turn-of-the-century daybed. The camera flash was evident behind his head like a halo or an H-bomb, depending on how you viewed it.

It had been a self-photo, snapped last week to remind himself exactly of this summer's precise muscle definition. Today, Zhubelovski was attempting a self-portrait.

One thing disturbed him. A combination of his long blond hair, well-built pecs and low skill level with oils meant the portrait was more feminine than masculine. Somehow the crotch wasn't working out. It reminded him more of a big-boned Lithuanian hooker he'd picked up last summer.

The canvas was six foot by four, so it wasn't as if he could turn it into a bowl of fruit or some impressionistic shit like all those French faggots did. Besides, there was a reason for the self-portrait. A reason that had been preying on his mind since his last business trip to Moscow and his chance meeting with the archivist.

He'd met the director of the Russian State Archive at a strip joint on Mayakovskaya. He must have sensed a kindred spirit because after the first bottle the conversation turned to how the Jews conspired to run the world in general and Russia in particular. They'd gone through the list of villains (Zionists): Trotsky, Bukharin, Kagonavich. And then the heroes, which in the main came up as one. Adolf Hitler.

'Did you ever hear of the loot the Soviets got from Germany after the war?' asked the archivist as he poured them each another 250 grams of vodka.

'No,' replied Zhubelovski, wondering if it was a toast.

'Care to see it?' asked the archivist.

'What sort of loot?' said Zhubelovski, more interested in the dancing on the stage which now involved four women all stripped to a G-string.

'Pictures, mainly. Priceless.'

'Not really my sort of thing. I'm more of a drugs and vodka operator.' Zhubelovski gulped another 250 grams.

'But you do hate the Jews?' asked the archivist.

'Too right,' said Zhubelovski.

'And you've gotta admire that Hitler fellow, right?'

'Absolutely.' Zhubelovski was transfixed. The strippers on stage now totalled ten, one of whom had no pubic hair at all.

'Paraphernalia?'

'What do you mean?'

The archivist was persistent. 'You got swastikas, medals, that sort of thing?'

'Some.'

The archivist lowered his chin to suggest that they draw closer over the table which was afloat with spilt drink and cigarette butts. Collecting had never been Zhubelovski's thing. He associated old things with his parents.

'What would you say to a few originals by the maestro himself?'

'What?' Zhubelovski was feeling frazzled. If it was some sort of deal the archivist was after, then the Up and Down Club with its $100 cover was not the right place.

'I have five original watercolours by Adolf Hitler in the state archive recovered by the retreating Red Army. Worth a fucking fortune.'

'How much?'

'Fucking millions.'

That had been what had decided him. That and the meeting the next day in the vaults of the state archives. Even Zhubelovski could recognise the great man himself from the self-portrait. Everyone knew he had a moustache. That and the fact it had A.H. in the corner. In the end, they'd settled on $1,000 a picture. The archivist had gone to so much trouble it hadn't seemed worth bargaining with him. 'For a watercolourist he made a great dictator,' said Zhubelovski.

The pictures were hanging in a cellar, next door to *his* cellar. Zhubelovski had made a gallery out of a couple of Third Reich flags and a swastika bought on his last trip to Moscow. The gallery had even encouraged him to start collecting some antiques, though at the present it was mainly fascist memorabilia.

That was where the idea of the self-portrait had come from. Painting was an impressive sort of hobby, thought Zhubelovski, and it was only fitting that he should leave a picture of himself to posterity.

His studio was in an upstairs bedroom, one of the fifteen that made up the dacha's first floor. He'd once read about a man with a terminal disease who lived in a house with fifty-two rooms in it so he could rotate and make his life seem to last longer. In Belugastan, owning a house that had fifteen bedrooms probably took about thirty years off your life, on account of what you had to do to get it. That was one of the reasons his security was so tight, including an armed guard at the gates and a twenty-four-hour patrol, as well as the dogs. These days you couldn't be too careful, especially at this time of year.

Zhubelovski stood up and padded in bare feet across to the window. The louvre windows were open and beyond the bars, at the back, he looked onto fields. At the front, opposite his house, was a row of ramshackle dachas, more shed than home. He had bought the plot of land there because, before his mother had stumbled out, he'd grown up in one, albeit one hundred miles away in Astrakhan province. It gave him real pleasure, amounting to a feeling of utter wellbeing, to know how far he'd come. And, more importantly, it reminded him that his mother, unless she was dead, was still living in poverty. He smiled and stroked his bare stomach.

III

'You're not working tonight then, dear?' Mrs Barinova spotted Anna coming out of the office marked manager at Come Dancing. She was wearing a short blue skirt and a V-neck T-shirt. She looked slightly flushed, as if she hadn't expected to see anyone she knew.

'I'm sorry?'

'Not working with the computers tonight. Night off, is it?'

'That's right,' said Anna.

'Are you meeting up with Feodor later?' Anna was wondering why Mrs Barinova still had her coat on. She went on, 'He said he might be out later.'

'No, I can't I'm afraid, I've got a meeting. You know.' Anna smiled apologetically.

'I'm meeting Erik in here for a drink. You might like to join us, if your meeting finishes on time.'

'We'll see.' Anna touched Mrs Barinova's shoulder and returned to her office. Mrs Barinova thought she was acting strangely, but then she thought most women under fifty acted oddly. She sat down at an out-of-the-way table and scouted for possibilities. The strippers were usually out of bounds, considering themselves too classy to pose in *Erik* because of the tips they could make at the club. Mrs Barinova was eyeing up a brunette barmaid when Erik walked in.

'What do you think?' She identified her by a glance.

Erik bobbed down under the table and looked towards the bar. 'No.'

'Why not?' asked Mrs Barinova. 'Erik, what are you doing down there?'

'Mrs Barinova, you might not know this, in many respects I hope you don't, but you can tell everything about a woman's body from her ankles. She,' he nodded towards the barmaid, 'has thick ankles.' He could see he had upset her. 'Sorry,' he said and produced two copies of the latest *Erik*.

'There you go,' said Erik, handing her a magazine. 'Do you want a drink?'

'Yes, please. A vodka and cranberry, double.'

'Make that two,' Erik said to a hovering barmaid who had good ankles but bad skin. 'So,' he said proudly, 'what do you think?'

Mrs Barinova and Erik spent an hour, four vodka and cranberry juices and two vodka and colas going through Edition 74. They both decided that, in the end, the nipples on page 14 worked. Mrs Barinova liked the Chandler Worthington story but objected to the problem page for being too medical. Readers wanted titillation not cures for thrush, she said. Like all good editors, Erik took her points on board. He finished with his usual speech and said it was too early to know if they'd broken the two thousand sales mark.

At the end of the meeting, Erik could tell Mrs Barinova had something more to say. But because he was still punishing her over the nipple incident he refused to ask.

In the end it burst out. 'We've got another response on the hunting page. Another e-mail.' Though he was interested – the Beluga argali argali had, after all, been his idea – Erik didn't approve of cabinet business in an editorial meeting. He did, however, pride himself on the fact that he never stopped working. Edition 75 was already suggesting itself to him. *Topless on the Mountain Top*. Erik *Goes in Search of the Mythical Sheep*.

'Go on,' he said.

'Well, it's all getting terribly exciting. Look.' She thrust two printed e-mails at him.

'You read it,' he said. 'I'm exhausted.' It was true, his eyes did hurt.

'There's two, one from Stella Anne something, we've heard from her before, and there's another one from, hang on,' she held the paper closer to her face, 'that's it. Someone called Seamus O'Shaunnessy, the world-famous sheep hunter from Donegal.'

'Really?' Erik sat up.

'And that's not all.' Mrs Barinova looked fit to burst. 'They're arriving on Monday.'

'You're kidding. I haven't even made the sheep yet,' said Erik anxiously.

'Well, I imagine it might take a long time before they spot it,' said Mrs Barinova. 'It is very elusive. In fact,' she said with a twinkle, 'it's hardly been seen by the human eye.'

'You can say that again,' said Erik. 'Fancy another drink?' Suddenly the barmaid's ankles weren't looking so thick after all.

The fax had arrived sometime in the middle of the night, marked, in English, for the attention of Anna Arbatova. Anna wasn't sure how many of the dancers spoke English; several had university educations. But in any case, when she'd come in this morning, it didn't look as if anything had been touched.

Her new cabinet position seemed to have quelled any lingering doubts on the Americans' side. Anna had asked Tim if there should be some sort of inauguration for her new government position. He hadn't seemed to know what she was talking about and told her that new members usually turned up on a when and if basis.

Outside her office, in the club, she heard the music start, a salsa tune that was played by every radio station and club in the country. She knew, every time she heard it, that it would make her think of this summer for years to come. She had started to distance herself from her scheme, as if she was already thinking of it in retrospect. Maybe because she felt duplicitous, maybe in case it failed.

Being a cabinet minister would improve her chances of success. It might even make it legal. Her ambitions were modest. She wanted wealth and security, a new home for her grandmother and Come Dancing to be reverted to a ballet school.

She turned the fax towards her and took out her lucky red Biro. If the salsa song was still playing by the time she'd signed, then she would succeed. She even took time to put a flourish under her name, with an unusual double line.

She looked up and smiled. The beat of the sliding, swaying song went on and on.

IV

Antoinette called first at 6.30 p.m. on the eve of Dominic's departure.

'Dodo, you will be on your mobile?' Dominic still associated the word mobile with something that used to flutter above his cot. He wanted to be under the mobile, tucked up, away from them all.

'I'm not sure it'll work there. But don't worry, I'll call.'

'Don't forget, you'll need to get in touch with your bank for the deposit.' She paused and changed from efficient to puzzled. 'Dodo, what exactly is a SNCF account? My bank manager hadn't heard of it.'

'It's short for speed. It's a fast, easy access, high interest sort of thing. It's new. Look, I've really got to get on and pack. I'll call you from the airport tomorrow.'

'Dodo, I do love you, you know.'

'I know,' said Dominic. 'And I love . . .' He started to imitate the beeping noise that his mobile phone had been making earlier, even though she'd called him on an immobile phone. Then he hung up. When he collapsed reflectively on his bed settee, the legs at either end came at him like jaws.

The gun question only occurred to him an hour later. Before

that he'd felt relatively calm, with a serenity brought on by a two-bottle lunch with a school friend, which had been maintained by half a bottle of Famous Grouse taken from his flatmate's drinks cabinet. He swore, if not to replace it, at least to augment it with cold tea. The calm was shattered when the gun question bubbled up into the right side of his brain.

He'd have to call Tony at home, which meant a prolonged argument with Gill as to whether she was able to give out the number. Dominic had Gill's home number because, as a sly way of forwarding it to Tony, she'd sent it as part of an office memo in her first week at SOS. The scrunched-up memo had remained in Dominic's breast pocket, sprouting out of the compost of fluff and castor sugar from his pineapple chunks.

Dominic thought people washed themselves and their clothes too often, spuriously encouraged by the multinational soap producers. As an act of rebellion he washed rarely. It was a conspiracy theory that met with little approval from Antoinette.

'I'll have to phone him and see if I'm able to give it to you,' she said. Dominic had called at seven fifty. She sounded cross, as if, when she heard Dominic's voice, she wished she'd kept the answer phone on. Dominic thought he'd disturbed her in the middle of a TV programme.

'For Christ's sake, Gill, it's me, Dominic, not fucking MI5.' Dominic noticed he had been swearing a lot recently.

'I'll have to get him to phone you.'

'What's the point? Just give me the bloody number.' He was speaking on his mobile. Dominic didn't know it had to be re-charged. It started to bleep in a Geiger counter sort of way. Dominic thought it might be related to radiation.

Gill seemed to relax. Perhaps the programme had ended. 'Dominic, I'm sorry, I don't make the rules. It is SOS policy that I am not allowed to hand out the numbers of other—'

'Oh, for Christ's sake.' He threw the phone on his bed settee and sat down. Soon after that it occurred to him that he could try directory inquiries. He spelt out the name. 'Beecham?' said the operator. 'As in powders?'

'I think so,' said Dominic, wondering if it was Beauchamp, as in Place. 'It's somewhere in Lewisham.'

After a pause, she came out with it. Dominic was as amazed as he had been when he'd discovered that London buses ran to a timetable.

He tried Tony at home, expecting an answer phone. He took a swig of Famous Grouse and started to construct a contingency plan. He was about to hang up when Tony picked up.

Tony recited back his phone number like Dominic's parents did, or like a character in a P. G. Wodehouse novel. Dominic cut him off to stress the importance of the call.

'Tony, it's Domin—'

'Dom! All packed?' He seemed pleased to hear from him. It annoyed Dominic because he made it sound as if he was going camping in Cromer for a week.

'No, I'm not frigging all packed. Look, you've forgotten one vital thing.'

'What's that, Dom?'

'Actually, two things, Tony.'

'Ye-es?'

'One. As far as I know, there aren't any fucking wild sheep in Ireland. Two, wouldn't the world-famous sheep hunter Seamus O'Shaunnessy take a gun with him on a fifty-thousand-dollar hunt?' Before the gun question arose, Dominic had been prepared to let the first point go. Now he felt differently.

There was a fractional pause. Dominic thought he could hear Tony putting together an alibi. He hadn't sounded surprised, which made Dominic think he'd thought of it previously.

Tony said, 'Well, yes, I had thought of that.'

'Really?' Dominic was being sarcastic.

'I thought that you could, sort of, hire one while you were there.'

'Hire one? They're not bloody roller skates.'

'Couldn't you say that they lost your luggage then?'

'What? And walk around in those frigging plus fours for two weeks?' Tony had given Dominic a suit of green Irish tweed, from a charity shop on Acton High Street, that he thought would help his disguise.

Tony was starting to sound apologetic. 'No, Dom, just say your gun bag has gone astray. You've got travel insurance. You never know, you could even claim on it.

Dominic sat down. 'I can't believe you said that.' There was a pause. Dominic wanted to hang up but he was reluctant to sever his last contact with the known world. Even though the known world only meant Tony.

'You got the dollars OK?' Tony asked.

Dominic ignored him. 'And another thing. What happens when these jokers discover that, rather than a world-famous sheep hunter I am Dominic Peach, undercover agent for some two-bit animal conservation organisation?' Dominic had seen a documentary about the Russian Mafia. The narrator had been at pains to stress their ruthless brutality. She'd even repeated the phrase.

'Dominic, please.' Tony sounded hurt. 'How will they find out?'

'Maybe when they realise I don't know one end of a frigging gun from the other? Never mind one end of a frigging sheep.'

'Dom,' said Tony, 'it's a great thing you're doing. It's a pioneering thing. Think of the sheep.' Tony also sounded as if he wanted to get back to his origami or *Inspector Morse*.

'Fuck the sheep.' Dominic knew it wasn't an appropriate response. Especially with Tony being Welsh.

'Are you taking your palm-top?' he asked.

'No!' said Dominic, shocked that Tony could think he owned such a thing.

'Laptop?'

'I haven't got a palm-top, laptop or any other bloody top,' said Dominic in despair.

'Oh well, you'll just have to fax the reports,' said Tony in a nil desperandum sort of way. 'Or phone them through.' He went quiet and then said cautiously, '*Dominic*, we are going to need reports, you know. If only to keep the muff divers off our backs. You do understand that, don't you?'

'Oh yes, Tony, while I'm being chased by effing wild sheep and the Mafia around some hellhole, I will, rest assured, attempt to keep the muff divers off your back.'

'Good boy,' said Tony. Then he went softer and even promised to 'air freight' him out if things got rough, saying it was part of his insurance package. Dominic said he had yet to hear of a policy that covered the fall-out from impersonating Irish sheep hunters in the former Soviet Union. Then he hung up.

Thirteen miles away just off Lewisham High Street, Tony hadn't been listening to Yoko Ono or *Inspector Morse*. He had been consumed by his latest project which he'd seen in a magazine called *Zen and Capital Markets*, left on the District line with an *ES* magazine.

Tony had taken photos of all the SOS staff – a word he used for ease of reference only, because really he meant family – on a twenty-four-slide film. He had developed the film into transparencies and clipped them into plastic mounts. The idea was to set the SOS projector opposite the white wall at the far end of the office and programme it to automatic on a one-minute setting. All day images of the workers would flash up in six square feet of technicolour. In order not to show any ranking structure he chose the order at random, though he thought it best to let Gill go first. Tony picked up Dwight's slide and held it up to the light. Maybe it had been the flash, but he looked very much as if he was asleep.

CHAPTER SIX

I

At thirty thousand feet Stella Anne Webster traced the arc of the airline at the back of the in-flight magazine and figured that they were just about to reach Europe. She was wearing camouflage. Not that United Airlines expected it of economy-class passengers, but Stella Anne wanted to present herself as a credible hunter at all times. And she had packed enough uniforms to cover all eventualities. She had Ultimate Greenleaf, Mossy Oak Full Foliage and Vanish Green, in case the terrain was summer. Then there was Sniper Fall Brown, Oak County and Skyline Apparition in case it was fall. For Hubba and Bubba she'd bought matching outfits in Vertical Reed, though neither of them had agreed to wear them on the journey.

Next to Stella Anne, in the aisle seat, Hubba was tuned in to the cartoon channel but Bubba, for whom the distractions of both children's fun pack and several measures of Bloody Mary were wearing off, was twitching irritably.

The fact that neither Hubba Hernandez, born Robert Emanuel, nor Bubba Peres, born John James Jr, had owned a passport hadn't surprised Stella Anne Webster. Apart from stays in young offenders' institutions, Hubba had left Texas only in order to visit family in Miami. Bubba had been to Mexico several times, smuggling white goods, but he hadn't figured on Mexico being a separate country.

121

Hubba and Bubba were as close to real family as Stella Anne had. She considered the boys part of her programme. The correctional facility where she'd found them considered her a freak.

Stella Anne's programme was simple but effective. Her husband Jeff, a plastic surgeon, whom Stella Anne had hated for more days of her existence than she hadn't, had been murdered in a drive-by shooting in 1998 coming out of a woman's apartment, a visit that, had he lived, he would have explained as a quote for breast enlargements. With his demise, Stella Anne inherited his multimillion dollar estate and a lifelong gratitude to the gang whose seven-millimetre bullet had hit him through the chest, killing him instantly.

It was inappropriate, from an etiquette point of view, and questionable, from a life insurance point of view, to repay the gang – four out of five of whom were behind bars – in cash. So Stella Anne decided to adopt boys from the Pennsylvania Correctional Institute at the rate of two every three years, excluding re-offences.

It was a two-way street. They got accommodation, food, a hundred bucks a week and lessons in game hunting. She got ground staff and gangland tips that might be invaluable in the field.

She chose them from the classified section of *Startling Detective*, figuring anyone asking for a future mate or a pen pal must be reaching out for a stake in the future. Hubba had first come to her attention as TEX 519-980 S CORRECTIONAL INSTITUTE INMATE. Single white male, 35, at times mysterious, loves animals, cooking, incarcerated, all letters answered, show him your beauty (bikini), willing to relocate.

Stella Anne hadn't shown him her bikini but offered to take him on the programme which he, along with his cellmate Bubba, agreed to join. Hubba, Hispanic looking and a one-time fitter, had been serving eight to twelve for the armed robbery of a garden centre, and Bubba, who in thirty-two years had notched up three wives and eight children, was doing five for receiving.

At thirty thousand feet the responsibility of it was starting to hit. Bubba was pulling the headrest of the seat in front of him and banging his knees. They were both wearing Yves St Laurent shirts, one lilac, the other pink. Stella Anne had been about to give them to the Salvation Army when she began her programme. Her husband had prided himself on his sharp dressing. For her it was the equivalent of dancing on his grace. Bubba had a leaking Biro in his top pocket next to a plastic gift from a packet of Pop Tarts.

Stella Anne passed Bubba a packet of in-flight peanuts as the pilot announced their descent into Moscow. With the instincts of a young mother, she pulled out a bag of boiled sweets from her shoulder bag. She checked neither of them needed to visit the bathroom before they landed because, as she explained, she wasn't sure of the facilities in the former Soviet Union.

Hubba turned to her, chewing peanuts thoughtfully. 'Ain't Russia where commies come from?'

'That's right, Hubba,' said Stella Anne. 'Rather, that *was* where communists used to come from. But now, just like me and your parole officer's trying to rehabilitate *you*, we Americans are trying to rehabilitate *them*.'

'You mean the whole freaking country's on parole?' said Hubba. 'Jeez.'

Stella Anne let it pass. Analogies were hard on them.

II

Heathrow had an over-lit, noise-contained sterility that sent Dominic's insides into hysteria, a collective angst of lost boarding cards and too much caffeine. He had an early-morning headache for which the Advil were yet to weave their neuralgic magic. In the end he'd decided to go with the baggage handlers' dispute to explain his missing gun bag. At the Lufthansa check-in he stood in line behind a tall teenager with floppy hair and an unopened copy of *The Decameron*. He filled up on double espressos from a fast food concession and sat down with a paper and Tony's document pouch.

The document bag was a pink see-through plastic envelope with a fuchsia pink button. It contained an e-mail of instructions for him on arrival in Belugastan, a burgundy-coloured visa with an incomprehensible alphabet and a list of numbers where he could be contacted, which he'd stapled to the inside cover of *The Hunter*, a small-arms contact magazine produced in Colchester.

Dominic's instructions were to expose the sheep hunting ring and get a photo of the sheep of newspaper quality, preferably with a hunter in the back or foreground. Tony assured him that hunters often had their photos taken at or around the time of the kill. Tony had gone security mad, and had banned any references to '*sheep*, per se'. Which was why he was calling it Operation Muff.

Dominic moved his feet out of the way of a milk float that was flashing and bleeping its way towards him with two pensioners in the back grinning as if they couldn't believe their luck. The man reminded him of Mr Orlovski and the photo from the Elderly Alert summer fete still in his back pocket. He pulled it out; it had become rounded to the shape of his buttock. Taking it with him, albeit accidentally gave him some reassurance. It was the nearest thing he had to a family snap.

The snap already had a faded look to it. Which was exactly why Dominic objected to having his picture taken. Not for reasons of vanity, he photographed exceptionally well, but because it produced an image of him with its own time frame. Which was also his objection to having children. Before you knew it, children are teenagers and you have become old. Or, in the case of photos, the picture is yellowing and you are the pensioner trying to remember when it was taken. According to Dominic, it obliquely speeded up the ageing process.

Overhead a foreign woman, possibly German, called flight LG 42 to Frankfurt – Tony said the only direct flights went from the States – to attention. Dominic put the photo between the pages of a Ryman's notebook which served as his address book and with his left hand made a quick checklist of the contents of his pocket – ticket, passport, money, mobile phone (switched off), Advil. He popped three of the latter and made his way to gate 13.

III

Tim spoke gravely in an effort to make it clear that he didn't have time to kid about. 'How are we going to do this, then?' He had a meeting at midday with the Gang of Four, Tim's name for the four most influential businessmen in the country. As far as economics went, Tim's governmental policy was laissez faire. He pretended he was basing it on the American model, but mostly it came from having little grounding in theory, which he left to Nasty, who in turn left it to the Gang of Four. For form's sake they met once a month and the bankers told Tim how exchange rates would be set and how high interest rates would be. The former interested Tim only when he was going to Moscow on a shopping trip and wanted to do a deal in dollars.

That morning, however, affairs of state had taken an unusual twist.

'How do you mean?' asked Erik. Both men were standing at the door of the garage looking in. Their faces were in shade but the sun pounded on their backs, making their shirts stick to their skin. Tim hadn't slept well the night before. It wasn't just because of the heat. He had been thinking of Natasha, how cool she looked in a cotton housecoat, and then about how she could only love a carpenter. Tim knew enough about women to know that no matter how misguided, they rarely changed their minds. He'd been so convinced of the point he'd borrowed a drill from

Pasha and tried a set of shelves in his hotel room. The result had made him irritable.

Tim looked at his watch. He said, 'Well, this *was* your idea. In case I have to remind you.'

'Yeah,' said Erik, not looking at him. 'And if you ran your so-called country better we wouldn't have to be doing it in the first place.'

Erik went over to the Dneiper, lifted it off its stand and pushed it towards the door. The lock-up smelt of oil, earth and dog food. There was a bench at the back but in the dark Tim couldn't make out what was on it.

Erik's garage was five kilometres from town, one of maybe a hundred in a shantytown of lock-ups used more often to store vegetables than cars. Despite, or perhaps because of, Tim's plans with the Yenesei, few of his countrymen owned a car. Only a Soviet bureaucrat could come up with the idea of a garage that required a half-hour bus ride to get to it.

'I'll have to get it outside, the light in here has had it.' Erik, who was using both his hands to push the motorbike, had a cigarette in his mouth as he talked. Tim thought about the fire risk. 'Anyway, what are you complaining about?' Erik went on. 'It's not your primary means of transport we're using for this.'

Tim ignored him. He'd left Pasha in the car waiting by the side of the road.

'Now what?' Tim stared at the bike. The black metal had a matt sheen to it and the seat was leather with a cut on the near side. The sidecar stuck out like a stabiliser. Anything Soviet seemed to be stripped down to its unembellished essentials, like a prototype that had been picked up accidentally and then gone into production. The bike was no different.

'Pass your mum's coat,' said Erik, fiddling with the handlebars. 'If we drape it over—' He stopped suddenly as the garage door opposite and one down to the right creaked from the inside. It made them jump. They heard a kick from the inside and the noise of a struggle as it was yanked up. A tall man in a brown suit of distinctly Russian origin emerged. He blinked in the brightness and the heat seemed to take him unaware.

As he reached up to pull the garage door down behind him, Tim thought he saw the glint of something metallic at his waist. Erik recognised him. Though they weren't doing anything immediately wrong, Erik, who generally had a guilty demeanour, threw the sheepskin coat in the sidecar and skulked back into the garage. Tim pretended to tinker with the engine.

'Good morning,' said the man.

'Good morning,' replied Tim and half raised a hand. The suited man had a natty crew-cut, probably more by accident than design. He self-consciously tugged his suit down at the corners, and pushed his hand over the contours of his head as if to smooth down his hair. As his hair was as long as the surface of a tennis ball it wasn't entirely necessary.

'Recognise him?' Erik had emerged from hiding in the garage.

'Should I?' said Tim.

'Third in command of the national police force, name of Colonel Nikolai Pertsov.' Erik pulled the sheepskin coat from the sidecar.

'What the hell's he doing sleeping in a garage?'

'You're obviously not paying him enough,' said Erik. The encounter seemed to have energised him. 'Right then, come on. Let's get to work. We've not got long before they get here.'

Erik was holding the coat out in front of him. 'Are you sure your mum doesn't want this?'

'Probably,' said Tim. 'But I'll get her a new one.' He touched the saddle. 'How fast does it go?'

'Faster than a sheep,' said Erik confidently.

'How fast do sheep go?' asked Tim.

'Fuck knows,' said Erik. 'Just hold the bike and pass me the scissors.' Tim held the coat to the side of him. Erik took the scissors and put his head down like a matador. With a flourish he said, 'Let the Beluga argali argali begin,' and charged at the sheepskin coat.

IV

The reflection of Kolya Pertsov's face, unless he stood on tiptoe, was split into two by the diagonal crack in the mirror of the second-floor toilet. The water was cold and Kolya had promised himself, after his military service in the Far East, he would never again shave in cold water. Even when the utilities switched the hot water off for all of August every summer, he used to boil a kettle. Or his wife had. The room was windowless and dark. It was quiet apart from the gurgle of the tank refilling. Kolya hadn't wanted to go to the lavatory in the garage. It had seemed bestial. More than that, it was unhygienic, and it looked as if he might be sleeping there for some time to come.

He lathered some soap and plastered his chin with it. A faint chemical smell of flowers took the stench of the toilets away. He wondered how they got so dirty when most of the officers in the police headquarters used the chief's en suite facility. Apart, of course, from Colonel Nikolai Pertsov.

When he finished shaving he removed the leftover soap with a towel and repackaged his soap and razor into a plastic bag and then into a wash bag.

If the garage hadn't worked out, Kolya's contingency plan was to try the yurt. The yurt was Kolya's accommodation of last resort. The animal skin tent belonged to a family of nomads who had befriended him last year after he'd arrested them for selling moonshine vodka, thought to have cost the eyesight of a dozen men and one elderly woman. The court case against them hadn't been proven and the family, Mongol in origin, had promised Kolya that he was welcome to stay with them any time he wanted. At the time he'd thought the prospect unlikely, but after three months with his wife, her lover and his mother, it had become increasingly appealing.

As it happened the garage was working out fine. He wondered why he hadn't thought of it before.

Kolya had been living in the lock-up for three nights. It had been a revelation. Not only was it close to the office, comfortable and most importantly lacked his wife's and her lover's nightly wails, but had turned out to be part of an entire community. And not just the drunks and down-and-outs. Kolya was already on nodding terms with a couple of men living in the row next to his garage, one of whom worked at the Kombinat and the other in the stationery shop on Chekhov Street. On warm summer evenings they sat on upturned crates, playing cards and listening to the radio. Despite the fact that they were all cuckolds, evicted from their homes by virile young lovers, it had the feeling of a band of outcasts, like a renegade army battalion. For the first time in several weeks, Kolya had started to walk with a spring in his step.

'Morning, Tatyana,' he said, bowing slightly and almost clicking his heels as he turned towards her. Tatyana was wearing her brown curtain dress which was creased over her thighs. Her wrist was moving up and down as she filed her nails.

'You're very chipper this morning,' she said, looking up but not moving her head. Tatyana's hair, Kolya noticed, was very neatly striped in layers of blonde and brown.

'We have work to do, that's why. Tea, please, in my office.' Kolya strode away and with a slight underarm movement guided his plastic bag to the floor next to his desk. Everything Kolya owned was kept in plastic bags. Precious things, like his Zenit camera, were sheathed in a series of plastic bags, like a matryoshka.

He opened his desk drawer and took out a green paper folder with the words 'Case 37, Unsolved' on the front. As he'd lain unsleeping on his camp bed the night before, he'd wondered if he should report his findings, in what he was calling the Mystery of the Disappearing Blondes (Chemically Assisted), to his superiors.

In the light of day, senior detectives on the national squad had very little interest in the activities of Colonel N. N. Pertsov, apart from the rare occasions on which they needed a figurehead, as when the US sent a delegation from the Drug Enforcement Agency. The Americans were convinced that they should be fighting the war against drugs in the countries of source. Belugastan was on a list that included Laos, Pakistan and Colombia. Kolya couldn't help thinking that Walter H. Theobold, who'd spent a month in the country, considered he'd drawn the short straw. It didn't stop him from giving Kolya a business card with what he called his co-ordinates on the front. On the back had been a photo of his family in front of a whitewashed house, looking vulnerable with parted lips, almost as a plea to him to do his best. Kolya, though he still had the card, considered it white propaganda.

The rest of the Belugastan police headquarters had very little interest in stopping the traffic in drugs. Hell, as Walter H. Theobold himself might have said, most of them derived their income from it. The picture of Walter and Kolya shaking hands was on the wall opposite him, underneath an American and Belugi flag.

Kolya decided to file a report on the case at the end of every second day and put it in the pigeonhole of his superior who he knew reported to the President every week.

When Tatyana came in, Kolya had his back to her and was studying the map of the capital with a tin of drawing pins in his right hand.

'What are you doing?' Tatyana collapsed heavily on the chair, making such a noise that Kolya spun round.

'Thanks.' He acknowledged the tea. 'I'm marking the places where the women who disappeared lived.' He reached for his tea. Tatyana was already drinking hers, dunking a plain biscuit into it.

'What are you doing that for?' she asked, lunging at a biscuit that threatened to crumble into her tea. Though Kolya hadn't eaten breakfast, he wasn't hungry. Even in the heat, he felt oddly charged. His sense of purpose made him more than usually annoyed with Tatyana.

'It's called detection,' he replied sarcastically. 'It's what the police tend to do.'

Tatyana humphed. 'No need to be like that. I got your big breakthrough, didn't I?'

'Yes, sorry, Tatyana, you did,' he recanted. 'Mostly, from what friends and relatives have said, the women all disappeared either on their way to or from work. In other words, within a short distance of where they lived.'

Tatyana continued eating while Kolya bent between the map and green folder until he'd stuck eight pins into the map. They were in the shape of an L.

'Well, well,' said Kolya trying to denote significance.

'What is it?' Even Tatyana picked up on it.

'All the places are in the centre of town.'

'Whompf,' said Tatyana sitting back, in a way Kolya guessed meant she was unimpressed. To emphasise the point she picked up another biscuit.

'But,' Kolya stood back from the map, 'the majority have been in the streets between the offices of the newspaper *Belugastan Today*, the Palace Hotel, and then the central square, near the old ballet school.'

'Come Dancing.'

'Sorry?'

'Come Dancing is what it's called now,' said Tatyana.

'Really,' said Kolya, touching his chin and realising how poor his shave had been.

'So what does it mean, then?' asked Tatyana.

Kolya looked at her. 'It means, I think we're going to have to flush him out.'

'Excuse me?' A fly had started to circle above Kolya's head.

'An undercover job,' said Kolya.

'Yeah, right,' said Tatyana, dunking another biscuit. '*You're* going to dress up as a woman and parade the streets.'

'No,' said Kolya patiently and giving her an odd, unseen look, 'you are.'

As he spoke the wet half of her biscuit collapsed into Tatyana's tea. A splash of soggy mush landed on her dress halfway up her thigh.

Georgina Wroe

V

Dominic wasn't what the travel sections of newspapers referred to as a seasoned traveller. Usually, on any sort of overseas trip, he took the back seat. Literally, when it came to the month he'd hitchhiked around Europe in his second year at university with a friend. Dominic had refused outright to sit in the front of the cars, claiming travel sickness. In fact it had been from a deep-seated desire not to talk to the driver. He had no interest in cross-cultural intercourse of any type.

On flights, while other passengers hoped for an upgrade, Dominic prayed to be seated next to Hasidic Jews who, in his limited experience, mumbled but never spoke. He also ordered vegetarian food, which came first. As it happened, flights to and from Frankfurt were half empty and light on Jews of any description. Dominic knew that because though he failed to score vegetarian food he was given two spare kosher meals and a halal one made up of prawns and smoked salmon.

He managed to dodge a conversation with a man who described himself as a professional soldier going to Germany to rationalise their weapons system, as part of a pan-European project. Dominic feigned deafness by shrugging and pointing to his ear. The man said fair dinkum and spoke of the army being a 'laugh'. As the pitch of the tannin-faced conversations rose after the second round from the drinks trolley, he described a ski trip to Norway when his blood had actually frozen.

Dominic drank a bottle of red wine, a double Baileys and ice and a fernet branca. Firstly because it took away the jittery feeling he'd had in his stomach since leaving the flat, and secondly because he wasn't sure when he would see food, or drink, again.

The man on Dominic's left, who had fallen asleep with a copy of *La Republica* on his pull-down table and had hung his tweed jacket up on the back of the seat next to him, seemed instinctively to rouse himself. As they buffeted through the clouds, Dominic looked out of the window and saw an evening sky the lilac of a suburban bathroom suite.

Dominic looked round hoping to see the army professional, but mid-flight his fellow passengers seemed to have changed. Half an hour ago they were well-dressed Europeans in tortoiseshell glasses, carrying the *International Herald Tribune*. Now they were a clump of manmade fibres lugging cardboard boxes from overhead lockers.

The glow from the 50 per cent spirits of the air was wearing off. It was time to come back down to earth. Dominic tried to get a glass of water but was told it was too late.

VI

The question of legality, like that of morality, very rarely occurred to Vladimir Zhubelovski. He had wondered how it might be to operate in a country governed by a framework of law, but it was difficult for him. He knew, though, that legislation was on its way. In ten or twenty years the countries of the former Soviet Union might be as regulated as Switzerland, for all he knew. He lived in very special times and it was up to him to make the most of it. He saw himself as a pioneer, like one of the robber barons of the Wild West. In the same way that he knew about laws, he also knew that some people were governed by a set of personal convictions. These had also somehow eluded him. He didn't feel bad about it – he didn't believe in God, nor had he ever been in love. Some people just didn't get the whole package.

He wasn't even sure where his attitude – or lack of it – had come from. Growing up in Astrakhan province, he couldn't remember his mother instilling anything in him. Distilling was more her thing. Even his father, about whom he remembered the smell of nicotine on his hands and the smell of smoked fish from his overalls, wasn't a tangible presence.

133

It was like when he'd gone back to the central store in Astrakhan last winter, the one down from the castle, and asked the shop girl if they had any Astrakhan hats. She'd looked at him blankly and said she'd never heard of them. That was how it was, something that might have existed in the past but now couldn't even be described.

Sometimes, though not often, Zhubelovski wondered why the hatred he felt for his mother, as real, focused and outward as a phobia was inward, was aimed exclusively at her. It was more than her polluted Zionist genes. His father had been a deadbeat too, spending his days at the local market selling things he'd picked up from tips to get enough roubles for another bottle. But other fathers were like that.

There'd been only one square metre of order in that bottle-full, dingy, ground-floor apartment that looked onto the communal yard, where the door was permanently unlocked for the drunks to stagger in and out. That was the area which, from the age of four, he had marked as his. A cardboard fence delineated the dimensions of his space, beyond which his parents weren't allowed to go. Not that they would have done; most of the time, Vladimir guessed, they took it to be an empty box.

Twice they'd been reported by the *dvornik* to the local authorities. Twice he'd been taken to the children's home, only to be retrieved by his father during the thirty days given to pick up a child. Why? He guessed because they used him to beg for kopeks on the local square. Shamefully, Zhubelovski remembered the hours he'd sat on a plastic chair bawling for his mother while the other abandoned children played around him. In his defence he'd been only five, but that was no excuse. It was weakness and betrayed affection for the person he should have known, even then, he had to hate the most.

He'd left the apartment at the age of fifteen, liberated by the profits from the sale of home-grown drugs, and taken up lodgings in a local *obszerzhiti*, along with itinerant families from the canning factory. That was why he had so much affection for drugs; they'd set him free. Now he had to stay free. Other people didn't understand how much he had to lose. That was why he had to be so strict. It was the only reason.

The gear stick of the Grand Cherokee strained to haul them further into the mountains. The driver's name was Jumbal, a native Kazakh with crinkled Asiatic features designed for the steppes – slanted eyes to keep out the glare of the sun and a short square nose to ward off frostbite. He was wearing a black felt hat with a green trim and dirty cotton trousers. At eight thousand feet the tarmac gave way to a dirt track. Behind them the feathery heads of the steppe grass shone gold in the evening sunlight.

As they climbed to the height of the golden eagles they saw an occasional group of yurts with a semi-permanent covering of corrugated iron, foreign-made cars parked at their sides and TV aerials poking from broken-down roofs. These were the homes of former herders who had given up the yaks to take care of Zhubelovski's fields, but he didn't have time to stop. Outside one a dark-haired girl of about six was playing in a house made from the discarded box of a German washing machine. It made him think back to his childhood.

They were waved through a customs stop, which police had put up after the visit by the American DEA. A man in a blue uniform with a cigarette in one hand and a Kalashnikov slung on his shoulder like a handbag squinted at them, his eyes painful against the low evening sun.

Zhubelovski pushed his shoulders into the leather seat that was as soft as a lover's embrace. He felt like a plantation manager on his way to view his cotton fields. He smiled and, though it might disturb the air conditioning, wound down the window to smell the night air, at first catching just the scent of the tall wild onion, then detecting the bouquet of maturing opium. Zhubelovski felt the supreme wellbeing of power wash over him with the draught from the opened window. He'd chosen well this year and not only in poppies. A few additions, a couple more adjustments and he'd be ready to harvest.

VII

Natasha liked the carpenter, but she knew it was still too early to say for sure. This time she wasn't going to rush in. Besides, she had the feeling that she wouldn't need to rush in. As far as rushing was concerned, it only took one, and that would be him. She'd read somewhere, or maybe it had been the homespun philosophy of her mother, who had been no expert, that the best relationships were when the man loved the woman more than she loved him. That type of relationship she'd never experienced.

For a change Natasha had decided to walk Whitey rather than to attach the lead to her steering wheel. The fighting season was almost over and there was no point in getting the dog all pumped up for nothing. Same, she thought, with men. She set off past the furniture shop, across the street at the store simply called 'Meat', and into the park.

She thought as she walked. He was big and she liked that; head and shoulders taller than her. And a carpenter, she liked that. No more uniforms. Uniforms had been Natasha's downfall, from the encounter with the brigade leader at Young Pioneer camp at Artek to Igor's dad the GAI officer. No more uniforms and no more authority figures. The next time she fell in love, it would be with someone without the slightest hint of power, a dandy or a poet. Someone like the carpenter.

Whilst Natasha was weighing up exactly how much she liked her new boyfriend, Anna was waiting for United Airlines flight 242 from Houston to land. She was dressed in her lucky navy two-piece suit, lucky because it was what she had been wearing when she'd had her last piece of significant good luck, and low slingback shoes.

She'd pinned her hair into a bun and even bought a crimson leather briefcase from a travelling Azeri sales rep for the meeting.

She wasn't expecting to see anyone she knew at the airport but, just in case, she hung back, standing behind a wooden trough of pot plants that gave the airport the look of a municipal building, like a hospital or a library. The board she had clamped under her arm with the black felt writing on it said, in English, John H. Easton Sr. There should have been a company name but Anna was worried that if anyone did see her, she'd be well and truly foiled. This way he could at least be a tourist, or something. She repositioned the board and hoped the lettering wasn't rubbing off on her jacket, which was dry clean only.

As if signalled by some imperceptible noise, a huddle of Armenian taxi drivers moved into the waiting lounge like vultures. It meant they must have spotted the plane from outside. Unlike Moscow, the only other airport she'd ever been to, there was only one booth for passport control, at that moment unmanned, and absolutely no customs, even though it was an international flight. There were two other people in the arrivals lounge, an elderly woman with a cat and its kittens, their heads poking out of a blue and white canvas bag, and a much younger man who had the bemused yet superior look of a foreigner. He had been staring at Anna so intently since she arrived that she'd checked on the arrivals board in case the flight had landed and he was, in fact, Easton. It hadn't, and in any case she'd known the young foreigner was too good-looking to have been Easton.

Anna was housing Easton in one of the two flats that had come into her possession on the death of her parents. One housed her grandmother's colony of tortoises, which on occasion spilt into the Pushkinskaya two-roomed apartment. It had the symmetrical look of the sixties: bold, tessellating patterns in orange and brown, combined with the flimsiness of a Soviet space project.

Easton could have stayed at the Palace, had Anna wanted the entire country to know about his arrival. She was going to sell him on the apartment by stressing the authenticity of a home visit. It would also suit their purposes better. What with the prostitutes at the Palace, and him so obviously a foreigner, it wasn't too much of a lie.

A woman's voice through the tannoy announced the flight's arrival. Anna decided it was safe to edge from the fringes of the pot plant and make her way over. She aimed to take cover behind two taxi drivers waiting with their car keys in one hand while the other pulled sunflower seeds from their jacket pockets. They spoke to each other out of the sides of their mouths and then spat the husks on the floor. She was just about to edge out when she saw him.

Her heart lurched. Erik also had a board in his hand. They really ought to communicate more, she thought. They shouldn't keep their scams to themselves. He was dressed as a chauffeur with a black peaked cap and glasses. She couldn't read the names on his card but as he waited he was met by a middle-aged American woman, dressed as a bush, with two sons both wearing baseball caps. Both were loping rather than walking behind her. One was absently pulling a length of gum from his mouth and the other, his shoulders hunched, was whistling nervously.

The woman was in her forties and pushing a luggage trolley confidently. Anna wondered if they'd come to Belugastan to take the mountain spring water, alleged to have healing properties. As they approached Erik, the other foreigner who had been staring at her joined them. It was the first time he'd taken his eyes off her.

Her absorption in the scene meant that Anna had missed the slight man who, even from a distance, looked as if he was going to smell of cigarette smoke. He had a pickled look and was wearing a large stetson hat. In one hand he carried a steel attaché case. As soon as she saw him she knew she would recoil from his touch and that his touch would be damp.

'Miss Arbatova?' he asked, sliding out a slim hand. She put her hand out.

'Mr Easton, very glad to meet you.' His hand was the size of a woman's though the grip was firm. 'Welcome to Belugastan, I hope you will enjoy your stay.' Anna's English was fluent.

'I have no doubts on that score, Miss Arbatova. Shall we go?' She had expected him to follow her, but it was Easton's low hips and stiff shoulders that led them from the airport lounge.

VIII

There had been things that had occurred to Dominic on landing. The heat as they left the plane was like the blast from opening an oven door. Then came the smell of baking tarmac and aeroplane fuel. The landscape was flat and wooded – not unlike Britain except it was uncolonised by farms and it wasn't divided into concrete car parks. In the distance was an unexpected row of snow-capped mountains. Apart from the Cyrillic lettering of the airport, the only words he saw were on other planes: Aeroflot, Caspian Air; a smaller one had Astrakhan Avia written on the side.

The passengers – there had been only five since Frankfurt, a middle-class family with a daughter with her hair in red pigtails and a tutu, and two men in identical black leather jackets – were taken to the terminal in a bus. It was not the short hop of a European airport, but a fifteen-minute drive around the runway. Dominic felt exhausted, not just from the early start but from the sensory overload, or was it underload? There was no movement, no colour, no advertising hoardings. He felt bleak. For comfort he ran his hand over the items in his pockets, his passport, mobile phone, cigarettes and wallet.

In his inside breast pocket was the copy of Kurosawa's *Seven Samurai* that Tony had given to him with a Japanese inscription on the inside. On the bus the duty-free bottle in his bag clunked reassuringly in the aisle beside him.

The arrivals lounge reminded Tony of a colonial lodge from the sixties. It wasn't just the heat; there were the khaki uniforms of the immigration staff and the carved wooden plant holders stocked with bulbous-leafed plants shooting green out of papery brown husks. Even the smell was faintly hothouse, like the school greenhouse where he had smoked crafty cigarettes among the tomato plants.

It made him yearn for a cigarette. As soon as the acne-pitted boy in a brown shirt waved him through passport control, he sank onto a plastic seat with the foam bursting out of it like pus and appraised the situation.

Tony's instructions told him he would be met at the airport. He consulted his travel documents case and pulled out the sheet printed from the Internet with the itinerary. 'You will be met at Belugastan International Airport by one of our trained tourism operatives.' He pulled a Camel light from his pocket. What happened next put him into a spiritual spasm. Effectively, it had the potential to wipe clean his internal CCTV tape of everything else not only that day but that year.

In his line of vision as he clicked the lid of his Zippo shut, he saw her, loitering under a coconut tree.

Dominic had read enough fiction, sat enough English exams, scanned through enough magazines, men's and women's, to know about falling in love. It was a one-off arrow to the heart, combined with a feeling that you'd known them all your life. You couldn't predict it and, like childhood diseases, it didn't happen to everyone and many people lived successful, happy lives without it.

He looked at her again, this time with an absolute certainty that he'd met her before. She was tall, slender, blonde, fragile and very, very beautiful. It was textbook stuff. Dominic was in love. The next thing he knew his cigarette had burnt out and an arc of ash had fallen on his shoe. He didn't bother to light another.

140

IX

'Do you always meet delegations on your own, miss?'

Anna opened the back seat of the Mercedes and waited for Easton to get in. His accent was thick and southern.

She walked to the driver's seat and waited until she was inside before she said, 'It depends, Mr Easton. We are a small country. We don't, what is the phrase you use? Stand on ceremony.' She couldn't drive in her jacket and it seemed hotter now than it had been at midday. In the mirror she noticed how his eyes, between the seats, focused on her breasts. She put on a pair of dark glasses so she could watch him better. She was unsure if she should encourage him or not. In the back his tiny body was drowned by the size of the seat.

'I'm encouraged to see a woman in the driving seat,' he said. The 'I' came out like a gasp. 'I had no idea you folks here were so progressive. The way it comes across in the States is that you're all hookers.'

Anna looked in the rear-view mirror. The man was speaking with his eyes shut. She carried on driving, taking the outside lane to overtake the airport bus belching clouds of black smoke and a green ex-Red Army truck, marked with the word 'People'.

Anna had an instinct about men. Mostly she didn't like them. There were exceptions. Tim was one even though he'd failed the cemetery test and, of course, Erik had charisma. The man in the back of her car she disliked more than most. She would do the deal, but he was going to get screwed. There was no need for him to know that.

She smiled sweetly. 'Or shot putters, isn't that how we are viewed? No, Mr Easton, we are a new country and we are opening up to all sorts of new experiences.' On the word experience her smile changed from sweet to suggestive. She ran her tongue over the left part of her upper lip, to make sure he saw it.

She watched him open his eyes and sit up. He was watching her

141

hand on the gear stick. 'Well, Miss Arbatova, looks like we're getting the measure of each other already.'

'Doesn't it?' said Anna as she indicated to turn into Pushkinskaya Ulitsa.

X

Dominic had expected to be on his own. The sight of three other foreigners infused him with a sense of gratitude. He was feeling infused all over, but he put that down to his recent experience of falling in love. Even though the woman had slipped out of his sight, he was confident, in the calm sort of way that he'd read about, that he'd see her again.

And there was more. He actually felt some sense of duty, hitherto unknown, as if he had to make the trip work for the sake of SOS. He stood up. He felt lighter. He felt noble. The man in the peaked cap was speaking. He was tall and well-built but sounded slightly robotic, as if he'd learnt English from a tape, or the Voice of America. He read from a card. The writing was in a flowing old-fashioned style.

'Ladies and gentlemen.' He smiled nervously. 'Members of the hunting community, all. I would like to welcome you to Belugastan, the foremost country for the killing of sheep.'

One of the two younger men started to giggle. The woman said, 'Now if you boys don't quit that I'm gonna put you on the next plane home.'

One muttered that he'd prefer it to being among a load of reds, then the woman cuffed him. Dominic was starting to wonder if he'd got the right group. He looked round.

The man in black continued, 'My name is Erik and—'

'Pleased to meet you, Erik,' said the woman. As if activated by remote control, she nudged her companions.

'Likewise,' said one.

'Me too,' said the other.

Dominic felt no cue to say anything.

Erik continued, 'I will be guiding you on the hunting tour for the sheep.'

One of the men began to titter. Dominic put his hand out. 'Pleased to meet you. My name is Seamus O'Shaunnessy, from London,' he started to shake hands, 'via Donegal.'

They all shook hands and the woman introduced herself as Stella Anne Webster from Texas with her two hunting guides Hubba and Bubba, the origins of whose names she didn't explain.

'Now we go,' said Erik. 'The car is waiting.'

'You know, there seems to have been some sort of mix-up,' said Dominic, in a speech he'd been preparing since Frankfurt. 'It appears that my gun case hasn't come through customs yet. I have the most terrible feeling it might have got put on the wrong flight.'

There was a slight pause then the man who turned out to be Hubba said, 'Hell, that's no problem. Me, Bubba 'n' Miss Webster's got enough guns to shoot most things in this whole damned country. Ain't that right, Miss Webster?'

Stella Anne Webster looked proud. 'Yes, Hubba, that is right. Mr Shaunnessy, why don't you borrow one of ours? Did you say you were Irish? I have relatives from Ireland on the distaff side. You seem to have lost your accent, Mr O'Shaunnessy. I pride myself that I would know a Donegal brogue any place.'

Dominic gulped.

She went on, 'Now, I take it you are acquainted with a Winchester .25-06? I used it to shoot some fine southern whitetails with 100 grain Nosler ballistic tips. I'm sure it'll do the sheep just as well.' Her whole face froze in a smile that Dominic associated more with apple pies than high-velocity hunting rifles.

He smiled back at her. 'You know that sounds just the type of thing I'm after,' he nodded and added, 'to be sure.'

'Goddamned faggot must be a fucking leprechaun,' said Hubba

and started to titter. Stella Anne Webster cuffed him.

'Shall we go?' said Erik. Dominic turned first. To his left Hubba seemed to lurch towards a duty-free kiosk while the other let out a whoop, though on reflection it could have been Stella Anne Webster.

Dominic tried to stay focused. Despite his new-found commitment to the SOS cause, all his efforts would be needed to track down the woman in the two-piece suit.

XI

'You don't have to wear the headphones,' said George, 'but they might help to drown out the noise.'

Tim was sitting opposite the DJ in the first-floor studio of Belugastan Radio. His knees were jammed uncomfortably under what George had called a mixing desk.

George looked up. 'When the song finishes I'll introduce you. OK?'

Tim smiled. 'Fine, great.' He was hoping Natasha wasn't tuned in.

When Ace of Base finished, George unexpectedly cut to an advert for soluble aspirin. When the jingle ended he introduced Tim with a reverence that Tim thought bordered on sarcasm.

Tim cleared his throat. 'Dear Belugis, this is your President speaking.' He took a sip of water. He had prepared a speech on the back of a Palace menu. 'You may have read in the newspapers this summer of the disappearance of several women. In fact you may know some of the women involved. I am appealing to you today not to panic and to be assured that the forces of law and order in the country are fighting round the clock to apprehend the person or persons responsible.'

He wasn't sure but he thought he heard one of the producers in the next room laugh at the 'round the clock' bit. He continued,

'That concludes the presidential address. Goodnight.' Tim looked at George. 'What did you think?'

'Great,' replied the DJ. 'Shall I play the national anthem?'

Tim tried to smile reassuringly. In truth he wasn't sure if there was one.

CHAPTER SEVEN

I

'What exactly am I supposed to be doing?' Tatyana was wearing her red two-piece. Sitting down, the skirt had ridden up over her knees. She didn't like it but, according to instructions, her hair was loose and laid strategically over her shoulders. 'It's getting in my mouth.'

Kolya thought that it wouldn't be the only thing getting in her mouth if she didn't shut up. They were already running late. 'Don't worry,' he said. 'You're undercover as my wife. Just keep the hair out. He must see the hair. And relax, I'll be there as back-up.'

They were sitting four seats down from the driver on the barely covered wooden seat of a trolley bus. A poster above them detailed their route by a single-line slug trail. It was next to an advert for Bank Zhubelovski. As Kolya spoke he passed two bus tickets to a young girl who accepted them mutely and passed them further down the bus. When it stopped, the trolley bus was stifling; it had the half-animal, half-vegetable smell of old people. Women fanned themselves with magazines or flattened palms.

'What sort of back-up are you? You haven't even got a walkie-talkie.' Her voice contained a hint of hysteria that he recognised from his sixteen-year marriage. She shook her head and Kolya got a mouthful of hair. She was morose. 'I really don't want to do this.'

'You'll be fine.' Kolya patted her knee. Tatyana knocked his hand away as if it was a sexual advance, which it was, though Kolya thought he'd disguised it as paternal. 'We'd better get off at the next stop,' he said, half standing.

Since the city trolley bus drivers had stopped getting paid in January, they no longer felt contractually obliged to keep to an approved route. Most were used for conducting personal affairs. As Kolya turned to look at Tatyana, he saw a moustache of perspiration. Close up and in direct light, her face had a waxy sheen to it, as if she had been dipped in a candle. It was much darker than the colour of her neck.

'Where are we?' asked Tatyana sullenly.

'It's OK, the driver's mother lives down here. I got this trolley bus last week. Come on. It's as near to the centre as he goes.'

Tatyana stood up gingerly. Kolya buffeted her down the crowded aisle, following in her wake. They were coming from the lock-up. Though he'd grandly pitched the after-work meeting as an operational briefing, he'd really wanted to show her off to the cuckolds. A meaningless gesture to men he didn't know, trying to show he could still attract the opposite sex.

But when they had arrived at just after five, the card table of an upturned Hitachi box stood alone. Tatyana had been predictably unimpressed by his new bachelor pad, despite the new drinks cabinet made from an abandoned microwave. They took their drinks outside on two canvas garden chairs.

'What's in it for me then?' Tatyana had asked as she sank onto the chair.

'What do you mean?' He hoped the springs were nipping her backside.

'I'm not risking my life for nothing.'

'Nor would I expect you to,' said Kolya. The orange fizzy drink he'd put in the vodka was flat, and the temperature of lukewarm tea. 'I expect there will be a commendation from the head of police in it.'

'What?' Tatyana had spluttered. Kolya had intended to both annoy and shame her. The shame bit hadn't worked. 'If you think I'm risking my life for the sake of some poxy thank you from—'

'OK, OK,' said Kolya. 'I hear what you're saying.' He stood up and levered up the garage door and disappeared into the cavernous lock-up. When he returned, Tatyana had finished her drink. From behind, her bottom on the canvas chair reminded him of a watermelon straining in a sack.

'What about this then?' The fur coat had been a gift to his wife on their second wedding anniversary. His wife was smaller than Tatyana but the coat was big. In any case, he guessed she'd sell it. Kolya wasn't a vindictive man. He'd taken the coat as booty, or at least his wife's lover's share of the rent.

Tatyana felt the quality of the fur and said, 'Beaver.'

'I beg your pardon?'

'Low-quality beaver.'

With Tatyana complaints were a formality. Kolya knew that. He waited. As she traced the stitching he saw that the heat and the drink had made her neck blotchy.

'All right, I'll do it. But if anything happens to me, I'll expect more than this to make it right.'

Kolya sighed and wondered if the DEA man, Walter H. Theobold, ever made payments to his staff in clothes stolen from his ex-wife.

Tatyana recapped, 'All I have to do is walk up and down—'

'And if anyone approaches you then you make the signal to me.'

'And you—'

'Pounce.'

'Pounce,' Tatyana had repeated unsurely. Then she'd asked for another drink.

Kolya followed Tatyana, part of a whirlpool of passengers spilling onto the pavement. One boy wearing a Nike baseball cap and with a skateboard under his arm scooted off towards the centre. Another middle-aged couple, dressed to go to the theatre, followed him on foot. In the interests of the operation, Kolya kissed Tatyana lightly on the cheek.

'What the hell do you think you're doing?' Tatyana asked, sounding as if he'd covered her in napalm.

'For Christ's sake, you're supposed to be my wife,' said Kolya, then remembered that had often been his wife's reaction as well.

'Have you got a gun?' said Tatyana urgently in his ear. Her breath was hot and smelt of tin cans.

'Of course, but for now just walk naturally.'

'You bastard,' said Tatyana. 'If you ever suggest anything like this again . . .' She tailed off and Kolya ignored her. It was just like being married again.

There could be no doubting that the July issue of *Erik* had been disappointing. In fact not only had they not broken the two thousand sales mark, they were considerably short of one thousand. Mrs Barinova put it down to the nipples, but as they hadn't occurred until page 14, Erik couldn't see how that could be the case.

The cover had been credible enough, a woman – his cleaner's daughter – draped in a stars and stripes flag. Maybe the topical issue – *Can IMF Loans Really Help the Former Soviet Union*? – hadn't been sexy enough.

Erik was on foot on his way to meet Mrs B at Come Dancing. Since the Dneiper had been converted into the Beluga argali argali he'd had to walk everywhere, apart from when he'd used Pasha to go to the airport, but that was official government business. The hunters hadn't been what he'd been expecting: an American woman old enough to be his mother with her two delinquent sons and an Irish man with an unpronounceable name.

Some people, honourable non-governmental people, might have felt bad conning the hunters out of thousands of dollars. Erik didn't. He was doing them a favour. Having their prey elude them on their first hunt, principally because it didn't exist, would just sharpen their appetite. The human condition ruled that people didn't enjoy anything that came easy. If they still wanted a trophy, Erik and Mrs Barinova had decided they could take a few pot shots at a few real Marco Polo sheep which actually did roam the mountains.

But tonight, Erik's mind was more on pornography than sheep. He'd overestimated how long the walk would take and he had time to kill. He sat on a park bench in some shade in the main square to watch the girls walk past. Some called it lechery, he called it research.

Erik liked skinny women with long, girlish legs and tight arses. If push came to shove, he also preferred small breasts. And yes, if truth were known, large nipples. He stood up restlessly and set off again, deep in thought. He turned automatically towards a newspaper kiosk marked Gazetti. Amid the newsprint, *Erik* was the first magazine his eye fell on. That was natural. They were all hanging along the back of the kiosk in a row; Erik was reminded of a coconut range. The other magazines were mostly American, but some were Dutch. He noticed for the first time how much *bigger* the girls were. One, kneeling on all fours with her rear to the camera, had an arse the size of a full moon beaming up at him.

He asked the attendant, a spotty, androgynous girl in a tracksuit, if he could have a closer look. She charged him a viewing fee, which he paid grudgingly. Erik didn't hold with the idea of men stoking up on sexual fantasies without paying the cover charge.

Inside the magazine, the breasts were large and pendulous, spilling out of bras, while nipples looked up at him as if they were drowning. The women were open-mouthed and expectant. Next to their brazenness, *Erik* looked like a shy teenager asking for a towel to change behind on the beach.

It made Erik think that he might have been missing the boat.

He thanked the kiosk girl and returned the magazine. It had been something of an epiphany. Maybe his girls were too thin for soft porn. Maybe it had been wrong to assume that his tastes were everybody's. Maybe it was nothing more than his vanity that was holding *Erik* back. The next *Erik* would be an experiment.

He had been ruminating with his head down. As he looked up, he saw her. Studied her backside as it rolled up and down as she walked. Even from behind, as she walked away from the club, he could tell her hunched shoulders were weighed down by the weight of her breasts.

Her ankles were thick and set the trend for the rest of her legs. She wore a red above-knee-length skirt and was walking purposefully from one end of the street to the other. As she did so, one straight arm went across her body synchronised with the other which carried a parasol, like windscreen wipers.

She was not Erik's cup of tea, but personal taste was no longer a part of *Erik*. As he caught up with her he admitted that to some, perhaps the older reader, she might have exuded a sulky sexuality. Erik had a crisis of confidence not experienced when approaching smaller women. He hesitated and lightly touched her arm just before she reached the kerb.

Although larger women were a new experience for Erik, nothing could have prepared him for her reaction. Until then he had been quite prepared to give the fuller figure a chance. What happened next put him off the double D cup for life.

He touched her lightly and said, 'Excuse me, miss, I wonder if I might speak to you—'

The woman turned and let out a scream, simultaneously endorsing the size of her chest. She then lifted the parasol and tried to perforate his chest with it before smashing it across his forehead and waving it above her. Erik pulled his head down and shot his arms defensively over his face and from that position he observed the approach of a man's legs in a brown Russian-made suit. He heard a whistle blow intermittently and the word, 'Halt.'

The woman's legs ran into a shop doorway where she collapsed onto powerful haunches. The parasol went up and she hid behind it. The man in brown took hold of Erik's upper arm. He was in his early forties, with grey crew-cut hair and the wiry strength of a cross-country skier. Erik recognised him.

'My name is Colonel Nikolai Pertsov of the Belugastan police,' he said gruffly. 'I am arresting you for attempted abduction.'

'What the hell are you on about? I only wanted to talk to her,' said Erik, trying to pull away from the police officer.

'About her blonde hair, no doubt,' he replied scornfully.

'About the size of her breasts, actually,' said Erik. From behind the parasol Erik thought he heard a sob. 'Look, I think there's been some terrible mistake. If you just hang on a minute, we can straighten this out. You see, as it happens, I am in fact the Belugi Minister of Culture.' Erik, as he gathered his wits, realised he was probably being charged for his procurement methods. He imagined that a model, possibly the nipple woman, had informed on him.

'Pah! And I'm the President,' said the policeman. 'You are going to prison and then you're going to tell me where all the others are.'

'Others?' asked Erik. 'What others? I only wanted to take their pictures. Ask Mrs Barinova.' Then he paused and tried another tack. 'Can we be civilised? Is this to do with the woman with uneven nipples? Didn't she like the spread or something?'

'You're a very sick individual,' said the policeman as he pushed him into the back of a Lada estate. Only then did Erik discover that the handcuffs he had been clamped into were fur-lined.

II

Nearly all the people who didn't know Hubba Hernandez and Bubba Peres from high-security institutions thought their names came from their addiction to 25-cent strawberry gum. In reality it derived from their ability, in any location, to construct a workable hubble-bubble pipe in less than an hour. In the Pennsylvanian

Correctional Institute they'd used a Fanta bottle and the metal from two tubes of spray-on cheese. Hubba had been psyched to learn that some people called the pipes hookahs, because on the outside he could get his hands on them too.

By eight o'clock, two hours and twenty minutes after they touched down in the country, Hubba and Bubba were lining up vodka shots on a table in the corner at Come Dancing. With only sixty minutes until the strip show started – Bubba had got the information by miming flicking off a front-fastening bra to a waitress – they were finding it difficult to keep their minds on drink. Multi-tasking was difficult for both of them. In addition they were both jumpy on account of not being armed. Neither of them had been out of doors since the age of eleven without an automatic weapon of some sort, or at the very least a knife. Since they landed, Stella Anne Webster had been very strict about access to the arms cache.

After two minutes Bubba said, 'Women here sure have got formidable legs. They got what you call *vital* thighs.' In the Pennsylvanian Correctional Institute Bubba had been a voracious reader of literature he thought had a high jerk-off index.

'How d'ya mean *vital*?' asked Hubba. 'I would have thought all thighs were vital,' he downed another vodka shot, 'unless you was in a wheelchair.' The bottle of Stoli was half-empty. 'Is that what you mean, Bubba?'

'No, that's not what I fuckin' mean.' Bubba thought about explaining it but could see no point. 'How much Miss Webster give us?'

'Twenty bucks.'

'A head?'

'Altogether.'

'Jeez. You find out how much the women cost here?'

'They're dual priced. One for foreigners, that's fifty bucks a pop, and one for Russians. The doorman didn't tell me how much that was.'

'Cheaper, right?'

'I guess.' Hubba sighed. 'Well, whaddya know?' Hubba had never heard of price discrimination when it came to hookers.

Bubba said, 'You remember that Romanian in the second annexe?'

'Screwball with four fingers?'

Bubba nodded. 'He reckoned the girls there did it for a plastic carrier bag.'

'No shit. Why didn't they just go to the store?'

Bubba was getting mad. Hubba was contributing diddly squat to the discussion. Plus his questions implied a kind of criticism.

'They did most for bags that had foreign writing on them.'

'Foreign meaning what?'

'Jeez, foreign meaning foreign.'

'This is foreign, right, Bubba?' Hubba pointed to the neck of the Russian writing on the side of the vodka bottle.

'That is foreign to us, but normal to them.' He shook his head sadly. 'Oh, man.' Then he said, 'Foreign to them is this.' He pointed to the top of his jeans where the label read Giorgio Armani. Bubba thought that, as usual, Hubba was missing the point. Hubba wouldn't know a gift horse if it pissed in his mouth. He said, 'You got that carrier bag your duty-free came in?'

'Yeah.'

'And I got one that Miss Webster packed my shirts in.' Bubba looked at Hubba. 'I propose we leave and go and score ourselves some one-on-one entertainment.' He stood up, picked up the three-dollar bottle by its neck, adjusted his belt, and started for the door. As he did so, an uncontainable bubble of satisfaction belched up inside him. In his opinion, this country was turning out to be one hell of a place.

'Ain't we gonna miss the strip show?' asked Hubba.

'Are you crazy? When we can have the real thing?'

Hubba reluctantly stood up. He preferred safe bets.

'You sure about this carrier bag thing, Bubba?' he said.

'When have I ever let you down?'

Hubba embarked on a description of a few occasions.

'I wasn't after no goddamned fucking list,' said Bubba. 'Now come on.'

As they went out, they saw the Irishman coming in. Both parties were touched to see someone they recognised. The Americans raised a hand and said, 'Hey.' Dominic acknowledged them with a wave.

So far, Dominic had seen little that he thought could form the first coded instalment of Operation Muff. The gargantuan hotel doorman had offered him the skin of a snow leopard for $10,000, along with a complimentary Belugi carpet to smuggle it through customs in. Away from his animal encyclopaedias, Dominic couldn't remember with clarity which species were endangered. He made a note of it, however, and then bought a kilo of caviar from the same doorman for $50. He was keeping it in the hotel room fridge along with a bottle of water from the hotel gift shop. Dominic felt safe in the hotel. There things were, if not normal, at least recognisable. 'Palace Hotel' was written in neon in English on the side of the hotel. There was a shop that sold Polish pot noodles and Cinzano. There was even a piano bar. Outside was a different matter. Dominic was keeping himself afloat, mentally, by slugs from his pewter hip flask, which held a half-pint of Ricard, and inhalations of duty-free Camel lights.

The 'Welcome to Belugastan' pack informed hunters that on the first evening their time was their own. Had it not been for his falling in love he would have gone straight to bed to bone up on a few articles from Tony's *Small Game Hunting Today*. By his calculation he had 157 hours to find the woman, pursue her and make her marry him. He'd been about to leave the hotel when his mobile, in his breast pocket, went off. He was already jumpy and the ring made him more so.

'Hello.'

'Dodo, darling. Where are you?' She spoke on the exhale. In the background was the fuggy noise of a bar, or a party. It mystified Dominic because London was four hours behind, making it teatime.

'Beluga frigging stan. Where do you think I am?'

'Great. How was the flight?'

The question annoyed him. Short of a hijack or a hurricane, flights were identical. You queued, you sat, you ate, you tried not to speak, and you disembarked.

'Great, really great,' said Dominic.

'How is it?' She was speaking in a way that made Dominic think she couldn't hear his replies. It crossed his mind to finish with her there and then.

Instead he said, 'Yeah, fine.' He knocked three times on the veneered bedside table. 'Look, there's someone at the door. I'm going to have to go.'

'Yes, but—'

His feeling as he hung up was guilt, which was strange, because usually when he hung up on Antoinette, it was relief tempered with dislike. It must have something to do with the airport woman.

Dominic showered and changed. He picked up a laminated map of the city. As he reached out for his credit card key, the ball of his left foot gave way. He was standing on a complimentary mango. It must have been unripe because rather than squashing, it sent him over, twisting his ankle as he landed. He swore and crawled over to the fridge for a gulp of water to swallow a couple of double-strength Advil.

The sprain put the kibosh on his plan to explore the city centre looking for leads – if she'd been at the airport she might be a travel agent, or even an air hostess. He limped past the doorman and out onto the pavement. Dominic wiped his shirtsleeve across his damp forehead and squinted towards the sun. To his right, a woman in red was hitting a man with a parasol. Dominic, who had since the playground avoided violence at all costs, reeled to the left towards a red and white awning stretched out over the pavement.

The letters were in Cyrillic which, despite Tony's protestations and a phrasebook, he'd failed to learn. As he got closer he saw the smaller words in English, Come Dancing. It had been his mother's favourite TV programme. There was the swirling noise of a salsa tune that he recognised. Inside he hesitated, blinded as his eyes tried to adjust.

That was when he saw Hubba and Bubba leaving. One had a gait that looked as if he'd just got off a horse, the other walked with his stomach held in and his shoulders pushed back. Dominic hadn't taken the pair to be ballroom dancing enthusiasts. It was probably why they were leaving.

By the entrance a man dozed behind a currency exchange booth with an empty Pepsi can on the counter. There was a smell of glue because the exchange booth doubled as a cobbler's. The door was flanked by two posters, one of the Sinai Desert and the other of Mount Fuji.

The place was larger than he expected and cooler. It was vaulted in one corner. The dampness was masked by the smell of cigarette smoke, spilt drinks and dry ice. On top of the bar a rotisserie was cooking half-chickens. Tinned sausages rolled on a griddle. Drinkers were huddled over tables in a proprietorial way. There was the unease of a fast food joint waiting for the gunman to appear. There were no sequined twirlers.

'Can I help you?' The voice was female, in English and behind him. Dominic swung round.

'I was just looking for somewhere . . .' It was too dark for Dominic to be sure, but instinctively he knew it was her. She smelt of lavender. In the half-light she seemed encased in a soft rosy glow, as if someone had put a coloured tint on his retina. 'I was hoping there might be a—'

'Ah, but I recognise you.' She sounded puzzled. 'You were the young man waiting at the airport this afternoon.'

'I, yes, that's right, I—'

'You are a foreigner.'

'Well, yes, yes, I am a foreigner.' Her voice made something move physically in his stomach, nervousness nibbled at him.

She said something else, which Dominic missed as he tried to follow the white orbs of her eyes and the movement of her lips.

'I'm sorry?' In his delirium Dominic thought that she'd called him a fishwife.

'Are you here for the fish or a wife?' she repeated. 'These are the two principal reasons why foreign men come to my country.' She must have narrowed her eyes because some of the marble white disappeared. 'It's not oil, is it?'

'No, none of the above. I'm actually, well, to tell you the truth I'm here for the sheep.'

'Sheep?'

'The Beluga argali argali?' Each word went up at the end, as if prompting her. She looked blank. Dominic dried the inside of his palm on his trouser leg before he extended it towards her. Though she was tall, Dominic was taller. His hand struck her right breast.

'Oh, I'm sorry. I'm – I mean my name is—' He stopped at the same time as the salsa ended. He boomed, 'My name is Seamus O'Shaunnessy, the Irish sheep hunter. You may have heard of me.' He was talking gibberish. Gibberish was all he could manage.

'Anna Arbatova, the Russian nightclub manager. I doubt very much that you will have heard of me.' Her hand was small and quivering. Dominic thought it an odd handshake. When he looked at her she was laughing. Dominic instinctively joined in.

'Would you care for a drink, Mr O'Shaunnessy?'

III

Natasha's other rule, second only to no more uniforms, was no sex before marriage. Or, at least, no *more* sex before marriage. By marriage she meant, of course, her second marriage.

That was why she was particularly cross to find herself astride Tim wearing only a pair of briefs as she kissed the perfect pale pink half-moons of his elegant carpenter's fingers, before clamping them to her breasts.

He groaned and with his free hand tried to tug at the inverted triangle of her pants. She groaned back at him and half-heartedly tried to stop him. Of all her imposed self-regulations, the sex ban was the hardest. Tim's chest, like the rest of him, was perfect. At least as far as her requirements went. Not the tautly sculpted chest of the GAI officer, beautifully defined by hours of directing traffic (the type she'd talked herself out of) but an older chest, a stable chest. Sexy but responsible. She seized his wrists and pushed them into a horizontal crucifix, her breasts fell into his face and she instinctively pushed down hard with her groin.

'I can't.'

'Can't what?'

'Do this,' she said.

'Do what?'

'*This.*' She put her hands on his chest and lifted her leg off him, as if she was dismounting a vaulting horse. 'Aside from everything else it's irreligious, what with you being a carpenter and everything.'

Tim levered himself onto one elbow. 'What the hell are you talking about?'

They were in Tim's hotel room at the Palace. He'd told Natasha he was able to make use of it because he was doing a job there. With the help of Pasha and an electric screwdriver he'd managed to get the shelves up.

His Rolex on the bedside table said 9.50 p.m. Natasha and he hadn't planned to go to bed, it had been more of a spontaneous expression of lust. Set off, as far as he could remember, by his explanation of a dovetail joint.

'Because I do it too early.' Early sounded good to Tim. 'I think that dooms my relationships from the start. This time I'm going to wait.'

Tim felt his testicles blanch in disappointment.

She went on, 'You should be pleased. It means I think a lot of you. But I can't stay the night because Whitey hasn't been fed and Igor's at a friend's until ten. They're laminating.' She traced his lips with her fingers. 'This is tough for me too, you know. It's the new me. No more men in positions of authority and no more sex too soon. Cheer up, it's like an honour.'

'I wish you'd told me that before,' said Tim. He didn't feel honoured. What was it with women these days? Was it possible that he had too much respect for them? 'Well, now we're here, what would you like to do?' he asked hopefully.

Natasha shrugged as if it was a new experience for her, too. 'I dunno. Talk?'

'OK,' said Tim, resigned to disappointment. 'You start.'

'I can't start just like that.'

'Hey, babe, this was your idea.'

'OK then, do you want to hear about Whitey's new collar, or Igor's plans for bus passes?' She giggled and put her head on his shoulder. It felt nice.

'Surprise me,' said Tim.

'Well . . .'

As he rolled over to face her, he put his hand under his head. The nugget from his ring jabbed his scalp. 'Ow.' As he moved it his phone rang.

'Feodor?'

'Mum, hi.'

'Is this a good time?' She sounded worried. Tim levered himself into a sitting position. His erection had gone.

'What's the problem?'

'Nothing to worry about. It's just that I was supposed to meet Erik tonight at the club at eight but he hasn't turned up. It really is most unlike him.'

Tim reached over for his watch and slipped it on. Natasha was sitting up beside him. He felt his erection returning. To spare himself further pain he turned away from her.

'I wouldn't worry, Mum. You know what he's like. Probably got a new—'

'No, dear, he never misses an editorial meeting. Anyway, it's worse than that.' She stopped as if trying to phrase it in a more palatable way. 'He's supposed to be taking those sheep hunters off tomorrow.'

'*What*? Christ, are they still coming?'

'Coming? My dear, they're already here. Erik picked them up this afternoon. Didn't you know?'

Tim didn't like to be caught out, especially by his mother. 'Yeah, yeah. I just forgot about it. OK then, the minute Erik calls, tell him to get on the phone to me.'

'OK then, dear.' She stopped, meaning she still had something to say. Something that was the real reason for the call. 'Not seeing Anna tonight then?'

Natasha was getting bored. A month after her marriage to the GAI officer had finished, over a bottle of Uzbek whisky, she'd worked out the uniform and sex thing. Uniforms equalled authority and authority equalled her father. Natasha had wanted her father's love, so she tried to please him. That meant that when it came to men, she was a compulsive pleasure giver. Pleasure giving was good short-term, but long-term you ended up screwed. It was, though, a hard habit to give up.

She reached out to stroke Tim's naked buttock and pulled him onto his back before sliding down the bed. Tim flinched, not knowing if he was more impressed by her lack of resolve or her tongue.

'No, Mum, I couldn't,' he said. 'Look, something's come up.' He groaned and reached down for Natasha's head. The phone fell onto the pillow so he didn't hear his mother say that she'd just left Anna having a drink with a foreign man in Come Dancing. By the time she got to the part about how intimate they looked, it was safe to say Tim couldn't have cared less.

IV

When the dancers came on, Anna knew it was time to move on or call it a night. Apart from the noise, she found it degrading and difficult to hold a man's attention when women were unlacing side-fastening knickers behind her.

'Would you like to join me for a drink somewhere else?' she asked.

'Yes, I mean that would be . . . Where?' asked Dominic.

'What about in my office? We can order something to drink from the bar.'

Anna liked the foreigner. For no obvious reason he made her laugh. She even thought he might be the second man ever to pass the cemetery test. He might be useful and, besides, she could tell he found her irresistible. She put her hand out to him as she led him from the bar.

Later in her office she found herself telling him things – things she rarely spoke of. Maybe it was speaking in a foreign language which seemed to set events at a distance. Maybe it was the foreigner himself with his finely arched eyebrows over grey-green eyes and perfect bow mouth.

She told him about the death of her parents, how she'd been brought up by her grandmother. She even told him how her grandmother, like the entire country of Kalkukia, had been exiled by the NKVD on Stalin's orders to Siberia in the winter of 1942, for allegedly sympathising with the Nazis. Thousands had died on the way and thousands more when they arrived in the gulag. Her grandfather, who had fought in the Red Army, had been captured by the Germans. Her grandmother, who had given birth to Anna's mother on the bare floorboards of the Krasnoyarsk prison barracks nine months after he left, hadn't seen him for half a century, though she refused to believe he was dead.

And the foreigner talked. He told her about a girlfriend he didn't love and a job he didn't like. As he drank more he told her about his father whom he hadn't spoken to since he returned from his mother's hospital bed to find him in bed with his secretary. His mother had died a month later of ovarian cancer. As the evening went on he looked her straight in the eye and told her he was afraid of being the sum of his parts.

V

Anna's grandmother had lived off tortoises for the last twenty years since Khrushchev had allowed her family, along with the rest of Kalkukia's population, to return from exile in 1953. Lived off them not physically but commercially. She felt a debt to them, which was why she liked to check on her charges at least once a week, even during their summer hibernation.

Because of the smell generated by more than one hundred comatose tortoises, she kept them boxed in a corner of the Pushkinskaya Ulitsa flat which Anna had inherited. Anna's grandmother hung on to the tortoises as security even though the orders had long since dried up, liking to think she could still turn a profit on a couple of dozen if she had to. She also knew that a few animal dealers at the Bird's Market in Taganka still kept her as a tortoise contact, if they needed a bulk order. Big orders were rare since Western authorities had clamped down on their importation. The tortoise's popularity was lessening everywhere. She'd even read in the local paper that Muscovites had taken to keeping alligators in their bathtubs. Tortoises were small fry.

She and Anna used to hunt them in the inland deserts at dawn in the late spring. She would carry the bag, an old milliner's sack, while Anna tossed them to her, their soft dappled underbellies cool whilst the landscape roared to a furnace. The tortoises moved in a drugged stupor, already sluggish and full of food before the hibernation which kept them out of the desert heat.

In the boom days of the early eighties, they used to make the two-day train trip to Moscow twice a month, packing the tortoises in the luggage cavity under the seat. At their height they smuggled 260 tortoises, losing only 12 to suffocation. Anna kept a log at the back of her maths book. She wrote the live entries in green and the dead ones in red.

Anna's grandmother had a lingering affection for the little creatures. Had it not been for the tortoises, Anna's grandmother didn't know how they would have survived.

She let herself into the flat. When she opened the door, her nostrils were primed to expect the hot scent of dried excrement and vegetation that, over the years, she'd got to like. Instead there was a musky smell that made her think the tortoises might have gone down with a shell infection.

'Darlings, Mummy's here.' As she spoke she took two heads of lettuce out of a brown vinyl bag. Strictly speaking tortoises shouldn't have lettuce when hibernating, but it was in case they woke up hungry. Anna's grandmother was a soft touch when it came to strays.

She sensed another person in the flat before she saw him. Something about the way the air was disturbed, as if a window was open somewhere. When she looked up she saw a man. Later, when she looked back, she thought if it had come to a fight she might have stood a chance. He was certainly no taller than she was and, in a pair of white Y-fronts, certainly no more muscular. His physique was feminine, his skin the colour of a hazelnut, and under two small breasts with a white line of untanned skin. His chicken-bone legs were paler than the torso. He looked dazed, as if he'd just woken up. With nothing on hand to defend herself, Anna's grandmother screamed and then cupped first one lettuce and then the next to her shoulder and pitched them at him.

She wasn't big, but like all girls at her school she'd been trained in the rudiments of shot-putting. By the time the lettuces hit the man they were travelling at speed and some velocity. Maybe she should have paused to examine the felled body, but she was an old woman and he was . . . She didn't know what he was. Before she left, locking the door on the outside, she broke off a couple of the lettuce's outer layers to push into the boxes of tortoises. On her way out she noticed a camel-coloured stetson hat and a silver attaché case.

VI

By six thirty the next morning Stella Anne Webster was already up. Wearing pink Ellesse sweat pants, she was stretching her calves in her hotel room by resting one leg then the other on top of the dresser. The first thing she had unpacked the day before, after the picture of her daddy leaning against a 14-point whitetail, was a piece of dog-eared card. She took it everywhere with her. It was inspirational. She'd extracted it from a hardback called *The Hunter's World* by Charles F. Waterman.

She started to read, automatically in her head changing the 'he' to 'she'.

Forty is the finest age of the sheep hunter. In her twenties and thirties she searches sheep, pursues them in the knowledge that the ram, which eludes her today, will have a bigger head next year.

But at forty she begins to plan around her physical strength. Still able to scale the slopes, although more slowly, she now feels more sharply the beauty of the high places and recognises that she cannot have it forever.

Stella Anne sighed. She knew that she couldn't have it forever. Stella Anne Webster had more than a hunch that time was running out on her. She was, after all, forty-three next fall and physically time was creeping up. She lay on the carpet and did one hundred abdominal crunches followed by fifty obliques on either side. Then she stretched. She showered and spent fifteen minutes at the window like an artist, trying to match her camouflage with the terrain outside. Accordingly, she laid out her Predator Spring Leaf. It was a personal favourite.

The sport of hunting had, for Stella Anne, always been about her daddy. She was the only one of three sisters who had any interest in the sport. While they played with dolls she was already lining up her first shots with a .303 Savage rifle. What she didn't know then was that her trips to Kerr County as a ten-year-old, and then to the Adirondack mountains, would leave her three decades later what her therapist would call an approval-seeking woman. All little Stella Anne had wanted to do was ride into the hills with her daddy to track aoudad. Her daddy had always told her that when it came to shooting, sheep made a whitetail deer look like a domesticated pig. He'd even seen a mature ram, upwards of 300 pounds, take ten or more shots from a .30-06 shooting 165-grain premium-hunting load and still remain standing.

The skins were reddish and sandy. He called it the colour of a Virginia autumn, even though they hunted them after the summer rut when their manes stuck out like the hair poking from a ripe sweetcorn. Her daddy wanted the horns and because that was what her daddy wanted, that's what Stella Anne wanted too, long, sweeping and elegant, like the curve of an elaborate staircase. Keratin with ridges of annuli, the ewes had them as well as the rams, one ridge for every year they were old, for every season that had passed, like on an oak tree. For humans, every passing year was marked by another belt notch round the waist and another pound on the scales, and there wasn't much glory in that.

Sheep liked the ground the rougher the better, either rugged mountain slopes or arid desert. They blossomed in adversity. Stella Anne liked that. Best of all, though, was the segregation of the sexes, the mature rams living in bachelor bands most of the year, only associating with the ewes at mating time.

Stella Anne Webster had a dream, not just to prove a point to her father, who had passed on eleven years before, but to her husband. She wanted to get into the record books in order to leave her mark on posterity. She had found the animal. Now all she had to do was to kill it.

At seven fifteen she went next door to knock for Hubba and Bubba. At first she wasn't convinced they were there. She felt a cattle prod of worry at the base of her neck. The curtains were drawn, but that could have been from last night. Then she smelt the sweet smell of alcoholic breath and trapped wind coming under the gap between carpet and door. Then she heard the snores. On the fourth knock, she heard a grunt.

'Hubba, Bubba, you get your butts out of bed now because we've got a big day ahead of us. Do you hear me now?' She started quiet but as her anxiety rose so did her voice.

There was silence and then a thud that she took for one of them falling out of bed. Hubba was usually the earlier riser.

'Hubba, is that you? Bubba?'

She tried the door, which was locked. She knocked harder and then started to bang. She put her body against the door to muffle the sound. When the door opened, the smell was so like the stench from her swing bin that Stella Anne unconsciously released her foot on the carpet tile to close it.

'My God, Bubba, what the hell happened to you?' At first Stella Anne hadn't been sure which one of her boys it was, but the blue Ralph Lauren pyjamas told her; Hubba's were lilac. One eye was closed shut; the side of his face was like raw steak. There was a purple haze around all of it, like the bloom of a plum. 'Where's Hubba, is he all right?'

'I guess.' Bubba jerked his head towards the twin beds. His voice was coarse.

'What was it, a fight?' Stella Anne went to touch his face but held back, as if not trustful of the bodily fluids coming out of the Pennsylvanian Correctional Institute.

'Yeah,' said Bubba.

'You need to see a doctor or something?'

'Nah, it's not much. It was an accident.'

'Excuse me?' Because of a split lip Stella Anne missed the last part of the sentence.

'It ain't nothing. We still huntin' or what?'

Stella Anne was shaking her head. 'If you boys think you can still make it. You think you can still make it?'

'Too right we can,' said Bubba. 'You got any codeine?'

By the time they arrived at breakfast – cold meat and a roll and coffee – an hour later, Bubba and Hubba had made a significant medical breakthrough. Smearing a tube of gelatine Carbomask over their faces not only hid the discoloration, it also helped the scabs form. Hubba had come across it in Stella Anne's medicine chest and took it to be antiseptic. As per the instructions, Carbomask was a state-of-the-art face paint made of charcoal and gel that concealed the face and locked in the human scent. Aside from turning them into Afro-Americans, it seemed to do the trick.

Into their third cup of coffee, which was hot water alongside a sachet of Nescafe, the Irishman joined them. He was dressed in pants that came to his knees, made of some thick green material that Hubba, Bubba, and Stella Anne did not recognise. As he appeared in the doorway, Hubba let out an involuntary, 'Jesus H. Christ.'

He was walking with a stick. 'Top of the morning to you, Miss Webster,' he said and sat down. 'Boys.'

'Good morning, Mr O'Shaunnessy. Is that an Irish tweed you're wearing? And that tartan tie, is it—?'

'It's a McNeill of the McFarlane clan. To be sure.' He did a double take when he saw at Hubba and Bubba, who glared at him sullenly. '*Entre nous*,' he said to Stella Anne, 'are you sure camouflage at breakfast is entirely necessary?'

'The boys are very keen, Mr O'Shaunnessy. Very keen indeed.' She dabbed her lips with a paper napkin with holly on the corners. 'Now don't forget that you'll need to come by and collect that gun from us. Our instructions state that we set off this morning at

169

eight thirty.' Stella Anne looked at her watch. It was already twenty-five past. 'I do hope that they haven't—'

As she spoke a woman in her fifties appeared in the doorway. She was wearing Adidas tracksuit bottoms and a green home-knitted jumper. In one hand she had a pistol and in the other she was brandishing a rolled-up glossy magazine. Bubba zeroed in on a picture of a large pair of women's nipples. She spoke in English. Her features were elfish.

'Members of the hunting community, you are all welcome to Belugastan. Please excuse us but we have experienced some problems with personnel this morning. However, the hunt will commence in approximately half an hour when we will be taken into our most beautiful mountains. Please finish your luxury breakfast and prepare to meet with me in the hotel lobby.' She finished with a slight curtsy then added, 'I am pleased to make your acquaintance. My name is Mrs Barinova and I will be your hunt guide.'

During her speech the woman had focused on a spot above their heads, not making eye contact. When she finished she saw Hubba and Bubba's blackened faces and jumped. Both returned her stare.

Bubba exhaled and said, 'I've seen everything now. Hunting grannies.' He lit a cigarette. 'This country's one goddamned freak show.'

'Sure seems to be,' said Hubba.

'You think we could get something together here?'

'Like what?' said Hubba. 'Hope you're not thinking anything to do with hookers and plastic bags. 'Cause that just about got us killed.'

'I wasn't planning on some pimp the size of a bus.'

Stella Anne Webster stood up and brushed the crumbs from her cotton polyester mix bib. 'You ready, boys? We got a lot of stuff to do today. For a start, one of you's got to make sure Mr O'Shaunnessy is tooled up.'

'Yes, ma'am,' said Hubba and Bubba in unison.

VII

Colonel Nikolai Pertsov was well aware of the good cop solidus bad cop routine. He'd seen it on *NYPD Blue* enough times. But another problem inherent in being the country's only incorruptible police officer was that he had to perform both rules simultaneously. Or he had to until he trained Tatyana.

He'd taken the decision at 10.30 p.m. the night before to leave the suspect in the cells overnight to 'let him stew'. Because of the hands-off approach to law and order encouraged by the Belugastan militia, the cells had been empty. Then Kolya had persuaded Tatyana to come back to his lock-up for a drink. At just after 11 p.m., in the wanton spirit of an arrest and after the best part of a bottle of Zhubelovski vodka, he'd got a kiss. No tongues, but he had felt his success, under a pale moonless sky, keenly, as a victory for the entire cuckold community. Then he drove her home.

The next morning at the station, as Kolya shaved in readiness to meet the prisoner, it had been a different matter. Tatyana was as moody as ever.

'Do you remember what we said?' he asked.

'That we were never going to mention it again?' replied Tatyana sullenly.

Kolya flushed around the neck and felt his expectations drop like a stone down a well shaft. 'No, not that. The suspect. The interview technique. You be good. I'll be bad. Got it?'

'Can't someone else do it? I'm paid to be a secretary.'

Kolya raised his eyebrows to remind her that she hadn't been paid anything for the last six months, apart from his wife's fur coat. 'Are you ready?'

'I guess so.'

Tatyana had never been into the cells before. Though the morning was as hot, maybe hotter, than any that year, there was a damp coldness. She put her hand out on a whitewashed wall to steady herself as they descended a staircase and swore as she

171

noticed a chalky mark on her brown dress. A draught from the opened door made the bare bulb swing. Tatyana shivered. 'Ugh! It stinks in here.'

When they got to the cell, Kolya looked in through the peephole. The suspect was rolled up facing the wall with his jacket pulled over his head. In Kolya's opinion it was the position of a guilty man. He heaved the cell door towards him.

'Stand back,' said Kolya to Tatyana, who was rubbing her goose flesh.

The suspect rolled round to face them in a sitting position. Kolya spoke gruffly as he bundled him into the interview room.

'I don't want any arguments from you. Keep quiet until I tell you to speak.'

Tatyana hung back.

Then the suspect said, 'Do you know who I am?' They ignored him. 'Erik Marchenko. In case you don't recognise the name, I am the Minister of Culture. You, my friend, are making a huge mistake. I demand to know why you have—'

'Shut up.' Kolya pushed him into a wooden chair with graffiti carved in the back. Kolya wasn't surprised the captive claimed to be a member of the government. It was highly possible. Most high-ranking criminals were. Everyone knew that the President had only sought office to dodge arrest for an illegal pyramid scheme.

Kolya sat on the table and flicked his jacket back to let the prisoner know he had a gun. Tatyana was pale. She sat opposite the suspect, her stomach falling in three even folds, the first of which Kolya thought in passing must have been her breasts.

Kolya put the prisoner in his late twenties with an educated accent and well-made foreign clothes. He had a pair of wrap-around sunglasses on his head.

'OK then,' said Kolya. 'Why did you do it?'

'Do what?'

'Try to abduct my undercover colleague, Miss Mastakova.'

'I wasn't trying to abduct her. I didn't realise she didn't want to come. They usually come voluntarily. I wanted her to pose for me.'

'Ha!' said Kolya.

'Would you like a cup of tea?' Tatyana asked the prisoner sweetly. Kolya scowled at her, not just because she was showing an unprecedented charm, but because it wasn't what he'd meant by good cop/bad cop.

'Yes please,' said Erik. He stood up. 'What's all this about? Has there been a complaint? If it's that nipple woman, she was only too happy to do it at the time. This is intolerable. I have to be somewhere by nine on official government business. I demand that you let me out.'

'Sit down,' bellowed Kolya. 'And shut up. How do you mean pose for you?'

'I'm the owner of a tasteful pornographic magazine called *Erik*. I choose local girls as models. Mostly they're pleased to do it.'

'Where do you keep them?'

'Under the stairs.'

Kolya scented victory. 'Aha!' He looked at Tatyana. 'How many?'

'All the back issues from May 1998.'

Kolya stood up. 'Not the magazines,' he shouted. 'The women.'

'What women?'

'The blondes,' said Kolya, moving his face closer to the prisoner's. 'The chemically assisted blondes.'

'I'm sorry, I've got no idea what you're talking about. I haven't kept any blondes anywhere. Really, you can ask Mrs Barinova.'

'Who's she?' Kolya flicked open a shorthand notebook.

'She's my deputy editor, in charge of production. She's also the President's mother.'

Kolya wrote down, 'Delusional and possibly psychotic.' He turned to Tatyana. 'OK, Miss Mastakova, we've heard enough. Is there anything you want to add before he goes back to the cells?'

Tatyana smiled at Erik and said shyly, 'I like your sunglasses.'

'Christ Almighty,' said Kolya, pulling the suspect to his feet. Just what sort of a detective was she?

VIII

Dominic's hunting outfit came with a cape, a sort of laird's poncho, that he hadn't considered appropriate breakfast garb. As he packed a short-stay haversack into the boot of the Frontera he didn't much care. That, he decided, was another element of being in love. He didn't even object to being jammed in the back with two men who looked as if they were auditioning for a walk-on part in a Diane Fossey documentary. All he wanted was the quiet of the journey into the hills to replay last night in his head over and over.

Her name was Anna. She was twenty-nine and was working as a manager until she found the money to reconvert the club into a ballet club. She had been brought up by her grandmother, whose husband had disappeared in the war. Her parents had died in a car accident. She had never heard of the Beluga argali argali. Dominic smiled as he remembered her face then he tried to straighten his leg, which since his accident in the hotel room had been in considerable pain.

'Hey, Hubba, could you tell the Caped Crusader next to you to move his ass across? I ain't got the room here to squeeze a tick's fanny.'

'Mister,' Bubba turned to Dominic, 'my friend's awful squashed. Could you budge up?'

Dominic moved further towards the window. The hunt guide, Mrs Barinova, was driving. The streets were dead, apart from a line of women selling vegetables who held cardboard over their heads to keep the early sun off them.

'Why you dressed like that anyways? You some sort of faggot?'

Dominic ignored them.

Miss Webster was sitting in the front passenger seat. She turned. In the daylight Dominic could see she was older than he'd thought. She said, 'Boys, you leave Mr O'Shaunnessy alone. And watch none of that Carbomask gets rubbed into the seats.'

The women in the front continued a conversation. Dominic felt like a naughty boy relegated to the back seat. Like anyone recently plunged into love, he resented being taken away from the object of his desire. To his left Hubba and Bubba giggled their way through the journey, wolf-whistling at women, until Stella Anne banned them from winding down the window.

The grey cityscape gave way to countryside that was flat and treeless. The only other road users were men on saddleless horses, twitching a tasselled whip and wearing hats like small fezzes.

Mrs Barinova inclined her head, indicating she was about to address the entire car. 'These are the natives of Belugastan. In the city most of us are of Russian descent. These men are the descendants of the Golden Horde; they can trace their ancestry back to Genghis Khan. Fine horsemen.'

Stella Anne said, 'You sure speak good English, Mrs Barinova.'

Dominic heard that she used to be a professor of English at the national university, then it faded out. Hubba and Bubba were asleep, converting last night's evaporating alcohol into twitchy dreams. He thought of Anna again and loosened his tweed collar. He couldn't shake off the idea that he'd met her before. She'd told him she'd never left Belugastan other than to go to Moscow. There was something about her height, her slimness and the imperious way she looked at him.

The jeep ground its way up the mountain path, battering Dominic's head against the window as it went. After an hour the feathery steppe grass became an inhospitable lunar landscape. After two hours Mrs Barinova pulled the Frontera off the track and headed towards a small settlement. Bubba had woken up. He yawned. His breath smelt bad.

'That where we heading to?' His scratching set Hubba off.

'Looks like a circus.' Hubba's hand went automatically down his trousers to rearrange himself. Dominic hoped Mrs Barinova couldn't see it in the rear-view mirror. She had blonde hair that had gone grey, pinned up in a loose bun. Dominic wondered how an English professor had become a hunting guide.

She parked the jeep alongside two horses so skinny their ribs were showing.

Hubba said, 'Well I'll be. There's a bunch of freaking camels over there. Bubba, you see them?'

Mrs Barinova said officiously, 'Of course. These people are camel herders. And yak. Please come inside.'

Hubba and Bubba looked at each other and followed her into the yurt. Inside, it was bigger than they'd thought and cooler, too. Painted wooden spokes met twenty feet above them in the centre of the tent. The outside was made of animal skin and designed, according to Mrs Barinova, so that the women could erect it in half an hour. There were benches inside and purple patterned rugs hung on the walls. Women sat in the centre with cooking bowls. They didn't seem to speak a language that anyone understood apart from Mrs Barinova.

'Please, you are welcome, sit.' The women were dressed in long, intricately embroidered kaftans. Dominic hoped no one was going to ask him to take his shoes off.

'It's a tepee.' Hubba turned to Mrs Barinova. 'These folks Apaches or something?'

As he spoke a dark-haired young woman with almond eyes and pigtails motioned for him to sit down and offered him a bowl of milky liquid. Then she said 'Tea' in English and smiled. The hunters sat down. Dominic was aware that the men, who wore dark felt hats, were staring at him.

'Well, hello there, little Miss Pocahontas,' said Bubba with a leery smile.

'The tea is a local Belugan tradition. It comes from fermented camel's milk, which is boiled with a few tea leaves and then butter and salt is added,' said Mrs Barinova. It stopped Bubba's grin.

'Well, well,' said Stella Anne, 'this is turning out to be one great big adventure. Can I ask these folks some questions about the sheep?'

'Later,' said Mrs Barinova. 'First we have tea. You like it, Mr O'Shaunnessy?'

'Oh, yes,' said Dominic. The tea was one of the worst taste sensations he had ever experienced. It was easier to drink it in one. But his bowl was quickly refilled by the woman with pigtails.

Mrs Barinova kept smiling. 'You see how the designs are derived from the curl of the giant sheep's horns. Please observe.' She traced a finger around the swirling pattern of the bowl. 'Also in the clothes.'

'Is this where we'll be sleeping?' Bubba asked. He was wearing a weird smirk that hadn't left the dusky waitress. It wasn't due to the tea, because Dominic had watched them both pour it outside through the vent of an opened tent flap.

'Please, some dumplings. They are fried dough.'

Stella Anne winced but took one just the same, to show her hunter's commitment to native cultures.

After the dumplings came a blue plastic plate of camel meat. Hubba and Bubba said that there was no way on God's earth that either of them was going to eat a camel. Dominic felt the same but took a piece. It was tough and tasteless. He used the tea to take away the taste of the camel and then used the camel to take away the taste of the tea. In that way he got through two bowls of tea and three slices of camel. He tried to remember if camels were endangered. He gave it 50–50.

It was just after midday when Mrs Barinova suggested they set off on horseback up the valley. Hubba and Bubba seemed happy to watch the native girls. Dominic touched his bad leg and shrugged in a way that meant, 'I'd love to, but . . .'

Due to a childhood accident, when he'd been bucked from his rocking horse, Dominic had a morbid fear of the species. He had hoped the hunt would be done on foot or from a car, like an African safari. Stella Anne, on the other hand, who had been bowing and smiling at the yurt people like a geisha girl, stood up and said, 'Sure thing, let's go shoot.'

He suddenly felt the bad leg might not cover it. Since falling in love, Dominic had felt differently about personal safety. It would be typical to have met his soulmate, only to be killed the next day in a freak riding accident. Or in this case a riding accident with freaks. Dominic started to groan and move his head from side to side.

'Christ, what the hell's gotten into the faggot?' Bubba nodded towards him.

'My head,' said Dominic with an odd cross-eyed look. 'It's altitude sickness.'

'OMG,' said Stella Anne softly. Dominic took it to be some sort of cure, then she said, 'Oh my God, it's because Ireland is so low.' She was crossing the yurt towards him when a man burst into the tent.

He was in his fifties, though sun exposure made it difficult to judge age. His felt hat was topped by a red pom-pom and there was a swirl of green embroidery round his hat rim which drew out the colour of his eyes. Stella Anne had been approaching Dominic from his left and now this man came at him from the right in a pincer movement. He held a bottle of alcohol at chest height with the intention Dominic should see it. But when he caught Dominic's eye, the man with the pom-pom lowered his head. The yurt was quiet; even Hubba and Bubba had stopped scratching.

The man handed Dominic a blue and white china cup and filled it to the brim before pouring his own. He curled his right hand round his cup, as if he was curing hiccups, and nodded for Dominic to do the same. Then he gulped it back in one. Dominic followed. The drink, which was vodka, burnt his stomach when it landed there and left a horrible taste in his mouth. Dominic's cheeks coloured and he involuntarily shook his head. The pom-pom man handed him a dough ball and smiled, revealing black stumpy teeth.

Dominic had taken it as a cure for altitude sickness, but within seconds the pom-pom man was setting them up again. Dominic stared a question mark at Mrs Barinova, who turned to a yurt man next to her. They spoke quietly and Dominic watched the contours of her face fall like a weather map detailing the onset of a depression.

Dominic slugged another measure and took another dough ball. He could see that Hubba and Bubba were getting edgy about being left out of the consumption of over-proof spirits.

'Hey, pal, you care to share that stuff around?' said Bubba. 'It's polite where we come from.' The polite came out as po-lite.

Dominic looked at Mrs Barinova. She touched Dominic on the shoulder and with her eyes, under a furrowed brow, gestured he should leave the tent. When Dominic stood up and stiffly stretched out his bad leg in order to hobble to the fur flap door, two things happened. Bubba made a lunge for his drink and a gasp from the yurt people went round the tent like water being poured on hot coals.

Outside the tent Dominic felt sick. It was hot and there was a stench of dried animal excrement and smoke.

Mrs Barinova followed him, looking grave. She said, 'Mr O'Shaunnessy, have you ever heard of the Mongol leader Dzhungar?'

'No,' said Dominic, shaking his head and belching into his hand.

Mrs Barinova tutted impatiently. 'He features in all Belugi folklore. He was a powerful warrior who rescued them from their enemies. The Belugis are great lovers of the folk tales.'

Dominic didn't want to appear uncultured, but he thought he was close to being sick. 'Really.'

Mrs Barinova looked at his shoulder when she spoke to him. 'The Belugi people believe that one day he will return to lead them from poverty to greatness. He will come on a black horse accompanied by two African slaves. This is not written down, the native Belugi is not a literate race, it is their oral tradition.' She looked up. 'If you understand?'

'Perfectly,' said Dominic.

'He will be wearing a traditional cloak and,' she looked at him earnestly, 'if you understand me, will have the limp.'

Dominic felt an electric charge at the bottom of his neck. He knew something terrible was unfurling but he wasn't able to work out what.

'In short, Mr O'Shaunnessy, you are he. The American delinquents, Hubba and Bubba, are your servants.'

Dominic leant against the yurt which, being made of animal skin, dented under his weight. 'But they're not Africans, they come from Texas, it's some charcoal camouflage stuff. This cloak is a comedy get-up from Acton High Street.' Dominic was pleading, 'The limp – it's from a complimentary mango.'

'That's as maybe, Mr O'Shaunnessy, but we have to work with the givens and the givens here are that you have inherited a race of people.' Her down-turned face was at odds with her sentiments. 'How do you say, look on the bright side. It will make the shooting of the sheeps much easier.'

Dominic reeled slightly. Then he thought about what Mrs Barinova had said. 'How will it make shooting of the sheeps easier?'

'Because I imagine they'll shoot them for you.'

As bright sides went, it wasn't encouraging. She led him back into the tent.

Stella Anne Webster knew weird; you weren't married to a cosmetic surgeon with a roving scalpel for twenty years without knowing weird. And this was definitely it. By ten o'clock the yurts were in darkness and she'd stepped outside for some air. She walked over to the horses tethered to a post and petted them, speaking softly in their ears. It was a beautiful evening; with no light pollution the stars twinkled as if they were a kid's drawing. The air smelt of a fragrant, flowery dew. She thought of the sheep in the hills and how she, Stella Anne Webster, would finally amount to something in her own right, other than as a daughter or a wife. How her name would be engraved in the giant sheep-hunting annals of history.

Stella Anne was a hundred yards from the yurt when the high beams of a car flicked onto her. To start with she didn't take fright; it was probably one of the native huntspeople or Mrs Barinova getting something from the jeep. She even waved in the light towards the car, knowing they could see her. She moved back when she saw the car was heading towards her, not fast, but downhill with the engine off. It was less than ten feet from her when it stopped. The brake lights shone red and she heard the creak of the handbrake go on.

It was only when she saw the size of the men who got out that she got scared; they were too big to be native huntspeople. But by then it was too late. Afterwards she thought it must have been chloroform, but at the time she was only aware of the smell of leather as she fell swiftly and lightly towards the earth held by an arm round her midriff.

CHAPTER EIGHT

I

Within the first minute of his coming to on the floor of the yurt, Dominic diagnosed it as a four, possibly five, Advil sort of hangover. *Surroundingswise*, Antoinette would have called it karma. Or she'd have said, gloatingly, what comes around goes around. Dominic's most extreme theory for not wanting to cohabit was that human society should, naturally, be based around bands of people, not nuclear families. There was something natural about the scene in front of him. If natural meant Hieronymus Bosch.

When he tried to raise his head, his brain was a spirit level with an air bubble of agony. Under him the ground was carpeted. Beneath his cape, which he'd tried to convert into a sleeping bag, his bad leg had stiffened. He badly needed to pee, but negotiating his way out of the yurt and losing fluid from his dehydrated body scared him. His hand was actually shrivelled from lack of water. The yurt smelt like one large unopened mouth, hermetically sealed in its rankness, in which Hubba and Bubba, blacker than ever in the early light, were a couple of rotten teeth.

Because of his itinerant lifestyle – vagrant and bum vied for Antoinette's favourite term of abuse – Dominic claimed he *liked* sleeping rough. Floors didn't bother him. Floors meant not being the sum of your parts. What bothered him more was the idea of his own bed in his own Georgian terrace refurbishment.

That was the theory. As theories went, Dominic thought, as he had tried to rub the carpet imprint off his face, it was bollocks. There was a comfort, not to mention a hygiene, issue of spending the night on the floor with eight other people. Dominic had been expecting some sort of segregation. For the sake of Miss Pocahontas, he'd very nearly suggested it. He had also thought that his new-found aristocratic status might have entitled him to a camp bed.

The night before, the yurt people had celebrated Dominic's coming with spirits ranging, as far as he could see, from Lithuanian beer to moonshine vodka. At one point he thought he saw Bubba take a tipple of eau de cologne. Dominic's eyesight had started to go at midnight – some sort of focal migraine-cum-blindness that made it seem he was looking out from behind windscreen wipers. That was when he'd stopped drinking.

Bodies had shifted in the night. Bubba, with a greasy wool rug pulled to his blackened chin, had levered and stretched himself towards where the woman with pigtails was sleeping. She was curled like a foetus and fully dressed. Dominic moved his cape aside. To his left, the pom-pom man was still snoring. Dominic looked at the brown ridges of his skin. His lips were freckled and vibrated as he exhaled.

To his right lay Hubba. The breathing was laboured but regular, a deep inhale followed by the sound of his lungs in collapse. As Hubba twitched his arm out of a cotton sheet, Dominic tried twice to generate enough saliva to cover his finger. He twisted towards Hubba and gently rubbed once more at the Carbomask on Hubba's outstretched arm. His skin, due to Miss Webster's cocoa butter cream, was surprisingly soft. The idea was to see if the Carbomask, which had spread down Hubba and Bubba's torso, would come off. If they weren't real African slaves, then the whole yurt people's theory fell apart.

The Carbomask's lock-in formula wasn't shifting. If anything it had dried to a tattoo, or thick matt paint. Dominic rubbed harder.

Hubba's arm had flopped directly underneath him like the thick tail of a Labrador. Dominic tried to dribble on it. He was working on an ad hoc idea that, based on snores per capita, he was the only person in the yurt awake. He was wrong.

A voice, which, not being Hubba's, had to belong to Bubba, said, 'What in the name of Jesus frigging Christ do you think you're doing, you faggot-balled freak?' It was low but reverberated with considerable menace. Then a shout, 'Hubba, you get your ass in gear, unless you want the Caped Crusader up it.' Bubba's alcohol-swollen black face looked as if it had melted.

Dominic recoiled with a slight scream. He used his feet as ballast to push his body away. He landed close to the pom-pom man. The noise triggered other yurt people awake. The men spat, spluttered and retched themselves into a sitting position. The women quietly stood up.

Dominic said, 'Nothing, really. I just wanted to see if it would come off.'

Bubba was sceptical. 'If what would *come off*?' Hubba was shaking himself awake like a dog. 'If licking my friend would *come off*?' Bubba was appalled. Not even in the Pennsylvanian Correctional Institute were inmates so brazen.

'I wanted to see if I could get the stuff off him. This black stuff,' said Dominic. The side of Bubba's face that he'd been sleeping on was lighter than the other.

'And how come you would want to do that?'

Hubba had sat up. Whereas he didn't much care for being licked by strangers, he wasn't as put out by it as Bubba. For his friend's sake he thought he should object. 'Yeah, why in the name of God would you wanna do that?'

'Because if you two stopped masquer— If you two stopped pretending you were slaves then that means they would stop . . . Oh, forget it.' Dominic flicked his cape to one side and stepped and heaved himself over waking bodies to get to the door.

What Dominic didn't know from the night before was that

185

Hubba and Bubba had, after reappraising their situation, absolutely no intention of giving up their disguises. They'd discussed it as they were competing to see who could urinate the furthest over the backs of the horses.

'You know what?' said Bubba, his arc not quite clearing the last animal.

'Whassat?' replied Hubba. Neither of them were strangers to over-proof liquor. When money had been tight and grocery stores thin on the ground, they'd once taken to drinking anti-freeze and OJ. But even they found themselves tested by the yurt people. Luckily they both rose to a challenge.

'I have a plan.'

Hubba was drunk but not so drunk that he didn't remember that Bubba's last plan nearly killed him.

'You do, huh?'

'Yeah. That queer Irishman they think's the Second Coming . . .'

Hubba swayed. 'Yeah?' By the thud of his pee, he'd hit a horse.

Bubba said, 'You seen that little dark lady with the hair in plaits? I reckon she's hot for me.'

'*No*,' said Hubba truthfully. 'Really?'

'Well, I'm telling you she's got a whole lot more friendly since they figured us for some sort of heroes.'

Hubba sat heavily on the side of the water trough. It sent a tidal wave that lapped up to his Lone Star belt.

Bubba went on, 'They think we're some sort of reincarnated somethings.' Bubba zipped his flies. 'Like we're disciples. I'm telling you, we could be in line for some action here, Hubba. Just you wait and see.' It was the first time either of them had been touched by glory.

Hubba looked up at the word action. 'Me too?'

'Sure, only they gotta think we're his African slaves. That way we're special.'

'So *black* people is special now, Bubba?' It went against all of their teachings. He belched loudly.

'For now, yes, they are.' It would take too long to explain.

It was 9.30 p.m. when he staggered to the jeep to search for the rest of Miss Webster's tube of Carbomask. Bubba thought he might have heard the gravelly engine of a four-wheel drive, but by that time he was too motivated to care. By 10 p.m., assisted by a 60-cent tub of boot polish after the Carbomask ran out, they were as black as the night sky.

Moodily, Dominic stalked out of the yurt. Outside was cooler than the yurts, nestled in the lee of a treeless hillock. He was wondering if the water trough was safe to drink from when he saw Mrs Barinova walking slowly and thoughtfully over the brow of a dusty mound.

'Good morning.' She was wearing the same clothes as yesterday, though her hair was loose. She looked too refreshed to have slept in the yurt.

'Morning.' Dominic needed something to eat and someone to blame in equal amounts. Mrs Barinova could help with both. He was about to ask about the luxury yurt breakfast when he saw how worried she looked.

'Couldn't sleep?' asked Dominic. She didn't reply. The sky was blue with a faint criss-cross of white.

'Everything OK?'

'Yes, I'm very well, thank you.' She stressed *I'm*, meaning not everybody was. He thought she was commenting on last night's party.

'Yes, I suppose we did all get a bit carried away.' Dominic paused. 'You *were* there, weren't you?'

'Yes, sort of.' She flicked a fly away impatiently. 'You haven't seen Miss Webster, have you? She wasn't in the yurt last night. I thought she was in the jeep. But she's not.'

Dominic was unable to list those present in the yurt. Mostly, his time had been taken up by refusing drinks offered by the pom-pom man. From midnight he'd been consumed by trying to regain his sight.

'Maybe she's gone for a walk,' he suggested, 'or after the sheep. She did seem awfully keen.'

'Awful?' Mrs Barinova looked confused. 'She seemed awful?'

'Awfully keen.'

'Maybe,' said Mrs Barinova, touching the sleeves of her green knit jumper. 'Or maybe she hasn't.'

The yurt's fur entrance flap stood at a ninety-degree angle. Bottles from the night before had been lobbed outside. A pretty toddler wearing only a pair of white pants collected them, pretending to drink the dregs until a woman, with a round, orange face like a space hopper, stopped her. The young woman with pigtails, called Lisa, stood with unbent legs over an aluminium pot, washing it with a beaker of water and a handful of earth.

Dominic was too worried about his short-term future to be able to think of anyone else. From inside the yurt, a whoop from the boys meant that they'd found a bottle that wasn't empty. Dominic's stomach knotted. He smiled at the space hopper woman and put out a shaky cupped hand, hoping he'd hit upon the international sign for water.

He hadn't. The woman fell to her knees and kissed his knuckles. Dominic's stomach tightened two more notches.

II

John H. Easton Sr had, in his line of work, travelled all over the world. Already that year he'd been threatened with abduction in Lagos and been kidnapped for two days by a gang of musclemen in Siberia. Hazards were part of his job. But never, even with twenty years' experience on the job, had he been attacked by an old woman throwing lettuces at him. The lettuces were not the worry; in fact, they had only stunned him. He hadn't even given much thought as to why a crazed old woman should have a key to the apartment. If John Easton dwelt on all the kooky things he came up against, he wouldn't get much work done at all. Lettuces were not the problem. The problem was being locked in.

At 10.30 a.m. Easton had a meeting planned with the delectable Miss Arbatova. According to the brief he'd given her, she was to pick him up from underneath the Lenin statue in the main square. There was a reason why, on his four-page résumé, Easton started his skill list with the phrase, 'can hit the ground running'. He showered in the metal bath using a handheld nozzle, which scalded him when he jammed it between his legs to lather up his shampoo. There was nothing much for breakfast, but Easton was used to that too. He hummed the theme from *Titanic* as he shaved and thought about his resilience level. He conjured up the image of his six siblings and his two-hundred-pound wife. Sometimes he wondered if he was the only person he knew who had achieved anything. Such were his thoughts before he tried the door.

Then he got the heebie-jeebies. Because John H. Easton Sr, international executive, overseas director (head of a fourteen-person division), and father of two, had an innate fear of enclosed spaces. To label it claustrophobia would have been giving in to it. Deep down he knew that he suffered from a phobia. But the fear was the fear of going back.

That was why, on the birth of his son, he had reached out for the suffix *senior* with more enthusiasm than he had reached for John Jr in the delivery room. He wanted to be senior because, out of seven siblings, John H. Easton had been the youngest. While the others paired up into three protective duos, he was left playing on his own. Which was why when it came to being rescued from the coal shed, holler as he might, no one ever came. That went a lot of the way to explain his fear of confined places. It also, in his mother's opinion, though she never said it, explained his vindictive arrogance. With seven children, Mrs Easton couldn't be expected to like them all.

He tried the door, which had two locks, methodically sixteen times in every locked/unlocked combination, before he felt the hot prick of fear in his stomach. He swallowed, pushed a hand over his perspiring forehead, picked up his attaché case, and instinctively made for the window. He yanked open a door onto a balcony, stacked high with the colonic irrigation from homes with no cupboard space. He unlocked the attaché's combination and, still calm, pulled out his cellular phone and his Psion 5. He tried every number he had for Anna Arbatova, none of which picked up.

He sat gingerly on the edge of the steel-framed balcony, looking out over an empty courtyard with blocks of low-rises on all four sides. Then he took his jacket off and hung it on a broom handle. He counted that he was fifteen storeys up. As panic threatened to launch itself from his stomach up his windpipe, he wanted to talk to his mother. He started to dial, but remembered it would be too early in Florida Keys. The thought of speaking to her brought on the contractions of a bowel movement. He squeezed his buttocks tight. He wasn't sure if he dared go back inside the flat.

III

By the first cup of tea and slice of dried camel there was still no sign of Miss Webster. Mrs Barinova asked the boys to check to see if her weapons were still in the jeep, in case she had gone sheep hunting. The next best idea was that she'd gone jogging though, as Bubba had pointed out, the countryside was a long way from being a Treadex machine. And besides, her cross-trainers were still poking out of the top of her daypack.

'Maybe she's just gone for a walk,' said Hubba. 'Miss Webster likes to walk.'

'Yeah, and maybe she's just been zapped by ET,' said Bubba sarcastically. 'Miss Webster ain't gone for no walk. She would've said.'

Mrs Barinova sounded stern. 'I can't remember seeing her in the yurt. It seems to me that she may have been gone all night.'

'I thought she was sleepin' your side of the tent, with the women,' said Bubba.

'Yes, and I rather assumed she was with you.'

Hubba and Bubba started to scratch themselves in a nervous reflex, in the same way people bite fingernails. Hubba was feeling chipper and not just because of the drink. It was one of the first occasions he could remember when something had gone wrong that wasn't down to him. 'Hey, that hooch sure was strong last night. Where's it come from?' he said.

Mrs Barinova was thinking. 'Some sort of mountain cactus, I believe.'

'No shit.' Hubba and Bubba, separated by different trailer parks, had practically been raised on the hallucinogenic plants of the Mexican deserts. They nodded, in a weighing-up information sort of way, and then glanced at each other.

Mrs Barinova sat with her elbows on her knees.

'She couldn't have been stolen, could she?' Dominic had read in one of Antoinette's magazines about cultures where men stole their wives. 'As a bride?'

Mrs Barinova shook her head. 'I would have thought she was a bit, how do you say? Long in the tooth for that. They are usually virgins.'

Hubba and Bubba sniggered.

'Kidnapped?' tried Dominic. 'Don't they kidnap people round here? I saw it on the TV. They chop their heads off.'

'That was Islamic fundamentalists in Chechnya,' said Mrs Barinova testily. 'In Belugastan we pride ourselves on having no religious detonations.' Dominic guessed she meant denominations. He let it pass. 'Anyway, why would anyone want to kidnap Miss Webster? Was she a big person?' She looked towards Hubba and Bubba, who were sniggering again.

'Big, how'd you mean?' asked Hubba.

'I think she means was Miss Webster important?' said Dominic.

'She knew the governor,' said Bubba. 'You mean someone from

191

back home could have done it?' He sounded slightly rueful, as if he'd missed an opportunity. A Tallahassee probation officer had once told him he had a scam default programme wired into his brain.

The heat in the tent was unbearable. Flies were hovering in the crater over the pail of tea. Dominic felt sick. He also thought he should be supportive. As he stood he said, 'Really, Mrs Barinova, I'm sure there's an innocent explanation for this. What could have happened to her? I mean no one even knows we're here.'

As if to prove him wrong, the muffled noise of a mobile phone rang from inside the top flap of Dominic's backpack. In the mêlée Dominic's bag had ended up at the other side of the yurt. 'Well, blow me,' said Dominic. Hubba and Bubba, who weren't familiar with the phrase, looked askance.

'Freaking queer,' said one as he picked up a tongue-shaped slither of camel meat.

The other said, 'Can you believe a cellular phone'd work up here? Shit, man.'

It was 4.30 a.m. in London. Dominic made for the door. Hubba said, 'Hey, watch it,' as he pulled his blanket away so he wouldn't stand on it.

'Hello?'

'Dominic, it's Tony here. Hello? Hello? Tony Beecham from SOS. Can you hear me, Dominic Peach?'

'Yeah, hi.' Dominic's expectations sank. He'd left his number with Anna. 'What do you want?'

'Wow. Dom, it's me, Tony. How's it going? Where are you?'

'Up a mountain somewhere.' He looked round; it was a grassy plateau between two hillocks.

'Look, we need something, pronto.'

'How do you mean?'

'A report, Operation Muff, something for the papers, and we need it now. The muff divers are onto us. They've spoken to the Lottery Commission and everything. We're in serious schtook if we don't get something out soon.'

Dominic raised his eyes heavenward. 'I appreciate that, Tony, but at the moment there's not much I can do. We haven't even seen a sheep yet.'

'What about the other hunters? Are they German?'

'No,' said Dominic.

'Shit.' Tony paused. 'In that case we'll have to leave the details till later. At the moment we just need you to bang out something. Like the bloody WWF does. You know, high on the roof of the world lives one of the most endangered . . . blah blah . . . until evil hunters . . . blah blah . . . slaughter innocent sheep . . . blah blah . . . impoverished country . . . blah blah . . . no excuse.' He stopped. 'Are you sure they're not Germans?'

'No, not Germans,' said Dominic.

'OK, well, have you got it, Dom?'

'What do you mean?'

'Do you understand?'

'I suppose.' It was too difficult to argue.

'We can use a library shot for the sheep. But we need it today, Dom. Repeat, priority for today.'

'Shit,' said Dominic.

'Sorry?' said Tony.

'I said sheep.'

'I can't hear you.' He went serious. 'Dom, you can do it.' His voice lowered to grave, 'Dom, don't make me wish I'd sent Don.'

Dominic wanted to ask if it was bad to eat camels or if snow leopards were endangered. But as he opened his mouth, the line went dead.

'Nothing bad, I hope.' Mrs Barinova was standing by the yurt door, frowning.

Dominic jumped and wondered how much she'd heard. When it came to work, Dominic didn't often form opinions. On sheep hunting he thought if he lived on a desolate mountainside in a tent he would kill sheep to keep his family alive. He also liked Mrs Barinova and Miss Webster, come to that. He didn't want to portray either as international pariahs.

'No, nothing, really. Just a call from home.' He smiled.

Mrs Barinova said, 'You are married, Mr O'Shaunnessy?'

'Me? No, no.' Then he thought his bachelor status might inflame the homophobes, Hubba and Bubba, and said, 'Well, sort of.'

'You're sort of married?'

'Girlfriend,' said Dominic definitely.

'Ha! You boys. You're like my son. Feet loose and fancying free.'

'Something like that,' said Dominic morosely.

Mrs Barinova looked down. 'You know, I'm really worried about Miss Webster. I think it might be best if I phoned my son. He will know what to do for the best. May I?'

'Does he work for the same hunting agency?' asked Dominic, passing her the mobile.

'Something like that,' said Mrs Barinova. Dominic tried to look benevolent as he watched the dancing liver spots on the back of her hand as she stabbed in a number.

IV

'There's no one here,' said Kolya. A search of the one-room flat had taken less than two minutes. 'Maybe he keeps them somewhere else.' He went over to the computer and wiped a layer of dust from the top of it. On top of the screen was a sticker for Spartak FC. 'Do you know anything about these?'

'What, Spartak? Russian champions last year,' said Tatyana.

'Not Spartak. Computers.'

The flat was everything that Kolya imagined a bachelor pad should be, down to the pornography on the walls and the overflowing ashtrays on the floor. A bad thought struck Kolya. If he could make the abduction charge stick, he could move in.

Tatyana shook her head. Only the secretaries on the third floor with walnut three-leaf tables and Panasonic faxes knew about computers. She said, 'I've seen these magazines in the kiosks. I thought they were foreign,' she said, picking up a copy of *Erik*. 'What are you doing?'

Kolya was trying to team up photographs of the missing women with the women in the magazine. He handed her four copies and four photos. 'Here, see if you can get a match. Then we would have some physical evidence.'

'Yeah, very physical,' said Tatyana. 'Anyway, I don't think it's him.'

'Well, you're not the one leading the investigation,' said Kolya. He held a page closer and screwed up his eyes. The woman he was looking at was sitting topless in a sidecar. He resisted for thirty seconds, then said, 'Why not?'

'Dunno. He's got an honest face. Call it woman's intuition.'

Kolya tutted. 'I just can't make out . . .' He bent the photograph back so a head was the only thing in it. Then he breathed out. 'Come on, let's do this back at the station. This flat is depressing me.' It was depressing him because it wasn't his. There was an unpaid phone bill on the bedside table with the ring of a coffee mug on it. Kolya pocketed it.

'Shouldn't you worry about fingerprints?' asked Tatyana from the other side of the room where she was rifling through the wardrobe. She pulled out a purple velour sleeve and smelt it. 'Mmm. Hugo Boss.' She held the shirt up against herself and half twirled towards him. 'Can I have it?'

'Jesus Christ, Tatyana, you're unbelievable. This man could turn out to be the worst serial killer since the Rostov Ripper and you want to know if you can wear his clothes.'

'Waste not, want not,' replied Tatyana sulkily. 'Anyway, it's better than recycling his dog-ends.' She frowned. 'Are those my tweezers?'

'I am not recycling his dog ends, I'm collecting a DNA sample,' said Kolya, hovering above the ashtray. 'It's evidence.' He bagged the cigarette butt in a plastic bag that had once held frozen peas and opened the door. 'You coming?' he asked huffily. Tatyana had to learn that she wasn't the only one who could do moody.

When they arrived back at the station after a forty-minute wait for a trolley bus that turned out to be taking the driver's son swimming, they were both irritable. Kolya had stumbled over a blue outstretched leg as they entered the foyer. A police guard was asleep, resting his cheek on his rifle butt. Then Kolya saw it hadn't been his leg but the tension from a length of string that had tripped him up. The cord went round the chair leg to disturb the guard if anyone went past. Kolya had heard of more high-tech security devices. As he tripped he kicked over a beer can that was an ashtray.

'Anyone been in, Pyotr?' As Kolya spoke, a copy of *Erik* slipped from under his arm. The guard picked it up. He was on page five before he said, 'Actually there was. Big chap. Reckoned he wanted to report a serious crime.'

'Reckoned he wanted to, or actually did want to?' Kolya grabbed the magazine. As he yanked it, the page ripped across a woman's torso.

'I think he actually did want to. I sent him to your office.'

Kolya and Tatyana headed towards the lift. Pyotr folded the ripped page, which crucially retained a pair of breasts, to fit into his top pocket. He shouted after them. 'He's still up there, you've only just missed him.'

The man waiting for them in Tatyana's office was as tall, dark and broad as a Soviet realist poster. Kolya disliked him on sight, not least because he sensed a sexual charge shoot through Tatyana that made her start flicking her hair. To annoy her, he resolved later to ask if it was her period that was making her irritable. The man's face was wide with sunken Tartar cheekbones and dark hair cut over his ears. He seemed familiar. A smell of French cologne had swamped the usual odour of packet soup and unfiled paper. Even

Kolya had to grudgingly admit the visitor exuded the aura of a famous person. He stood up when he saw them.

Kolya clenched his buttocks and said in a no nonsense way, 'Good afternoon, my name is Colonel Nikolai Pertsov of the Belugastan police force. This is my assistant rookie officer, Tatya—' Then he looked up from the handshake. 'Don't I know you?'

Tim said, 'I don't think so, my name is Feodor—'

'A good detective never forgets a face. I remember you from the other day. You live in the lock-ups out by Timiraysevskaya.' Kolya smiled, glad to have got the measure of the man. The measure being cuckold. 'What is it, your wife got a new lover? Kicked out by her latest boyfriend? Don't worry. Happens to the best of us.' He looked at Tatyana and smiled. Tim had no idea what he was talking about.

He said, 'Ah, yes, Erik said you were a policeman.'

Kolya squinted, '*Erik?* But you were alone.'

Tim wondered where this was going. Most of the time he was glad that the police operated on a skeleton staff. On occasions, like this one, he wasn't. 'No, my colleague Erik was inside the garage.'

'*Erik?* You know a man called Erik?'

'Don't tell me it's an offence these days.' Tim had known the militia would be a waste of time, but his mother had insisted.

'No, but it is an unusual name. Wouldn't you agree?'

'Yes, I admit it's an unusual name, but—'

'Tell me, are you a consumer of pornography? Mr?'

'Barinov. Look, what the hell's that got to do with anything?' Tim stepped towards Kolya, who stepped back.

'This man, let us call him Erik,' said Kolya ponderously. 'He owns a lock-up?'

'That's right. And his name is Erik.'

'What were you doing there?'

Tim thought of the Beluga argali argali. 'Well, to be honest, it's quite a long story.'

'What's the number?'

'*What?*'

'The number of his garage. Think. This is a matter of life and death.'

'Sixty-seven, I think.'

'A lock-up. Exactly. What an idiot I've been. Come on, Tatyana, we're going to the garages.'

Tim stood in front of him. 'But I'm here to report a crime. It's urgent.'

'I'm sorry, but I'm afraid we really must go.'

Kolya grabbed his jacket, which he'd only just thrown onto the back of the chair, and took Tatyana's wrist. They headed for the door. He turned to Tim. 'Please, write down what's happened and I'll attend to it when I get back.' Kolya thought about arresting the man as an accessory, but first he had to find the women.

Tim hadn't expected much from the police. Now he found it easy to understand why the country's crime clear-up rate, according to a report left on his desk last week, was four per cent. In theory he'd had two, not one, missing persons to report. The first was the American Miss Webster and the second was Erik, who had been absent for two days. Tim thought about waiting for Nikolai Pertsov to return, or trying another officer, but the place was deserted. He picked up a pen, which had the name of a pharmaceutical company on it, and wrote out a missing persons report. Left to the police, Miss Webster stood about as much chance of being found as a Beluga argali argali.

Scenarios were mapping themselves out in Tim's head. Erik's disappearance, though regrettable, was not as doom-laden as the American's. Tim knew what happened when Americans disappeared overseas. They sent gunboats and Exocets. Then the whole country would fall under the international spotlight of *Time* magazine, as would the President and his criminal record.

Had Tim's thoughts not been focused so keenly on Erik and Miss Webster as he mooched out of the station, he might well have missed the voice wheedling its way into the corridor. Tim wasn't an inquisitive type; he was enough of a Soviet not to want to stick his neck out. Now he tried hard not to stray from the collective. If you leave the flock, expect to get burnt by the sun, his mother used to tell him. So he would have ignored the noise, had the voice, or the choice of expletives, not been familiar.

'Will some bastard let me out of these Godforsaken cells?'

It was Erik. Tim did an acoustic double take.

'If you don't let me out, I'll have this whole frigging place closed down. I am, if anyone cares to check, the Minister of Culture.'

Tim pulled open the door that seemed to lead down to a cellar.

'Erik, is that you?' The stairs he called down smelt of plaster and dampness. There was a pause for an echo or thought.

'*Tim?*'

'Yeah. For God's sake, where are you? What the hell are you doing down there?' Tim felt for a light switch inside the door. 'Jesus, thank God for that.'

The keys were hanging up on a nail next to a 1994 calendar. Tim scanned the cell which, apart from his friend and an iron bunk bed with a mattress on the lower bed, was empty. A hole he took to be the latrine had an upturned family-sized Fanta bottle jammed into it. There were no windows but mosquitoes swooped in and out of his earhole.

'At last,' said Erik. 'What kept you?'

'What kept me? What happened to you, don't you mean?' said Tim, incredulous and offended. As a knight in shining armour he wasn't getting much credit.

'Where is that fucking madman policeman?' Now he was released, Erik made no effort to flee. He sat on the lower bunk with his head down. He tried to rub the creases out of his Dockers.

'Pertsov?'

'There's another one?'

'I dunno, he ran off. I think to check your lock-up. Look, why

199

are you here? Mum's worried, you were supposed to be off with those hunters yesterday.'

Erik looked at him. His eyes were red and his chin was stubbly. 'I'll sue him. You know I'll fucking sue him for wrongful arrest.'

Tim was getting impatient. 'Just tell me why you were locked up.'

'How should I know? Totally random. Totally random. One minute I'm on my way to Come Dancing, the next some nutter is attacking me with an umbrella. Then that detective starts on at me about women going missing. I asked him, *do I look like a psycho?* I'm the Culture Minister.'

'OK, mate, don't worry,' Tim put his arm round him. 'Come on, let's get you home.'

Erik shrugged him off. 'What's up with you? I haven't got dementia. Stop treating me like I'm deranged.'

'I understand.'

'Sure you do. When was the last time someone put you in the cells?'

Tim thought he was seeing a side of Erik that he'd never seen before. In the spirit of liberation he put it down to low blood sugar.

Erik pulled on a brand of shoe called Doctor Martina's; Tim guessed they were Czech. 'The bastard even took my laces.' He flopped up the stairs. As they were leaving, he kicked the sleeping guard viciously and then went back to retrieve his shoe.

Erik fell over his shoe and onto the pavement. He squinted and pulled his sunglasses on. 'You got a car?' he asked. 'I need a burger.'

'Yeah, over there,' said Tim, pointing to the Shogun, pulled up on the pavement. They stood in silence. They both knew he had to ask. Tim said, 'You didn't have anything to do with it, did you?'

'Yeah, right. I've been kidnapping women for years. It's like a hobby.' He looked at Tim against the sun. Tim saw his own distorted reflection in the wraparound glasses. Both were silent though Tim was aware of kids trying to climb on the bonnet of his car. Erik said, '*No*, I didn't have anything to do with it. What do you take me for? Have you got a cigarette?'

'OK then,' said Tim. 'I didn't think so because another one's gone missing.'

With his back sunk in the mulberry, leather-look interior, Erik said, 'Pull over at the kiosk, I need a smoke.'

'One of the hunters.'

'The *hunters*?' On the dashboard Erik's hand was shaky due to lack of nicotine.

'They all went into the hills yesterday.' Tim looked at Erik. 'In your absence I had to send Mum with them. Then today she phones to say the woman has disappeared.'

'Hang on, rewind. You sent your *mother* off with a bunch of psycho hunters?'

Tim was all for dissent in a democracy, but sometimes he wondered who was President. He said, 'It seemed like a good idea. Anyway, she was keen.'

'Why couldn't you go?'

'Affairs of state,' he said, trying to put an end to it.

'Yeah, or maybe just affairs,' said Erik.

Had the pyramid scheme gone the other way, Erik would have been the head of state. Sometimes he liked to remind Tim of it.

Erik said, 'OK, then. So who would want to kidnap the American lady?'

'That is the question. I thought you might look into it.'

'*Me?*' Twenty-four hours ago he hadn't known anything about disappearing women, now he was some sort of Sherlock Holmes.

'Well, you can't have the President of a country running around for some serial abductor.'

Erik was far from conceding the point. 'What about that Pertsov guy?'

'I wouldn't trust him to find a nuclear submarine in a bathtub.'

Erik nodded. Tim parked beside the kiosk. Eric came back with a packet of full-strength Marlboro. He lit one and suckled on it.

201

'Why should I be the one to try and find her? She could be dead by now, for all we know.'

'Yeah, and how that would help to raise this country's international profile,' said Tim sarcastically.

Erik was annoyed. 'Before you get all principled about this, just remember why you tried to get elected in the first place.' He pushed his glasses to the top of his head. Inside the car it was so hot the air was difficult to breathe. 'It was a question of political immunity, if my memory is correct.'

'Well, think about it. That's exactly why I don't want the whole world looking into my background, just because some stupid American chooses to go missing here.' Tim flexed his elbows against the steering wheel and exhaled. A fly walked up and down in the space between his palms. 'Do you know what a timocracy is?'

Erik stubbed his cigarette into the pullout ashtray. 'No.'

'It means a political system in which love of honour is the guiding principle. It's Greek, *timokratia*, from *time*, meaning honour.'

'Amazing.'

'Wouldn't that be nice?'

'I can't see it, but I suppose so.'

Neither of them spoke. Eric lobbed his cigarette butt from the window and lit another.

Tim said, 'None of us would come out of it very well if we were investigated.'

'Speak for yourself,' said Erik.

'You wouldn't be able to run *Erik* from inside Butyrskaya.'

He thought a while and said, 'I guess not.'

Tim looked at him. 'Does that mean you'll look for her?'

Erik wasn't sure how he'd suddenly got his back to the wall. 'I suppose so.'

Anna had been waiting twenty minutes before she started to worry. Because of Easton's size, she'd taken him to be precise and orderly. To that she added the knowledge that Americans were rarely late.

It was one of the many things they liked to lord over Russians. By 10.20 a.m. it was already too hot to wait for him on the square, especially as the shadow given by V. I. Lenin was in the wrong direction. Like the GAI, who had been catcalling her since she arrived, she retreated to the fringe of trees. In the shade she looked at the building that had once been the ballet school.

It was like a diminutive Bolshoi, the same socialist blueprint that erected theatres over eleven time zones, done in Greco style with a chariot on the top of four columns. A gang of young men draped themselves on the steps out of the sun, drinking beer and smoking. Some watched girls go by, others watched boys go by. Even in communist times the steps of the ballet school had been a gay pick-up point, so much so that Anna's grandmother dropped her off after school at the blue door at the back. It was the same entrance she used for Come Dancing.

The paint was splintered and the old rubbish bins, shaped like acorns, overflowed. She watched a couple of her dancers head towards the door. Even though they were fifty metres away, she thought she recognised Lisa, a part-time underwear model, and Galya, who, never fully believing that communism might not return someday, kept up an unpaid job at the Kombinat. Used to jeering, neither of them flinched when the young men called to them.

Anna was about to flick away the car pulling up beside her when she realised, from its size and colour, that it contained Tim and Erik. She swore as she smiled. If the deal was going to come off she needed to get rid of them before Easton showed up.

'Hi,' said Anna. Tim was looking shifty. Erik smiled at her. She said, 'You're about early.'

'Business,' said Erik from the passenger seat.

'How are you?' asked Tim. 'We haven't got together for some time.' By 'got together' Anna understood he meant sex. She wondered if his marriage proposal still stood. From his nervousness she guessed not. It didn't depress her, it just meant her judgement had been spot on.

'Well, very well. Busy. The club's doing really well. I saw your mum in there the other day.'

'Yeah,' said Tim. 'She's often there. What are you doing on a street corner?'

'Just looking at the club's entrance. I thought I might do it up for the celebrations day.'

'Good idea,' said Tim.

There was a silence that Tim didn't seem keen to fill. Neither did she, but she had to get them on their way.

'I don't want to keep you,' she said.

'No,' said Tim.

'We're looking for a woman,' said Erik from the passenger seat.

'Really?' said Anna. 'This early?' Despite herself she was intrigued. More or less.

'No,' said Tim, blushing. 'An American woman, on holiday here. She's sort of disappeared. Let us know if you see one. She's forty-something.'

'OK, will do.' The Shogun reversed and then pulled away. From the passenger seat Erik gave a desultory wave. Anna put her hand up, automatically, but kept her eyes looking down. She had a hunch that Easton would join the missing list soon; she wondered if anyone would connect the two.

V

Sonya didn't usually turn tricks in the morning. It wasn't that she couldn't; in terms of space it was perfect, because both her parents were at the factory. It was because the quality of the men was not outstanding. Most were Estonian riggers with a week off, or horny overweight husbands before work. Sonya liked the evening clientele better – young businessmen who tipped well, sometimes a foreigner if the girls from the Palace ever let them get past their cordon insanitaire. This morning it had been a Monday regular,

Comrade Belykov. Comrade Belykov was hardly old enough to remember Soviet times, and at nineteen Sonya had only heard tales, but he insisted that she act like a Young Pioneer. He even bought a uniform with a red hat. Sonya enjoyed it because she liked dressing up and the sex was quick. She'd bumped into Comrade Belykov the other day in the central store looking at computer manuals. He was with his mother. He introduced her as a work colleague. She knew he was a programmer for an Italian phone company. That was how he could afford her.

At nineteen and three-quarters Sonya had a dream. It was the same dream she'd had at seventeen and a half, when her cousin Alla had emigrated to Canada. Sonya's dream was to make enough money to join her in Toronto. According to Alla, there were as many Russians strolling the leafy boulevards in Toronto as there were eating ice creams in Gorky Park. Like all her friends, Sonya felt the urge to emigrate as natural, like learning to walk.

But emigrating wasn't the whole of Sonya's dream. Alla had quit Belugastan by marrying a man who had selected her from a picture on the Internet. She was twenty-three and he was forty-seven and, like Comrade Belykov, was something in computers. By all accounts, namely Alla's, it was a good match. She kept him in above average sex and below average cooking and he kept her.

Alla also had a dream. By keeping his diet typically Russian, high in carbohydrate and saturated fat but low on greenery, in three years she had snaffled away nearly $20,000 in housekeeping. In another year, if he didn't die first (that would be too much for even them to dream of), she would divorce him and open a business of her own.

From the age of five both girls had had a keen interest in animals. Whereas Sonya took pleasure in disembowelling them with a kitchen knife and slatted spoon (only the dead ones from her grandparent's smallholding and, even then, it had only been a phase), Alla loved to dye them. In texture and disposition animals were perfect, only colour could improve them.

The plan was to open a store called Pets to Dye For. Alla had already experimented. Light ones, usually cats, were the easiest. The darker ones could only take low lights or peroxide, whereas a white cat, say, could effectively go the colours of the rainbow. The cats' temperament – Alla swore they were vainer than dogs – also took to it better. Hamsters' coats were too thick.

They planned a partnership. Sonya opened her exercise book and added another $50 to the running total. Then she stuffed it inside a zebra nightdress case that Alla had dyed pink some fifteen years ago. Sonya was $1,800 short of her twenty grand but with every hand job and every twenty thrust into her garter at the strip club, she got a little closer. She smiled to herself as she reapplied plum lipstick all but sucked off by Comrade Belykov.

She was in an extra good mood today. There'd been a letter brought up by her father from the green tin postbox in the hall. Sonya's English, apart from the hooker's phrases, was limited. That was why every week Alla sent her a list of sentences to memorise by heart. Sonya opened the envelope and marvelled at the colours of the stamps. Mostly the letter was in Russian: gossip, boys Alla fancied, TV programmes. Sonya skipped down to the English writing which was still unfamiliar but getting easier.

She watched her mouth in the mirror of her compact as she tried out the sentences. She glanced at the heart-shaped clock in the kitchen. She had half an hour before her shift at Come Dancing. She inhaled crossly and blew glistening make-up and a long blonde hair out of the hinges of the compact. Then she started, slow and self-conscious. 'Excuse me, your poodle should be what colour today? Pink or the blue?' She stammered over saying *the*, checking the mirror to put her tongue between her teeth. 'Our dyes are non toxic and last up to three months.' Hell, she thought, that *three months* bit was hard to say.

She was still trying two hours later as she walked across the square to Come Dancing. When the car drew alongside her it startled her so much she even bit her tongue. Two minutes later perfecting her English seemed irrelevant.

VI

Dominic's body was as rigid as a ramrod. Next to him Hubba and Bubba were so weak from laughter their black bodies were flaccid as slugs. After two days of Carbomask, it seemed unlikely their skin would ever return to flesh-coloured. They seemed pretty chuffed.

'Why don't you two shut the fuck up?' Dominic's neck under the weight of the hat had started to go into spasms. 'Can't you do something useful like throw yourself off a mountain top, or go and look for your mother?'

'She ain't our mother,' said Hubba. As he spoke a piece of gum was ejected in mirth onto his belly. He put it straight back into his mouth. 'We *will* go find her, only this is too good to miss.' He wiped his mouth on the sleeve of his Calvin Klein shirt.

'What did I tell you, Hubba? Didn't I always say this faggot was some sort of queen?'

'You sure did, Bub.'

'And was I right?'

'You sure was, Bub.'

Mrs Barinova was standing by the door. She said, 'It certainly does suit you. But I can see many big troubles ahead.' She still had Dominic's mobile phone in her hand.

'How do you mean?' said Dominic. 'How much worse do you envisage this getting?'

Most of the yurt people had gathered for the ceremony, which was directly at odds with what Dominic had been hoping – that they'd forgotten about the reincarnation thing.

'Well, put it this way, Mr O'Shaunnessy. If *you* had waited a thousand years for the return of your spiritual leader, how keen would you be to let him go?'

Despite the weight of the pom-pom, Dominic tried to stand up. It was like balancing a tray on his head. The pom-pom, which Mrs Barinova had explained was traditional yurt attire, was unstable.

He'd very nearly had enough of Mr Nice. SOS had booked the

trip in good faith, expecting sheep, not for him to be crowned king of the yurt people. He tried to convey a level of ominous threat. 'Mrs Barinova, you really *are* going to have to explain. Tell them that these two reprobates,' he pointed towards Hubba and Bubba, who were grinning and pulling strands of chewing gum from their mouths, 'come from a caravan park in Texas not bloody Zanzibar.'

'Believe me, Mr O'Shaunnessy, I have tried.'

'Tell them I've got to go home in a week.' He stopped, he was fed up with going through an intermediary. 'Which one here is the head guy? Tell him I really need to speak to him.'

A man with a moustache wearing wellingtons and a Kookai T-shirt set a full glass in front of him.

'Not now,' pleaded Dominic.

Bubba tried to sit up. 'So much for native hospitality. How's come we don't get none?' He looked at Mrs Barinova. 'How about telling them if it wasn't for me and African slave Hubba here, then the king of the faggots would never have made it back to his homeland.' He had thought about changing their names to Hubbongo and Bubbongo, to give them an African twist, but the natives didn't speak English anyway. He winked at Miss Pocahontas.

Dominic repeated, 'Shouldn't you two be out looking for Miss Webster?'

Hubba said, 'He's got a point, Bubba. We should be out looking for Miss Webster. Something bad might have happened to her.'

Bubba's loyalty to Miss Webster was not as profound as his friend's. Whereas finding her would be good, he couldn't help wonder how her property would be divided up on her demise. Maybe the Tallahassee probation officer had been right.

The yurt people were silent, watching the scene like a TV set. Every five minutes or so, though Dominic never knew what triggered them off, they would laugh or gasp like a studio audience. Irritability was a terrier snapping at his heels. He didn't like the women's passivity or the men's spitting. Or the way they forced dried camel on you and tea made of butter and fermented mare's milk. One of the men last night had spent an hour trying to find out how much he weighed. Dominic knew from Don that ethnic cultures had an automatic right to Western respect, but it was all so in your face. And the smell was terrible.

The man in wellington boots stood up and craned his head like a guard dog. Half a minute later they heard a car pull up. Dominic thought it was a Ford Fiesta sort of rasp. Outside he saw a motorbike and empty sidecar.

Mrs Barinova gave a delighted shriek as the driver dismounted. He wasn't wearing a helmet and his hair was slicked back on his head. It was, thought Dominic, the airport chauffeur, though this time dressed head to toe in Gap.

'Hello again. How are you?' His English was nowhere near as good as Mrs Barinova's. His accent and the sinister way he rolled the Rs made him sound like a member of the KGB. Which, Dominic thought, on current form he probably was.

'Hi,' said Dominic weakly. Inside the yurt he heard a woman's shriek and a lusty laugh from one of the boys. 'Are you here to help find Miss Webster?'

He nodded.

The tension in Dominic's shoulders relaxed. 'Fantastic. You're what? Police? Security services?' The last word came out in three slow syllables.

'No, no, no. I am a, how to say?' He looked at Mrs Barinova, perplexed. 'I am a professional pornographer.'

At first Dominic thought he'd misheard him, maybe he'd said *photographer*. But then, he thought, he probably hadn't. His head fell back as he looked to the skies in a gesture that he hoped meant abject despair in any language. Which was why Dominic was the first to see the red pom-pom coming over the brow of the hill.

There were five in the group, all bow-legged on chunky, disconsolate piebald horses. At first, from a distance of thirty metres, Dominic thought the bundle resting sack-like at the base of the horse's neck was a body.

Instinctively a cold wash of fear rinsed over him, worried it was Miss Webster. Then he saw the bundle was fleecy, with legs either side of the horse. As the group rounded the hillock, Dominic saw the enormous spiralled horns on the other side and an animal's face with a trickle of blood coming from its mouth.

They came closer and the moustached man said something to Mrs Barinova. She turned to Dominic and said, 'It is formidable. They have done a great honour for you. They have slaughtered the sheep for you. See how big his horns are?'

'A Beluga argali argali?' asked Dominic faintly.

'Oh no,' said Mrs Barinova, her spirits visibly raised. She even giggled. 'That would be impossible. Because . . .' She waggled her head from side to side and then said, 'Well, it doesn't matter. This is the Marco Polo sheep.'

Dominic nodded and tried to smile.

'It really is the highest honour, Mr O'Shaunnessy. I'm sure I don't have to tell you there are less than one thousand of them in the entire world.'

'Nine hundred and ninety-nine,' said Erik.

'Holy shit,' said Hubba, falling out of the tent with a large cigarette in his hand. He looked at the animal. 'That's one helluva son of a bitch.'

Someone tossed the sheep at Dominic's feet. It was the size of a small donkey. Its eyes were opaque and looked as if they'd been crying.

Mrs Barinova said, 'Now, perhaps I can take your picture with the beast. To remember this big day.' She spoke in Russian to Erik who handed her a Kodak Polaroid from the sidecar. Dominic tried to object, but before he knew it she snapped him.

Whether newspaper quality or not, Dominic, in a lime-green pom-pom hat, was snapped standing over the sheep in a way that a caption might call 'proudly'. SOS's plan had gone very astray.

VII

Ordinarily, something about the sight of Natasha in a sky-blue front-fastening bikini would have been enough to make Tim shelve his problems. Had it not been for the fact that shelving was one of his problems. The others, in descending order, were the disappearance of the American, another government reshuffle in Moscow that meant he might be called to the Duma, and the end of an old girlfriend and the start of a new one – one who could only love a carpenter, and then not to full intercourse.

These problems were mentally highlighted in marker pen. Others, the sluggish economy, the preparations for the country's anniversary day parade, the civil servants not being paid, were there but simply underlined in pencil.

Natasha had called him at just after 11 a.m., soon after he'd dispatched Erik to the hills. He was listless in a guilt-ridden way. His defence for not going, should anyone ask, was that it was conduct unbecoming for a president. He'd found the phrase, which he used in English, in the Starr Report.

Back at the Palace he'd got a can of fizzy drink and fidgeted. He thought about paperwork, or checking with the printers about their latest Belugastan brochure that had been delayed due to the July issue of *Erik*. Nasty had mentioned a Kazakhstan trade delegation due in town next week, so he could chase them up. When his phone rang he was looking at the National Day Parade plans that so far incorporated two ambulances and a bus. It was a long way from civic pride.

It was Natasha. 'Hi, Tim. You're good with your hands?'

'Kind of,' said Tim, hesitantly.

'Good, because I need a carpenter. I've got some shelves and I can't get them up. The instructions are in Portuguese, or something. Maybe Hebrew. Can you come over? I'll make it worth your while.'

'I thought there was a sex ban.'

'Who said anything about sex?'

'What then? You're going to laminate me?'

'Wait and see,' said Natasha.

Tim thought, what was it that made women think that men would do anything for sex? He was about to ask her, haughtily, but what came out was, 'See you in thirty minutes.'

An hour later, the shelves were still on the floor. To her credit Natasha had been good with the spanner, and it had been DIY of a sort, just not the sort of do-it-yourself that got flatpacks up.

Tim asked as he rolled off an aluminium bracket, 'How long before we can make *actual* love?'

Natasha kissed her way up his chest. 'What are you complaining about? Wasn't that good?'

'I guess.' He paused. 'This hasn't got anything to do with Monica Lewinsky, has it?'

'Who's she?' asked Natasha, resting on her shoulder.

Two hours later and sunbathing on the roof, Tim was cataloguing his worries. Natasha took his hand and kissed it.

'You're not much of a carpenter,' she said.

'Well, I tend to do my own stuff, you know, furniture – chairs, tables.'

'I know what furniture is,' said Natasha, turning over.

'Yeah, well.' She gave him a look that meant he was talking rubbish. Tim felt contented. As he drifted off to sleep, he thought about how good it would be if he could stop being President and re-train, maybe as a carpenter.

VIII

For most of her life, no man had credited Stella Anne Webster with enough sense to do anything. Apart, that was, from Hubba and Bubba. Even her daddy had only let her ride with him in the absence of sons. He never asked her if she thought the hot weather would keep the whitetail in the forest, or if re-loading made more sense than not.

Her husband hadn't even got that far. Mostly she didn't know what he did every morning after she had stoked him up on granola and five fruit groups. Not that she minded. When things got very bad and her neighbours at the local mall started to look at her in a sympathetic way, she switched from putting ground-up Prozac in his food, which improved his mood around the home, to laxatives.

Since their honeymoon, when the smell of his beard made Stella Anne sure he had strayed with the gamine chalet maid, she'd hidden three cloves of garlic in every evening meal. Like the laxatives, she had regulated the garlic one week on, one week off, in case his system got used to it. It had been her way of leaving her mark.

Now she had the hunting. Such were her thoughts after the chloroform had finally worn off. Stella Anne was underground, that much was clear. In fact she was in a sewer. There was light from a bare bulb attached to a multicoloured electrical lead. There was a steel wall to her left and right, as if she was in an underground tank. Something dripped and she thought she could hear a mechanical whirring noise. Perhaps it was a car or a subway. She felt groggy, from the chloroform. Her limbs were stiff and she massaged them and did her morning routine of stretches. Her voice, when she called out, bounced back off the chamber.

Two years ago, when filling in a survey that asked her to use five words that described herself, Stella Anne had written wife, daughter, member of the women's institute, bridge-player and overweight. She tapped her foot on the ground to see if it was solid. If she had to describe herself now she would have said a hunter, patron of the disadvantaged, a champion bridge-player, fit and plucky. Plucky she liked best of all. She wasn't scared, more intrigued. She revelled in the fact that she didn't mind rats. And although neither her father nor her husband had credited her with any sense, she had, in the inside bib pocket of her camouflage suit, her hand-held global positioning system. The Waco storekeeper hadn't sold it on its effectiveness in the event of an abduction, he'd just said every serious huntsperson should own one. Stella Anne knew the GPS wouldn't work underground, it just gave her comfort. She was fingering it when she saw the book.

It was a hardback, A4 sized and very thick, poking out from the corner of a good quality German eiderdown. On the front was a mother with her hand and face inclined towards a baby. It was in both English and Russian. The English bit read *Childcare the Spock Way*.

Stella Anne frowned.

CHAPTER NINE

I

It was the hot flushes that finally decided Mrs Barinova she had to get off the mountain. A volcanic eruption of molten hormones was coursing through her body, so hot that she thought she would fry to death on the slopes. Her heart started to beat normally again at twelve ten. The nurse at the polyclinic had told her to time the attacks and eat more yams, even though neither she nor the nurse had ever seen a yam. By half past she resolved to quit. At her age, she couldn't help thinking her son should be the one doing her the favours. They were his hunters, not his menopausal mother's.

She slumped in the shade of an unbridled horse and looked at her CCCP watch, which beat out the time with a hammer and sickle. Yesterday one of the black boys had whistled and said, 'Cool logo.' It shrivelled her pride, even though she knew from her school days that Americans were educationally disadvantaged. She couldn't blame them, logo was all it was now. She resolved to give one of them the watch before they left. Just because the Soviet regime was shot away didn't mean it hadn't made good watches.

To get her plummeting oestrogen level off the mountain, she decided they should make a composite picture of Miss Webster. Erik was near the jeep, anxiously chewing on a blade of grass. He argued that in terms of today's crime detection a composite picture was too low-key. She offered to put it on the Web. Apart from the photo-fit, they didn't have any other leads. Erik nodded. He knew an artist but they'd have to go back into town. Mrs Barinova smiled and gathered up her belongings. She said a poster campaign around the square might jog memories, or in case Miss Webster had got disorientated and wandered off, it might help her get her bearings, despite the information from the black boys that Miss Webster wasn't the wandering off type. Especially not if there were sheep to be killed.

From midday, when Hubba and Bubba had gone to search the scrub around near where the Irishman had found the camouflage toilet bag, they had been acting weird. At first Mrs Barinova thought it might have something to do with the contents of the bag, but on inspection that only held a plastic container of multivitamins and an electric toothbrush with 'Designed with floss in mind' along the side.

What Mrs Barinova didn't know was that while the boys said they were looking for signs of an abduction, they were after the familiar dragon-jaw leaf of an hallucinogenic drug group. Hubba was unshakeable in his belief that Miss Webster had been taken away in a spaceship. He was a firm believer in alien abductions, ever since a cousin on his mother's side in Spokane claimed to have been sexually molested by extraterrestrials. She had even woken up with carpet burns on her thighs and an overall sense of having been violated. Also her Dutch cap had disappeared.

Bubba was sceptical. 'Why they choose Miss Webster? As a human specimen, she ain't exactly all that.'

'They like women,' said Hubba. 'They want to know how we reproduce.'

Bubba didn't like that. It smacked of disrespect to the abducted. He aimed a stone at Hubba's head and then launched himself at him. He had already decided that, no matter what, they were taking the sheep home. If Miss Webster had come to a sticky end, he planned on using the horns as the basis for a memorial.

Had it not been for the fight, they might not have spotted the zigzag leaves that spelt grade A drugs. As he fell under the weight of his former cellmate, Bubba nearly eradicated the entire crop.

'We sure as hell ain't got time to dry them,' said Bubba. 'Should we chew them?'

That was when Hubba spotted the blackening cauldron over a log fire where the yurt people were boiling the sheep's head to strip it of flesh.

'Let's put them in there.' Hubba nodded at the pot. 'It'll be a sort of opium broth.'

After a ten-minute wait, they siphoned off two steel mugs of it. Bubba wiped his YSL sleeve across the top, trying to mop up the mutton fat and white froth. After three mugs they were two bundles of black simpering joy, so sedentary that neither Erik nor Dominic could shift them into the Frontera.

By 11.20 p.m., when the drugs really kicked in, Hubba and Bubba's altered state made them identify the dead sheep so closely with Miss Webster that they became one and the same. They started to mew and cry when the meat was handed around. From then until they passed out they tried to rip the flesh from the greasy hands of the yurt people.

'What the?' said Mrs Barinova.

'They're vegetarians,' explained Erik, 'probably.'

'But what's the matter with them?' asked Mrs Barinova.

Erik could guess, but said, 'Most likely altitude sickness. Maybe we should leave them here in any case. You never know, she might return to the yurt.'

'Well, dear, if you say so.'

'We'll leave the Dneiper up here, in case they feel better and want to come back into town.' He looked at Hubba and Bubba, both slouched dazed against the water trough, and doubted it. He went on, 'We're not doing any good up here. Let's go back into town. See what Tim says. Do the photo-fit.'

Mrs Barinova said, 'What about the hunt?'

'The hunt's off.' He nodded towards the Dneiper. 'I had to dismantle the Beluga argali argali to get up here.'

'What a pity, I was looking forward to seeing it.'

Erik put a consolatory hand on her shoulder. 'Don't worry, there'll be other hunts.' Erik was thinking of the $100,000 they'd already made. He nodded towards Dominic. 'Do you think he'll want a rebate?'

'I doubt it. He says he couldn't dream of hunting while one of the party is missing. Apparently it's some sort of Irish hunting tradition. Actually, he seems very keen to leave the mountain. I think this whole reincarnation thing has really got to him.'

'Reincarnation? What are you talking about?' They had studied ethnic Soviet cultures at school. Erik liked the central Asian ones best because the females didn't always cover their top halves. It might have been the embryonic germ of *Erik*.

'It's ridiculous,' said Mrs Barinova, 'but these mountain people seem to think he's some sort of reincarnated leader.'

'You're joking.' He looked up from packing the jeep. 'He comes from somewhere in Ireland.'

'They didn't seem to care. It was the black boys, the African slaves that were with him that did it. The leader always came with a couple of servants. They even sort of performed a crowning ceremony.' She looked straight at Erik. She could tell he was ferreting the information away, in an only-to-be-used-in-emergencies file.

Erik said, 'But those guys were white when they arrived here.'

'Really?' Mrs Barinova was moved, but not amazed. 'I didn't know that could happen.'

Erik said, 'You don't think he'll sue, do you?' Ever since Russian politicians had started suing magazines for libel, Erik had been extremely sensitive to litigation.

'Shouldn't think so, dear.' She walked towards the jeep. 'Should we give these people anything? They've been very kind.'

'Not necessary.'

'Why not?'

'It's a tradition among Belugi natives. They have to accommodate strangers without asking any questions. It's worked out well for us. Kept overheads really low. I think we'll bring the next lot here. What do you think?'

'Oh Erik, you mean you haven't paid them anything? They didn't even know why we're here? You are naughty.' Mrs Barinova believed in fair play.

'I'll leave a few copies of *Erik*. Anyway, they should be pleased to help their country. I bet they don't pay any taxes up here.'

'No, Erik, but you know perfectly well that no one in Belugastan pays any taxes,' said Mrs Barinova. 'The government doesn't do anything for them and they don't do anything for the government. I think Tim quite likes it that way. He says it makes him feel less responsible.'

Erik said, 'Then it's time they contributed something. I mean, they're welcome to come to the National Day Parade. That'll be free. Come on, let's go.' Erik was anxious to leave. He wanted to discuss August's *Erik* with Mrs B in the car. He couldn't see them recruiting much raw material for the discerning gentleman among the yurt people.

As he drove down the mountain, he dabbled with the idea of an eco edition set on the mountains. But as they approached the city, under a cloud of sulphurous smoke from the Kombinat, with an overflowing dumpster on every street corner, he sensed green issues were not that important to his readers.

By ten past four Erik, Mrs Barinova, Dominic and a chain-smoking woman called Oksana, who drank neat vodka and smoked simultaneously, were in the foyer of the Palace Hotel, hunched over a chrome and smoked-glass coffee table. Oksana earned a living painting caricatures of American presidents on concentric matryoshka dolls and exporting them to a firm in Seattle. Their unique selling point was the inner Monica Lewinsky doll in a G-string. Oksana found the rounded, shapeless contours of the wooden doll suited her purpose well. Not only that but her boyfriend, who had a degree in physics from MGU and had worked on the Mir space shuttle, designed the doll's mouth so that it opened and could be slotted onto a wooden stump under the belt of the outer Bill Clinton doll. He called it the erection projection.

For Dominic's sake they spoke in English. Oksana had a rasping voice like a late-night cabaret singer. She was bare-legged and wore a skirt so short Dominic thought he could see the red pimples from a recent bikini waxing. They watched her painted nails glide over the sketchpad.

'Her hair was more . . .' Dominic flicked the back of his hand over his head and made a little kink at the bottom

'Don't make her nose so big,' said Mrs Barinova. 'It was like this.' She pushed her nose into a retrousse shape. Oksana's pencil worked light and shade in long sweeping arcs. 'No, that's terrible, it looks like Ronald Reagan,' said Mrs Barinova. 'More like this. May I?'

'Oh sure,' said Oksana sourly. 'Who is the artist? Pah!' She tossed her pencil onto the table and spat phlegm into a glass ashtray. 'Here, why don't you do the whole thing?'

'Oh, I couldn't do that, dear. It's just that she was more . . .' She rubbed out a line and picked the pencil up. 'Well, less rounded, I suppose.' She held the pad up. 'And her clothes were all leafy, weren't they, Mr O'Shaunnessy?'

'Camouflage, yes, that's right.' Dominic looked at his watch and started to fidget. 'I wonder if I could be excused? It's just that I've got a few things to sort out.' Dominic was wondering why he was in a distant hotel lobby, helping with an e-fit that looked like General Noriega. 'It's a question of my MRSA.' An MRSA was a drug-resistant infection his mother had contracted in hospital after the removal of her varicose veins.

'Of course,' said Erik who, since litigation had occurred to him, was pleased to get rid of the foreigner. 'Please take my big apologies for the hunting. When we find Miss Webster, then we can return to the mountain and chase those sheeps.' Erik mimed a shotgun pointing in the air and said 'boom' as he pulled an imaginary trigger.

Oksana laughed boisterously and lit another cigarette. Dominic said, 'Absolutely, you just let me know when.' He clicked his thumb against his forefinger. It was only 2 p.m. in London. If he worked quickly he had enough time to catch Tony.

II

Anna wanted to report Easton missing. Sonya, who hadn't turned up for her ten thirty shift, was just the excuse. Most likely she'd got a good paying client who'd wanted to spend the morning with her. Even then Anna didn't want to report Easton missing as such, she just wanted to see what might have happened to him – a foreigner in Belugastan. She pulled her Mercedes into the *stoyanka* parking spaces of the police station. That was the problem with doing business in Belugastan, especially when it wasn't one hundred per cent legit, everyone wanted a cut of it, especially the police.

She couldn't phone Easton because the flat wasn't connected and she hadn't been able to get through on his mobile. At just after eleven that morning Anna had buzzed Easton's heavy double door. When she tried the outer steel door, covered in red Burgundy plastic like a Bulgarian sofa, it was locked. He must have gone out. She prayed it was just that, and that he hadn't been caught up by a scumbag like Zhubelovski, who considered kidnapping a legitimate negotiating tool. She frowned and stubbed out a cigarette on the ground of the car park. She'd been so careful about Easton's trip. No one but her knew about it.

The police station smelt of sour milk and uncollected refuse. The building was deserted. A guard slouched over the TV listings sent her up to the third floor. Her mules on the wooden floors echoed so much that Anna kept to the occasional lengths of threadbare carpet. She was surprised when anyone answered at room 212. The woman behind a bare desk was wearing a red suit, too warm for the time of year, and had the damp, flushed look of someone carrying an extra thirty pounds.

'Detective . . . ?'

'In there,' she said, gesturing to another door with her head. There was a Snickers ice-cream wrapper in front of her. She had the kind of poisonous attitude that Anna was used to from other women. 'Go straight in.'

Anna smiled condescendingly. The woman reacted by finishing the ice cream in one.

The room was sunless but light enough for her to notice that the man had holes in the soles of his shoes which Anna noticed because his feet were on his desk, six inches higher than a pornographic magazine. He flung it, like a glossy bird, across the room. The centrefold splayed open on the floor. Embarrassed, the man aimed another piece of paper at it to cover it up.

'I'm sorry,' said Anna unsurely, 'the woman – your secretary? – she told me to come straight in.'

He blushed. 'Witch,' he breathed.

'Which?' asked Anna. 'The one out there, of course.'

'You're supposed to knock. She knows that. She victimises me.' He stood up. 'Do come in. I am Colonel Nikolai Pertsov of the Belugastan police. Sit down. How can I help you?'

On his feet he was tall and thin. He was what her grandmother would have called effete.

'That magazine,' he pointed to it on the floor, 'it's actually to do with a case I'm working on.'

'Really, there's no need to explain. I manage a strip club,' said Anna and smiled sympathetically.

'Really?'

'Come Dancing, maybe you know it?'

Kolya nodded and waved his hand dismissively. He meant he knew it but couldn't admit to knowing it.

Anna looked down. 'Actually, that's sort of why I'm here.'

Kolya uncapped his Biro. 'The club?'

'Sort of.' She paused. 'Some people have been disappearing, haven't they?'

Kolya looked up. 'What do you mean?'

'I would have thought that was pretty obvious.'

'Tell me.' Kolya knew from *NYPD Blue* that people visiting doctors and police rarely gave the real reason why they were there straight off. This woman, though, seemed quite definite.

She said, 'Some people have been disappearing. Which aspect of that do you find difficult to understand?'

Kolya wondered if the young woman in front of him was in some way related to his wife.

He said, 'How do you know?'

'Well, for a start it's been in the papers—'

'Go on,' Kolya interrupted her.

She looked exasperated. 'And on the radio. And one of my girls has gone missing.'

'Really?'

'Yes, really.' She was cross. In Kolya's experience this was not uncommon. 'Now tell me what's been going on.'

He sucked his teeth. 'I'm afraid I can't say too much while the investigation is ongoing.'

'You Soviet.' Anna used the word as abuse to mean he was overly bureaucratic to the point of obduracy.

'Thank you,' replied Kolya. 'Now, what is it you want to know?'

'I don't want to know anything.' She crossed her legs in irritation. 'Is it only women or have men been going too?'

'*Going?*'

'Yes, going.'

The detective was standing by the window plucking at the tomato plants.

'Look, for God's sake, I'm not asking for secrets from the Soviet archive. I just want to, feel *entitled*, to know, as a citizen of this

223

country, and incidentally the Minister for the Environment, some information.'

Kolya thought, what was it that made everyone suddenly think they were cabinet ministers? Despite her charms he felt unmoved.

'Miss . . . ?'

'Arbatova.'

Kolya stood up and rubbed the creases from his suit. 'What have you heard?'

'Nothing,' said Anna crossly. 'I want to know if it's just women, or are men disappearing as well?'

'Tell me. Are you a natural blonde, Miss . . .'

'Arbatova,' reminded Anna. 'Yes, of course.'

'Then you have no reason to fear. Our assailant only likes women with chemically assisted blonde hair.'

'No men?' Anna held her breath. 'No foreigners?'

Kolya frowned and sat down. 'Not as far as I know. Now, your friend?'

'She wasn't my friend, she worked for me, she's a stripper. Sonya Krestyaka. Her shift started at ten thirty this morning and she didn't show up. She's one of my most hard-working girls. Never misses a shift.'

'Have you tried her home?'

'Her mum and dad were at the Kombinat until two this afternoon, but they haven't seen her either. Most of her friends work at the club. They're as much in the dark as the rest of us.'

Kolya looked down at the tea tray left by Tatyana. 'Is Sonya Krestyaka a blonde?'

'Ish.'

'Ish?'

'It varies. She likes to experiment. Last week was pink, but now she's definitely gone back.'

'To blonde?'

'Pinky blonde. I think so.'

Kolya said, 'I think I'd better take down her details.'

III

As a rule, Dominic liked to file the concept of scruples in the abstract part of his brain. But since he'd started playing a video of Anna on a loop in his head, all that had changed. He felt as if he'd had a blood transfusion, or at least an oil change; he had the fearless competence of a man in a shaving advert. He wanted to find Miss Webster. He even wanted to help SOS. From the perspective of the hotel room and after a superior Swedish jet shower, he even had a passing concern for the yurt dwellers – if only on the proviso that there was at least three hours in a Japanese jeep between him and the nearest camel meat.

At the times when work raised its ugly, though rarely seen, head, Dominic liked to compensate by making himself as comfortable as possible. After the shower he put on a clean pair of Y-fronts, drew the curtains and got into bed. After a night in the yurt, even the polyester undersheet felt like Egyptian cotton. He withstood the lure of TV by throwing the remote out of reach. It struck the door by the laminated fire instructions and spewed its batteries. Later, Dominic would take it as a sign. A lightning bolt that meant he should leave the mass media alone.

For several reasons, a significant one being that he, Dominic Peach, had hastened the breed's demise, the report couldn't focus on sheep. The photo of him behind the dead animal might haunt him like Lee Harvey Oswald with the shotgun, or Clinton embracing Lewinsky. It was too risky. He needed an alternative. Animal abuse with a human touch.

It had come to him when he'd tried to order a cheese sandwich from room service just after they'd arrived back.

'We only have cheese and ham,' said the receptionist whose elongated es and hard h made her sound as if she had learnt English from American TV.

'No, no ham, just cheese,' said Dominic. 'Please.'

'Only have cheese and ham.'

225

'Couldn't you just leave out the ham?' asked Dominic.

'Impossible.'

'I can't have ham, I'm Jewish. No ham.'

In the background he heard shouting. 'One cheese and ham?' asked the receptionist.

'For fuck's sake.' His eyes scanned the menu and he saw the caviar burger. It all fitted into place.

What had Sasha the doorman said when he'd sold him a kilo? 'Just fifty dollars to you, my friend. In the West it would cost more than a thousand.' The plastic bag had squelched with grey-green primordial slime.

Dominic prodded it with his finger. 'Has it gone off?'

'No,' boomed the seven-foot doorman. 'It is stolen by the Dagestan fishermen. They take their boats at night. In the spawning time.'

'Stolen?'

'No, no stolen. It is poached.' Poached had come out in three syllables but Dominic got the drift.

Dominic wasn't a species rights executive without knowing that poaching was the mass murder of the animal world. On Palace Hotel headed notepaper, which ironically included the silhouettes of two sturgeon, he started to write:

In Belugastan, part of the once great former Soviet Union, even the name means caviar. Now the country earns hard currency in the only way it can, from poachers. Caviar that graces the tables of the rich and famous can be bought here on every street corner for less than £30 a kilo. The Acton-based environmental agency Save Our Species is the first to highlight this abuse. Speaking from the heart of the country, SOS executive Dominic Peach, 29, said: 'Everywhere I turn I am being offered cut-price caviar. It is poachers who are turning this evil trade to their own advantage. Something must be done to stop them.' SOS was recently saved from bankruptcy by a vital £50,000 Lottery Commission grant.

Dominic wondered whether to make a jibe about the muff divers, but he knew from a week-long course in Advanced Press Relations in Harrogate that it wasn't his job to editorialise. By the time he'd bumped the report up to one thousand words, Dominic was feeling chuffed. Actual detail was thin on the ground, but it was a press release. He tried the SOS office but got no reply.

He felt absurdly let down by SOS. How dared no one be there? Then he took an unusual step. Nothing was as irksome to Dominic as having done some work and getting no credit.

Disgruntled and fired up, he decided to go straight to the newspapers. One of the sofas that Dominic had lodged on around the May bank holiday belonged to a sub-editor on a London tabloid. Dominic fanned back the sheet and pulled his Ryman's spiral notebook which was his address book from his pouch of travel documents. The number was listed in black pen under 'Bob (wk)' and alongside it in blue, '(poor mattress, noisy girlfriend)'.

When he got through on an echoing line to the newspaper, he was met by a female W8 accent and told that the subs didn't get in until 2 p.m. The reporter was stunned by his gaucherie to the point of sounding hurt. Dominic was nervous and annoyed.

He said, 'I'm sorry, I'm in Belugastan.'

'Where?'

Dominic repeated, tiredly thinking of his next move, 'Belugastan.'

'Where's that?' asked the reporter.

It was the first time that Dominic realised he didn't know where Belugastan was.

'Russia.'

'Russia, as in the country?'

'Yes, Russia as in the country,' said Dominic. 'Listen, I've got a hot lead. I was going to tell Bob but I might as well tell you, now I've got you.'

'Is it ordered?'

'It's fairly ordered.' Dominic thought she was asking about his prose style.

227

'This is a terrible line, I'll put you through to copy.'

Dominic waited. After three minutes an older woman with a south London accent said, 'Copy-takers, which basket?'

'I don't know about baskets,' said Dominic, 'I'm in Belugastan.'

'Sport?'

'Foreign,' guessed Dominic.

'What's it called?'

'Caviar-poaching in the former Soviet Union.'

'One word,' she barked.

'Caviar,' said Dominic.

After a twenty-second wait, the woman said, 'Get on with it then, I haven't got all day. I'm holding for a three-thousand-word feature on fire-walking classes south of the river.'

'OK then, here goes.'

After Dominic had stumbled his way through the piece, the copy-taker sighed heavily and asked, 'Is that it?'

Dominic felt insecure. 'What do you think?'

'It's not up to me, lovey.'

Then she asked if his details were on file, to which Dominic replied possibly. After that she put the phone down.

The experience of work had left him in a desultory, suspended mood. He wandered around the room, flicked the kettle switch on, tried to mend the remote, thinking of Anna. Out of nowhere an image of Mr Orlovski came to him. Maybe it had been calling London. On one level, quite a big level, Mr Orlovski was now his only tie to the UK, now that, in his mind at least, he and Antoinette had parted. The picture from the Elderly Alert garden party of the two of them together had fallen out of his address book. He sat on the bed and looked at it, rotating it in his hand and using the corner to gouge yurt dirt from his fingernails. Since it had been taken he'd crawled another week closer to his thirtieth birthday. But for the last few days his age had stopped worrying him.

He needed air. On the way to forcing open a balcony window he wafted air at himself with a melamine wardrobe door. Inside smelt of plastic sheets and cardboard. He used the same loose-armed movement to tug at the grey and purple curtains. They stuck midway. He cursed. He hadn't spotted the curtain-opening pulley system.

He found the baton and yanked the left-hand side hard. It jammed.

Dominic said out loud, 'Why in God's name do you need a bloody stick to pull a pair of frigging . . .'

When he finally made it through to the glass, he was glad he'd surfaced like a sluggish burrowing animal rather than a top-of-the-bill curtain-raiser. Later, he even thanked the Oslo architect who had installed the curtain-pulling baton. By slithering, he appeared slowly. As he peered out of the window onto the square, he gasped. Below him were a dozen, possibly two dozen yurt people. He furled himself slowly back into the dusty curtain; the last thing he saw as he rotated was a red pom-pom. He started to crawl towards the bed.

IV

When Sonya first came to, she felt groggier than she had done after the two-week R&R break of a crew of Uzbek oil riggers. Her body was stiff, as if she'd been beaten up. She was lying on her front, the ground underneath was hard and there was a cold breeze that reflexively made her think of the industrial fan, bought at a Kombinat discount sale, that they used at Come Dancing. They were told it was air conditioning though the girls knew it was to make their nipples stand up and their hair look as if it was in a breeze.

To the left of her a bright light was shining and she felt hands massaging her back. She didn't know the surroundings, though the touch was familiar. Usually it meant more sex was required.

Sonya tried to push herself over on her hip. She could hear a voice but it was indistinct, as if it was coming from a long way away. Even when it slipped into auditory focus it was in a language she didn't recognise. She knew, though, that it was a woman. That scared her. She'd never done a trick with a woman before. That was her last thought as she drifted off again.

The body had arrived three hours ago, Stella Anne guessed. In the absence of a clock she kept time by reading. She estimated, ignoring pictures, it took her two minutes to read every page of Dr Spock's child-rearing handbook. She had been on page 14, weaning, when the woman was lowered into the sewer through a manhole. Now she was on page 100, terrible twos. It was gripping stuff. Had it not been for the sheep she might have thought she was missing out on something. Stella Anne had never had children of her own. When first married she'd queried her failure to conceive. Her husband, the cosmetic surgeon, had told her with more savagery than was necessary that he didn't do tubes and she should see a specialist if she wanted to get pregnant. He said it in a way that suggested he wouldn't care if it was the specialist who impregnated her.

The specialist was a second-generation Pole who kept a game of Buckaroo in his surgery that he claimed put women at their ease. Stella Anne saw straight through it. It meant he avoided eye contact with his patients. Stella Anne wanted to talk about irregular periods with someone she could trust, not a plastic bunking bronco.

In any case, by the time a plastic spade caused the Buckaroo to rear up, she knew she'd lost the urge to reproduce with her husband. She'd never much cared for the word mother anyway. It reminded her too much of smother.

Down the sewer, reading the book with its soft focus and smiling babies didn't make her broody. She was glad that on top of everything else she'd never had the parent/child dynamic to deal with. She had her focus and her focus was sheep.

The woman's body had been lowered in an elaborate knotted cat's cradle, like something a stevedore might use. Stella Anne had yelled up at whoever was on the other end of the ropes; she thought from the voices that they were men. They had ignored her, but that was no surprise. Stella Anne knew from her true crime magazines that kidnap victims had to engage their abductor, make a connection that aroused his sympathy. Then she reconsidered. That was never going to happen; it hadn't even worked with her husband, never mind a crazed psychotic.

At any rate, she'd failed to engage the criminal, though to his credit the woman had come with four bottles of drinking water and six bars of Russian chocolate. Most significantly, when they'd shut the manhole, a chink of light shone through. It wasn't anywhere near enough to mean she didn't still need the torch, but it filled her with hope. She'd felt for a foothold – the manhole was only twenty feet or so up – but it was impossible. The walls were sheer and slimy.

The woman was more a girl than a grown-up. She was dressed in tight blue jeans and white sneakers. There was English writing on the front of her sweatshirt, probably a baseball team, but face down Stella Anne couldn't read it. The woman looked fit and sensible. The sort of person she'd want to be captured with. She covered her in the eiderdown and carried on trying to massage her awake. She uncapped a bottle of water, ready.

When the girl started to shake herself awake, groggily raising her head six inches off the ground, Stella Anne reached for the torch. She shone it at the roof so as not to blind her. She started to make sympathetic noises to try and calm her down, but her co-captive seemed calm. She spoke in Russian, garbled and frenzied, then, hearing Stella Anne's English, said, 'You pay me honest. Fair's fair.' Stella Anne smiled in a motherly way. She put it down to the effects of chloroform.

V

The missing person's report was still on the floor. Kolya had lobbed it towards the magazine to cover up the shame of the centrefold – his shame, not the model's. It was the first time he'd seen it. It was in neat capital letters and written in a style either intended to emulate that of the police or take the piss. It described an American woman in her forties who had been seized from a camp on Pik Lenina, late yesterday.

Since the disappearance of his prime suspect, Kolya had been losing interest in the case. One of the boons of being the country's only incorruptible police officer was that nobody expected a result. But now that a foreigner, and the best type of foreigner to boot – an American – was involved, the stakes were raised. Solving the crime might get an FBI recommendation; it might get a reward. A reward would mean a new flat. He dialled the number on the report and called Tatyana in. He felt the unmistakable symptoms of an *NYPD Blue* surge. He wrinkled his forehead in an I-mean-business way. He was turning it sombrely towards the window for a long sweeping camera shot of his profile, when Tatyana came in.

'Second-storey loos are blocked again,' she said.

Kolya looked at her and shrugged. 'No one ever said it was going to be easy.'

Tatyana looked at him in a way that suggested he'd nipped out to the kiosk for a bottle of mandarin liqueur.

They left the station, with Tatyana fanning herself with a dress pattern. She walked a few feet behind him, more due to unsuitable shoes than respect. Kolya saw it first, a photocopied sketch of a woman, taped to a telegraph pole. He was reading it when Tatyana caught him up.

'Yuk,' she said, 'who's that?'

Kolya ignored her, still reading.

Tatyana said, 'Hang on a minute, I recognise—'

Kolya snatched the artist's impression and carried on walking.

Tatyana said, 'I've got it. Yeah, hang on, it's that American president.'

Ahead, Kolya shook his head.

VI

Sergei Kapustin had been the editor of *Belugastan Today* for eleven years. At first the perks had been communist – modest but significant. He had a three-room apartment in the new part of the city, plumbing that always worked and a sober concierge. He had been able to shop in high-domed grocery stores that sold German sausage. They got to spend the summer in the better parts of Sochi; there'd even been an overseas trip to Bulgaria. With a wife like his, having anything the neighbours didn't ranked as a Stalingrad-type victory. As she liked to remind him, her marriage had caused her to change a name meaning swan to one meaning cabbage. She had a right to demand compensation.

Now, of course, things had improved significantly. There had been an uncomfortable period after the end of communism and the fall of TASS when they hadn't known quite what to write. Then stories paid for by factory owners became all the rage; journalists would recommend the latest fizzy drink or tinned meat. Often the bills were settled in kind. Kapustin had put on ten kilos a year from 1994 to 1997.

But now the paper had a proprietor who looked after his journalists in an unprecedented manner. He also told them what to write. Typewriters had been replaced with Apple Macs, the office furniture was Swedish-made, they had a revamped canteen, they even had a huge plastic bottle of water in the middle of the room, for which there was no Russian word. Life, thought Sergei Kapustin, as he rhythmically pushed his groin up and down between the swivel chair and black ash table, was Italian-imported peachy. The only cloud on the horizon came in the shape of the proprietor. Unfortunately the cloud was sitting opposite him.

'Hot today,' said Kapustin.

Vladimir Zhubelovski sat with his knees apart. At university, before he met his wife, Kapustin had been a keen geometry student. He had wanted to become a draughtsman. Zhubelovski's legs were at a 120-degree angle. It was a good chunk of any pie chart, or any pie. In contrast, Kapustin nursed his testicles nervously between crossed legs.

Zhubelovski said, 'It's been a hell of a summer. I don't remember the weather being this hot since the good old days.'

'The good old days,' concurred Kapustin. 'Even the weather was better then, eh, comrade?'

'You mean you preferred it in communist times?' asked Zhubelovski. His body had pulsed a few centimetres towards him. 'Before the advent of democracy and freedom?'

'Well, of course there's two ways of looking at that one,' said Kapustin. 'Materially we're better off, of course, but spiritually . . .' He hovered.

Kapustin didn't think much, he tended to believe in what he was paid to believe. As regards opinion, he'd based a thirty-year career on nodding and echoing the last words of his superior's sentence as they spoke it. It also worked with his wife.

'We are bereft?' hinted Zhubelovski.

'Bereft,' he echoed, still not sure which way it was going. 'Well, possibly.'

'Mr Kapustin, I am the son of a drunken slut mother and a worthless father. Not what you might call the product of a glorious empire. I was born into a barbaric system where for the first year of their lives babies were straightjacketed in swaddling. Fathers were not even allowed to visit their babies in hospital. Imagine the effects. Morally, communism was bankrupt. You would do well to remember that.'

'Exactly,' said Kapustin. His groin was pulsating like a metronome. Though he didn't know it, his nervous reflex was the reason women employees didn't go into his office alone.

'So, Kapustin. How's things?' Zhubelovski asked, pushing back from the desk.

'Well, thank you, really well,' said Kapustin with a forced smile. 'The water cooler gets jammed and the tiles in the bathroom are loose over the third stall—'

'I meant with the paper.' Zhubelovski flicked his blond ponytail over his shoulder. Despite the heat, he hadn't taken his coat off. A bodyguard in a double-breasted leather jacket stood behind him, in posture and stature like an upright Buddha in Armani shades.

'Good. Excellent, in fact. Circulation is up, advertising is up, everything is up.' Kapustin hoped up was good. In case up was bad, he kept his face engaged, as if he hadn't finished. 'Drink?' He exhaled in relief. A secretary set down a tray with a bottle of Zhubelovski vodka and three glasses. The tray had a socialist medal on it showing the date 1945–1995, to celebrate fifty years since the Great Patriotic War.

Zhubelovski picked the bottle up by its neck. 'Every bottle has a hologram of me on the label, to prevent forgeries. What do you think of that?'

'Incredible,' said Kapustin, shaking his head in disbelief.

Zhubelovski creased his forehead. 'Are you all right? You're sweating like a pig.' He poured three glasses and handed them round. 'Cheers,' he said. 'To us.'

'Us,' said Kapustin.

While Kapustin and the guard wiped a hand over their mouths, Zhubelovski produced a green silk monogrammed handkerchief from his breast pocket. 'Excellent vodka. Very smooth indeed, very smooth. Now, business.'

Kapustin felt his mouth go dry and the sound of blood rushing through his inner ear.

235

'There's been too much of the paper devoted to these Five Years of Belugastan celebrations and that half-witted President. I want more space devoted to me. In fact you might as well know that I shall be running for President myself soon. When are the next presidential elections here?'

He'd caught Kapustin off guard. 'I'm not sure they have any pattern to them as such.'

Zhubelovski's eyebrows furrowed and his facial warts pointed in a downward V.

'Next year,' said Kapustin definitely.

Zhubelovski shook his head in disgust, signalling that next year was too far off.

'Or next month,' corrected Kapustin. 'I think there are probably some preliminaries next month. In fact tomorrow's editorial mentions them specifically.'

'Good,' said Zhubelovski as he got up to leave. 'I don't suppose I need tell you which way *Belugastan Today* will be leaning, need I?'

'No, absolutely not – Zhubelovski for President,' said Kapustin, so sure he'd got it right he put his fist in the air.

From the door, the proprietor said, 'I'm aware that some women have been going missing recently. You really should hi—'

'*Hide it*,' said Kapustin, 'more towards the back of the paper?'

Zhubelovski frowned. 'Highlight the menace of this man who is responsible. Stress the fact he's a fiend. Otherwise you'll be for the high—'

'*Jump*,' said the editor.

'Exactly,' said Zhubelovski. 'Glad there's something we can agree on.'

After he'd left, Kapustin delved into his briefcase for a can of air freshener. His secretary said Zhubelovski smelt of French aftershave, but Kapustin detected the faint odour of sulphur. Under the can was a shopping list from his wife. He sighed. He would have to leave now if he was going to get it all.

VII

Dominic was trying to set fire to his caviar story when he heard room service at the door. To validate his exposé he was trying the caviar burger.

'Anna, my God – what a surprise – my God, come on in.'

'I hope I'm not disturbing you.' Dominic was still in his Y-fronts. He reached out for a Palace Hotel robe. He tugged at the curtains, pulled shut to eclipse the menace of the yurt people.

Anna sniffed the room. 'Has there been a fire in here?'

'No, I was just seeing to some paperwork.'

'Don't tell me you're a spy, Mr O'Shaunnessy.'

'Me? No, good heavens, no. I work for a refuge. A refuge for victims of domestic violence. How did you know we were back? How did you know where I was staying?'

'We are a small country, Mr O'Shaunnessy,' said Anna. 'Few things happen here without us all knowing about it.'

Dominic tucked his hair behind his ears. 'That must be nice. Please, sit down.'

'How do you mean nice? On the contrary, I find it parochial.'

Dominic wasn't sure what parochial meant. 'Sure, me too.'

'How was your trip?'

'Good, yeah, very good,' said Dominic. 'Well, actually, bad. One of the hunters disappeared.'

'Really?'

'Yeah, she was really nice, I mean is really nice. American.'

'Oh yes, I heard about that. A hunter that was hunted. It is ironic, no?'

'I suppose so, I hadn't really thought about it. Look, would you like to go for a walk, or something to eat?' Dominic felt overpowered by her presence in the room. Then he remembered. 'Actually, maybe not. I can't leave the hotel room.'

'Is it spy business?'

'No, it's daft really.' Dominic sat on the edge of the bed.

'There's been a terrific mix-up. Where we are staying the people thought I was some sort of reincarnated native leader. Absolutely crazy. It was the limp that did it. I told them it came from a complimentary mango but they wouldn't have it.'

'I'm sorry,' Anna frowned. 'Sometimes my English skills are really not so good. In the mountains the native Belugis thought you were some sort of leader?'

'Yes. Barmy, isn't it?'

'But you're back here now,' Anna said definitely.

'Exactly, that's what I thought too, but there's a gang of them outside.'

'Oh, but this is absurd. You have no right to roam. You British love the right to roam.'

Dominic nodded. 'I thought I'd just hole myself up here until my flight but—'

'When is that?' Anna interrupted him.

'Sunday,' said Dominic with an unexpected flutter in his stomach.

'The day after Belugastan National Day,' said Anna pensively.

Dominic decided to be bold. 'Besides, the only reason I had for leaving the hotel was to find you.'

Anna didn't seem to have heard him. 'This is preposterous. I insist you stay with me. Well, if not with me, then with my grandmother at her dacha. She will show you a good time.'

'Really?'

'Yes, pack your things. There is a back entrance to the Palace that I am familiar with.'

She waited while Dominic packed around her. He still didn't know why she was here. 'Did you want to see me about something?' He had already mapped out his dream reply to this question while he'd been packing his shaving foam. It wasn't quite as he had hoped.

She said, 'I have a gentleman visitor from overseas that I can't locate. I was wondering if it is the experience of foreign gentlemen, in general, to undergo any problems here. Tell me, have you been approached by anyone?'

Dominic felt as deflated as the travel pillow he was squashing in his hand.

'Other than the yurt people, no. Oh, the doorman asked if I wanted a blonde. Other than that, no.'

Anna had her head down. 'Good, excellent.' She looked at him. 'Oh, and I find myself attracted to you, strangely,' she added.

'Attracted to me strangely?' Dominic repeated and sank onto the bed. Kneewise, he felt like a block of flats being demolished. 'Or strangely attracted to me?'

Propelled by his weight, the Polaroid of Dominic and Mr Orlovski at the Elderly Alert summer fete slid frictionless towards him. Anna picked it up. 'Either. We were taught not to split infinitives.' She studied the picture. 'Who's that?'

'Sorry?'

'The man, he's familiar.'

'Yeah, well, it's me.'

'Not you, the older one.'

'That? He's an old bloke I visit in London. He's a Pole.'

'It seems like I know him.'

'Well, old people can look alike, can't they?'

'You can be very insensitive, Mr O'Shaunnessy. It is not attractive.'

Dominic smiled apologetically and in his head wrote 'I must be more sensitive' one hundred times.

VIII

The girl was acting as strangely as a whitetail in the rutting season. Apart from her husband's young mistresses, Stella Anne had very little experience of female teenagers. She'd tried to quieten her with a maternal hug, but she'd whimpered worse than a dog missing its master. She spoke low and evenly.

'My name is Stella Anne and I am American. We have been

abducted and we must be brave. What is your name?'

Sonya trusted the woman sitting next to her in the gloaming; in the torchlight she had a kind smile and a faint double chin. Seated, she had the spreading thighs of an older woman who wouldn't threaten her.

Sonya had much to convey. Her English skills were limited to her call girl work and Pets to Dye For. She said, 'My name is Sonya. I dance just for you?'

'Well, that would be lovely, honey, and I'm sure it would keep you warm, it's just maybe a bit impractical.' She patted Sonya's thigh. 'You dance later.' The girl showed pluck, she liked that. 'Now, why don't you have a drink of water, Sonya. We need to keep our strength up and our fluid level high.'

'You buy me a drink?'

'No, honey, why don't you just take a sip of this.' To make her feel more at home, she passed her the Dr Spock book. 'Here, darlin', you have a look at this.'

The next phrase made Stella Anne think either the chloroform had had some pernicious lasting effect or that the girl was deranged.

'Cats take the dye best. Your hamster should be blue.'

'Sure it should, baby.' Stella Anne put her arm round the youngster.

IX

'Who the fuck is Dominic Peach?' Jimmy 'Good-oh' Little's reputation as a newspaperman was based on his skill as a headline writer, not rewriting. He was a rangy man with a penchant, since his wife Joan had left him, for drip-dry easy-iron garments that he stocked up with from the ROP adverts in the sports section. Maybe it was a property of the fabric that made him look particularly well-endowed. It caused the all-female features department to come up with the double-page piece, 'Tackle or Sack-all? Ten ways to guess the size of a man's packet.'

Jimmy had joined the staff of the *Daily Rail* in 1995. Since its relaunch the paper had become a market leader, in part because many thought it was dedicated to British Rail news in suburban areas. The newspaper was in fact devoted to asserting consumer sovereignty.

'Dominic Peach? No idea.' Gayle Barratt was the paper's health correspondent, credited with leading a middle-class revolt against immunisation in the under-twos. Even though doctors feared she might be single-handedly responsible for an epidemic in childhood measles, her stuff got letters and that's what counted. Due to cutbacks she was also the paper's food and wine editor. She was due to meet her boyfriend Teddy at a pub on the river in Richmond at 10.00 p.m. She wanted to leave early because she and Teddy had rowed that morning over the fat content of Coco-pops.

'Well, whoever he is, he can't write. Here, Gayle, do something with this bollocks, can you?'

Less than thirty seconds later the story appeared on her screen. Gayle groaned. 'Oh, Jimmy, can't you get someone else to do it? I'm health.'

'Holidays, Gayle. You're food, aren't you?'

'So?'

'It's about caviar. Do it to five hundred, it might make a page lead.'

'All right.' Gayle put down the A-Z, where she was looking up the Richmond pub.

'Good-oh.'

She scanned the copy. 'But this is foreign. We don't do foreign.'

'It's caviar, not foreign.'

When the subs got the story at 11 a.m., by which time Teddy and Gayle had made up their differences over Coco-pops, Dominic's piece was very different.

X

Tim looked at himself in the mirror above the handbasin as he urinated. He yawned. With his free hand he massaged his features awake. He was naked, the door behind him was open. There was a religious icon propped up on the top of the cistern, next to a Russian-made shiny loo roll. According to Natasha, the stencilling in the bathroom, based on an idea from an Italian interiors magazine, came from nipple prints. Tim said he didn't know she spoke Italian. She agreed she couldn't. Looking at the finish, it explained a lot.

'You got to get back?' Natasha had a sheet pulled up to her chin on the sofa bed. Igor had left the radio on before he went to bed and there was a salsa tune playing. The dog was asleep in his hammock on the roof.

'I should, really.' He felt reluctant to go.

'Why do you do it if you don't like it?'

Tim washed his hands and splashed water on his face. 'I dunno. First it was the political immunity, then I felt I should give something back. Now I guess I just feel responsible.'

Natasha sat up. 'What the hell do you mean? Political immunity? What sort of a carpenter needs political immunity?'

'Oh, shit,' said Tim and flushed the lavatory.

CHAPTER TEN

I

The jockey moved Erik, and it wasn't just the shape of her perfect ankles and calves, slim but muscular, like the fetlocks of a pedigree racehorse. Nor was it her life story which, though touching, was not remarkable. Erik stretched a leg out from under the sheet and rotated his ankle lazily.

More likely it was because she made love as if riding a winner coming down the home straight. Even her whip arm had twitched when she came as if she was galloping past the winning post.

The jockey's name was Larissa. She was a Muscovite who, until the age of twenty-one, had worked as a deputy manageress in a glittery Western concession in GUM that specialised in camcorders and bread-making machines. Then the rouble devalued and the Italians pulled out swiftly in a way that the Russian store manager said helped explain their performance in the war. Larissa didn't understand that, but she did understand that she needed a new job. The following Monday she answered a classified advert in *Komsomolskaya Pravda* wanting women aged eighteen to twenty-three with a size ten dress size to work as waitresses abroad.

The job was for waitresses, and it was abroad, but it turned out to be topless in a Coney Island strip joint. Skipping the stripping part, she got her passport back by bribing a Brooklyn doctor to write a letter saying she needed a mastectomy. The pimps had agreed. No one wanted a stripper with only one tit. The problem was that in Moscow the recruiting agents would see she was still double-breasted. The agents were fierce – Larissa knew they killed some girls – so she'd moved to Belugastan last year.

'The rest,' she'd said with her head on Erik's chest, 'is history.'

They'd met the day before at the rundown *konezavod*, the Soviet pony factory where she was mucking out the stables. Erik had been meeting an advertiser who exported horsemeat. Erik was determined not to let on that *Erik* possibly wasn't the sort of flesh magazine the exporter was after, because he paid $400 for a half-page. Erik had liked Larissa immediately.

Now he was trying to recruit her for a double-page spread. She had agreed on the proviso the magazine wouldn't be seen in Moscow.

'I swear,' said Erik, 'that no one north of the Volga delta will see you still have two breasts.'

'OK.' She paused and smiled. 'But I'd want to have the horses in it. Those are my conditions.'

Erik lit a cigarette. 'You mean like a Catherine the Great thing?'

'*No.*' She took a drag. 'I mean something tasteful. Maybe me on horseback. If I write anything it'll be about the plight of horses in the former Soviet Union.'

'Excuse me?'

'You heard.' She clipped on a bra. 'How much do you pay?'

They agreed on two hundred bucks.

'When can you start the shoot?' asked Erik.

'What about today? I don't have to be at work till midday. There's no time like the present.'

'I guess not,' said Erik.

As they walked towards the magazine office in the same low-rise block as *Belugastan Today*, Erik noticed how tiny she was. It made him wonder about her stripping; unless you got a front row seat, you weren't going to see a lot. Logistically Erik knew the horse thing was going to be a nightmare. Saucy bank tellers were one thing, recreating Ben Hur was a different ball game. But he liked the idea. Edition 74, topical issue, *Horses – The Forgotten Victims of the Soviet Break-up*.

He faced her. 'So, what made you come to Belugastan?' he asked. The morning was hot. The sun shining on her hair made it jet-black.

'You mean after New York?'

'Yeah.'

'Well, like I told you, the breast thing, and also the horses.'

'Really?' Erik paused to let an ancient Zhiguli drive past. 'I didn't know there were any horses here.'

'Idiot,' said Larissa and smiled, 'you've never heard of the Donskaya? The Buddenovskaya? They have the best horses in the world here. They used to breed them. Give them away to foreign presidents. Then the money ran out and now they're all dying.'

'So you came here and became a jockey?'

'Something like that.' She walked in a pert way, swinging her hips and shaking her hair, like a horse.

'What's the pay like?'

'Lousy, though we sometimes get to rig the races. That helps.'

'It would,' said Erik. 'Got a *krisha*?'

Larissa looked at him as if he was mad. 'Sure I have. Has Boris Yeltsin got a shrivelled liver?'

Erik smiled. 'I mean, who is your roof?' A roof was security. A gang that protected you from the threats of other gangs. Often they were gangsters turned security firms, sometimes they were former special forces. Larissa mentioned the name of one.

Erik said, 'That's Zhubelovski's lot, right?'

'They used to be, but they've set up on their own now.'

When he caught sight of the crowd in the corner of the square it was already so hot that the air was shimmering above their heads. Erik took the crowd to be a bunch of communists, the only ones dumb enough to believe in the power of demonstrations. Then he wondered if it was National Veterans' Day or the International Day of the Pensioner. As he and Larissa got closer, the smell helped place them – smoke and sour milk – then the national dress, then the horses.

Erik guessed there were twenty altogether. The men stood, while the women, about half a dozen in all, squatted on their haunches. Immediately Erik thought visual. Play his cards right and it could be a backdrop – large, unpaid, ethnic crowd scene. In the far corner of the square two old ladies, not yurt people, were arguing. One, in an orange bib, brandishing a twig broom, was the municipal street cleaner. The other, in her seventies, was threatening her with a shovel. It was so heated, Erik contemplated breaking them up. They were arguing over the rights to horse dung.

'Hello there,' said Erik. He recognised the one with the red pom-pom hat. 'Aren't you hot in all that gear? It's gotta be thirty-three degrees out here.'

The man ignored him. Erik continued, 'What brings you into town?'

Three men were grouped around a bottle of Stolichnaya vodka, huddled like bullies around a weakling, wondering what to do. Erik could tell from the label that it was moonshine, probably pure alcohol and water, guaranteed to send most people blind. The three drinkers didn't seem to notice. Shoulders hunched for another round, they didn't even seem that drunk. It wasn't the tipple most would choose for mid-morning in a heat wave.

Erik tried again. 'Remember me?'

The pom-pom man was the oldest. Beneath the hat he had a moustache and narrow eyes. He was powerfully built, like a wrestler. His T-shirt under a fleecy vest read 'Hard Rock Café, Tehran'. He extended a hand.

Erik said, 'So, what brings you lot into town?'

The man spat before he spoke. 'We've come for Dzhungar.'

Out of the corner of his eye, Erik noticed that the makeshift encampment was using the newly lit eternal flame for boiling water. Benches around the square were piled high with plastic bags. A pile of fur rugs covered the plaque of war dead, as high as the victims of the Afghan conflict.

'Dzhungar, that would be who, exactly?' He spoke slowly and before the sentence was out it came to him. The reincarnation shit. Erik didn't like it, it made him nervous. Losing one foreigner was bad enough, losing two was a disaster. 'You mean that tall foreign guy, the hunter?'

The red pom-pom nodded.

Erik asked, 'What are you going to do when you find him?'

'Take him home,' said the pom-pom man. 'We still have his servants. Dzhungar would never leave them. If he doesn't come back with us, then we will keep them.'

'Is that right?' Erik scratched his head. Suddenly the debit list was reading four foreigners. It was a PR disaster. He could see this was going to take some serious negotiations to wriggle out of without either bloodshed or a lawsuit.

Erik looked him straight in the eye. 'How do you know he's still here? It was a short hunting trip. Chances are he's already gone home.'

'This is his home,' said the wrestler. 'Besides, the doorman told us he was in the hotel.'

Next to him Larissa was showing no signs of impatience. He liked that. It meant she was used to waiting for people to do their business. Or maybe horses required patience.

Erik walked closer to the men. Behind them the women were sharing out two loaves of bread and a lump of Russian sausage.

He said, 'Where are you camped?'

'Peace Square.'

'Yurting, I suppose.' Erik wasn't sure if it was a word. The man nodded. One of the women with her head covered in a headscarf shouted at Larissa to join them. She smiled and reluctantly bobbed down cross-legged.

Erik still required more information. 'What are you going to do with this man once you have him? As I understand it, he can't even speak Russian, never mind whatever it is you people speak.'

The pom-pom man looked blank. 'Worship him,' he said.

Erik gulped. 'What if he doesn't want to be worshipped? You can't make him.'

The man shrugged and turned his back on Erik.

Erik called to Larissa, 'Come on, we're going.'

Larissa didn't move.

'Come on,' he shouted.

As Erik tried to think of a way out of the yurt conflict he felt the jelly of worry in his stomach harden. You only had to trip over in the West and someone paid you thousands, he thought. How would it be if you went abroad to hunt sheep, in good faith, but were kidnapped by native herdsmen who thought you were a reincarnated leader? And then were forced to spend the rest of your life there. The compensation would run into millions. He had to think very hard. Larissa noticed his frown.

'What's up with you?' she asked.

'It's nothing,' Erik lied. 'Well, actually, I forgot. I meant to borrow one of those horses, for the shoot.'

Larissa raised herself on tiptoes and kissed him on the chin. 'Ah, you were just thinking of me. How sweet you are. Look, don't worry, we can steal one. There's some tied up round the corner. We'll take one.'

Erik shook his head.

Larissa said, 'But I'm not doing the shoot outside. I don't want everyone watching me. It'd be embarrassing.'

Given that she was going to be seen topless by thousands – well, maybe two thousand if circulation picked up – that was a hard one to justify, thought Erik. But he'd made enough bad location decisions in his time at *Erik* to be able to recognise one straight off.

Five minutes later she was breathing up a piebald's nostril. The horse had followed her as if he'd been attached to her since birth. He was more donkey-sized than a fully fledged horse, which meant that – though squashed – they all fitted into the lift. Larissa went in first, then the horse, then Erik. Larissa said, 'Which floor?'

Passing the third, she said, 'You know what we put in a horse box to calm horses down if they're nervous?'

'Surprise me,' said Erik.

'A sheep.'

'Really,' said Erik. Since the Beluga argali argali, he'd been off anything ovine. 'What did you say to the guard downstairs?'

'I told him,' said Larissa, 'that one of the yurt people was tampering with his car.'

'That's the way ethnic hatred starts,' said Erik.

As he spoke the horse's breathing speeded up. An arch of saliva dribbled onto the lift floor. It was mopped up by the centre pages of a discarded newspaper.

As the doors opened on the tenth floor Larissa said, 'Everybody out.' As they clip-clopped past the editor's office Erik felt the tingling of a brainstorming idea. He told Larissa to wait.

He walked through the air-conditioned editorial office of *Belugastan Today*, which was the usual ferment of non-activity, and straight into Kapustin's room.

'Hey, cabbage man. I've got a great story for you.'

Kapustin looked up from the copy of *Russian Cosmo* from which he was carefully peeling off the free shampoo.

'What is it, Marchenko – the bottom fallen out of porn?'

'Good one, fatman. Listen, this is a scoop.'

Kapustin looked in some pain. 'Like what?'

'Like the next President of Belugastan is going to be an Irish hunter reincarnated from Dzhungar.'

'I'm sorry?' Kapustin was the first to admit he didn't understand much about hard news, but even to him it sounded far-fetched.

'You've seen those Belugi natives in the square?'

'Yes?'

'I don't suppose it occurred to a journalist of your calibre to wonder what they were doing there?'

'I thought they were something to do with the National Day Parade.'

'Wrong. They're here stalking a foreigner in town, because they want him to be the next President,' said Erik triumphantly. 'When are the next elections?'

'Next week, actually.' Kapustin's brain felt over-heated. They went years without a hint of an election and then suddenly, in the last twenty-four hours, everybody wanted to be President.

'Exactly,' said Erik. 'And you're going to do a piece on how this foreigner is the front runner.'

Kapustin looked up; the shampoo had come free. 'I don't get it, why would a foreigner be running in the election?' Things, he reflected, were so much easier under communism.

Erik said, 'It's an ethnic thing. Trust me. All you have to do is say that he's running.'

Kapustin smiled. 'I can't do that.'

'Why not?'

'Because Zhubelovski's running.'

'*Zhubelovski?*'

'You heard,' said the editor. 'So, naturally, we're supporting him.'

Erik had to do some very quick re-thinking, rather like the time when the February front cover was ready to go to the printers and the model phoned up to say her boyfriend with the AK-47 objected.

After thirty seconds Erik said, 'Well, I'm sure Zhubelovski wouldn't want to run unopposed. This way it'll look like an actual election.' He paused. 'And obviously there's something in it for you.'

'What?' asked Kapustin. As he spoke he heard a whinny from the corridor and a shriek from the classified department.

'Something not even Mrs Kapustina's got.'

'Such as?'

Just then, as if she'd guessed why they were here, Larissa walked in with the horse. Erik could see, as ludicrous as it was, that Kapustin was assessing the animal. The cogs were cranking in the avarice department. The way Kapustin saw it, Zhubelovski couldn't object to them just *listing* the candidates. The piece would mention this foreigner before launching into the paper's full support of Zhubelovski's candidacy. Also, his wife had always wanted a horse, mostly because the neighbours didn't own one.

'All right,' said Kapustin, 'I'll do it. Just one thing.' He'd heard journalists say it in the newsroom. 'We'll need a photo.'

Erik remembered the Polaroids shot by Mrs Barinova on the mountain.

'No problem,' he said.

Kapustin frowned so that a roll of fat, as if he'd been garrotted, showed around his neck. 'What about the current President? Is he standing again?'

'Leave him to me,' said Erik.

II

As it happened, elections were a long way from Tim's current first division list of worries. It looked as if he was about to be dumped for the second time in seventy-two hours, which was a record only beaten by the time Masha Lyubova had dumped and reclaimed him four times in a week at Pioneer camp in 1977, variously in favour of the *zolotaya molodezh*, the golden youth of the Party officials' sons. That, for Tim, had marked the end of his affection for communism.

'I'm going for a walk.' Natasha got up off the sofa sulkily. 'Whitey needs some exercise.'

'Can I come?' Tim got up at the same time. 'Or I could help Igor laminating?'

'Do what you like. You always do.' She looked very unattractive when she frowned.

251

Tim hadn't expected anyone to take the news of his presidency so badly. From memory, not even the candidates he had beaten had seemed this upset. He needed to establish if she was pretending to be pissed off or if she really was. From where he was sitting his money was on the latter. It was a pity because she was wearing the same denim shorts she'd had on when they first met. He really hoped he hadn't blown it.

'OK, babe, I lied. I'm sorry, really. But what could I do when you'd just told me you didn't like men in positions of authority?'

'You could have told the truth.'

'Right,' Tim said sarcastically. '*You* don't like men in authority, which is why you finished with your husband, the traffic cop. And then I announce, "By the way, honey, I'm President of the Republic"?'

'It was wrong of you,' said Natasha. 'Thank God I never slept with you.'

Tim shook his head in despair. It wasn't time to mount the fightback, but it was getting close.

He still had a lot in his armoury. Natasha was a single mother with an income derived from pit bull terrier fighting. He was one of the richest men in the country. He had read that some women were moved by morals, but like the Beluga argali argali, he'd believe it when he saw it. He really hoped it wasn't going to come down to the lying thing.

By the door she said, 'You *lied* to me.'

Tim groaned.

Natasha said, 'Come on if you're coming. I've got to lock up.'

'What about Igor?'

'He's on the roof, he's got his own key.'

At the lift a man in a khaki army uniform smiled at Natasha. She smiled back. He was clinging to a bag, which at first, given his clothes, Tim took to contain grenades. Then he saw they were bread rolls.

'Who's that?'

Natasha said. 'He works as a security guard in the bread shop.'

'Your bread shop has a security guard?'

'Sure. Anyway, why should you care?' said Natasha, very sarcastic. 'I mean, it's not like you're the President or anything. Oops, sorry.'

On the pavement he said, 'Natasha, will you let up a minute?' Whitey was straining on his leash. Tim knew from previous walks that the lead was the one contribution that the GAI officer had made to the family home. It was designed in case Whitey got caught up when running alongside the car. If he really tugged, he came off it.

The streets were quiet but it was still early. There was a huddled flea market on one corner, a couple of old cars parked by a kiosk. The only movement was two beggars – a father in a striped army vest with no legs who propelled himself by his knuckles on a homemade cart. His war wound made him the same height as his eight-year-old son, to whom he was speaking as if to an adult. Tim thought the children of disabled war veterans must grow up quickly. In the background the jagged screams of kids in the city swimming pool could be heard.

Natasha hadn't seen the beggar. 'Hot, isn't it?' she said in a matter-of-fact way. 'Has your water gone off yet? No one in this *microrayon* had hot water this month.' She made a sarcastic face. 'I guess you don't have to worry about that, though.'

Tim pulled her elbow. 'What is making you this upset? The fact that I'm President or that I told a tiny white lie? Christ, I thought women were supposed to be turned on by important men.'

Natasha stopped in her tracks and turned to Tim. If you drew a vertical line between his belly button and shoulder she would have come halfway up. It was an exaggerated look of earnestness that made him think he'd got her beat. It also made him realise how much he didn't want to lose her.

'I'll tell you what it is,' she said. She looked around. The lead was fully extended, but she couldn't see Whitey. 'Where's he gone?

Oh my God, where's he disappeared to? Quick, do something.'

Tim scoured the landscape between the low-rises. 'Look, stay calm. All you have to do is follow the lead. Where does it go? Pull it.'

She yanked it hard. The leash was strained taut. 'He must be stuck somewhere. I'll just . . .'

She kept pulling. It gave way at the same time that a car backfired. Momentarily, she was catapulted backwards, off balance. They both looked down at the lead; it was limp like a line that had lost its kite. Natasha looked at him, her voice bitter. 'This is your fault.'

For the second time that morning Tim thought she was being unfair. He said, 'Don't worry, babe, I'll find the dog. Give me the lead.'

He looked round the lunar landscape. The leash curled across the burnt grass and round a climbing frame. One end led to nowhere in particular, while the other was attached to him. Viewed from above it would have been like one of those games in a kid's puzzle book – which string led to the bad man? In this case everything pointed at Tim.

III

On the second floor of the Belugastan police headquarters Kolya said, 'Can you meet me there in five?' As he spoke he drummed his fingers impatiently on his desk.

'At five?' asked Anna.

'No, in five minutes. I'm sorry to rush you, ma'am. What you might not be aware of is that crimes are most often solved in the first twenty-four hours.' Kolya winked at Tatyana, who was leaning against the door jamb, picking her teeth. 'I need to get to the scene of the crime immediately. You are a key witness.'

'But I wasn't even there.'

It was a wail that smacked of insubordination.

'Do you want to be treated as a hostile witness in court?' asked Kolya.

'I don't want to be treated in court as any sort of witness. I'm busy.'

'Miss Arbatova, I will see you outside Come Dancing in five minutes or you will be on a contempt charge.'

'How can I be on a contempt charge?' Anna was sure that only applied to courts.

'I have made my ruling, Miss Arbatova.'

He put the phone down. He felt a warm bristle of pride. Colonel Nikolai Pertsov of the Belugastan National Police was determined to get the American woman back. Since he was on a roll, he thought he might as well press home the advantage.

He looked towards the door. 'What have you decided about my washing, Tatyana?'

'I've told you, a dollar a kilo, and that doesn't include underwear. You pay for the powder. If it's Russian powder the price goes up to two dollars a kilo. Those are my rates.'

'It's daylight robbery.'

'Fine, wash your own clothes.'

'Two dollars for three kilos.'

'No way, the hot water's off.'

Kolya shook his head. How many great detectives of the twentieth century had to wear their underwear three days in a row, inside and out, to make full use of it. It was undignified, especially in his line of work. What if there was an accident?

'Come on then, we'll stop by the lock-ups on the way.' He picked up his jacket from the back of his chair.

'I'm warning you, any dirty Y-fronts and I throw the whole lot out,' warned Tatyana.

Anna flicked her mobile back into her purse and went outside. Dominic and her grandmother were sitting under an apple tree drinking black tea. Anna softened. Dominic had even managed an entire bowl of the kasha and sour milk her grandmother had cooked for breakfast. The language difference didn't seem to hamper them. Her grandmother pointed to things and said their name in Russian. Then Dominic mispronounced them and they laughed.

She said to Dominic, 'That was that idiot detective on the phone. He wants to see me at Come Dancing. I should go. I've got some paperwork to do in any case. Do you want to come?'

Dominic was wearing a white T-shirt and chinos. His feet were bare. Anna was a sucker for men's feet. Dominic's were suntanned brown with an ant's trail of dark hair leading to perfectly formed toes. Tim's toes had been irregular, the third one actually bigger than the first. The nails had been square. In her opinion, it was the sort of thing on which successful marriages hinged. As for respect and love, she looked elsewhere.

He wasn't as muscular as Tim, but in the cotton T-shirt she could make out the shape of his long spine and the crease of dark skin in the back of his neck. They were good signs. Very soon she would have to start wearing her lucky knickers.

'Come Dancing?' he said. 'That's near the hotel, isn't it?'

'Mmm.' Anna sat on the arm of her grandmother's chair. Due to the heat the old lady was wearing a Nike baseball cap on Anna's insistence. Anna studied Dominic. When he looked down, his eyes paused for a second too long and his eyelashes cast a shadow on his cheek.

'That's where the yurt people are. Maybe I shouldn't. Is it OK if I stay here?'

'Oh! I forgot. Of course you can't, no, you stay here and keep Granny company. I will not be long.' Anna turned to her grandmother and said, in Russian, 'I'm going into town. It's OK if he stays here, isn't it?'

'Of course, darling. I like him. So do you.'

'Oh, for God's sake, I felt sorry for him. He's being persecuted by yurt—' She stopped. 'Actually it's quite a long story and I must fly. Will you be OK?'

'Of course.'

'Don't feed him too much kasha.' Anna kissed the top of the cap and stroked her shoulder.

She waved at Dominic and delved into her shoulder bag for the car keys. As she set off to the car, parked further up the dirt track, her grandmother called her back. 'Anoushka, I almost forgot, what with all the confusion. I went to the Pushkinskaya flat to check on the tortoises. There was a man there.'

Anna looked horrified. 'And?'

'I'm afraid I might have disabled him with a lettuce.'

'Oh, Christ,' said Anna.

'What's the matter?' asked Dominic.

Anna ignored him. 'Give me the spare key,' she said. 'Now.'

IV

Stella Anne was a religious woman. It had been her unerring belief that had got her through her marriage; faith, and the ground-up Prozac. She knew the Good Lord would lead them out of the sewer somehow. What she was not expecting as a conduit from God was help in the shape of a large, muscular pit bull terrier. The dog entered their lives on page 216 of Dr Spock, coping with their first day at school.

As a rule Stella Anne hadn't liked pit bull terriers since she'd split up a fight outside a Pasadena diner. While one of the owners, an accountant, had drawn a loaded pistol from his breast pocket, she had sprayed the animals with soda from a siphon taken from the diner. The memory of the trails of saliva and the rat-like incisors lived with her. And that was just the accountant.

Luckily, Sonya had no such qualms. The minute the dog plumped down beside her, too startled or winded to bark, she started to coo like a mother with her newborn.

'Gee, honey, you be careful,' said Stella Anne, instinctively edging away. 'They can be dangerous animals.'

'No, no,' said Sonya. 'He good boy. Good boys pay well.'

'You betcha,' said Stella Anne, who had grown accustomed, even fond, of the youngster's homespun philosophies.

Sonya was petting the dog, saying, 'Good dog. You prefer blue or pink? Dark colours best.'

Two things occurred to Stella Anne with the advent of the dog: firstly, that if things got very bad they could eat him, and secondly that he would warm them if they had to spend another night there. It was only after she'd settled down to try to doze off that the third possibility came to her. The dog had fallen through the manhole and what had come down could go up again.

'Honey, do you have a lipstick on you?' she asked Sonya. As she spoke she mimed a ring round the outside of her mouth.

Sonya said in a shaky voice, '*Blow job?*'

'Heavens, sweetheart, the things you do come out with,' said Stella Anne. 'No, lipstick.' She made the charade of a small cylindrical object.

Sonya shrugged but squeezed her hand into her jeans pocket and came out with a blue and gold mascara case labelled Channel.

'That'll do just fine, sweetheart,' said Stella Anne and started to rip the acknowledgements page out of the Dr Spock book.

She knew the message ought to be in Russian, but she couldn't trust Sonya to write anything that would make much sense, so she wrote, using the mascara wand in English, 'Please help, we have been kidnapped and are in the sewer.' She reread it. Somehow it should say more. She wrote 'p.t.o.', flipped the paper over and wrote, 'One of us is an American.' She smiled. That should do it. She gestured to Sonya that she wanted to attach the note to the dog's collar. Sonya deftly unbuckled the collar. The dog was more placid than Stella Anne had expected. Maybe it was still in shock.

The next bit was going to be tough. She had to somehow hurl the pit bull through the manhole cover. Kneeling on all fours, she started to crawl towards the animal. The dog growled low and fierce. Sonya cooed harder. It was good luck that, as Stella Anne lunged for the beast, the cover above them was jerked back and a rope dropped down. Stella Anne stopped crawling and twisted herself protectively towards Sonya as the man slid down the rope in a practised military way. His size filled the space, accompanied by his leathery smell. He was wearing a balaclava, though Stella Anne could see his pink rubbery lips poking through the mouth slit, forming angry words she couldn't understand. Stella Anne reached for Sonya's hand. The pit bull, only recently settled, started to bark. In shock the man reached out with the butt of a pistol and smashed it over the dog's head. Then Sonya started to whimper. The man was wearing woollen gloves and black combat pants. He unlocked the padlock on the steel vault door and, pushing them from behind with the gun, made them walk forwards.

V

By midday Anna had checked the Pushkinskaya Ulitsa flat. While there was evidence – a half-unpacked Samsonite suitcase, a short-band radio and Hilfiger moisturiser – that Easton was still in residence, the man himself was absent. He had disappeared, along with the contents of one of the cardboard boxes full of tortoises. When it came down to it, there wasn't much she could do. The news that her grandmother had been responsible for the American's temporary incapacity came as a relief to her. And today's absence meant that at least he must have been well enough to move. Unless the tortoises had eaten him, and she didn't think that was possible.

The reconstruction of Sonya's abduction outside Come Dancing had been predictably unsuccessful. The detective had used Anna as the victim, making her walk up and down the pavement in front of 'would-be' witnesses – his phrase. It had caused a cacophony of wolf whistles among the lads who were camped out drinking beer on the steps of the theatre, but not much else. One boy, pale with platinum hair, said he thought he'd seen a black jeep drive past at the time, possibly with the letter Z in the registration. That, as the detective had pointed out, didn't narrow the field in a country which had more Cherokees than a Red Indian reservation. Anna had smiled at that. She wondered if she ought to be worried about Sonya, then she decided against it. For all she knew she'd saved up enough money to get a visa for Canada and skipped the country to join her batty cousin. It did happen, strippers weren't renowned for their loyalty to their employers.

She glanced in at the newspaper kiosk as she crossed the square. She had a sugar low and wanted an ice cream. Anna was rarely moved by the headlines in *Belugastan Today* but today their lunchtime edition caught her eye.

The headline was 'Election Announced', then underneath in smaller font the strapline said 'Candidates line up'. There was a large picture of Zhubelovski, the one he used for all his publicity shots with the facial warts air-brushed out, and then a smaller one of Dominic with his foot on a sheep. She did a double take and bought a copy.

Halfway through the article, which mainly recited the as yet unpublished virtues of Zhubelovski, she wondered where this left Tim. She hadn't seen him for so long, maybe he had decided to throw in the towel with politics. Deep in thought, she looked up slowly. Maybe it was the heat, possibly she'd been working too hard, but she could have sworn that across the square she saw the editor of the paper leading a black and white pony from the building.

VI

'I mean it's fucking ridiculous.' Tim spoke as he hauled a cardboard box from the top of a skip labelled 'Soviet property'. Something told him that Soviet property was an oxymoron, but today he had other worries. 'It's probably not even legal.'

The skip was empty but for a huge advertising mock-up of

German laxatives. Tim looked at Erik, who was wearing a baseball cap with Lakers on it and swigging from a can of gin and tonic. A copy of *Belugastan Today* was rolled in his right hand like a baton.

Erik said, 'Are you talking about the dog or the election? If it's the election, I'm sorry, but I didn't think you'd be that upset. If it's the dog, then it's a lesson for you to stop getting involved with kooky females.'

'So this is my fault?'

'Look, if you want to go for the presidency again, just say so. Just because the foreigner is running doesn't mean you won't get in.'

'How do you think it makes me feel seeing the candidates for my job in the paper, with no mention of me?' Tim used two discarded iron poles like giant chopsticks to pick up half a lavatory seat in a desultory way.

Erik protested, 'People obviously assume you're running again.'

'And Zhubelovski.'

'And Zhubelovski,' said Erik, 'but you can't blame me for that.' He looked around. Tim's pale linen suit had a grass mark down the front of it. 'Besides, it's not as if you are.' He took another swig from the can.

'What?' Tim replied miserably, flinging a brick in the direction of a pile of rubble. He was carrying the dog's lead in his left hand like a lasso.

'You're not exactly *presidential* these days. I mean, what exactly are you doing now?'

'Looking for this dog.'

'My point entirely. How long do you think Lionel Jospin spends moving rubble on the Champs Élysées looking for lost pets?'

'Who's Lionel Jospin?' asked Tim, grumpily.

'Also,' continued Erik, 'what about some perspective here? You're no Nelson Mandela. Your presidency has served its purpose and now it's time to move on.'

'If I don't find this dog,' muttered Tim, 'I'll be moving as far as the morgue.'

In sympathy Erik kicked a couple of beer bottles across the wasteland. Tim looked at him. 'Thanks for your help.'

'Where is the owner of the pooch?' Erik asked.

'She's too upset,' said Tim. 'She's gone home.'

'Great. How long have you been at it?'

'Since I got back from taking her home.'

'It could well have gone miles,' said Erik, trying to cheer.

'I know that.'

They walked round the skip shoulder to shoulder in silence. Tim's foot narrowly avoided a used condom.

He said, 'Why is Zhubelovski standing?'

'He's a crook, all crooks stand for political office. It gives them respectability and immunity from prosecution.' Erik looked at him. '*You* should know more about that than most.'

'Yeah, but why now? He's always been a crook.'

'Who knows? Honestly, mate, I thought you'd be pleased. You do know why I did it, don't you?'

'Remind me,' said Tim. 'It's to do with your demented sheep hunting.'

'Sort of, but like our own little insurance scheme, to stop us getting sued for millions.'

'Who's getting sued?'

'No one yet, as long as we stick to the plan,' said Erik. 'OK. This is what might have happened. After a week of virtual house arrest, the Irishman goes home, gets a lawyer and sues us not only for the invasion of the yurt people but for not ever having seen a sheep in the whole time he was here.' He paused to draw breath and take a swig from the can. He carried on, 'Believe me, this happens. I read about an American who bankrupted Paraguay after spraining his ankle on a miniature bottle of rum.'

'But that would be his insurance company that had to pay, right?' Tim had given up the search and was sitting with his back against the skip.

'Wrong,' said Erik. 'They sue everyone. So this way we make it look like the hunter wanted to stand for President. If anything happens, we point out that he's even got his picture in the paper. He complains, we say the guy had delusions of power. You never know, we could even call him a spy.' The more Erik thought about that, the more he liked it.

'Then we'd be in the clear,' said Tim.

'Right.'

'OK, Einstein, there's one other thing you've forgotten.'

'Which is?'

'Which is that there's a real live American that has gone missing, possibly dead in this country. How are you going to explain that?'

'I was coming to that.'

Tim pushed himself to his feet with his elbows against the skip and started to walk again. Erik followed him – he crushed the G&T can in his hand and kicked it with his left foot. With his right hand he drew a small Beretta from a shoulder holster and aimed.

'For Christ's sake, don't do that here,' Tim said. 'You might shoot—'

'I don't believe it,' Erik said, looking over the dusty field. 'The can has disappeared.'

'You missed, more like.'

'No, seriously.' Erik was a few metres away from Tim. 'Look here, there's a bloody great hole.'

Tim walked towards him. 'Must you swear so much? This is a playground.' He wasn't fooled by Erik's diversionary tactics to get him away from the list of presidential candidates.

Tim looked down. 'Christ alive,' he said. 'You're right.'

VII

Dominic wouldn't have heard his mobile go off had he not stepped inside for a jug of water. He liked Anna's grandmother but as with all old people, even without a language barrier and her sharing a quarter gene pool with the woman he loved, an hour was his limit. When he heard the phone he had a doughy feeling inside because he knew it must be Anna. He was wrong.

'Peach, what the hell do you think you're playing at?' It was Tony. If he was demonstrating a new Japanese management technique, it was definitely on the Hiroshima end of the scale.

'Tony, hello. Hi, I tried to call you yesterday.'

'And?'

'And I couldn't get through.'

'So?'

'I, um, what do you mean, Tony? I thought we were on a deadline. I had to get the piece across ASAP.'

'Yes, Dominic. So you did what?'

Dominic was getting sick of questions that implied failure, especially when full-scale praise was in order.

'I gave it straight to the paper.'

'The *Daily Rail*?'

'Yeah. You see, my mate Bob works there and – look, Tony, what's your problem? I was trying to get the muff divers off your back.'

'Oh, you've definitely done that.' Tony was both apoplectic and sarcastic.

'So what's the problem?'

'The problem is you've got every animal agency from the WWF to fucking Sturgeons R Us on my back. It's already been picked up by the *Standard*.'

'What has? What are you talking about?'

'What am I talking about? Do you have a fax machine there?'

'No, well, yes, there's one in the hotel.'

'Give me the number.' When Tony got very angry it brought out his Welsh accent.

'Hang on,' said Dominic. 'Look, why don't you just read it to me?'

'Because I want you to see all of it. How you, Dominic Peach, have single-handedly made SOS the laughing stock of every right thinking member of the animal welfare community.'

'Now hang on there a minute, I—'

'Fax number.'

Dominic read from his Ryman's notebook, into which he'd transcribed the number from a box of Palace Hotel matches. 'Eight, nine, seven, four, double five.'

'Code?'

'Dunno.'

'Dominic, I think it's safe to say you can consider yourself no longer an employee of Save Our Species.'

'But—'

'Principally because as of tomorrow there will be no more SOS. Not only has the Lottery grant been withdrawn, it has been done with the additional proviso that the muff divers open a refuge for the victims of lesbian on lesbian violence here.'

'In the SOS office, you mean, like a joint venture?'

'Yes, in the bloody office but not with SOS, you moron. We're out on our backsides. Think about that.' He paused, though Dominic could tell he was mid-flow. 'Thanks to you, Dominic, it's species advancement nil, dykes one. Happy? I'm sending the fax.' The line went dead.

Dominic felt stung. What could have happened to his story? He walked pensively back into the garden. He was intrigued enough to try a trip to the Palace, yurt people or not. The evening before, when he'd arrived, he'd seen an old bike outside the dacha, propped in the porch with a crossbar. He put his address book gingerly on the chipped table. He looked at Anna's grandmother, who was dozing.

Dominic said, 'I'm sorry to bother you, but I don't suppose I could possibly borrow that bicycle on the veranda?' He mimed a bicycle and the old woman smiled.

He slipped on a pair of trainers and set off along the dirt track into town.

Georgina Wroe

VIII

Oksana Menshikova graduated from Moscow Art School with a distinction. The distinction she had from the other students was that she was more prepared to perform oral sex on the male tutors. To Oksana fellatio was simply an art form as valid as any other. While her fellow students joined American advertising agencies or set themselves up on Red Square painting for tourists, she maintained the savage irony of real art. She was a product of post-Soviet society and yet like all great artists she stood apart, as an observer.

Oksana often stood apart because very few people, employers as well as friends, could withstand her monologues, or her tolerance for soft drugs. Many simply said if she wanted to chronicle the ironies of post-communist Russia she should go off and chronicle them. Others were more brutal. To date, as an artist, the only catalogue she had created had been a catalogue of failed romances which had driven her southwards until visa restrictions prevented her going further.

She met Pavel during a piece of performance art in Peace Square. It was a one-woman show detailing the collectivisation of the kulaks using twentieth-century consumer props and some, though not total, nudity. Pavel, depressed since the abandonment of the Mir space shuttle, was the one who best helped calm the crowd riot.

Apart from painting matryoshkas for the Seattle company, Oksana advertised in the local paper under 'Artist, 39, all commissions considered. Nudity appreciated though not essential. Best rates.'

Oksana accepted the proposal on the phone at 10.10 a.m., so early that she'd not even had her first Winston of the day, never mind a joint. So early it was difficult to remember her name, never mind what she did. Luckily the man on the phone helped.

'I need you to finish a self-portrait. Do you do portraits?'

'Portraits, as in canvas, or portrait as in performance?' The

266

phone was by the bed. Sunlight came into the room in concentric circles through tie-dye curtains.

'You do *performance* portraits?'

'Sure, man.'

'What, you act out what you think the person looks like?'

Oksana hadn't thought of that. It sounded interesting. Performance portraits in the past had meant using her naked body as the canvas for others to paint. In her opinion it had revolutionised the whole model/artist dynamic. In Saratov, one pensioner using soured cream and a roller claimed it had redefined the way he looked at art. Or at least that had been Oksana's interpretation.

Oksana said, 'Not exactly.' Pavel passed her a joint. She inhaled deeply.

The man said, 'You just have to finish off a self-portrait for a client.'

'Radical. Self-portraits by another artist.' She looked over at Pavel, who grinned encouragement and nodded sagely.

The man said, 'Just shut up. If you'll do it, I'll send a car for you. Tell me where you live.'

Oksana reeled off an address and a list of instructions, fluent like a drunk in a taxi.

The man asked her to repeat a couple of roads.

'Is that out by the Hippodrome?'

'Kind of.'

'It'll be there at midday. Make sure you're ready.'

He was just about to hang up when Oksana said, 'Will I need to bring my paints?'

The man whistled. 'Of course you'll need to bring your own paints. What sort of a fucking artist are you?' Then he hung up.

'A professional,' said Oksana and took the joint out of Pavel's hand. 'Peasant.'

By midday Oksana was in a mood conducive to portraiture. She'd taken two Estonian Quaaludes and a Russian Valium to steady her and the best part of a bottle of vodka to ignite her imagination. By twelve thirty a black jeep had dumped her outside a house so big it reminded her of the Hermitage, which like the dacha in front of her she considered bourgeois. The door was chestnut wood and arched.

Two hired hands stood on either side. Under dark glasses they had the hurt, determined look of men recently disciplined. Or maybe they always looked like that, Oksana thought. She puffed on a full-strength Winston cigarette.

'If anyone should ask you, you've never been here.' The driver was the same man who'd set up the commission on the phone.

'Who am I going to tell?' replied Oksana sullenly, thinking that in terms of hassle it rivalled a recent project to replicate the nouveau riche in Gzhel pottery. The mobile phones always came off in the firing.

Her model was spread out lying on his side, waiting for her on a chaise longue under the slatted window of a room on the second floor. Even for Oksana, who was no stranger to the human body in its myriad forms – including the Saratov pensioner who insisted he got naked too – *model* was a loose description. He was middle-aged and warty like a toad. His torso was as undefined as an Easter Island statue. A giant toad in green silk boxer shorts with a white stomach flopping to one side. Luckily Oksana's mood, due to the Valium, was benign.

'You know who that is?' asked the driver.

'He can't speak?' asked Oksana, putting her paints on a stone floor.

'He can speak, he's just choosing not to,' said the driver roughly. 'Answer the question.'

Oksana looked at him. He was familiar. It was a Pavlovian thing; when she saw him she instinctively had the taste of vodka in her mouth. Or maybe that happened anyway.

'No.'

'*No?* You don't get out much, right?'

'I am an artist and most of my cognitive processes are internal.'

'Yeah, well, keep them that way. You see this?' The driver whipped a muslin cloth off an easel. Behind it was a watercolour, the type you got experimenting with paintbrushes and higher apes. A white splodge in the foreground, trees in the distance.

'Primitive,' she said.

'It's not finished.'

'You're not kidding.'

'Don't be a smart-arse. You've got to finish it. Make it so it looks like the gentleman on the sofa.'

Oksana protested, 'Can't I just start again? I can't finish a work started by someone else.'

'Listen, lady, you've got to. Otherwise it wouldn't be a self-portrait.'

'But it's ridiculous.'

'Five hundred dollars,' said the driver.

'Seven fifty.'

'Six fifty.'

'Done,' said Oksana. 'Where can I wash my brushes?'

Throughout the portrait the man on the sofa didn't open his mouth. He maintained the rigidity of an unblinking lizard sunning himself on a rock. Apart from an occasional self-satisfied smile, and the inflation and deflation of his gut, she might have thought he was dead. He seemed oblivious to her being in the room.

Oksana's palette was a chipped dinner plate that had been used as an ashtray. She didn't mind the ash, in fact mixed with saliva it had a charcoal feel to it. She wanted to portray the toad man's air of superiority as well as the toadying attitude of his lackeys, through an olive-green watercolour wash. Like all great portrait artists, her job was to present the whole man. She looked around. That also meant his trappings of wealth. The juvenile Kandinsky lithograph on the back wall, the hideously rococo Fabergé eggs she'd seen on an inlaid table.

Because the toad man had ignored her persistent requests for an ashtray she had to flick her cigarette butts out of the window behind him. Like all Oksana's packets of 'going out' cigarettes, her twenty Winston consisted of ten tobacco cigarettes and ten custom-made ones where the tobacco had been swapped for high-quality skunk. It was a fiddly job that Pavel, with his physicist's eye for detail, excelled at. She chose to smoke most of the skunk hanging out of the window.

That was why at just after 3 p.m. she saw, at least she thought she saw, a young woman with pink hair, carrying a pit bull terrier in her arms, emerge from a manhole in the courtyard below them. The young girl was followed by an older woman in an outfit fashioned from the flora of the forests. They staggered, blinking, when they emerged. Behind them a man in black leather wearing a black balaclava hauled himself up. He used his right hand to steady himself; as he did so he laid a pistol on the ground. Oksana looked away and looked back. The women were being forced into a split door, like a stable, at the back of the house.

Oksana frowned and threw the roach out of the window. The man on the chaise longue was coughing impatiently, signalling she should get back to work. As he coughed, his slab of stomach wobbled. She giggled and went back to the easel. She suddenly had an idea where to paint the Fabergé eggs. She giggled a bit more. After all, Russian slang for testicles was egg. He might not like it, but she was the artist.

IX

Dominic thought he knew the way back from Anna's grandmother's house to the Palace Hotel. It was just a case of keeping to the dirt road until you hit the weather-cracked tarmac that led to the main square. The pot-holed track was edged by silver birches with bark that was blowtorch blistered. Beyond that, flat marshy plains burnt by the sun filled the landscape as far as the mountains in the distance, with just one crag still covered in snow.

Dominic cycled round a parked truck bursting with watermelons, where a man with a dark face, creased like a well-worn belt, hacked the fruit open with a machete. Dominic was aiming for the high-rises on the edge of town. Apart from an occasional slow Lada, there was no traffic. Nearer town he was overtaken by carelessly driven flashy jeeps.

Before his trip Dominic had imagined everyone in the former Soviet Union was poor, and yet some of the brick houses going up around Anna's grandmother's cottage were huge, like the Home Counties palaces of just married royals.

The polemic got him lost. He veered right, heading for the town centre, but the road ended in a pentagon shape of grey tower blocks. He spun the cycle, gearless and with a seat like a knife, round. He was drenched in salty sweat that got in his eyes and made them sting. After an hour, close to collapse, he stopped and paid ten dollars for a hunk of watermelon from a group of gypsies wearing an array of bright scarves and aprons that, from a distance, made them look like a giant basket of potpourri. Close up they weren't as fragrant.

Only after he'd left them, his stomach knotted with the fear of being completely lost, did Dominic realise the watermelon sellers were only a block away from Peace Square. The relief of seeing the Palace Hotel so near was tempered with the dread of an approaching two-lane junction. Dominic was unaware of the square, or the people in it.

When he looked up, the sight caused him to sway drunkenly on the bicycle. The moderate collection of yurt people had swollen overnight into something more akin to the final scenes of *Zulu Dawn*. Worse still, they were chanting *Dzhungar* and waving photographs on poles.

Head down and pushing his bicycle, he approached a group where a woman was nursing a baby. While the woman called on

271

her husband to wind the child, Dominic stole a glimpse at his placard. He couldn't read the writing but the picture was of him with the sheep, only blown up to poster size. Other, smaller, versions, clung to by children, seemed to have come directly from a newspaper.

Ahead of him the neon sign signalling the safety of the Palace Hotel beckoned. He reached in his pocket for the last of the duty-free Camels. To cross the square unmolested, he returned to the watermelon people and paid fifty dollars for a headscarf and two aprons which stank of milk and smoke. Ten minutes later, one scarf knotted babushka-style under his chin and two covering his chinos, he was slouched in the Genghis Khan lounge behind a triple Ballantine's.

'You foreign? Here fax.' The receptionist's name tag said Nina over her left breast next to a Union Jack and the French flag. It also said next to a smiley face, 'I speak English.'

Dominic thanked her. Even the typeface on Tony's covering sheet looked angry. He waited for the whisky to take effect before he read it.

X

Anna's grandmother didn't know much about the odd young man but she liked him because she sensed he was in love with her granddaughter. Maybe that was just sentimentality, because on the whole she hated foreigners. It wasn't just xenophobia, her hatred was more tangible. Foreigners had caused nothing but upset in her life. Then again, Russians hadn't been much better. But that had been Stalin, and the coarse Georgian had made everyone suffer. As usual, thinking about the past made her pulse tremble in anger.

She pushed herself out of her chair using her knuckles on the table to steady herself. She paused halfway up and then stacked the teacups on a tray. Shaky from the heat and the memories, she knocked one over, spilling scaly black tea on the odd young man's address book. She cursed and pulled a handkerchief from her sleeve and started to mop at it. The pages were wet and so was the photograph. She picked it up by the corner to lay it out in the sun to dry. A glance turned into a look and she had to sit down again. She stared so long that her eyes ached and the picture started to go fuzzy around the edges.

CHAPTER ELEVEN

I

Tim called the dog three times before he told Erik to throw a lit match down the manhole.

Erik looked at him sideways. 'There's a rope, why don't you climb down?' The match hadn't illuminated much apart from a gloomy sense of damp walls and the promise of rats.

'I'm not climbing down a sewer.' Tim was lying down with his head peering in. 'If the dog had fallen down we'd hear him barking.'

Erik wanted to avoid a scenario that had disaster written all over it. Since the photo shoot with Larissa and the horse, where his reflective umbrella had been trampled under hoof, he'd finished with the absurd, even if the pictures did promise a unique chapter in the development of soft porn.

'Not if he's broken a leg and is unconscious,' said Erik. 'Or dead.'

'Cheer me up, why don't you?' Tim pulled his head out of the hole, his hair falling at unusual angles, which only made Erik more convinced he didn't want anything to do with the scheme. To make up for the umbrella, Larissa had promised to go out with him to the kino centre where they were playing a Bruce Willis double bill.

Tim continued, 'Have you got a lighter? I think I can see something.' He threw a stone down to see how deep it was.

'I think that only works in wells,' said Erik.

'Why don't you do something useful, like ask at that kiosk if he's got a torch.'

'OK.' Erik got up. Tim wasn't expecting compliancy. He stuck his head back down the hole. It was possible the dog had fallen down it. If it had tugged hard then the lead would have come off automatically. Tim rolled over onto the grass. The wasteland was empty. In the far corner an empty sea-green jeep was melting in the heat. Four by fours tended to hunt in packs; a solitary car, away from a block of flats, meant a gang out collecting extortion money. It was as close to taxation as the country got.

Tim stared up at the sky. A light wind was whipping itself into something stronger as it was funnelled between the high-rises. He was pissed off with Erik out of habit. The news of his political demise had been a shock, but on reflection, having a list of presidential candidates that didn't include him could pan out very nicely. What better way to ingratiate himself with Natasha than to claim he'd renounced political life for her? It was almost true; he had had enough of politics. Let Zhubelovski run the country.

With his head on the ground, Tim heard the crunch of Erik's return before he opened his eyes.

'Torch,' he said, flicking the button on and off. 'It's costing ten bucks an hour plus batteries, so whatever you need to do, hurry up.'

Tim pulled his legs into his chest and released them, letting the weight rock him into a sitting position. Then he put his hand out for Erik to grab.

'Why can't she find her own dog?' asked Erik. Erik was hot and fractious from having to walk everywhere. The Dneiper was still in the mountains.

'Who?'

'Natasha, or whatever her name is.'

Tim's sigh was exaggerated. 'Erik, haven't you ever wanted to do something for someone just because you wanted to help them? Make them happy?'

'No.' Then Erik thought. 'Well, yeah, maybe once.' He paused. 'I take it you and Anna are history now?'

Tim didn't hear. His head was down the sewer shaft with the torch.

'Shit,' he said, bobbing up. 'My RayBans have fallen down there.'

'What can you see?' asked Erik.

'Not much. There's something down there but I don't know if it's the dog or not.'

'Is it smelly?'

'It's a sewer,' said Tim, his head down. 'What do you think?'

When he came up again, Tim's face was red and open-pored, his features puffy from too much blood. He said, 'One of us is going to have to go down there.'

'That means you.' Erik was adamant. 'I've got a date tonight.'

Tim flattened his hair. 'I don't like pulling rank, but remind me again which one of us is the President?'

That did it. 'You are,' said Erik maliciously, 'until Sunday.'

Tim frowned and his eyebrows went into L shapes. 'What do you mean, Sunday?'

'That's when the elections are going to be. Zhubelovski wants them as soon as possible.'

Tim, shocked, sat up and rested his arms on his elbows. He reminded Erik that Sunday was the National Day Parade.

'So?' said Erik. 'What difference will a couple of fire engines and a primary school parade make?'

'So, it's a bit early, that's all.' Tim had less than three days as President, unless he stood again.

Erik saw he was upset. Recanting, he said, 'OK. Look, why don't we both go down the hole? How about that?'

Tim looked at him. 'You go first,' he said sulkily.

Erik hitched his shorts up higher round his waist. 'You don't think there's going to be anything horrible down there, do you?'

'Like what?'

'Bodies and shit.'

'Shit, definitely, bodies, probably.' Tim pushed him in the back and told him to get on with it.

'You shine the torch,' said Erik.

When he was halfway down the hole, the kiddies' climbing frame that the rope had been attached to jolted an arm's length towards it. Erik's scream was muted by echo.

'How deep is it?' called Tim.

Silence.

Tim called again. 'Is the dog down there?'

When the voice came back it was distorted by damp air. 'Come and have a look,' shouted Erik. 'It's weird.'

'Yeah, but is the dog there?'

Silence. It was not the right time for Erik to throw a moody. Tim knew he'd have to go down as well. He cursed. When he was little Tim had liked climbing ropes because the sensation of the cord between his legs was erotic. It was his first sexual charge, before he moved on to trees. Given the upshot of his latest amorous liaison, he wished he'd stuck with branches and goal posts. They were less demanding.

The hole was no deeper than five metres, which meant that as soon as he'd started dangling he was practically there. The space was enclosed, manmade with iron walls like a septic tank. There were a couple of cushions on the floor and above the smell of ammonia, the smell of people.

Tim said, 'It's OK, it must just be a hideout for kids or homeless people.'

Erik, with his head down, said, 'Yeah, but look at this.'

He held out Whitey's dog collar and shone the torch on it.

'What the hell – where's the dog then?' In the torchlight Erik's face cast a ghastly shadow.

'That's not all,' said Erik. 'What do you make of this?' He showed him the Dr Spock book.

'Kids,' said Tim.

'So how do you explain this?' He handed him the acknow-ledgement page with the cry for help in English. Behind Erik the steel door was still ajar. 'How many people do you know around here who would leave a message in English?' Erik grabbed the torch and flashed it along the sewer. 'I reckon we've found that American woman.' Erik's face was gritted. 'Come on, this is our chance to stop the world's worst PR disaster since Chernobyl.'

'*And* retrieve the dog?' said Tim, sceptical. 'Maybe we should get some help.'

'Like who? Colonel Pertsov of the Belugastan police?' Erik said.

Tim hung back, unconvinced. Erik grabbed him. 'Look, do you want this bloody dog back or not?'

Tim didn't see that he had that much to lose.

II

Dominic wasn't sure how it could have happened; how an animal welfare story could have become so warped. On instinct he'd crumpled the fax after he'd read it. Two minutes later he tried again. It read:

Caviar – Are You Paying Ova The Odds?
British consumers are paying up to twenty times more for caviar than other Europeans, the *Daily Rail* can reveal. Despite millions in IMF loans from British taxpayers, we uncover the truth about Russians' champagne lifestyle. How the so-called peasants are dining out on the exclusive fish eggs night after night. Today, the *Daily Rail* asks, why?

British holidaymaker Dominic Peach said: 'I can't believe it. You can buy it on every street corner here. It's so cheap. I'd come back, just for the caviar.' Mr Peach, 29, works for an Acton-based charity called SOS. Wiltshire-based caviar expert Bruce Harris, 42, said: 'There's no doubt that we are paying too much. Why should Russians get it so cheap?'

The piece went on to detail how the cost of an ounce of caviar and the price of a brand new Ford Mondeo differed in Britain, Belgium, Denmark and Canada. The evidence was compelling; Britons were paying too much. Readers were asked to phone an 0800 hotline if they agreed that British consumers were disadvantaged when it came to fish eggs. It also called on fed-up caviar eaters to canvas their MPs.

Every time Dominic read it he felt his lower intestine twist, not because he was responsible for it, but because it portrayed him as such a loser. The image of Dominic Peach he'd spent more than twenty-five years constructing was in tatters – no longer the urbane sophisticate but the bargain hunter who crossed the Channel to buy slabs of cat food from Calais hypermarkets. The sole reason he worked for SOS was to cultivate an image of a 1990s great white hunter, with the same derring-do but with none of the inhumanity. The article in the *Rail* had landed a body blow to his reputation. Overnight he'd become the sort of person who snipped money-off vouchers from free newspapers. Being three thousand miles away helped. He no longer wanted to go home.

Oksana's artistic expression had never before met with such negativity. It was a poor reflection on turn-of-the-millennium Russian culture that irony, the foundation stone of all great modern art, should be so dead. That was what she was saying when she hit the pavement at just after 2 p.m. She yelled the word *peasants* to them as the jeep pulled away but the only people who took any notice of her were, ironically enough, a huge group of peasants camping out on Peace Square.

'Not you,' said Oksana apologetically as she stood up and dabbed saliva on a grazed knee. 'Those bourgeois pigs.' She stuck her middle finger up at the tarmac left in the jeep's wake. Because of the accumulative effect of the marijuana and the Valium, which relaxed her body and eased her fall, the sight of so many Belugi natives caused her very little angst. In fact as she sat gingerly on the corner of a bench, moving aside a jar of sour cream and half a cabbage, delving into her special packet of Winstons for another joint, she was hardly aware of them.

As she inhaled she muttered, 'They ask me to be the artist, yet they don't care for artistic expression.'

The artistic expression she referred to was replacing the model's testicles with depictions of two Fabergé eggs, and giving her subject the face of a toad, along with a mobile phone in a webbed hand. To her it was a perfect representation of the collapse of collective mentality in favour of oppressive individuality.

She spoke to no one in particular. 'Look around you. Crude materialism everywhere. This is what my art demonstrates.' She pulled on the joint and kept the smoke as long as she could in her lungs before she released it in a gasp. 'Everywhere, consumerism, advertising.' She looked up. 'Is advertising the only artistic expression of the age? Pah! I spit on them.' She spat on the pavement. Then with a clarity of thought brought on by the soft drugs, she saw the advertising billboard for Zhubelovski Vodka. There he was, the toad man himself, his grotesque features twelve feet tall and beaming at the square.

At the same time, closer to her field of vision, the photo-fit she had drawn of the missing American, nailed onto a telegraph pole under a plea to return a missing black cat, fluttered into view. With the benefit of time, even she could see its similarity to Ronald Reagan, but that was not the point. She saw how she could take her revenge on the cultural pygmy.

She slowly extended her left leg and tried some weight on it to see if she was still capable of walking. With the drugs and the fall, though mainly the drugs, she'd taken quite a pounding. At the head of the square, close to the Palace Hotel and at the foot of the Lenin memorial, an officer in uniform was creating a cordon out of what looked like dirty washing. He was trying to keep the crowds from spilling onto the main road by use of a megaphone. Oksana took him to be GAI until she got close up and saw the olive-green uniform of the Ministry of the Interior. She took another drag and stumbled towards him.

'Good afternoon,' said Oksana. 'I wish to report a very serious crime.'

The man spoke to her through the megaphone even though she was less than three feet away. 'Stand back, madam. I am in charge of crowd control and cannot permit you to come any further forward.'

Even when on a full-scale acid trip, things like this didn't always happen. She tried to remember the precise narcotic alchemy that had produced the effect for future use. Usually in these circumstances, Oksana would have sat down, smoked another joint and gone with the flow. But she had artistic indignity burning in her breast.

'But I have to report a crime.' As she'd approached the front of the square she'd ripped the wanted poster from the telegraph pole. She brandished it. 'It is regarding the disappearance of the American.'

The officer was still speaking through the loudspeaker but his voice had gone up half an octave. 'Please come through. My name is Colonel Nikolai Pertsov of the Belugastan police.'

'Hello.' Dominic hadn't seen Anna approach him. 'Why are you dressed like that?' she asked matter-of-factly.

His heart fell down a lift shaft.

'I didn't want the yurt people to see me,' said Dominic nervously. 'Have you seen how many of them there are?' Dominic's voice had an unfocused edge to it. He was feeling slightly numb around the brain. He looked at Anna. 'Why have they got pictures of me on sticks?'

'Ah, well, that's because you appear to be standing in the

Belugastan elections.' Anna was forthright. It wasn't the sort of information you could dress up.

'How come?' Dominic asked weakly.

Anna sat down next to him. 'Actually, you know, I don't know. Did you tell anyone you wanted to be President of Belugastan?'

'I don't think so.' Dominic suddenly felt unsure.

'Not on the mountains?'

'No!' He looked at her. 'Look, what am I going to do?'

Anna took his hand. 'Come on, let's go home. What can you do? Those crazy Belugi natives, ignore them! They can't stop you from flying home, can they?' She was wearing pedal pushers and a scoop neck T-shirt. The ease with which she could put him on the flight home worried him as much as returning to Britain. His heart sank to his lower intestine.

For the next seven minutes neither of them spoke. Then Anna smiled. 'Please, though, do me a favour?'

'Yes?' said Dominic.

'Take those ridiculous aprons off.' She flicked one up and her hand rested briefly on his groin. He couldn't tell if she'd noticed or not. Seconds later she said jauntily, 'Come on, we'll disappear out the back.'

'I can't,' said Dominic, struggling with a knot. 'My bike's parked round the corner.' He explained, embarrassed, that it wasn't his bike but her grandmother's.

Anna frowned and tapped her finger on the table. 'You can't leave it here, it belonged to my grandfather. We must be quick, though.'

He stood up too quickly and his head throbbed as if gripped in a vice. He doubted if there was any water left in his body, just a mixture of tea, watermelon juice and whisky. Since he'd arrived in the country the colour of his urine had ranged from weak tea on a good day to viscose amber today. He felt as if he was being reduced down, the way his mother made stock, to a more concentrated version of himself.

Outside, they skirted the edge of the hotel with Anna nearest the road. There was a smoky sour milk smell coming from the encampment. A couple of fires had been lit on the pavement and groups of men sat on their haunches, drinking vodka and spitting out sunflower husks. Their attitude, to Dominic, appeared malignant rather than adulatory.

Anna turned to him and took his hand. 'They've come from miles around,' she said. 'You should be pleased.'

Dominic kept his shoulder clamped to the hotel's cool marble cladding. As they turned the corner they relaxed enough for Dominic's shoulders to fall visibly. He exhaled. After the faceless sea of mankind they'd just left, he was amazed to see a set of features that he recognised.

It was the hippie woman with the phlegm who'd painted the photo-fit of Stella Anne. She was floppy like a rag doll, and was being held up by a policeman holding a loudspeaker. At every fourth step he paused and drew a hand over his forehead to mop up the sweat. Given the situation – that Dominic had been holding the hand of the woman he loved for an uninterrupted five minutes – they were an easy duo to ignore.

Away from the square, Anna and Dominic's pace had slackened. His palm in hers was sweaty so when they broke free level with the bicycle Dominic tried surreptitiously to dry it on his trousers. Which was why he didn't notice them, despite the half-human, half-animal noise that was their accompaniment. Later, Dominic thought it was because Anna's ear was more in tune with their dialect that she became aware of them first. Though after ten seconds the refrain was quite easy to pick up.

'Dzhun-gar, Dzhun-gar.' It came out as two distinct words.

Dominic felt his stomach back-flip. His mouth went dry. He turned to Anna.

'What are they doing? They can't—'

When the yurt people spilled round the corner Dominic saw that, predictably, the red pom-pom man was the chief rabble-rouser. The expressions of the crowd, taut faces with open mouths, looked more angry than worshipful. Dominic's knees buckled when he saw three men, led by the red pom-pom, break away from the crowd.

'Quick,' said Anna, hauling Dominic away by the hand. The grasp held as they split to run round a pile of horse manure. Anna led, dragging him towards a mosquito-brown Lada into which the policeman was trying to coax the hippie. When they got to the car, Anna hit the roof with her flattened palm.

'Get in,' yelled Anna. She pulled open an unlocked door and bundled Dominic onto the back seat while she opened the driver's seat.

The policeman's expression looked ironed out with shock. He said, 'I was just about to find—'

'Give me the keys,' Anna yelled over the roof of the car.

'But this is Belugastan national property.'

Before the sentence ended the policeman spotted the first of the yurt men appoaching. To make them easier to carry, they were holding their election banners waist high, giving the impression of battering rams. He wiped a line of sweat from the grooves of his forehead.

'Oh my goodness.' He shoved Oksana into the front passenger seat and started into the back next to Dominic.

'The keys!' Anna yelled again and the policeman bobbed up and hurled them at her. She jammed the car into first gear and pulled awat just seconds before the first fleecy tabard reached them.

Anna's foot was on the floor of the Lada. 'Can't this go any faster?'

'Relax,' said Dominic, 'they're not going to catch us now.' Anna looked at him in the rear mirror. He was clutching the back of the passenger seat. He'd trapped some of Oksana's hair in his clenched fists. When they went round the corner, her head was dragged back.

'Watch it, pig,' said Oksana.

'Do you mind if I ask a question?' Kolya was appreciating the opportunity to speak in English. Before he'd joined the police force he'd wanted to be an English teacher, but Kolya had grown up in Orphanage 126 and, in common with other orphans, he had been encouraged to repay his debt to society by going into public service. 'Why have you stolen my vehicle?'

Anna slipped the gear stick into third while she overtook a 1959 black Chiaka piled high with spindly furniture, probably a removal job. The elderly driver steered his worthless cargo with unwarranted care. Then Anna accelerated into fourth and the megaphone on Kolya's lap jammed into her back. She sat back sharply, hoping to dislodge it.

Kolya didn't wait for an answer. 'Having said that,' he smiled at Dominic, 'if you hadn't come upon me like this, I would have to have found you.'

'Really?' said Dominic, still pale with the start of a dehydration headache gnawing behind his eyes.

'I am acquainted with your lady friend.' Dominic liked the lady friend bit. He wondered if the detective was aware of the half-empty bag of dirty laundry between them. 'But I don't think we've met.' Kolya put his hand out to Dominic.

'Hello,' said Dominic. 'I'm with the hunting party.'

Kolya nodded. 'So you are acquainted with the American?'

'In a manner of speaking,' said Dominic, then he turned to the window, hoping the detective would take it as a sign he didn't want any further conversation.

Kolya leant forward. 'Miss Arbatova, we meet again. It is a coincidence because I was on my way to find you.'

'Why?'

'Because Oksana here has some information for us.'

'Really?' replied Anna, taking a sideways glance at Oksana who was re-rolling a joint that had become unstuck as the car had overtaken. She was balancing it on a box of Russian soap powder.

'Oksana has vital new evidence in the case of the disappearing women. It might be that she knows where your friend Sonya is.'

He smiled at Dominic. 'Were it not for her, we would be in a worse position.'

Dominic smiled back, weakly.

Anna asked, 'How come?'

She'd slowed down, driving along Kievski Boulevard past the railway terminus. She was convinced the yurt people couldn't catch them, unless they saddled their horses and she didn't think that was very likely. She breathed a sigh of relief. Oksana handed her the joint; she accepted it and inhaled.

Anna turned to her and asked, 'So what do you know?'

Oksana said, 'OK, I'm an artist, right? Some guy calls me at home.' She was trying to make it sound significant. 'He wants me to finish off a picture of him. He gets one of his heavies to pick me up, then he takes me to some dacha on the outskirts of town.' She passed the joint back to Anna. 'We get there and the guy's disgusting, a big fat toad. But it's weird, every time I look at him I think of vodka.'

It didn't surprise Anna, who had already spotted a bottle poking out of her patchwork suede shoulder bag. She swerved to avoid an Armenian family crossing the road. The youngest kid, a boy, held a violin by its neck.

'Then,' Oksana continued, 'because the guy has no aesthetic sense, he doesn't like the picture. So he gets one of his bulls to drive me into town and dumps me on the pavement. Disgusting, right?'

Anna didn't say anything. In the wing mirror she was watching the boy with the violin set up a busking pitch.

'Anyway,' said Oksana rubbing her elbow, 'while I'm up at the house, I see them.'

'Who?' asked Anna. 'Sonya?'

Oksana wound down the window and threw her cigarette butt out. As she did so, a line of ash blew back into Kolya's face. 'The woman I made the picture of, in the tree costume, and a younger girl. With hair sort of pinky.'

'Pinky?' Anna glanced at her over the gear stick.

'Yeah.'

'Well, that must be Sonya.'

'Who's telling this story?' Oksana spat out of the window.

Anna pulled over so she could concentrate better. They were parked by a twenty-foot bronze dedicated to victims of political oppression, facing a statue of Dzerzhinsky, former head of the secret police. A man was sunbathing, shirtless, standing up between them.

Anna shifted her body round a few degrees to face Oksana.

'The pinky one had a dog with her.'

'A *dog*?'

'Yes, a dog, what is the matter with you?' asked Oksana heatedly.

The car was silent as they thought about what to do. On top of Dzerzhinsky's head a pigeon was trying unsuccessfully to mount a mate.

'What do you think?' Anna asked Dominic. She translated the main parts of the story for him.

He said, 'I think we should call the police.'

Anna looked at him, astonished, and then pointed towards Kolya with her eyes. 'That is the police,' she said.

'But,' said Dominic, 'what *can* we do?' He had a slight edge of hysteria to his voice. Anna thought of her grandfather's bicycle left outside the hotel. She didn't want to leave it there.

'He's right, maybe we should go home,' said Anna, reaching for the ignition.

Kolya had been quiet. He pushed himself up higher in the sinking back seat with his fists. A pair of fur-lined handcuffs poked out of his top pocket. He knew he should have a plan, but he needed more time to think. He also knew there wasn't enough petrol in the car to mount an operation. It was his job to think of things like that. He opened his mouth to address the car, but nothing came out. Anna swung the car round and started to drive back into town.

III

In his turret room, Vladimir Zhubelovski looked at the self-portrait again. He'd started painting it as a fortieth birthday present to himself, a monument to his achievements – a gift to the man he'd become, from the boy he was. Nothing, especially not the painting, was going to tarnish the celebration of the most important day of his life. When he looked as it he felt a swarm of locusts in his head, a black cloud of anger, made up of all the people who had tried to sap his genius over the years.

It wasn't the Fabergé eggs that maddened him; he liked to be associated with wealth. It was more the reptilian hue that the idiot woman had given him and the emphasis on the facial warts. He probably should have locked her up with the rest of them, harvested her as well. He would have done so had she not been a redhead. Her pigmentation would upset the balance.

Ritual was very important to Zhubelovski, whether in the rotational order that they harvested the opium crop and packed it en route to the processing plant in Baku, or in the way he selected his clothes in the morning. Order was everything to him. Control was what mattered. At last, on the last day of his thirties, the final hours of his fourth decade, it was coming together perfectly.

It would be his final harvest in order to cleanse himself before he stood in the elections. It would rub out his past once and for all. The youngest should be presented to him first; they would confess their sins and beg forgiveness, which he would deny, and then they would be taken from him and shot. Zhubelovski had no interest in the killing itself, just the fact that they would be dead and with them the terrible actuality of his previous life. Then he reconsidered. The oldest should go first. The one that knew most about what she'd done.

He didn't know whether to keep their hair after they had been killed as a trophy. Not a scalp, that would be obscene; maybe a lock or two from each woman, as a fetish, although that sounded like something a pervert would do. He smiled to himself, a wrap-around smile of cunning and self-satisfaction. With the latest two additions, women who had only just completed their induction in time, he had seven in all. Seven women to represent the seven ages of his degradation. He wondered about what he should wear for the ceremony, perhaps a Nazi uniform or some military regalia. It would be appropriate for the women to see him for what he was – a self-made man, a success story, despite their worst efforts.

When he thought of what he was about to do he started to tingle nervously. It was an anxious feeling that he knew he could savour because soon he could have relief from it. The years and years of bitter resentment were soon about to be over. The swarm of locusts in his head would be gone. He looked at the self-portrait again. Suddenly it didn't seem so bad, the Fabergé balls and the mobile phone. It even seemed comical. He looked at it hard. Then he started to giggle, a saliva-filled titter. Before he could catch his breath the laugh had become a bellow.

IV

When he saw the body curled under the branch of a willow tree in the courtyard, two choices occurred to Khanbaba Balzanov. There might have been more options but Khanbaba didn't like to over-complicate things. His Uncle Vlad, a Hero of the Soviet Union for sheep breeding, often stressed Khanbaba's need not to over-complicate things. Khanbaba, until he saw the cut of the man's suit, had taken him to be a drunk. That meant he could rob the man, or he could help him. In some people the choice would have been automatic, but to Khanbaba things were never that clear cut.

He'd already lost one horse today, a black and white Aranzal belonging to his uncle, who had opted to stay in the mountains to watch the herds. His uncle was sceptical about the reincarnation of a real-life Dzhungar, but champion sheep breeders were renowned for logic, especially when it came to genes. He knew what his uncle would say when he confessed to the lost horse. 'Boy, I wouldn't trust you to protect a whore's virtue in a brothel.' If he could soften his uncle's blow with some hard currency, it was more likely Khanbaba would be allowed out of the yurts and into town again to see the Bruce Willis double bill.

The man was a foreigner, though whether he was Russian foreign, or foreign foreign, Khanbaba couldn't tell. The shoes used to give it away but now some Russians and even native Belugis were so rich it was impossible to tell. The guy on the ground was wearing brown tasselled loafers. His socks had pictures of teddy bears on them. Khanbaba thought, rich Russians were crooks and crooks didn't get sentimental about cuddly animals. That meant the chances were he was an American.

A lot depended on whether or not the man was dead. If he was dead then robbing him would make a lot of sense. If he was alive, altruism might be more in order. That would be taking the long-term view.

Khanbaba approached him downwind on instinct. He was lying by a wooden children's slide decorated with a woodland theme, his arm underneath him, so that unless you'd been looking for a missing horse you probably wouldn't have seen him. He couldn't have tripped because there wasn't anything to trip over, unless he'd plummeted from the climbing frame. And something about the man's posture said that he wasn't a climbing frame sort of person. It might have been a heart attack. He definitely hadn't been shot.

Khanbaba knew he was alive because when he peered over his left shoulder he could see a bubble of spittle go up and down in the groove of his mouth. When he looked up, past a first-floor balcony stacked high with empty jars, he saw the man must have fallen. Above him, tied to the metal surround of a balcony way above him, several sheets were knotted together.

Khanbaba shook the man. As he did so he saw the unmistakable shape of a shiny mobile phone in his left pocket. The urge to steal it was gnawing at him, but a voice – his uncle's – was reminding him of the long-term gain. He shook the man by the shoulder. His hair was thick and cut in the shape of a crash helmet. He was of slight build, whereas Khanbaba was stocky. He fetched the other Aranzal and, pulling the man up by his shoulders, got the horse underneath him. The booty wasn't going to make up for the loss of the other horse, but it might help. Khanbaba set off back to the square.

Khanbaba had taken the tortoises dotted around the ground – some the right way up, others upside down – to be carvings, part of the children's woodland playground. But as he walked the horse and the American away, he saw them edge sleepily into the shadows. There were approximately twenty of them. Khanbaba frowned to himself. He doubted if even his uncle would have a logical explanation for that.

V

From the door Sonya was amazed how much the room resembled backstage at *Come Dancing*. Women sat in groups, gossiping. Others sat alone on top of rolled-up mattresses with their backs to the wall and their elbows resting on their knees. It was a cellar, Sonya knew that from the stairs they'd been forced down, but it didn't have the mouldy vegetable smell of the cellar her father had dug underneath their lock-up last year to store potatoes. The floor was concrete and the walls plastered and whitewashed. It must have been custom-made for the job, but now the walls were getting dirty. It made Sonya think that the cellar had been in use for some time.

There were pictures cut from magazines around the room as well as religious icons. Two hand sewing machines were against the far wall operated by women, knees draped in material. The room smelt of sweat and urine and trapped female hormones combined with anxiety.

When they were pushed into the room, some of the women fell on them, foul-smelling and full of questions. Others hardly looked up. The guard in black had said only, 'Ladies, this then completes the set.'

Sonya had no idea what he meant. She looked around at the women. She guessed she was one of the youngest there and certainly the prettiest; her companion the foreigner would have been the eldest. She staggered as Whitey fell out of her arms. The bare-bulbed brightness of the room after the sewer was too much for Sonya. She also hadn't eaten since the morning before. A hard-looking woman in her mid-twenties with harshly dyed hair approached her. Beside her the foreigner squeezed her hand. Sonya felt the floor move underneath her and the start of a whirr of one of the sewing machines became unbearable. She tried to inhale but her head felt fuzzy, as if a bomb had gone off in it. Still clinging to the foreigner's hand, she fainted.

VI

From the back seat, Kolya contemplated the detection experience of the people in the car. Straight off, there was him. That amounted to fifteen years, including a credit from the Belugastan training centre. Then there was Anna Arbatova, who struck him as a capable sort of girl but not to be relied on in a crisis. Then there was the junkie Oksana and a foreigner.

Despite his calculations it was Arbatova who had turned the car round and started driving out again towards the palatial dachas, the suburb of the caviar poachers and *narcomafia*, on the outskirts of town. After five miles of sulky silence, she'd said she'd a duty to ensure her staff's safety. She didn't look too happy about it.

The woman drove as if she was only used to German cars, where the gear stick moved like a knife in butter. In his 1982 Lada she jammed and crashed the gear stick, which had always been temperamental in third. He tried to ignore the damage being inflicted on his engine, while he examined the evidence. Mentally he flicked to a new page of a spiral notebook and licked a fictitious pencil. The criminal case was, allegedly, that one of the country's most influential businessmen, about to stand for President of the country, was behind a series of inexplicable abductions. On what was this based? The testimony of a so-called artist who, even now, was smoking her third joint in half an hour.

The extent of Kolya's narcotics knowledge came from his week with the DEA's William H. Theobold, who had been keen to impress on him that Belugastan would soon rival Laos for a tangential spot on the Golden Triangle. That was the hard evidence. On a personal level the effects of drugs were more of a mystery. From Tatyana, whose brother Ivan had gone off the rails in Semipalatinsk, he knew that hallucinations were common, even sought after. Oksana was easily influenced and highly strung. He studied the back of her head. Her red hair was coarse and, in the words of Western shampoo manufacturers, unmanageable. It was not a head of hair that would stand up in court.

As they headed out towards the swamp lands on the edge of town where the plushest dachas were located, he put his face between the two front seats and turned to Oksana, who smelt strongly of tobacco. He asked with trepidation, 'Do you remember which one is his?'

'Kind of,' said Oksana.

This confirmed Kolya's worst suspicions. To stress the point he asked tiredly, 'Kind of you do, or kind of you don't?' He looked out of the window. Clouds were frothing up on the horizon. 'You were only there an hour ago.'

'You shut up, you pig. I am an artist, not a taxi driver.' Oksana rolled down her window and spat.

'OK,' said Anna, conciliating. 'Not all of them are lived in. What about that one on the left? You see those cars on the forecourt,' she pointed, 'are they familiar?'

There was a smell coming from the sack of dirty laundry that Kolya hoped the foreigner hadn't noticed. Apart from watching Arbatova, the foreigner had been silent.

'Yes,' said Oksana, 'that is it.'

Anna stamped her foot on the brake and pulled off the road. The car's chassis hit the dirt ground as the car slowed down over a hollow and then a ridge. Kolya winced. To the right of the car, slumped in a sentry post, a teenage guard was eating yoghurt off a Biro. When he saw the car, a white liquid blob dropped onto his AK-47.

'Hi.' Anna's voice went into a register that Kolya hadn't heard before, but must always have been there, like the upper case of a typewriter. 'I wonder if you could help me?'

The guard, with red raw acne and permanently flushed, wore the blue and white striped cotton shirt of an army private. There was an unmade camp bed in his sentry box and a TV set, smaller than a portable, was playing a fuzzy American film dubbed into Russian. There was a samovar on a folding table. From the back seat Kolya couldn't help thinking it looked pretty homely for a guardhouse.

'What?' His tongue had a white crust on it. His chubby knuckles, squeezed round the Biro, had crude prison tattoos on them in bluey black. Kolya didn't like taking a back seat when it came to matters of detection. Next to him Dominic wound down his window. For the first time in months Kolya felt the air was fresher, even chilly.

Anna said, 'It's embarrassing, really.' In the wing mirror Kolya saw she was engaging in a lot of eye contact and smiling in a way that revealed a lot of teeth. At training camp one of the sergeants had told the women recruits that, either attractive or ugly, they had an unfair edge over male officers. Suspects would tell them their secrets because they either fancied them or felt sorry for them. At the time Kolya had reported him to the camp commander for demonstrating an anti-women bias. Now he saw that the sergeant had a point.

Anna continued, 'My friend has just come from here.' She nodded towards Oksana. As if to explain she said, 'She's an artist.' The guard looked at Oksana who was attempting a smile, which came out as a nervous grimace. Clearly it wasn't a facial manoeuvre she often attempted.

'Unfortunately, she left her stuff behind,' Anna smiled. 'You know, paints, that sort of thing.'

The guard nodded. He said slowly, 'Who are they?' pointing to the back seat with a knife, which he pulled from the fleshy pulp of a watermelon.

'Well, they are . . .' She showed more teeth and her tongue ran over the front row. Kolya knew it wasn't in the interests of the collective, but hoped she would make a fool of herself, to highlight the difficulties faced by a detective. 'They are the—'

'They are models, for God's sake.' It was Oksana, galvanised by a lagging chemical that had suddenly hit a neural home run. 'They are my life models, which is why I need my paints. I must paint.' She shook her hair. And then her head fell forward.

'Why has he got a megaphone?'

'She paints at a distance and we use it to communicate with her,' said Anna plainly, as if she shouldn't have to state the obvious.

'You model too?'

Anna said, 'Of course not, I am her assistant. Look, please, we are losing the light. All we want to do is recover our property.'

The guard was loosening something stuck between his teeth with his tongue. He was dividing the threat posed by a car full of misfits into the sum of not wanting to upset an attractive woman. It was a difficult equation, not helped by Anna twisting her hair as he computed.

'Sure, go on up to the house.' He flicked a switch under the counter, which activated the two ornate iron gates.

Dominic, who hadn't understood the exchange, gave a regal wave as the car sped past.

'Now what?' asked Kolya. The recently gravelled forecourt spat up stones at the paintwork as the car drove in. Kolya winced.

'You're the detective,' said Anna to the rear-view mirror. The house was fairytale, only it belonged to the ogre. It had a second floor that looked too big to rise out of the first, with two slate-grey turrets at the front. The woodwork was painted black and the brickwork was herringbone in panels. To Dominic, who was keeping quiet, it was a Gothic Barrett home. Two rows of silver birches either side put the drive into shadow. Cars, mostly Japanese, were parked three deep at right angles to the door. The Lada spluttered towards them sheepishly. There were two apple trees nearer to the house, bowed down with fruit. They comforted Anna, reminding her of what Russia had been before four-wheel drives and Hugo Boss.

Kolya said, 'How likely is it do you think that this man is responsible for these crimes?' He looked at Oksana, whose head was still forward.

Anna was agitated. She snapped, 'Just show Zhubelovski your police card, say it's routine, and have a quick look round. Then we can go home.'

From the back of the house a dog started to bark deeply enough to suggest it was very big. It was followed by the metallic rustle of a chain rattling.

Kolya placed his hand nervously on the door handle. 'Maybe I'll have a look around first. Oksana said she saw them at the back of the house. I'll try there first.' He pulled the door handle and the window wobbled dangerously. He turned back, anxious not to leave the safety of the car. 'Do you think there's anyone here? It looks deserted.'

Anna ignored him. She turned to Dominic. 'You go with him. It'll look better that way.'

Dominic looked up, shocked to hear someone speaking to him. 'Where's he going?'

Anna reached behind her to the back seat. She rested her elbow on his lap as she stretched to open his door. As she did so her hair fell across his knees and her face was inches from his crotch. It was simultaneously both intimate and repelling. It left Dominic confused as he fell out of the car and staggered towards the detective. When he righted himself he was less than a metre away and joined him as two bull-like men circled them.

Anna instinctively dropped her head. The men must have come from the back of the house. They were tree-trunk big, with the unmistakable gait of the ex-military – a back-leaning lurch, as if they'd just been released from a heavy backpack. They also held their weapons with the easy familiarity of men who signed up for wars without the need for conscription. Like most of the country's young thugs, they were the newly fat. They wore their extra layer with the same pride as their cashmere blazers. One was wearing a leather cap, like the Moscow mayor Yuri Lushkov.

Anna held her breath. Since she was a little girl she'd believed stopping breathing made her invisible. From the driver's seat she watched the scene in the wing mirror, past Oksana's rising and falling stomach. When the sun came out from behind a bank of clouds, the four men cast long, afternoon shadows that put their faces in darkness. Anna sank further down in her seat as she heard Dominic shout out in English and look towards the car.

The thug in the leather cap raised his revolver and with his special bandy-kneed walk, bouncing on tiptoes, crunched over to the car. Anna felt her stomach go through a mangle. He stuck the gun nozzle against the window, which meant she should speak to him.

In the background she saw Dominic and the detective scuffle on the gravel. The Englishman's movements were slow and exaggerated, the detective's jerky with indignation.

'You're just in time for the party,' said the peaked cap. His face was coated in podgy fat that made her put him in his late thirties, though he was probably ten years younger. He spat out the husk of a sunflower seed. His garlic breath invaded the car.

'Get out of the car,' he said, lips curled in the expectation of sport, 'and bring your friend.'

CHAPTER TWELVE

I

Even with the memory of the pressure of the gun in his back still physical, what Dominic felt, pushed into a cellar of women, was the hot poker of embarrassment. It reminded him of the 10.30 p.m. start of the slow dances at the school discos, 'Nights in White Satin', with a dozen pairs of female eyes assessing him.

'Jeepers creepers,' said the detective beside him in English. 'What the fuck?'

The cellar was no more than ten metres square. In front of him Anna and Oksana were roughly pushed aside for the women to get a look at the men. Dominic thought he was going to be sick, a combination of fear and the smell that reeled him back to school canteens and the fungal infections of changing rooms.

He could have been in there a minute or half an hour before he was aware that he'd moved. A volley of wolf whistles kept him pinned to the chalky whitewash of the back wall. His nervous second glance around, this time more fact-finding than instinct, made him spot the American. The relief of a familiar face, almost a compatriot, made him extend his arms and sink to his knees beside her.

Anna was talking to a woman with peach-coloured hair. She was sitting on a wooden-backed chair with her knees apart; the other woman was crouched on the floor. She was using her hands a lot.

While they spoke they both intermittently patted a large pit bull terrier which, other than a gash on the side of its face, seemed quite happy.

He turned to Stella Anne. 'My God. How are you?' He paused. 'We were so worried.'

Dominic saw immediately that the American realised that he'd forgotten her name. With the impeccable manners of her national-ity, she re-introduced herself. Stella Anne's hair was pinned off her face, with a couple of strands falling over her eyes. She was still in her camouflage. The bib was creased around her lap, but hid the dirt well. Her first question was about Hubba and Bubba, whom she referred to as 'her boys'. Dominic assured her that they were well, and had elected to keep up the search for her at base camp in the mountains. He didn't mention their altered states.

'Are they eating enough?' she asked.

'They seemed pretty satisfied,' said Dominic, truthfully.

Stella Anne was reassured. With her head on one side, she hummed a tuneless campfire ditty.

Dominic was agitated at being dismissed so soon. He said, 'What is this all about?' Unintentionally, his words came out with the nervous froth generated by the hot bolus of fear in his stomach. Not yet panic but very close. 'I don't get it. Why are we here?'

Stella Anne looked at him. His question hadn't been existential. Her answer was philosophical.

'Did you get a sheep?' She was sanguine and smoothed the creases over her knees, which were as round as grapefruit halves.

'I'm sorry?'

'The Beluga argali argali – did you hunt one?'

'No, well, yes, they . . .' He shook his head and glanced at Anna, who returned a watery smile. 'Is this relevant?'

'What do you mean? Yes or no, did you get a sheep?' The word *get* came out as *git*.

'No, I didn't,' said Dominic, 'but they sort of got one for me.'

Stella Anne sucked her teeth and shook her head in a gesture of lost opportunity. Dominic felt he should cheer her up. 'Not a Beluga argali argali. Something named after an explorer. A Machu Picchu or something.'

'A Marco Polo?'

'Yeah, something like that.'

'Shucks,' said Stella Anne. The American's face was dirty on the bottom of her chin and another strand of hair had come loose.

'Absolutely,' agreed Dominic. 'Look, more to the point, why has somebody nabbed you? What's it all about? Is it kidnapping or something?'

'How big?'

'How big what?' Dominic swatted a mosquito away from his face.

'The horns, you banana boat.'

'Christ knows,' said Dominic, convinced the American had gone stir crazy. 'They were all curly.'

Stella Anne looked at him as if he had confessed to being a paedophile.

'*They were all curly*? What sort of a hunter are you?' she said. Her flaccid face had tightened in dismay.

'At the moment a kidnapped one,' said Dominic petulantly. 'And if it wasn't for you I wouldn't be here. If it's ransom then I don't see why we should all be dragged in.'

Stella Anne rotated her camouflaged shoulders five degrees and looked him in the face. 'You are one selfish son of a bitch. Take a look around. I don't think the man who brought us all here is interested in money.'

Dominic looked; she had a point. The women were at the very low end of the glamour scale.

'Then what is it?'

'Well, for a start, before you turned up here, we all had something in common. We *were* all women. That strikes me as significant. As a hunter, he has chosen only the female of the

301

species. That, as any hunter would know,' she said it in a way that meant Dominic should know, 'is very unusual.' She went on, 'It's very bad hunting. And most of them are young. In hunting, as opposed to in life, young females do not produce the best trophies.'

'Really?' Dominic felt dazed, as if he'd cornered the wrong person at the party.

He fell silent. He shifted from one buttock to the other. His left leg had gone to sleep against the concrete, so he jiggled it nervously. The dance alerted Stella Anne who, nudged out of her sheep dreams, motioned with her eyes that the conversation was over.

Anna was good at estimating numbers. First there had been the tortoises, approximately forty-five to a full sack, and then women. It came from working out the rota at Come Dancing and a limited experience of choreography that demanded six women to fill the stage. In the cellar, at first glance she saw five women by the far wall and four clustered around a table. When she and Oksana were pushed into the room they made it too full. The confinement reminded her of the train trips she used to take with her grandmother to Moscow with the tortoises. The smell of the carriages wasn't dissimilar: sweat, stale breath and cigarettes made from newspaper. The bubble of fresh air when the door had been opened had been inhaled in a collective gasp.

From experience Anna disliked groups of women, made dysfunctional by their synchronised hormones and man jealousy. At the age of nineteen she'd dated a Kirghizian prison guard, who'd told her that they drew straws not to have to work the women's section. A couple of women here had the blank expressions of troglodytes, eyes unable to focus on anything more than a metre away. Their skin, waxy from lack of vitamins, was more dead than alive. Others must have just arrived – their clothes were cleaner and their faces more optimistic. A few were wearing make-up turned grotesque under the light of a bare bulb. Even though they'd been pushed down a flight of wooden stairs, the room was stifling. Mosquitoes swarmed and an arch of cockroaches migrated across the far wall.

The guard with the gun had said something as he pushed them inside. Anna hadn't heard him. The women's expressions had gone from shocked interest to resentment in five seconds. To emphasise the fact that there wasn't enough room for any more, a woman Anna's age had stood up, her hands resting on her hips like an anchor. Before she could speak, Dominic and the detective had been pushed through.

When the men arrived the mood in the cellar had changed. The women's hard, ugly mannerisms softened. Hostile postures of aggression doubled up on themselves, bodies levered to draw the men into the room. Two of the older ones, stooped over a sewing machine, wolf whistled.

The detective was sweating, Dominic looked as if he was about to faint. Anna watched him turn to a woman whose face was familiar, but in the last five minutes the sequence had turned dreamlike and she was no longer able to identify reality. As she kicked an ashtray aside to make room for herself, she heard a voice she recognised. It was Sonya, lying with her cheek resting on a dog. She went over to her. Her eyes bulged large in a gaunt featureless face.

'Sonya?' Anna spoke slowly. 'What are you doing here?'

'I don't know,' she wailed. 'I was on my way to work when this car stopped. I thought it might be a client but then they put a rag on my face and I woke up underground, with that mad woman.' She pointed towards where Dominic was sitting.

Anna put her arm over her shoulder. 'It's OK now, Sonya, don't worry, it's all going to be all right.'

Sonya scowled. In the few minutes she'd been with the women in the cellar she'd learnt a lot.

Sonya hoisted herself up by her waist; she looked hurt as if she'd been slapped. 'What do you mean, it's going to be all right? Don't you know? It's today. The horrible man's birthday is today. That's when he's going to kill us all.'

Kolya recognised the chance to shine when it presented itself to him. And this was it. In less than half an hour, after using his police ID, held up like a crucifix in front of a coven, to silence the cat calls, he had completed his preliminary inquiries. The information, though somewhat incoherent due to the educational level of several of the captives, was significant.

The density of bodies in such a confined space reminded Kolya of the orphanage he'd been brought up in. He spoke in English. 'Ladies and gentleman, my name is Colonel Nikolai Pertsov of the Belugastan police. For the English speakers among us, I speak in their tongue. Then in Russian.'

He repeated the bit about Russian in Russian. There was some jeering, especially from a cigarette-smoking woman squatting on large thighs. Then Anna hushed them. Oksana who, more than anyone, looked at home in the room, was sitting with her head lolling on the back wall.

The detective went on, 'We have been catched by the man Zhubelovski.'

Stella Anne, due to her camouflage, had gone unnoticed by the detective so that he looked startled when she corrected him. 'Caught,' said Stella Anne, raising an arm to wave off the detective's bow of thanks.

'Does it matter?' said Dominic irritably. 'We know that. What we want to know is how we're going to get out.' Dominic extended his leg and pulled back the foot. The cramp had seized his entire leg.

'He's right,' said Stella Anne. 'Don't forget I am an American citizen.'

'Great,' said Dominic under his breath. He was deliberately hitting Stella Anne's leg with his elbow as he roughly massaged the leg that had gone to sleep. He was venting his anger on the

American, but really he wanted to know why Anna was sitting with a pink-haired woman and not with him.

'Unfortunately, that is not something I can know you,' said the detective.

'Tell you,' corrected Stella Anne. 'Can I make a suggestion?'

'No,' said Kolya and bowed again. 'It also appears that if it were not for the fact that I am a detective, we would all be for the chop.' He smiled at his grasp of the English colloquialism. 'However, I have a plan.' He raised his eyebrows. 'But now, I am scared I must translate for the others.'

As he was speaking, Dominic turned once more to Stella Anne for an explanation. 'I don't get it. What does he want with a bunch of women? It's mad.'

This time, Stella Anne's reply was more focused. 'He makes them stitch things,' she nodded towards the sewing machines, 'and knit.' She looked towards a table in the left-hand corner. 'Then there's the babies.'

'What?'

'The plastic dolls. I've watched the women put them in diapers. They have to make them look good before the guards give them any food. They sort of present them.'

'Oh my God,' said Dominic. His stomach felt itchy with nerves. Every time he considered his position his body went limp and sweat started to seep through his palms like cowardly stigmata.

He watched the detective who was demonstrating to the women how to use knitting needles as a dangerous weapon. He used his left hand to hold down an imaginary assailant and the right as a dagger. Dominic knew a lot about knitting; he'd had to learn it at the village school he went to until the age of eight. He knew that baby clothes, the type the women had been knitting, required thin needles. With chunky knit or Arran they might have stood a chance, with number 11s the result was a foregone conclusion.

'I bet you wish you'd never come here,' said Dominic. He'd made eye contact with Anna, who smiled but didn't move towards him. She nodded towards Oksana, who was snoring.

'Are you kidding?' Stella Anne paused as she re-plaited her hair. She was about to continue when Dominic felt a new atmosphere in the cellar wash over them; change from nervous excitement to terror. As the women became silent and instinctively turned their faces to the door, Dominic heard the hollow thud of boot steps on the wooden stairs.

II

John H. Easton came to in the shade of a tent, stuffy and smelling so strongly of sour milk that for a full ten seconds he thought he was a child again. From his vantage point on the earth floor he instinctively looked round for the door. A section of the tent, which was high enough for a man to stand in, was raised to let air in. Easton's left side ached and he was stiff across the shoulders so that it hurt when he tried to raise his head. His hip had a dull pain that told him he'd been sleeping on his mobile phone.

He tried to think back. He remembered throwing the tortoises to try to attract someone's attention, then tying the sheets together. He couldn't remember the fall. A dark-haired boy stood over him. He squeezed some evil smelly white liquid from a poultice and reapplied it to his forehead.

Before he fell asleep again he thought the boy's stare was not entirely benevolent. But then, even in illness, he had an instinct for such things. Before he slipped from consciousness, he considered adding it to his résumé.

III

Three men appeared at the door after a series of metal bolts had been dragged back. Their sheer physical bulk filled the cellar, together with a puff of aftershave. Two were flunkies; the one in the centre was the honcho, even though he stood a full head shorter and wider than his henchmen. Long blond hair billowed over a belted black full-length leather coat. His height was no comfort; it just reminded you that most evil was carried out by men who lacked the goodness to grow larger.

He kept his hands rooted in his pockets as he spoke. 'Ladies, the time approaches. Please form a line by the door.' No one moved. He went on, his voice low, his chin up. 'Please do as I say. I want you to form a queue with the youngest at the front. Then my friends here will handcuff you.' When he smiled, a triangle of warts on his chin formed a straight line. Then his voice became denser. 'I repeat, I want to see the youngest leave first.'

IV

The sewer was made of limestone. Tim and Erik limped along a ledge on the right of a gully more than five metres across. The water was stagnant. The smell was otherworldly but the darkness was the worst, the thick matt black of the dead.

Erik walked behind with the torch. Every ten yards he flashed it down the tunnel. 'For pity's sake, shine that thing in front of me,' said Tim. He kept his balance by leaning his left shoulder against the wall. He might have cared about ruining his suit had he not already done so searching through garbage skips. Tim was now unable to say the word dog in his head without prefacing it with the word fucking.

'It's amazing,' said Erik. 'Did you know this place existed?' Erik was thinking of potential shoot locations. Obviously it would require a lot of lighting.

'The sewers? Yeah. It's where the Jews hid from the Nazis in the war.'

'You're kidding.'

'No, my mum told me. They had to spend months down here.'

'When?'

'Before the country was exiled. In nineteen forty-two, I think,' said Tim.

Erik stopped. 'Where did they sleep?'

Tim was forced to stop. 'I dunno, some of them level out into sort of caverns.'

Erik shook his head. 'Wow, I had no idea.'

Tim turned his head. 'No one ever accused you of being much of a history man, did they?'

Erik didn't like his intellectual credentials being questioned. He deliberately flicked the torch up and down the vault. Tim missed his footing.

He swore. 'Jesus Christ, will you give me the torch? I'm the one who's supposed to be following these footprints.'

'Right,' said Erik sarcastically, 'that's why we've been walking around in circles for the last hour.' His voice echoed.

'Are you saying we're lost?'

'Are we?'

'Give me the torch.' It had become a sort of unwritten rule that whoever carried the torch, at the rear, could not be the navigator so could not be blamed in the event of being lost.

'On one condition,' said Erik.

'What?'

'You don't go on about this presidential thing.' Erik shone the torch directly in Tim's eyes. 'About Zhubelovski standing, and me putting that foreigner in the running instead of you.'

Tim shrugged and wrapped his arms round his chest. The sewers were cold. He said, 'There's not a hell of a lot I can do about it, is there?' In the light of the torch bouncing off his own face, Tim saw Erik's features freeze.

'Jesus Christ.'

'What?'

'Something just ran over my foot.' Erik started running on the spot. He reached for his pistol. 'I think it was a rat.' He shot twice into the darkness.

Tim moved against the sewer wall. 'For God's sake,' he said, agitated and loud, 'don't shoot in here, you idiot, you could kill someone.'

Erik said urgently, 'Quick, take the torch. We have to get out of here.' Erik slapped Tim with the torch with such force that he twisted an extra clockwise quarter turn.

Tim sank his fingers into the rubber torch. 'It's only rats.'

With the torch in his left hand, Tim turned to see an antechamber leading off to the right. He flicked the torch up. The rungs were green slime on top and rusty fawn underneath. A stalactite of green slime dripping perfect crystals of clean water had formed at the top, next to a manhole cover.

V

Hubba looked at Bubba, a bleary-eyed look of dazed but supreme satisfaction. Had they retained the ability to speak, they would have agreed that this was the most fun they'd had since a week on Highway 90 between San Antonio and El Paso. In the desert the hallucinogenic cacti were free and plentiful, and they had passed out for a week in the lea of an adobe wall.

In this state, the boys' two minds worked as one, united in the urge, primeval like a newborn's quest for mother's milk, for more of the jagged-leafed panacea. Their antennae met when they saw the truck pull off the track.

When the driver climbed down from the cab and started to adjust a nut on the nearside wheel, the boys inhaled the sour sweet smell of Grade A drugs. With an imperceptible nod to each other they took their chance as the driver relieved himself in the bushes.

They'd had enough of the mountain, in any case. 'Specially the hygiene level,' thought Bubba as he clambered into the back of the truck with the remains of the hunting arsenal strapped to his back. As the truck pulled away, Bubba reflected that the driver never did wash his hands.

VI

Tim's jacket ripped under the arms when he slid the cover to one side. When they hauled themselves up and dusted themselves down, and their eyes had adjusted to the glare, the men were in the middle of a courtyard. Facing them, a double garage had been constructed so recently that a cement mixer stood alongside it, with sand spilling from a gutted sack. The garage was empty, with the doors yanked up. On the forecourt of one someone had written 'Masha 4 Me' in wet concrete. It made Tim think the forecourt required another layer because it didn't look like the type of home where you messed around with wet concrete.

'Thank God for that,' said Erik. Under his Lakers baseball hat, he'd grazed his nose. 'I can't stand rats. They make me, I don't know, they . . .' He looked around. 'Where the hell is this place?' Even in the sewers he'd kept his sunglasses on; now the weather was overcast but bright.

Tim scanned the courtyard, deserted but for a bag of workmen's tools. He said, 'Those dachas at the Krilatskoye end of town, I'd guess.'

'The big ones?'

'Yeah, take a look,' said Tim, sarcastic. They were walking round the garage, and the house appeared in front of them.

Most people knew the dachas on the edge of town were unlived in, deserted by their dollar-rich owners who'd fled to the south of France or Brighton beach. Others were mortar skeletons belonging to drug smugglers whose wealth had outlived them. Tim had a theory that they'd only ever been built for show, that the Russian peasants' love of the kitchen table was too ingrained for them to be happy in large museum-silent rooms.

So it was a shock for them to run into anyone. It was more of a shock to see, in front of them as they turned out of the courtyard into an alley that ran towards the dacha, a dozen women, as scruffy as kulaks going to Siberia, being marshalled at gunpoint away from an outhouse. At first Tim took them to be hired hands, maybe the workers who'd built the garages. Then he saw the gun. A split second later he saw his former fiancée.

CHAPTER THIRTEEN

I

'Anna?'

What disturbed Tim most was seeing her holding hands with a tall guy with floppy, practically feminine, hair. Erik's reaction was more instinctive. He pulled his Beretta from the left side of his blazer.

Two henchmen pivoted towards the noise of the pistol being cocked. At the same time, somewhere among the group, a mobile phone chimed out the William Tell overture. Erik couldn't imagine the unprofessionalism of a gunman who didn't switch his mobile off before he did a job. Or maybe he couldn't afford to keep out of touch. For a hired killer that showed a lot of clout. A couple of women screamed, but they gave the impression of a group who could scream no more.

The phone was still ringing when one of the guards, heavyset with Mongol features in striped Adidas tracksuit bottoms and a pea-green jumper, grabbed a woman in her mid thirties with dark hair streaked with grey and locked her head in the crook of his arm. His fingers were too stubby to thread their way through the trigger hole of his gun, so only one digit made it. The pistol was aimed at the woman's temple. She was taller than the guard and slimmer. She didn't scream because she looked like the sort of woman for whom this wasn't the worst thing that could happen.

Still handcuffed by the wrist to another woman, her hair fanned out over the guard's green jumper as her spine bent backwards. It was an exchange that didn't require dialogue. Erik thought he would provide some nonetheless.

'Let her go,' he said. Given the circumstances, his power to issue commands was limited.

Tim, ahead and to the left, turned back, astonished. They'd both recognised Zhubelovski at the back, his black leather coat flared open from the waist. His hands were wedged in the pockets of black trousers. His warts danced as he smiled and then frowned when he saw Tim.

'Well, well, the President, if I'm not mistaken. If I'd known you were going to join the party, I'd have laid on something more spectacular.' He looked at the women. 'Not to say you're not welcome to join us.' He flicked his hair over his shoulder. 'In fact I demand it. How did you know it was my birthday?' A machine-gun rattle laugh fired out of his loose-lipped mouth. 'Have you brought me a present?' He smiled. 'Or is yourself enough?'

Erik still held the pistol waist high. 'What shall I do?' He spoke to Tim.

'What do I know? You're the gangster.'

Erik looked back at Zhubelovski. The women had started to talk in a low-level vibration of nervous excitement.

A man Erik recognised as Colonel Pertsov stepped forward. 'Please be aware that this man is a psychopath,' he said. 'He makes the women dress dolls in nappies.'

Tim felt a throbbing in his temple. Then he spotted the American hunter at the back of the line. She was handcuffed to a girl who, under her right arm, was struggling, on razor-thin hips, to control a pit bull terrier he recognised as Whitey.

Tim felt as if a neural suspension bridge in his brain was about to snap. He said, 'Anna, has he hurt you?' Then, without waiting for an answer, 'Zhubelovski, what the hell do you think you're doing? Let them go. What's the point of this?'

'The point?' Zhubelovski repeated the word as if he'd never heard it before. His body was edgy, twitchy, and his face was pained. 'You, him, come here, now.' Zhubelovski walked towards them. 'Today, gentlemen, is my birthday and I have a little party planned. That's all.' He stopped in front of Tim. 'Of course, you are invited. I am your host.'

Tim put his hands out in a way he'd read meant non-aggression in higher primates. With Zhubelovski it was possible he was making too much of an assumption.

'Mr Zhubelovski, this is crazy. You're standing to be President. This is no way to treat your people.'

'On the contrary,' said Zhubelovski, 'I have to do this in order to free myself *to* lead the country.'

Erik was a long way from putting down his weapon. 'What do you want me to do?' he asked. 'This guy's a freak.'

A whip-crack shot, more firecracker than bullet, drilled into the tarmac in front of their feet and ricocheted into a sandbag behind them. It had come from one of the heavies. It helped Erik make up his mind.

'Drop the gun,' said the guard with the woman in a headlock.

'Yeah, I have done this sort of thing before, you know,' said Erik. He shot a look of blame at Tim and tossed the gun on the ground. One of the guards stepped forward and handcuffed them together before pushing them into line.

Tim asked, 'Where are we going, anyway?'

'To my party. Right here at the front, on the lawn.' Zhubelovski was leading them and spoke over his shoulder. 'When I was a kid I used to dream of having a birthday party outside, with all my friends.'

Behind him Erik muttered, 'Fucking Virgo.' He shook his head. 'That'd be right.'

Tim looked at him; he was anxious to talk to Anna. '*What?*'

'I do the horoscopes for the magazine, right?' said Erik. 'Saddam Hussein happens to be a Virgo.'

They walked in silence for two metres until they rounded the left end of the alley. The dacha loomed in front of them. The surface turned to gravel. Even though his brain was spinning, Tim felt sorry for the women, most of whom were barefoot.

Zhubelovski raised his hands and looked down the line. His face softened and he sounded surprised. 'You see? Everything is ready.'

In the centre of the lawn, under the branches of an apple tree, a long dining table had been erected, draped in a white linen tablecloth. Two places were set. A bottle of champagne, French not Russian, was in a silver bucket in the centre. Strung from the tree, in bunches of tri-coloured balloons, was a banner that read, in English, 'I am 40'.

'What the?' gasped Erik.

Some of the women giggled with nervous relief.

Zhubelovski muttered, 'It is the perfect spot for an execution, don't you agree?'

Erik turned to Tim in dismay. Now they were at their destination, the guards had joined Zhubelovski. Some of the women regrouped. Tim edged over towards Anna.

'What the hell happened, how did you end up here?' he asked. Not waiting for a reply he said, 'Who's he?'

Anna knew that, given a choice, even minutes from death, Tim was more interested in the man she was shackled to than her welfare. It made her think she'd made the right decision. She tried to smile at Tim.

'He's one of the hunters. Zhubelovski's been taking these women, I lost one of my dancers, so we came up to have a look.'

'*On your own?*'

'No,' said Anna. 'That detective was with us, and another woman. Look, does it matter?'

Dominic had remained silent for so long he had the sensation that he was watching a video. Even then he made the distinction. It wasn't the sort of movie he'd pay to see at a cinema. He said, in English, 'Who's he?'

Though tall for a woman, Anna was dwarfed by the two men. Ahead of them Zhubelovski was talking to one of the gunmen. The other watched over them.

'I'm sorry, this is Tim,' said Anna. 'Actually, he's the President of Belugastan.' She waited, head down.

'Pleased to meet you,' said Dominic and yanked up his hand, handcuffed to Anna, to shake Tim's hand.

Tim turned to Anna and with a stab of outdated jealousy, said angrily in Russian, 'Are you seeing him?'

'Am I *what*?' Anna's face was frozen in disbelief. 'We're about to be shot by some madman and all you're interested in is whether I'm seeing—'

'Are you seeing him?' Tim repeated to Anna, but his eyes were on Dominic. Then he looked at Anna and started to nod. 'My God,' he said. 'I get it. He's the one standing for the presidency. Is that why you're with him?'

Erik tried to move between him and Anna, touching her elbow. He said, 'Come on, Tim, relax.'

Tim didn't hear. 'What is it with you and presidents?' He said, 'Is it the power?'

Tim's last fistfight had been six months before his election at Come Dancing, with the head of the gang of itinerant Turkish bricklayers who had refused to obey the 'no touching' rule. Tim had come out worst. He moved towards Dominic, face first.

'For God's sake.' Anna put herself between them, using herself and Erik as a buffer. She said, 'We're kidnapped at gunpoint and you just want to start some macho fight.'

Erik said in Tim's ear, 'Come on, this is silly.'

Some of the women had noticed the start of a scuffle, but Zhubelovski was too busy surveying the garden and suggesting changes with his hands.

Tim kept looking at Dominic. Anna said, 'Besides, Erik told me you were seeing someone else in any case.'

Erik looked at his feet.

Tim said, 'That's not the point.'

'*Really?*' said Anna. 'Then what is?'

Dominic had edged back as far as the crocodile would allow him. He said to Anna, 'Your friend is very,' he rubbed his chin contemplatively, 'physical.'

'I'm sorry,' said Anna, 'he's a little nervous at the moment.'

'Nervous?' said Dominic. 'Of me?'

'No,' said Anna, patiently. 'Because we are all about to be killed by a lunatic.'

'Don't be ridiculous,' said Tim, understanding the English. 'By Zhubelovski?' He looked round. 'It's some sort of game. He's a psycho, but he's not dangerous. He's standing for President, for God's sake. It's a party, that's all.'

Erik said, 'It's probably some sort of publicity stunt.'

'Yeah,' said Anna sourly, 'a party. Course it is. That's why he's kept these women in a cellar for the last six months. To get them in the mood.'

Tim had never noticed a bitter streak in Anna before. He put it down to her latest escort. He was about to comment on it when Zhubelovski raised his arms to the level of his hairline. The lining of his leather jacket was a purplish green. He twitched a cloud of thunder bugs away from his face.

'We are close to the start,' he said, not loud enough for everyone to hear now that the wind had picked up, 'or should I say the end?'

'Jerk,' said Erik. He looked around for an approving audience but the women were too scared to take their eyes off Zhubelovski. Erik trusted women's judgement. Their terror-struck expressions made him re-evaluate the situation.

Someone spoke. 'I demand, for the final time, that you let these women go free.' It was Kolya. 'Otherwise the consequences for you are going to be very unfortunate.'

Zhubelovski looked as if he could hear the words but not understand their gist.

'Shut up, you are guests at my party. No.' He smiled. 'You are gatecrashers at my party. You have made it messy. I prefer neatness.' The last three words he said distinctly as if each warranted its own sentence, or he was trying to convince himself. 'I am going to start with the ones who deserve it most first. Then I shall work my way down to the youngest.' He scanned the line. 'You will take a glass of champagne with me at the table. I will explain how you sinned. You will attempt to explain your actions and beg my forgiveness.' He spoke as if reading from a script. 'Then, when I tell you, you will take up position next to the killing pit. Then I will shoot you.'

Half a dozen of the women started to cry. They moved on the spot nervously, trying to squeeze out of the handcuffs.

Tim said, 'You freak, you can't do this.'

Zhubelovski smiled. 'Can you see anyone here who's going to stop me?'

'No, but—'

'Then shut up,' said Zhubelovski. 'Killing the President will also suit my purpose admirably.'

Though it had started to rain slightly, Zhubelovski had shed his coat, revealing a bulge of fat which lapped over his belt, and handed it to the younger henchman in the leather cap.

Zhubelovski spoke to the group. 'You may watch or you can come as summoned in birth-date order.' He turned to the older guard. 'Zhenya, you have the list?' Then he stopped. 'But I'm forgetting, the first should naturally be the oldest one. The *Amerikanka*. Bring her, please. Then we can begin.'

Erik sighed. 'I can't believe it, he's shooting the American. This is a fucking PR disaster.'

Stella Anne had understood none of Zhubelovski's speech. She'd been comforted by the picnic scene as they'd rounded the corner and was trying to comfort Sonya, who sobbed in large breathless gulps. The youngster was so distraught she had dropped the pit bull, which whimpered next to her, licking her bare ankles.

319

'Now, honey, there there,' said Stella Anne, stroking Sonya's hand with the one that was handcuffed. 'Everything's going to be all right. I'm an American, nothing bad can happen to us. It just can't, you wait and see.'

When the gunman walked towards them, some of the women cowered, but Oksana, who had rallied considerably in the last five minutes, emitted a lump of spittle that landed unabsorbed on the guard's green acrylic jumper.

Stella Anne said to Sonya, 'Now, honey, you must hush up, we don't want to upset these gentlemen any more than they already are, now do we?'

Oksana's face was black from sewer dirt and smudged mascara. She looked Stella Anne full in the face.

'No, you stupid. You old bag. They kill you first,' she said.

Compared to the rubbish she had been spouting, it was admirably to the point. Her prediction was also borne out by the rough way Stella Anne was being pulled from the handcuffs by the guard in green.

The grip was ferocious. It reminded Stella Anne of the way her husband used to physically chastise her in the kitchen when she'd talked too much at dinner parties. The memory unleashed a spasm of anger that she had thought a six-month course of therapy, as well as four trips to a psychic surgeon, had vanquished.

'Now you just hold it right there.' She tried to keep her biceps close into her chest and her feet rooted next to Sonya. She had, as a last resort, hidden her GPS and a knitting needle up her sleeve, but there wasn't time to mount a small-scale skirmish.

The young guard went to hit her. Dominic, in front, turned to stop him with his free arm. The guard kneed him in the groin. With the same movement he slipped a hand round Stella Anne's arm and pulled her towards the front. Erik yelled at him to leave her alone.

Stella Anne had quite forgotten the strength of men and it dispirited her. She relaxed her torso to stop it hurting so much, telling herself she was biding her time like the consummate huntswoman she was.

She had been dragged to within three feet of Zhubelovski and was weighing up his improbable shortness when the iron gates at the front of the house swung open. The gravel crunched as a lumbering ex-Red Army truck gear-crunched its way along the twenty-five-metre drive from the road. The back of the truck had been customised and stripped of its awning at the back. It was piled high with bales of just ripe hay. The women gasped at the distraction. Some waved at the lorry while others whooped.

As the truck approached, the driver's face came into focus above the steering wheel. He was a Belugi native with sun-dried features and large dark-rimmed glasses with one lens missing, wearing a grubby T-shirt with the Nike slug of a black tick on it. The rain was increasing, falling in large nipple-shaped drips on the wind-screen. Either the wipers didn't work or the driver had reached his destination and hadn't bothered to turn them on.

Stella Anne used the disruption to mount her struggle. She wriggled her torso, hoping to shake down the knitting needle. Watching her with a twitchy anxiety like a hungry man waiting for meat to cook, Zhubelovski caught sight of the truck last.

As the driver disappeared from view to lever up the antiquated handbrake and climb down from the cab, the women saw that salvation was not at hand. The driver's T-shirt was pulled up over his nut-brown stomach to his chest, for ventilation. He pulled it down self-consciously, which indicated that he believed he was the spectacle, not them. Nothing the driver saw at the dacha shocked him. Before his feet hit the ground, Zhubelovski roared.

'For Christ's sake, man, get that stuff out of the wet. What are you trying to do, ruin me?' The driver's face fell. 'Hurry up, you fool. Get it in the garage.' Spits of Zhubelovski's saliva mingled with the rain.

Then he bellowed to the guards to take firmer control of Stella

Anne. The truck had thrown him off balance. His mood wors-
ened as he tried to regain control. Sensing it, Stella Anne knew
she had nothing left to lose. She clenched her abdominal muscles
and summoned the black hole of hatred in her stomach that she
kept for all men. The noise she made was immense, a rhinoceros
wall of sound. She didn't expect it to be answered. Later, when
she retold the story, she described what happened as the instinctive response of the young members of the herd to an elder in
distress.

Bubba was the first to leap from the truck. Even buried in
opium, he and Hubba had recognised, if not exactly the screams of
their mistress, the chance for a fight. It also helped that their
perceptions were already dangerously heightened.

The roar as they leapt from the back of the van was as resonant,
maybe more so, as Stella Anne's. Strapped to their chests was most
of the hunting armoury left with them on the mountain. In the
fading afternoon light their eyeballs and teeth gleamed white
against the Carbomask. For two men who had been ingesting
drugs for the last seventy-two hours they assessed the situation
with military precision, homing in on the firepower as if their wiry
little black bodies were magnets.

As they leapt, Stella Anne was ready with her knitting needle
which she rammed with force into Zhubelovski's groin. She used
her GPS to batter him about the head. Handcuffed women
inched over to him and kicked him to the ground while Hubba
jammed a rifle butt in the face of the first guard and then the
second. It took them less than forty-five seconds to defray the
situation.

Women pinned Zhubelovski down, sitting on each limb with an
intimacy that Hubba and Bubba thought was rightfully one of the
victor's spoils. Oksana landed row after row of spit gobbets on the
young guard's acrylic jumper. Hubba used a meat cleaver stolen
from the yurt to split the handcuffs while Kolya, bent over
Zhubelovski, stretched out on the ground to read him his rights.

Then, satisfied the prisoner was restrained, the detective went to the mosquito-brown Lada and brought out a pair of handcuffs. Only over the shoulder of a weeping Stella Anne as she embraced them did Bubba spot that they were fake-fur lined. He mentioned it to Hubba and they both agreed it was a nice touch.

CHAPTER FOURTEEN

I

Mrs Barinova tingled, not, for once, with hot flushes, but because of the change in the weather. Her own mother, whose brother and father had both died mid-month, always said August was the most dangerous month of the year. And Mrs Barinova believed her. The air had a charge to it, one that galvanised the healthy and killed the weak. Her mother said it was caused by the change in atmospheric pressure as the summer turned; the positive ions turning to negative. All Mrs Barinova knew was that the light cleared in the same way as the fuzziness of her Soviet black and white TV disappeared when she tuned it in. It had been the same when she'd visited Boris Pasternak's grave in Peredelkino, with Feodor next to her, then still a rangy boy. A precise light burst through the cemetery trees, half an hour's walk from the train station, on the fresh grave loaded with red carnations bunched in even numbers.

In the main hall of Come Dancing, she adjusted the flowers on the tables, moving them from the centre of the table, where they might get in the electorate's way, to the edge. They were plastic pansies, from the Caspian Canteen on the third floor of the Palace. It wasn't ideal, because they would get stolen. But, even though it was cooler outside, she knew that fresh ones would wilt during the twenty-four-hour poll. There was no time to erect polling booths for a secret ballot. Three years ago in the last election they'd made screens by dissecting a giant advertising mock-up of a box of Croatian aspirins brought in from the chemist's shop window. One of the election candidates had complained that the chemical fumes had affected the voters. She remembered telling him that it had been the $100 offered by her son to everyone who voted for him that had done that.

This time, though, with all the excitement, constructing separate booths would take too long. Igor, the barrel-chested bouncer, had helped her move the tables in the main hall of the club and clear last night's ashtrays. By the sticky feel of the tabletops and the overflowing cigarette butts, it looked as if some had started the National Day celebrations a day early. All things considered, she wasn't despondent that her political career was drawing to an end. It gave her more time to concentrate on her hobbies. In the three days since the kidnapping, Erik had applied himself to the magazine with added verve. Yesterday, he'd announced he wanted an Internet edition of *Erik* by October. She was to head it.

Erik was due to help at the polling station, but he'd left a message with the woman at reception to say that he was in a high-level meeting and would be late. Mrs Barinova looked at her watch; there were only fifteen minutes until they opened at 9 a.m., and the ballot papers still hadn't been delivered. Of course Mrs Barinova knew the problem. The most favoured presidential candidate was languishing in a high-security mental institution in Moscow. But even though he had been prevented from attending yesterday's hustings, Zhubelovski had not yet withdrawn from the election.

She finished the tables and looked around. One of the girls had draped a crepe paper fringe along the stage and strung up a poster that read, 'Dear Residents Happy National Day and Good Luck in the Ballot'. It was Soviet in sentiment and too verbose to fit on the banner so there was only room for the word 'Ball'. Mrs Barinova smiled with patriotic pride anyway. She was glad her son wasn't standing again. It was time for him to settle down and leave all that politics nonsense to the professionals, or she'd never get any grandchildren.

Handbag tucked under her arm, she marched over to the Palace Hotel. The Belugi natives were still camped out on Peace Square. In the early morning chill the breath of humans and animals was opaque. She nodded at a couple whom she recognised from the mountains and smiled as Sasha, the Palace doorman, pulled the glass door open for her. He told her that her son was in a meeting in the presidential suite on the thirteenth floor.

She said, 'I know that,' and headed for the lift, wondering if she'd miss the pomp when she returned to ordinary middle age and unruly hormones.

'Read it to me again.' Tim's feet were crossed lazily on the walnut table in one of the hotel bedrooms that he'd converted to an office. It was called the Square Office in deference to the American White House. Really it was more of an L-shape, but linguistically that didn't work. His hands were behind his head. An onlooker would have called his position relaxed. Erik knew that he was as tight as an elastic band and about to flick himself upright.

He cleared his throat. The report was a photocopy of a fax. It had been delivered early and left in Tim's pigeonhole downstairs by Colonel Nikolai Pertsov, who Pasha reported was driving a Cherokee jeep, which Erik guessed was Zhubelovski's. The letter had come with a handwritten note from the detective:

To Whom It May Concern

Please find enclosed the report from Dr Scherbakov of the Tserbski Institute in Moscow relating his findings as to the mental state of V. S. Zhubelovski. I think you will agree it testifies to a disturbed mind. Zhubelovski's, that is, not the doctor's.

In addition to the psychiatrist's report, Zhubelovski faces a criminal trial following his full confession. I have decided in the interests of furthering the investigation to base myself in the dacha recently made empty by the arrest of Mr Zhubelovski. Should you need to contact me, or my secretary Tatyana, you can do so at that address.

'Jesus,' said Erik, 'he moved quickly.' He scanned the page.

A combination of poor interstate phone lines and the doctor's writing made it very difficult to read. The paper was headed the Tserbski Institute, Sadovaya 24, Moscow. Erik skipped the psychobabble. He read, 'V. S. Zhubelovski, blah blah, endured a failed relationship with his mother which left him psychologically isolated and unable to form meaningful relationships with adults. He sought release from this in an unusual way by abducting women who physically reminded him of his mother – who it transpires had dyed blonde hair – and attempting to rehabilitate them into good childcare practice by books and dolls. If he believed that the women failed to learn childcare skills, and in his eyes those kidnapped all failed to do so, he determined to kill them. His profound psychosis allowed him to believe that murdering the women would prove cathartic and allow him to reach a further stage in his life.'

Erik shrugged and said, 'There's some more medical stuff, his current medication, that sort of thing, but in essence that's all.'

'He can't be all that mad,' said Tim, flexing his feet backwards and forwards. 'Because if he was he wouldn't have put his name forward for the elections.'

'Meaning?' said Erik.

'You know what it means.' Tim groaned. 'If he's elected here, which he will be, then he gets immunity from criminal prosecution.'

'But surely, even here, they're not going to elect a bona fide nutter to be head of state?'

Tim ran his hand through his hair. 'Much as I would love to agree with you on that, I'm not sure I can. I mean, they did vote for me.'

'But the guy tried to kill eleven people. He abducted a seven women and made them read childcare books,' said Erik persuasively. 'All you did was create some phoney pyramid scheme.' Erik needed Tim to think it was his decision not to stand again. It was man management.

Tim shook his head. 'Crime doesn't bother the Russian electorate. In fact, they prefer a criminal. They think there's something trustworthy about someone who screws the system.' He shrugged. 'Besides, he's offering a half bottle of vodka for anyone who votes for him.'

'*From prison?*'

'I don't know. Via the newspaper, I think.'

Erik walked over to the window and turned. He said casually, 'So, there's only one thing for it – you'll have to stand again.'

Tim had started shaking his head before the sentence came out. 'No way. Absolutely no way. I've just about salvaged Natasha with the return of that bloody dog, there's no—'

'Yeah, yeah,' said Erik, sucking his teeth in disapproval. 'More like you don't have to stand again. Just think, though, what'll happen if Zhubelovski gets in.' He tapped his front tooth with his forefinger, while Tim put his hands up to show he didn't care.

After two minutes of silence Erik said, 'Well then, it's going to have to be the foreigner.' He looked at Tim. 'Would you prefer it if he got in?'

Tim sat up. 'You mean Anna's boyfriend?' He pulled his feet off the table. Talking about Anna's new boyfriend made his stomach light and his body restless. He was about to ask who in hell would vote for a Westerner with hair like a poof when he remembered how he'd had to park his jeep four blocks away because the square was full of Belugi natives chanting for the Englishman. In fact a delegation of Spanish missionaries, staying on the seventh floor, had already started to complain about the smell.

Tim shook his head. 'He'll never do it and, besides, I'm no constitutional expert but doesn't the President at least have to be a

Belugi national? That foreign guy's going home today.' He looked into Erik's eyes. 'Isn't he?'

Erik looked away which should have prepared Tim. Erik said, 'Yes.' He paused as Tim's shoulders relaxed. 'And no.'

'What do you mean?' said Tim, his voice a semi-octave higher. 'Yes and no? He's either getting on a plane today, or he's not.'

Erik said, 'Natasha's great, isn't she?'

Tim frowned and stood up. 'She's OK, but what's—'

'You're really lucky to have found her,' said Erik. 'You've moved on, you're making sense of your life.'

'Does this have a point?'

'I'm just saying that living in the past isn't good for you. I mean, that brush with Zhubelovski taught us how lucky we are to have what we have. You know, me and the magazine, you and Natasha.'

'What are you trying to say?'

'I'm saying that the foreigner *can* stand for the presidency,' said Erik, 'if he chooses to.'

Tim sat down again. 'How come?' After ten seconds of silence he repeated. 'How come?'

Erik steadied himself by gripping his armrest. 'Well,' he said, 'because he's married a Belugi.'

'Who?' The word came out on an exhale, as if he'd been winded.

Erik tried to make it light. 'Anna.'

Mrs Barinova let herself in. 'Hello, boys.' She put her handbag on the table. 'Have we decided who's going to be President yet?'

CHAPTER FIFTEEN

I

At a few minutes after midnight Anna said, 'If we go into the garden we should be able to see the fireworks.' She was sitting at the head of the table with her grandmother on one side and Dominic on the other, wearing a white two-piece trouser suit with no shirt. Dominic hadn't seen it before and it reminded him how little he knew of her wardrobe. Figuratively speaking, there might be a whole lot she kept under wraps. But Dominic was determined to think about that another day.

'How do you know there'll be fireworks?' he asked. The room was lit by candles that almost flickered out when a guest went outside. Anna's grandmother insisted that Hubba and Bubba smoked only on the veranda. Given that what they were smoking had come from Zhubelovski's truck before the detective took it away for forensics, it was just as well.

'There are always fireworks on a memorial day,' said Anna, 'it's predictable.' She smiled at Dominic. 'Let's call him again.'

'No.' For once Dominic wasn't thinking of his mobile bill. He didn't want to overexcite the old man. 'Why didn't he tell me he wasn't Polish?'

Anna shrugged. 'He thought you were. Or that you were practising the language. In our country it would be odd to send a

331

young person to visit an old one. Granddad thought he was doing you a favour.'

It was the first time she'd called Mr Orlovski Granddad.

Dominic said, 'It's odd, though, isn't it?'

They sat in silence for a minute.

'Why odd?' asked Anna. 'Many from our country got dispersed after the war. There were three million Red Army prisoners; some retreated with the Germans, some to Italy, some to France working on the canals. Why shouldn't Granddad have ended up in London?'

Dominic moved his head back and took her hand. 'But for me to know him? You have to admit, it's a coincidence.'

Anna tutted. 'You have no idea. What is it, coincidence? It's a word. For you it's coincidence, for Grandma and me it is fate, that's all.'

Beyond Anna's stern profile he saw Mrs Orlovski staring into the deep red of a glass of Moldovian wine, planning what would happen when her absent husband returned to her.

He said, 'Why didn't he look for her? I mean when the war was over.'

Anna turned to him patiently. 'Dominic, my whole country was exiled for a decade, along with millions of others. He searched but didn't find.'

Dominic nodded. 'No wonder you looked familiar to me. There was a picture of your grandmother on Mr Orlovski's mantelpiece. You're just like her.' He nodded at the old woman. 'When she was young.'

Since the kidnapping, Dominic had felt like a different person. He'd read in newspapers how car crashes and tube disasters changed people. He'd assumed they meant they'd become more appreciative of birdsong or the taste of chocolate. Nothing like what he felt. He felt physically incapable of leaving Belugastan. When he was sober, it was as if he couldn't remove himself from the country where he'd experienced so much; when he'd had a few, he felt as if his fate was inextricably linked to that of the fledgling country. The Orlovski connection proved it. His proposal to Anna had been after dinner two days ago, a few minutes after Anna's grandmother had told them she knew the man in his photograph. He'd been amazed when Anna had accepted his proposal without hesitation. But it had been an amazing week.

Next to him Anna's face was half pout, half frown, depending which eye he focused on her. He wasn't sure she viewed their nuptials in quite the same way as he did.

He put his hand out for his bride again. She pulled away slightly and sat up. 'Now, another toast. Please, Dominic, now you must make one.'

Stella Anne Webster, not in camouflage but a floral dress designed with nature in mind, sat next to Sonya. Stella Anne had told him that she was hoping to invite the youngster to stay with her in America. They hadn't discussed the details, but Stella Anne felt that the English language had so much more to offer Sonya than she already knew. She planned to enrol her on a crash course. Only then were they going to discuss the possibility of Pets to Dye For. Stella Anne hadn't ruled it out, she liked to be fair with all her charges.

'Yep,' she'd said, handing Dominic her coat when she'd arrived. 'Hell, now I know how the darned sheep feels.' She was wearing make-up that brought out the grey of her eyes.

Dominic stood up, clenching his knees to stop his chair falling over backwards. Oksana, who had arrived with her boyfriend, had bought a small cassette recorder and a pirated tape of the Red Army band playing the top twenty Soviet anthems which, given the nature of the event, she considered ironic. As he waited for the room to quieten Dominic picked out the melody of Kalinka tooted out on a euphonium. There'd been six guests at the wedding ceremony, done by special licence in the city hall, including Stella Anne, the boys, Sonya, Mrs Orlovski. Colonel Pertsov was there too. He used the authority of his *propusk* to get the authorities, in their case a large Georgian woman called Judge Inga, to open her office.

Dominic turned first to Mrs Orlovski and put his hand on his heart. He meant it as an apology, because the toast would be in English. Dominic had taken to the Russian toast – a lengthy construct dedicated to international hope and friendship – with enthusiasm. It seemed to convey so much more than 'Cheers'. He thought, if he put his mind to it, he could turn out to be quite a Slav; they had a tendency to wallow in sentimentality that he thought he might like.

He started slowly and got slower. 'Ladies and gentlemen. Before today, before I came to Belugastan I thought of marriage,' he looked at Anna, 'as something to be avoided.' He knew it was the vodka talking, but he didn't care. He paused. 'I was scared to nail my colours to the mast. In the sense of,' he looked at Anna, 'I mean – the mast being a woman.'

Anna's hair, when she shook her head impatiently, fell around her face. It was straw-coloured in the light of the candles. Four seats down to the left, Hubba said, 'Git on with it,' and banged a fork on the table.

Dominic smiled. 'Marriage means being the sum of your parts.' The last four words ran into each other. He put his hand on Anna's shoulder. 'And today, I'm very happy.' He raised his glass. 'Very happy to say I am part of my sum.' His smile met blank faces around the table. Hastily he added, 'To Anna.'

The women, apart from Anna who was sticking to orange juice, drank the toast in Russian champagne and, when that finished, peach liqueur.

'Hear hear,' said Stella Anne.

Hubba belched. 'What the hell's he talking about?'

The men drank from two bottles of Zhubelovski vodka. In some ways having the madman's head on the table, in the form of his picture on the label, was eerie but fitting. Vodka shots were followed by a bite of brown bread, or a piece of salted tomato.

Oksana had a square of chocolate in the bottom of her flute.

By one o'clock the noise of the party had reached a crescendo of conversations made forceful by too much alcohol. Bubba was miming something to Mrs Orlovski and Oksana was encouraging Stella Anne to take part in a piece of performance art.

Dominic turned to Anna. 'One question.'

Anna smiled.

He nodded towards a man with his legs on either side of the corner of the table. He was dressed in an orange poncho and had three days' stubble. 'Who *is* that?'

Anna made a nervous twist of her hair. 'His name's Easton. He's from an American oil company. He came here to sign a deal on the Caspian rights.'

'What Caspian rights?'

'It's nothing for you to worry about.'

'But why is he *here*?' asked Dominic. 'At our wedding?'

Anna looked at him. Stella Anne was dancing to a guitar instrumental of the Soviet national anthem with Oksana. 'He's my guest. I sometimes help with that sort of thing.'

Dominic frowned and waited for the information to sink in. 'What have Caspian rights got to do with you?'

'Nothing. It's nothing for you to worry about. But if you must know, all the countries that border the Caspian have a claim to the oil there.'

'So?'

Anna tutted. 'So. I am the Minister for the Environment. In Azerbaijan there's going to be enough oil to make everyone there a multimillionaire. I was going to sign with Easton. I think we deserve the same.'

'We?'

'Belugastan, of course.'

Dominic picked up a glass of red. After another minute and a trombone version of 'The Volga Boatmen', he asked, 'Why's he dressed like that?'

Anna waved her hand in annoyance. 'He climbed out of a window and banged his head. Then he got picked up by a young boy from the Belugi natives and he's been living with them. He called me yesterday.'

'Right,' said Dominic.

'I think he's lost his mind. He tried to get people's attention by throwing tortoises at them. Can you imagine the cruelty?' She looked grave. 'Not only that, but they belonged to my grand-mother.' Anna pushed her chair back and motioned with her head that he should do the same. Her white suit was immaculate and uncreased. In the distance towards town, he heard the dynamite fizz of fireworks followed by a sharp crack.

Anna said, 'Dominic, we have to talk.'

Her expression and the tenor of the instruction made him think of Antoinette. It was the first time he'd done so in days.

'Yes, darling?' He blinked to try to clear his cataract of drunken-ness.

'You know you'll have to do it.'

'What's that?'

'Stand in the election.'

'*What?*'

'Erik called me. If you don't stand then Zhubelovski will, he'll be President and then we'll never . . .' She stopped herself. 'Well, that would be terrible, that's all.'

Dominic blinked. He said, 'How can he stand if he's awaiting trial? I thought he was behind bars.'

'Dominic, in our country it's the law. Half of the Duma are only there to get out of prison.'

He wasn't listening. He needed to focus on the implications for himself. 'You can't seriously expect me to be the President. I mean, it's ridiculous. What do I know about it?' He was starting to feel ever so slightly set up. Maybe that was what married life was all about.

Anna smiled. 'You won't need to know anything, I'll help.'

'But who's going to vote for me?' He took another drink. 'You *do* have to be voted for, don't you?'

Anna put her hand on his knee. 'You silly thing. You've already attracted a very strong power base in the regions.'

'*What?*'

'The yurt people.'

They fell into silence. He felt as if he was being given a breather, to catch up with the news.

'Dominic.' Anna was cross; he knew that because the crosser she was, the more she lengthened the last syllable in his name. 'Marriage is about responsibility. Didn't you just say that? You have a responsibility to me now. You have to do what I want.'

'Within reason.'

'Do you want that man to get off, how do you say, Scotch free?'

'No, he should—'

'If you are President then he will stay in the Tserbski Institute forever.' She was now plaintive. 'See our guests, Dominic.' He looked round the room. Oksana was on Hubba's knee. The tape had gone back to Kalinka. 'Zhubelovski wanted to kill them.' She looked into his eyes. 'He wanted to kill me.'

'But I'm foreign – I can't even speak the language.'

'Don't worry,' wheedled Anna, 'I'll help.'

She allowed him another two minutes. Then he said, 'Anna, this isn't what marrying me was all about, was it?'

She smiled and tutted at the same time. 'No, of course not.' Anna's intonation fell at the end of the sentence, making it difficult to question her. 'It is about doing what is right.'

They stopped while Oksana fell heavily onto the wooden floor.

'Right,' Dominic echoed her, chewing the idea over. Anna took it as agreement.

'So, that's settled then.'

'Wait, no, but in any case the election was today. The polls are closed, aren't they? Isn't it too late?'

'Trust me,' said Anna. She grabbed his mobile phone and

stepped over Oksana to go onto the veranda to pick up a signal. Even in their unseeing stupor, Hubba and Bubba watched the cheeks of her bottom swing past, their heavy laden eyes drawn to her buttocks like a magnet.

II

Since he'd appointed Larissa head of classified advertising on *Erik*, they'd spent a lot of time in production, usually with Erik on the layout table and Larissa astride him. He liked it; the position gave him a certain hands-free autonomy. She'd dismounted a full ten minutes before and was dressing, coyly, in the ladies' when his mobile went off.

Anna said straight off, 'He's agreed.'

Post-coital, Erik struggled to dovetail the left and right sides of his brain together. This required logic. 'Excellent.' He paused. 'Actually, it's just as well. Have you seen the first edition of the paper?'

'How could I? We're at my grandmother's.' Erik could hear the noise of the party in the background.

He said, 'Well, let's just say it worked out very nicely.'

'What about Tim?' asked Anna.

'Well, he's back to being Feodor Barinov. Actually, it's OK. He's working things out with Natasha.'

There was a fifteen-second pause before Anna said, 'How did the National Day Parade go?'

'Oh, you know, with a bang.'

'Fireworks?'

'Sort of,' said Erik, looking towards the door.

Anna reduced her voice to a whisper, more shrewish than she'd hoped. 'You're sleeping with her, aren't you?'

Erik said, 'You married him.'

Anna checked to see if anyone could hear her. 'It was part of the agreement. It's always suited us best like this.' She paused. 'I had to. This way I'll get the ballet school.' Anna smiled in the darkness. To try to make up she said, 'Easton's signed, so the oil deal is in the bag.'

'How much?'

'Twenty million.'

'Dollars?'

'Of course.'

'Fifty-fifty.'

Anna gave a short laugh. 'Sixty-forty.'

'Excellent,' said Erik. She could tell from his voice that he was smiling. 'You did a good job.'

'Don't I always?' said Anna, then, not wanting to end the call, 'Here's to another term.' She paused. Erik was silent. 'You know it'll always be me and you, don't you?' said Anna. 'You were the only one that passed the cemetery test.'

Just before he replied, Larissa swung through the double doors, fully dressed. 'I know,' said Erik. 'You and me.'

From the top of Natasha's roof, with their backs against Igor's laminating factory, they watched the night sky light up.

'Who pays for the fireworks?' asked Natasha.

'There's a budget for it,' said Tim. Strictly speaking he was Feodor again, and he'd paid for the display, but he didn't want to complicate things.

'Wow, a firework budget,' said Igor. 'I wish you were still President.' Natasha looked at him sternly.

'*I* don't,' said Tim. A fountain of sparks sprayed across the dark. Whitey was downstairs with Mrs Barinova.

He glanced at Natasha's profile, expecting a smile to be lit up by the light of a rocket. Tim tried to get her to look at him. Something under his rib cage told him he was doing the right thing. It hadn't yet connected with his brain, but adjusting to new lifestyles always took time. On Monday he was getting

Pasha to teach him how to make shelves.

When the display had finished and Igor had gone downstairs, Natasha turned to him.

'Now, I think it is time we made love.' She started unbuttoning her shirt as she stared into his eyes.

Tim pulled at his shirt. He couldn't have agreed more.

Sergei Kapustin was working late, but his wife had chosen the National Day celebrations to throw a party for thirty-five. To show off her new horse, it had started early with champagne and vol-au-vents in the garden of their dacha. For Kapustin, the elections had provided an excellent alibi. At 2.15 a.m. he felt it was safe to return home. Behind him, sticking out of the office lost and found box, was a striped parasol.

He was stuffing his briefcase with half a dozen pairs of counterfeit nylon tights with the label Guchy, given in payment for a quarter-page classified ad, when his secretary, Olga, came in with an armful of first editions.

The headline was in 20 point and took up half the page. 'BELUGASTAN ELECTS NEW LEADER.' Underneath in 15 point it said, 'FOREIGNER ELECTED TO TOP JOB.' It was followed by a strap line, 'Zhubelovski Out, Awaiting Abduction Trial, Doctors Say He Must Never Walk Free.'

'Yeah, great,' said Kapustin, not looking up from his bag. He'd already discussed the potential benefits of having a Westerner in charge with Mrs Kapustina, who agreed that the potential for travel outweighed any downsides. Since the gift of the horse, there was no doubt that he'd irrevocably upped the stakes. He kicked himself. Now six pairs of fake tights would just be thrown back in his face.

He frowned and looked up, suddenly very serious. 'Olga, you're a woman. What do you think? Would you prefer six pairs of knock-off tights, or a parasol?' He brandished the latter like a swordsman.

III

Dominic went outside for some air. He stepped over Hubba and Bubba who had collapsed on the porch. He thought of his friends inside and his new family and smiled. Anna had suggested he start a caviar export business to keep him busy. When he mentioned he thought he *was* the new President, she said he was better not worrying about that sort of thing. He looked at the sky and wondered if Tony might want to take control of the London end of things. He smiled certainly. It appeared to be that being a caviar-exporting president was the sum of his parts. Developmentwise.

Slaphead

Georgina Wroe

Terry Small wants a woman. And he's seen a catalogue full of them. They're in Moscow, employed by REDS IN YOUR BEDS marriage agency. Armed with his best Calvin Klein underpants and his new abdominiser, Terry, the most dynamic conservatory salesman in Basingstoke, is on his way.

Awaiting him in Moscow is Katya, the agency's Russian representative. The only mate Katya cares about is her delinquent six-year-old, Sasha – and Terry, probably her most unprepossessing customer ever, isn't going to pose a problem for a woman who's already despatched a redundant husband to Siberia.

But Katya hasn't bargained for the intervention of Fate. Not to mention Moscow's latest entrepreneur, Professor Modin, formerly Lenin's embalmer, now specialising in providing a mounting pile of dead Mafia bosses with the flashy, unforgettable funeral they so richly deserve . . .

Fast, confident and fantastically funny, *Slaphead* introduces a writer of anarchic brilliance to the fiction-writing scene.

'A female Carl Hiassen' *The Times*

0 7472 6203 9

HEADLINE

Icebox

Mark Bastable

Here's the deal.

Give Gabriel Todd your brain, and you'll live forever. Gabe'll freeze your head in a flask – and three hundred years from now, you'll be reborn in a new, perfect body. You will be immortal.

Unity Siddorn wants in. She has her own plans to save the world – with genetically pumped tomatoes, as you ask – but she's already thirty-bloody-one years old. In actuarial terms, her life is 41.3% over. She'll do anything – ANYTHING – for more time.

Don, her squeeze, is less keen. A pack of smokes and a gambler's shot at seventy years – he can live with that.

Suddenly, Gabe's theories are about to be put to the test – though circumstances are admittedly less than ideal. The police tend to take a professional interest in a freshly severed head. It's not something you can easily hide . . .

0 7472 6839 8

HEADLINE